D0468746

THE KASHMIR SHAWL

Rosie Thomas is the author of a number of celebrated novels, including the bestsellers *Sun at Midnight*, *Iris and Ruby* and *Constance*. A keen traveller, she has climbed in the Alps and the Himalayas, competed in the Peking to Paris car rally, spent time on a tiny Bulgarian research station in Antarctica and travelled in Ladakh and Kashmir to research this novel. She lives in London.

By the same author:

Celebration
Follies
Sunrise
The White Dove
Strangers
Bad Girls, Good Women
A Woman of Our Times
All My Sins Remembered
Other People's Marriages
A Simple Life
Every Woman Knows a Secret
Moon Island
White
The Potter's House
If My Father Loved Me
Sun at Midnight
Iris and Ruby
Constance
Lovers and Newcomers

ROSIE THOMAS

The Kashmir Shawl

HarperCollins*Publishers*

HarperCollins*Publishers*
77–85 Fulham Palace Road,
Hammersmith, London W6 8JB

www.harpercollins.co.uk

First published in Great Britain by
HarperCollins*Publishers* 2011

9

Copyright © Rosie Thomas 2011

Rosie Thomas asserts the moral right to
be identified as the author of this work

A catalogue record for this book
is available from the British Library

ISBN: 978 0 00 728596 9

This novel is entirely a work of fiction.
The names, characters and incidents portrayed in it are
the work of the author's imagination. Any resemblance to
actual persons, living or dead, events or localities is
entirely coincidental.

Set in Sabon by Palimpsest Book Production Limited,
Falkirk, Stirlingshire

Printed and bound in Great Britain by
Clays Ltd, St Ives plc

All rights reserved. No part of this publication may be
reproduced, stored in a retrieval system, or transmitted,
in any form or by any means, electronic, mechanical,
photocopying, recording or otherwise, without the prior
permission of the publishers.

Mixed Sources
Product group from well-managed
forests and other controlled sources
www.fsc.org Cert no. SW-COC-001806
© 1996 Forest Stewardship Council
FSC

FSC is a non-profit international organisation established
to promote the responsible management of the world's forests.
Products carrying the FSC label are independently certified
to assure consumers that they come from forests that are managed
to meet the social, economic and ecological needs
of present and future generations.

Find out more about HarperCollins and the environment at
www.harpercollins.co.uk/green

For my father

The mountain sheep are sweeter,
But the valley sheep are fatter;
We therefore deemed it meeter
To carry off the latter.

ONE

Mair made the discovery on the last day at home in the old house.

The three of them were upstairs in their father's bedroom. They had come together for the melancholy business of sorting and clearing their parents' furniture and possessions, before closing up the house for the last time and handing over the keys to the estate agent. It was the end of May and the lambs had just been taken away to market. Out on the hill the sheep were bleating wildly, loud, incessant and bewildered cries that were carried in with the scent of spring grass.

Mair had made a pot of tea and laid a tray to carry upstairs to her sister Eirlys. Their brother Dylan came behind her, ducking as he had had to do from the age of thirteen in order to avoid hitting his head on the low beam on the landing.

Eirlys's energy was prodigious, as always. The floor of the bedroom was squared with neat piles of blankets and pillows, towers of labelled boxes, crackling black bags. She stood at the foot of the bed, resting a clipboard on the bedpost and frowning as she scribbled amendments to one of her lists. With the addition of a white coat and a retinue of underlings, she could easily have been on one of her ward rounds.

'Lovely,' she murmured, when she saw the tea. 'Don't put it down there,' she added.

Dylan took a cup and wedged himself on the windowsill. He was blocking the light and Eirlys flicked an eyebrow at him. 'Drink your tea,' he said mildly. 'Go mad, have a biscuit as well.'

Mair sat down on the bed. The ancient pink electric blanket was still stretched from corner to corner, and she thought of the weeks of her father's last illness when she had come home to the valley to nurse him, as best she could, and to keep him company. They had enjoyed long, rambling conversations about the past and the people her father had once known.

'Did I ever tell you about Billy Jones, the auctioneer?'

'I don't think so.'

'He had a stammer.'

'How did he manage?'

Over the top of his spectacles her father had glanced at her. 'We weren't in such a hurry, you know, in those days.'

In the low-ceilinged room the old man seemed very close at hand, and at the same time entirely absent.

Eirlys was pointing out which bundles were to be taken away to charity drop-offs and what exactly the house-clearance people could be left to deal with. There was a question about the linen bed-sheets that had been stored in the same cupboard for as long as they could all remember and were mysteriously kept for 'best', probably according to some long-ago edict of their mother's. But when the sisters had unfolded the top sheet they saw that it was worn so thin in the middle that the light shone straight through. Eirlys pursed her lips now and briskly consigned it with its partner to one of her graded series of bin-bags.

The sun was slanting through the window, painting Dylan's jumper with a rim of gilded fuzz.

Mair found that she couldn't sit still any longer and let the wave of memories engulf them all. She jumped up and went to the bow-fronted chest of drawers facing the end of the bed. Their mother had inherited it from her own mother – she remembered hearing that. Gwen Ellis's clothes had been stored in here after her death, until at last her widower and her elder daughter had recovered sufficiently to be able to give them away.

The pair of split drawers at the top was empty. Eirlys had even removed the lining paper. The middle one had recently held their father's vests and pants and folded shirts. As he had grown weaker, Mair had helped him dress in the mornings. In the vain hope of making his bones feel warmer, she would hold the underclothes in front of the electric fire before handing them to him. A heap of these things now lay on the floor.

'We'll have to put those bits and pieces of his in the bag for recycling.' Eirlys nodded. 'They're no good for anything else.'

Mair slid open the bottom drawer of the chest. She saw a few yellowing pillow-cases, and the tablecloth with the cut-work centre panel that was taken out once a year without fail to be smoothed over the Christmas dinner-table. The white fabric was stained in places with rust. Reaching beneath the cloth, her fingers came into contact with tissue paper. She lifted out the cloth to investigate what lay beneath it.

The tissue paper was very old and limp.

When she folded it back her first impression was of wonderful colours. Silvery blues and greens sprang at her, like a distillation of lake water and spring skies, with starbursts of lavender and vermilion flowers caught in the depths. She looked more closely and saw the intricacy of the woven pattern; the sumptuous curved teardrop shapes with curled tips, the ferny fronds and branched stems and tiny five-petalled flowers. The only sound in the room was the distress of the sheep as Mair shook out the layers of soft wool. It was so light that it seemed to float on the air.

The shawl was a lovely thing, and she had never seen it before.

An envelope had fallen out of the folds. It was an old brown one, ordinary, creased in half, with the glue long ago dried from

3

the flap. Gently Mair eased it open. Inside there was a single lock of hair. The curl was very fine and silky, dark brown, with a few coppery threads shining in it. She pinched it between her fingers.

'That's Grandma Watkins's shawl,' Eirlys said, in her authoritative way.

'It's so beautiful,' Mair whispered.

Eirlys was the only one of the three who had known their mother's mother, and even she had no recollection of her because she had died when Eirlys was still a baby. All any of them knew was that she had been out in India with her much older missionary husband. The couple finally came back to Wales and had had their only child when Nerys was already in her forties. That daughter, Gwen, had married a neighbour from the same valley, handsome Huw Ellis, when she was only nineteen. She had always said to her own three children that she didn't want them to grow up with elderly parents, the way she had done.

'Whose hair can this be, do you think?' Mair wondered.

'I've no idea,' Eirlys said.

Mair thought about it. Grandma Watkins wouldn't have kept her own hair, would she? Was it her husband's, then, or more probably her child's?

No. This wasn't the hair of an elderly missionary, and it wasn't Gwen's either, she was fairly sure of that – hers had naturally been a quite different, much lighter colour.

Whose, then?

The question intrigued her, but it seemed to have no answer.

She pressed the shawl to her cheek. The fabric was so fine that she could enclose it in her two fists. For the first time, she breathed in its faint scent of spice.

'We've still got a lot to do,' Eirlys said, as she finished her tea.

Thoughtfully Mair slipped the lock of hair back into its envelope.

Later, when most of the packing and boxing were done,

the three of them gathered in the kitchen. The back door stood open and midges floated in on the breeze. The noise of the sheep grew louder and more plaintive as twilight crept up. Dylan had opened a bottle of wine, and Mair was putting together a picnic supper of cold ham, with baked potatoes from the microwave. Dylan had bought it for their father a couple of years back and Huw had used it regularly to heat up supermarket ready-meals for one, declaring that they were very tasty. Eirlys had disapproved, pointing out that ready-meals were high in fat and salt.

The machine pinged and Mair took out the potatoes. She could just see their father winking and silently going *heh-heh-heh-heh*.

Without warning, tears threatened to spill out of her eyes.

They all knew that this was the last evening they would ever spend together in the old kitchen. Mair was determined not to make it more sorrowful by indulging in any fit of weeping. She smiled instead, at Dylan who was sitting with his hands in the pockets of his jeans and then at Eirlys, with her hair hooked behind her ears and her eyes looking very shiny behind her glasses.

'Should we eat in the other room?' Mair asked.

The table in there was a better size for three than the drop-flap one wedged in the kitchen corner, where the memory of their father sitting alone with his cup of tea and the newspaper was very clear.

The business of taking the food through and finding the last pieces of unpacked cutlery carried them through the moment. Dylan found some candle stubs and Eirlys put them in a saucer. The glow made the stripped-out room look inviting again, blotting out the dust squares on the walls where pictures used to hang.

'We should talk about the good things,' Eirlys said, when they were all sitting down.

For a second Mair thought she meant the happy times they had spent as a family, and the uncharacteristic sentiment startled her. Then she realised that her sister was talking about the two or three pieces of furniture and old silver that were all there had been of real value in the house. Since the reading of the will they had known that the proceeds from selling the house were to be divided equally between them. The smaller items they hadn't really talked about.

There was the grandfather clock, with a painted face showing the sun and moon, whose sonorous tick had measured out the long afternoons of her childhood. Huw had mentioned it once, in the last weeks, referring to it as 'Dylan's clock'. Mair had deliberately ignored him because she didn't want to acknowledge what he meant.

'You'll take the clock, Dylan,' Eirlys said. 'Mair?'

The other two were married, and they owned houses with hallways and alcoves and shelves. Mair was not, and she lived happily in a rented one-and-a-half-room flat. She didn't need, or even want, her mother's bow-fronted chest or silver teapot. They would find a better home with Eirlys. She laid down her knife and fork and cleared her throat.

'I would like to have Grandma's shawl,' she said. 'If that's all right?'

'Of course it is.' Eirlys nodded. 'If you agree, Dylan?'

He looked at Mair. There were quite deep lines at the corners of his eyes, these days. He and Eirlys were both short-sighted, and Dylan tended to screw up his eyes when he was concentrating.

Awareness of how much she loved her brother wrapped round her like a blanket. All her life he had been her ally, whereas as children she and Eirlys had constantly squabbled, mostly because they were each other's embodied opposites. Not that they had quarrelled recently, of course. The loss of their adored father had made them considerate of each other, even wary.

'Do you know where it might have come from?' Dylan asked her.

She said, 'No. But maybe I could try to find out.'

6

This idea only came to her as she gave voice to it. She was surprised by the curiosity that the mysterious shawl aroused in her.

That night Mair and Eirlys went to bed for the last time in the room they had shared as children. Mair could tell that her sister wasn't asleep, although she didn't twist and turn between the damp sheets like Mair was doing. In the end she whispered, 'Eirlys, can't you sleep?'

'No.'

'What are you thinking about?'

'The same as you, probably. Once your parents are both dead, you really are it, aren't you? You're responsible, because there's no one standing in front of you. Do you know what I mean?'

Sympathy flooded through Mair. Her sister had been behaving responsibly for her entire life. She had been a prize-winning medical student and had just been appointed to a consultant's post at her Birmingham hospital, yet she had still found time to marry and have two boys. All her life she had been studying and looking after other people, and now her vision of this latest phase of their lives was of yet more weight falling on her shoulders.

Mair thought, Ever since I could walk and talk, I've been skipping away from the path my sister and brother trod ahead of me. Instead of following them to a good university she had left home and Wales at seventeen, fulfilling a long-standing promise, halfway between a family joke and a rebellious threat, to run away and join a circus. And at Floyd's Family Circus she had met Harriet Hayes, or Hattie the Clown. Together they had worked up a simple trapeze act. Their nights at the circus were a long way behind them now, but they had been close friends ever since. In the intervening years Mair had also been a dress-shop manager, the singer in a band, a receptionist, a PR, a nursery assistant, a bookseller, and several other incarnations in the job market, with varying degrees of success, but usually some satisfaction.

No, even Hattie wouldn't call me responsible, she acknowledged. And Hattie was quite a lot more frivolous than Eirlys.

Mair's heart began to pound against her ribs and a white light blazed behind her eyes. Her body felt suddenly as light as a feather, and she realised that what she was feeling was *free*. She wanted to capture this blessing, and at the same time she longed to share some of it with her sister. Her fingers reached out and touched the fringes of the shawl, which lay on the chair beside her bed. 'Yes, I do know what you mean,' she said. 'Eirlys, I've been thinking. I might do some travelling. You know, now Dad's gone and, like you say, there's just us left behind. I was wondering about going to India – perhaps see what I can find out about Grandma and her shawl. I'd be unravelling some family history. Why don't you come with me? We could spend some time together. We haven't done much of that lately.'

There wasn't so much as a second's hesitation before Eirlys replied, 'I couldn't possibly. There's the hospital. It's difficult for the whole team, with the latest cuts. And who'd look after Graeme and the boys? You should go, though, if that's what you really want to do. I saw the way you looked at the shawl.'

Mair knew there was no point in trying to change her sister's mind. Eirlys was decisive enough for two people. 'I do think it might be interesting,' she said.

She didn't try to articulate the feeling of rootlessness that had troubled her since their father's death. Eirlys and Dylan were settled, and she was far from being so herself. Perhaps uncovering some family history might help her to feel her place again.

'You might not find out anything at all. India's a big country. But you deserve a break and a new horizon. Grief can take all sorts of different forms, you know. And you took on most of the burden of looking after Dad. Dylan and I are really grateful for what you did, giving up that job and everything.'

Mair blinked hard in the darkness, but hot tears still escaped from the corners of her eyes. After the funeral Eirlys had remarked that the baby of the family was so busy being unconventional that it didn't leave much time for her to focus on anything else. That had stung Mair, but now she reflected that grief did indeed take many forms. Eirlys's caused her to be more tart than usual. The realisation made her sister's kindness now seem even more touching and valuable. She murmured, 'It was a privilege. I'm glad I was free to do it.'

'Take some time, have a trip to India. If you need a reason and the shawl gives you one, that's fine,' Eirlys concluded. 'Now, can we go to sleep?'

Outside, the bleating of the sheep had finally subsided. Mair knew why. Once night had fallen, the ewes understood that their lost lambs could never be called back. The occasional despairing cry still rose to the stars, but the flock was settling into silence.

Mair woke up and lay in the narrow bed, trying to work out where she was. She had been dreaming of a dog barking and animals stirring in response, a rustle of alarm passing among them before the leaders broke away and scudded across the bitten ground. Then sunlight flooded a hillside with sudden colour and the moving animals flowed into grey-on-green paisley patterns against the grass. A sheepdog chivvied them towards a stone enclosure where a farmer was holding the gate open.

In the way that dreams unfold, a familiar and beloved place had become merged with another she hadn't yet visited. The room was cold and she shivered, pulling the blankets round her shoulders. As she did so the first call of the muezzin broke through the shutters.

The skin at the nape of her neck prickled, not just with the chill but with anticipation.

She remembered.

She opened her eyes wider, struck by anxiety in the grey dawn. The hotel room was cramped and liberally strewn with her belongings. Last night she had burrowed through her bags, searching in a power blackout for pyjamas and bed socks. But the shawl was safely there, neatly folded over the back of the room's single chair. The light wasn't strong enough yet to reveal the colours in their full glory, but they were vividly printed in her mind's eye.

Mair pushed back the covers and sat up. It was too early, but she knew she wasn't going to fall asleep again.

She had decided to give herself a full day to acclimatise. So, after a solitary breakfast in the hotel's chilly and deserted dining room, she made her slightly nervous preparations. Into her shoulder-bag went the sketch-map of the town that the smiling Ladakhi receptionist had given her, a bottle of mineral water, some antibacterial gel and a well-rinsed apple. She was uncertain enough of what lay ahead to experience a breathless flutter beneath her diaphragm that had almost nothing to do with the effects of altitude.

Mair had never been to India before, not even to the beaches of Goa or the sights of Jaipur, let alone to a remote town in the Himalayas. Nor was she – in spite of her declared independence – at all used to travelling alone. Holidays, when she could afford them, had in the past usually involved the Greek islands or Spain, with a new boyfriend or one who was on the way out, or some looser combination of friends almost always including Hattie. As usual, Eirlys had been right when she had pointed out that Mair didn't often break off from her studied absence of routine.

Mair smiled again as she locked her hotel-room door. She was free now, wasn't she? Days and weeks of formally unallocated time stretched ahead of her. Thanks to the sale of the old house in Wales, she had some money, and time to spare for the strange project that had gnawed at her imagination for months in a way she didn't properly understand. She hadn't talked very much about the undertaking, even to Hattie, because it would have been too difficult to make her compulsion sound intelligible.

Just the same, the vaguest of vague plans had brought her all the way here to Leh, on an open ticket, with no fixed return date in mind to confine or comfort her.

She walked down the concrete path from the hotel, past beds of zinnias and cosmos and gaudy marigolds, and out into the street. Heading towards the centre of town, she gazed round her in fascination. It was the end of September, and she saw that Leh's short tourist season was practically over. Already many of the craft shops and travel agencies lining the road had rolled down and locked their permanent metal shutters ready for winter, and the Internet cafés that catered to backpackers and trekkers were almost deserted. The high peaks ringing the town glittered with fresh snow, and the poplar trees in hotel gardens rustled with dry golden leaves.

In a month's time the real snows would come, and the high passes linking the Ladakhi capital with the Vale of Kashmir to the west and Himachal Pradesh to the south would be impassable until the spring thaw came. For six months the only way into Leh would be by air, as Mair had arrived yesterday, flying from Delhi into the little airport beside the Indus river. As she walked she was trying to picture what it would be like here in midwinter, when the narrow alleys of the town would be clogged with snow and the roof of each house piled high with sheaves of dried fodder for the family's animals. But she was distracted. The imminent disappearance of tourists meant that the town's salesmen were urgently trying to make a last few rupees. In the main street three of them cut off her progress with a practised pincer movement.

'Hello, madam, where you from? Look at my shop, please.'

'I have beautiful pashmina, I make you a very good price today.'

The third man pouted when she experimentally shook her head. 'But looking is free, madam. Just looking. What is the great hurry?'

She was in no hurry, that was true. Laughing, she followed the nearest merchant up the steps into his cluttered shop and let him show off his stock. From Tibet there were trays of silver, coral and turquoise jewellery, from China painted Thermos flasks and furry nylon blankets in electric hues. There were prickly hats and waistcoats, locally knitted from goat's hair, woven bags with tassels, and racks of T-shirts in every size and colour – mostly bearing a machine-embroidered yak on the front and the slogan 'yak yak yak Ladakh'. Her eyes were acclimatising to the dim light of the shop's interior. Against the walls there were ramparts of samovars and copper dishes and crewel-work rugs.

'It's very nice. Thank you for showing me. I'm not shopping today, though.'

The man was Kashmiri, and therefore born to sell. 'You want pashmina.' It wasn't a question. At the back of the shop floor-to-ceiling shelves were stuffed with layers of folded fabric.

'Show me.'

Immediately he began to whirl shawls off the shelves. A drift of colour built up on the tiny counter, yellows and blues and fuchsia pinks. 'See? Feel, beautiful. Best quality. Pure pashmina.'

Mair knew a lot more about fine shawls than she had done four months ago, when the exquisite piece that was now locked in the hotel safe had first come into her possession. She understood the quality of the craftsmanship, and its likely value. 'Pure?' she said. 'Really?'

'Yes, pure silk pashmina mix. Twelve hundred rupees. Look, this pink one and this lovely blue-turquoise. Christmas is coming, think of gifts for your friends. Three for three thousand.'

'Do you have any *kani* woven shawls? Or embroidered pieces?'

The man looked up. 'Ah, yes. You know the best, madam. I show you.'

12

He unlocked a cabinet and brought out another pile. Like a magician he shook out more coloured breadths of fabric, whisking and flourishing them in front of her. Mair picked up the nearest one and let the folds slide through her fingers. She bent her head briefly to examine the floral design in reds and violet, then wound the shawl over her shoulders.

'So nice,' the Kashmiri approved. 'These colours just right for you.'

It was nothing like the other one. This fabric felt stiff, lumpy around the margins of the flowers, and it hung awkwardly, with none of the fluid drape of her shawl. When she took it off again she could almost hear the crackle of the fibres. She didn't know for sure how the design had been woven, but from a glimpse of the reverse it looked like cheap machine work. 'Thank you,' she murmured.

'Nine thousand. Good price.' He knew she wasn't going to buy. 'And this one, see, embroidered. By hand, all of it.'

Royal blue, this time, with a band of white flowers sewn at either end. The flowers had certainly been done by hand, but the design was haphazardly stitched and threads trailed on the reverse. The outlines of the blocked pattern were visible beneath the stitching. It could not have been more different from the other, on which the double band of floral embroidery was worked over the woven design in the same shades and in stitches so tiny that they were invisible to the naked eye, all of it executed so perfectly that the right side and the reverse were indistinguishable. The effect of such minute and effacing work was to emboss a broad swathe of the woven pattern, giving the paisley shapes and entwined foliage an opulent three-dimensional effect.

'It's very nice,' Mair repeated.

The man looked offended. She wanted to get out of the shop now, back into the sunshine. She picked out a pair of coral earrings from the display stand next to the door, paid for them quickly and made her escape.

'Come back soon,' the merchant called after her.

The other two salesmen reattached themselves to her side, but half-heartedly. She was able to sidestep them and make her way on down the sunny, dusty street past a row of women sitting at the kerbside with baskets of cauliflowers and apples for sale. Shoeshine men with their brushes and tins of polish set out on squares of sacking tried to attract her attention, even though her scuffed Converse were clearly visible. Scooters and rickshaws jolted over the potholes in the road. The noise of traffic was deafening. Mair peered up the shadowed alleyways leading off the street and chose one at random to explore. A mangy dog loped by, its distended teats swinging.

It was cooler in the shade and she pressed deeper, past barbers' shops and butchers' stalls where goats' heads oozed on wooden slabs. A black, buzzing object nailed to a beam revealed itself as an animal's severed tongue, presumably fixed there to draw flies away from the rest of the meat. Mair glanced at it, swallowed, and groped in her bag for her bottle of water. She took a determined swig and pushed on. Canvas tarpaulins were laced overhead now, and the alley grew dimmer and narrower. Overripe vegetable remains and less identifiable waste squished underfoot. Women in saris brushed past, and others in *burqas* hurried in the opposite direction. Stallholders called out and children vaulted over the gutters. It was a busy, cheerful scene and every aspect of its unfamiliarity served to highlight her alien status.

The alley opened into a square and she squinted as the sunlight struck her face. To one side a small brown bullock grazed with apparent relish on a pile of smouldering refuse. To the other, a crimson and gold prayer wheel was mounted beneath a painted canopy. As she stood there an ancient monk in saffron and burgundy robes wandered out of the crowd and set it turning clockwise. He stepped with it as it rotated, murmuring and counting the beads on his rosary. Mair took a photograph of him, then wondered if she had been intrusive.

She moved off down an alley, which ran in yet another

14

direction, into the heart of the bazaar. Down here the stalls were heaped with white trainers and brown plastic sandals. Overhead, backpacks and holdalls swayed in their hundreds like misshapen fruit. Girls' dresses made of glitter and tinsel hung in electric tiers.

And it was here, framed against the blue smoke rising from a food stall, that she first caught sight of the Becker family. The trio would have presented a striking picture anywhere, but in the chaotic market they made a tableau so unearthly that it had an almost religious quality to it.

They were the only Westerners she had noticed since leaving the main street. The woman was tall, slender and ethereally pale-skinned. She had a mass of red-gold hair that sprang over her shoulders. She was wearing a loose white shirt over a tiered blue linen skirt and a pair of mud-encrusted boots. She was talking, pointing and laughing all at the same time. The man with her was looking in the other direction. He was even taller than his wife and suntanned, with coal-black hair and eyebrows and a half-grown beard. Between them was an angelic child, a little girl of about two. She had the same curling mass of hair as her mother, but the colour was white-blonde. Her head rotated as she looked from one parent to the other. Then she stuck her tiny arms into the air and yelled, 'Carry.'

The woman was still laughing and gesturing. She stooped and, with the other arm, swept the child off her feet. She settled the little girl astride her hip and strode across to the food vendor. The air shimmered above a vat of boiling oil. The child pulled out a coil of her mother's amazing hair and peered down through it, as if it were a veil, at the heads passing beneath her.

The man turned to see what his wife was pointing at. The vendor fished in the boiling vat with a ladle and brought up some shiny toffee-brown squiggles. He tipped them into a paper cone and handed this over in exchange for some rupees. The woman dipped in her fingers and extracted a deep-fried squiggle. She blew casually on it, then handed it to the child. The little girl bit into whatever it was with relish.

The woman tilted her head back and dropped some of the food into her own mouth. She chewed eagerly and laughed, wiping the grease from her chin. Health and satisfaction seemed to shine out of her. Her free hand floated lightly to her husband's hip and rested there. It was a gesture of possession and affection, as intimate as it was casual. She steered him away from the vendor, and from Mair's scrutiny, even though none of the three had so much as glanced in her direction. They strolled deeper into the maze of stalls. She followed them with her eyes, the red-gold and black heads, with the child's pale one bouncing between them, until they turned a corner and passed out of her sight.

She stayed rooted where she was, despite her urge to run after the family. The food vendor shovelled another scoop of his mysterious wares into the cauldron; the oil sizzled and spat.

In the hubbub of the market Mair's loneliness intensified.

She had plenty of friends, and had had the usual series of relationships, but there had been no one she could imagine spending the rest of her life with, not the way her sister Eirlys had undertaken to do with her Graeme, or Dylan with his Jackie.

She made herself take a deep breath of bazaar smells, and noted the ambling cows, the hens scratching on a hill of rubbish, the Buddhist monk returning from his trip to the prayer wheel, and the steady surge of people going about their business. Colours and scents and fresh impressions flooded her head, and her spirits floated again. She turned and retraced her steps, deliberately heading in the opposite direction to the glorious strangers.

The drive out to Changthang, eastwards from Leh, almost to what had once been the border with Tibet – and was now China – took the best part of a day. The other members of the sightseeing tour in a small Toyota bus were two portly, middle-aged Dutch couples and three Israeli boys, who managed to be rowdy yet noticeably unfriendly. They sprawled in the back, guffawing over the separate accompaniments of their MP3s. Curled up in her seat and braced against the jolting, Mair had plenty of opportunity on the long drive to reflect, and remember.

Before leaving for India she had done as much research as she could into her grandparents' history. Three months ago, in the on-line edition of a book called *Hope and the Glory of God*, subtitled *With the Welsh Missionaries in India*, she had read the entry for *Parchedig Evan William Watkins (1899–1960)*.

Evan Watkins had been educated at the University College of North Wales, and the College of the Presbyterian Church of Wales. After his ordination he had heard the call to work in India, and in 1929 he had travelled out to Shillong in what was then Assam. Subsequently he served as district missionary to Shangpung.

Since reading his clerical biography, she had regularly tried to conjure images of Evan Watkins, in his black coat and dog collar, as he gamely preached Nonconformism to the people of remote Indian hill villages. Had he thundered from his makeshift chapel pulpit on a steaming day with the monsoon rains drumming on the tin roof?

Since her arrival in the Indian Himalaya she had tried harder still to picture him, but the clash of cultures was too brutal to generate any kind of image.

According to his entry in the book, Parchedig Watkins had returned to Wales in 1938, where he had met and married Nerys Evelyn Roberts, born in 1909. In 1939 the couple had sailed from Liverpool, bound for Bombay, aboard SS *Prospect*.

That was easier to picture. Mair saw the sunset over the Suez Canal, and heard a band playing for the dancers in the second-class saloon. Probably the minister wouldn't have had much time for the foxtrot, but she wondered if the young

Mrs Watkins had been of the same mind, or whether she had sipped her lemonade and watched the laughing couples with a touch of wistfulness.

The Reverend Evan and Mrs Watkins were subsequently called to give service to the new mission of Leh, far up in Ladakh, where the minister became responsible for the work of missionary outreach throughout the region. Many roads in his territory were impassable for seven months of the year, the biographer noted, and electricity was almost unknown.

Mair looked out of the bus window at the stark landscape, and the purple-grey mountains rearing into the empty blue sky. The unmade road ahead zigzagged towards a distant pass in a series of pale hairpins scratched out of the rock and dust. Along this road giant trucks with painted fronts like fairground rides hooted and skidded. The small figures of the Welsh preacher and his wife still refused to take shape in her imagination, here or anywhere else in the Himalaya.

The rest of the entry was brief. After the war, the clergyman's poor health had forced him to return to Wales. Evan Watkins retained a strong interest in the work of the missionary services, but his health never recovered from the rigours of the Indian climate and he had died in 1960, leaving his widow and one daughter, born in 1950.

That daughter had been Mair's mother, Gwen Ellis, née Watkins.

Gwen had died suddenly from a cerebral haemorrhage when her youngest child was barely into her teens. It was one of Mair's greatest regrets now that, as an averagely self-absorbed and dismissive thirteen-year-old, she had never asked her mother to tell her a single thing about Evan and Nerys's exotic years as missionaries in India.

The bus pulled in at a roadside stall selling tea and snacks. The Israeli youths leapt up at once and barged their way past Mair and the Dutch couples. Before climbing out to ease her cramped legs, Mair picked up the rucksack from the seat beside her and slipped the strap of it over one shoulder. She

18

kept it pinned to her side with the pressure of her elbow.

'Where are you from?' one of the Dutch wives asked her, as they sipped heavily sweetened tea from the vendor's Thermos. A column of Indian Army trucks ground slowly past, part of the border defence forces. Young soldiers with guns at the ready peered at them over the tailgates.

Instead of saying 'England,' and naming the pleasant south-coast market town where she lived within easy reach of Hattie and several other friends, and where her most recent job had been located, Mair surprised herself by answering, 'North Wales.' Her childhood home was now occupied by a businessman from Manchester and his young family, so there were no ties left, except her brother and sister and their memories. But even so, or perhaps because of this, the valley and the years of her childhood lived within its limits were much in her mind. She missed home, now it had been sold and she could never go back. She clung to the thought of her grandparents and their lives in this strange place.

'And you?' Mair returned quickly.

'Utrecht. Are you on holiday?'

'Ye-es. Just travelling.'

The rucksack lay against her hip. The shawl was folded in a pouch inside it.

The woman sighed. 'We are not finding it so easy on these roads. My husband is unwell.'

From behind the bus came the unmistakable sound of someone throwing up. Between themselves, the Israeli youths found this uproariously funny.

The bus ground over one more high pass and a huge vista opened ahead. Their destination was a high, flat, remote place north of the mountains. Geographically, it was part of the Tibetan plateau although still within India.

Changthang was where the nomad peoples of eastern Ladakh traditionally herded and grazed their flocks of goats. Up here, the climate was so cold and harsh that the animals

19

produced the densest, lightest fleece to insulate themselves. The nomads moved the flocks throughout the year in search of the sparse grazing. The goats' fodder and the water they drank were unpolluted, and their wool was the purest it could have been.

From her reading, Mair knew that this was where the finest *pashm* came from, the raw material for Kashmir shawls, so it was from here that her precious, mysterious shawl had almost certainly begun its journey as the wool of a pashmina goat.

When she was finally alone in her tent at the tourist camp, she took the pouch out of her rucksack and examined the shawl once more by the light of her head-torch. The faint spicy scent caught in the soft folds, she now knew, was the scent of India itself. The central motif of the shawl's woven design was a peacock's tail fan. A deep double border enclosed the centre panel, with lush paisley shapes filling the angles, and there were broad bands of exuberant foliage at either end. The bands, which were partly embroidered, gave an almost brocaded effect. For all its beauty, though, the shawl was battered and worn. There were lines of fading that showed where it had lain for decades in the same folds; the intricate embroidery was unravelling in places, and in others it was rubbed away altogether. There were blotches of ink in one corner, an irregular yellow stain in another. Mair drew it over her knees, absently tracing the arabesques of embroidery and smoothing the knotted fringes, trying to read the shawl's history as if it were a map.

Early in the morning their guide rounded up Mair, the Dutch and the Israelis while it was still barely light, and drove them up a track that was no more than a slightly less rocky channel between the grey boulders littering the plain. They reached the shores of a vast lake, where the water was filmed with ice and the ground was powdered with snow. At the lake's edge stood a handful of single-storey houses, little more than huts, set between a line of bare poplars. Yaks, with their long hair almost brushing the snow, moved ponderously between the rocks. In preparation for winter the Changpa nomad families were bringing down their herds from the more remote pastures. There were circles of low stone walls close to the lake, and the early arrivals had flung goat-hair tarpaulins over these to make shelters for themselves and their animals. Smoke rose in thin columns from the ventilation holes at the apex. A woman with a bent back trudged up from the water's edge carrying a full bucket.

The goats stank – there was no other word for it. The nomad camp was also redolent of kerosene and animal dung and woodsmoke, but the dominant, throat-clogging smell was of unadulterated goat.

A display was laid on for the tourists. Three men in rough tunics and yak-skin boots drove a handful of their animals into a stone-walled enclosure. Mair pulled the flaps of her fleece hat over her ears and shivered in the keen wind. She could almost feel the layer of ice thickening on the lake. The goats were shaggy creatures, white and brown and black, with curved horns and disturbing long-pupilled eyes. They allowed themselves to be hobbled and tipped on to their sides where they lay, stiff-legged and reeking. From the recesses of their garments, the men produced wooden implements like hair-brushes, set with fierce, incurved stiff metal prongs. With synchronised vigour, they each set to work on a goat, rasping and tugging at the wool of the throat and chest. Matted clods of hair began to yield to this treatment, coming away in chunks with the embedded dirt, dung and grease. The goats protested and the men countered with a throaty, ululating song.

'They are singing to the goats, telling them to give some good *pashm* in return for the sweet grass they have eaten and the good water they have drunk,' explained the guide.

A woman gathered up the tufts of hair as the men disentangled them from the combs, taking care to retrieve every last wisp,

21

and stuffed them into a frost-stiffened polythene sack.

'Each family has between eighty and two hundred goats. The animals are combed in May and September. Each animal's combing yields approximately two hundred grams of raw wool,' the guide intoned, in his chipped English. At least she didn't have to translate all this again, Mair reflected, unlike her companions.

'How much money do they get?' asked the Dutchman who hadn't been travel-sick.

'Sixteen hundred rupees for a kilo,' the guide told him. 'Maybe more, maybe less, depends on quality. After cleaning and processing, that kilo of raw wool will yield only three hundred grams of pure fibre ready for spinning.'

Mair stared at the sack. It would take a lot of combings to add up to one kilo and probably a whole herd of goats' combings to fill that one bag. And it was very hard to conceive how those filthy, greasy bundles could ever be transformed into the feathery elegance of her shawl.

'So what happens next?' asked one of the Israeli boys, although he didn't sound all that interested.

'The wool traders come out by truck from Leh. They buy the *pashm*, and take it back to town for processing,'

Another of the boys had retrieved a rusty can from the detritus scattered across the Changpa camp. He set it on a rock and aimed pebbles at it.

'Is that all?' his friend wanted to know. A fusillade of stones clattered against the can until it bounced off the rock.

The guide looked offended. 'This is the traditional way for the people. It has happened like this for hundreds of years.'

'But is this all there is to *see*?'

'This afternoon we will visit the monastery. There are some fine paintings.'

'Yeah.'

The demonstration over, the men freed their goats and chased them out of the pen. Their leader waited for a cash hand-out and the others hastened towards the nearest tent enclosure.

Mair hoped they were going to spend the rest of the day sitting by a log fire, singing goat-herding ballads and drinking *chang*. She unbuckled her rucksack, checking yet again that the shawl was wrapped inside, and took a five-hundred-rupee note out of her wallet. The man's blackened fist rapidly closed on it, but not so quickly that the guide didn't see how much. He would think she was a careless Western pushover because the tip was far too generous, but she didn't care.

'*Julley*,' she murmured. It was the all-purpose Ladakhi word for 'hello', 'goodbye' and 'thank you'.

'*Julley*,' said the man. He was already on his way over to the Dutch.

Mair had planned to unwrap her shawl and spread it on some sun-baked rocks, with the goats browsing in the background, to take an artistic photograph of its beginnings to show Eirlys and Dylan – but she would have had to weight it with small rocks to stop it blowing away and there were pellets of windborne ice pinging against her cheeks. The whole scene was just too bleak for anything more than a mental acknowledgement that this was where the fine, light wool had originated perhaps seventy years ago. Nothing would have changed since then. And she was glad she had made the visit. She contented herself with taking a picture of the lake and the trees, with a white-wool long-haired goat glaring in front of them.

There was no way to capture the smell, but that wasn't a matter for regret.

As for her grandparents: now that she had been here herself it seemed implausible that even an emissary from the Welsh Presbyterian Mission to Leh would have penetrated this far. Surely Evan Watkins would have found enough preaching to do in the villages along the Indus and Zanskar rivers without pursuing the Changpa people out here. He couldn't have reached this spot in winter, because the snows would have cut it off.

Her companions were trudging back across the plateau

towards the white speck of the Toyota. Mair took one last look at the goats and their backdrop and headed after them.

'Back in the bus, guys,' the leader of the Israeli boys shouted. The other two tramped eagerly after him.

TWO

Back in Leh, Mair spent a day trying to find the caretaker who held the keys to the European cemetery.

'This afternoon maybe he will be here,' predicted an old man, sitting on a step with his hookah.

But in the afternoon there was no old man, and no caretaker or keys. Mair stood in frustration on the wrong side of the fence as leaves like gold flakes rattled from the trees and drifted over the gravestones. In Ladakh, she was learning, life was lived at its own pace. She walked back into town, intending to go to a café to drink *chai* and make a plan.

In the main street in front of the mosque, she caught sight of red-gold hair, blazing above the white caps and grey backs of men heading for prayers. The woman and child were fully occupied, the child in having a tantrum that screwed her face into a crimson knot and the mother in mildly remonstrating with her. There was no sign of the saturnine husband.

'*Non, non!*' the child cried, kicking her feet in the dirt.

'That's enough,' the woman ordered, in American-accented English. 'Stop it right now.' There was amusement as well as resignation in her expression. Her arms were weighted with shopping bags, and she put down one load in order to have a hand free for the child. But the little girl had already noticed Mair watching her. She blinked her eyes, in which there were no signs of tears, only outrage. The yells changed from private fury to operatic display.

Mair glanced round. There was open space behind and in front of her. She lifted one finger and locked eyes with the child. The tantrum abruptly faded as curiosity took over. As soon as she had the little girl's full attention Mair drew a breath, gathered herself up and executed a standing back-flip.

It was quite a long time since she had attempted one, and she rocked on landing, but otherwise it was fairly satisfactory. The child's mouth fell open and her eyes made two circles of amazement. Mair clapped hands at her, and did two forwards linked hand-springs. Hattie and she had synchronised this routine as part of their act, and even now she could probably have done it in her sleep. The second somersault brought her up quite close to the mother and child. The little girl grabbed Mair's leg and gazed up at her. A smile lit her face.

'Again! *Encore une fois!*'

The mother was laughing. 'That's pretty neat. And it's way better than a candy bribe.'

Mair was slightly embarrassed to realise that her intention had probably been to attract the mother's attention as much as the child's. They had also drawn a fair-sized crowd of onlookers because there weren't many other distractions on offer in town on this end-of-season afternoon. She hoped the spectators would quickly move away.

'It seems to have done the trick. Can I give you a hand with these?' Mair brushed dirt off her hands and picked up the shopping, leaving the mother to scoop up her daughter and settle her across her hip with the same easy movement she had used in the bazaar.

'Jumping lady,' said the child in wonder, stretching a small hand to pat Mair's face.

'That's right,' her mother agreed. 'Pretty amazing, huh?' Her voice had a touch of the American south in it.

'As a matter of fact it was rather shaky. I'm not quite sure what came over me. I wanted to stop your daughter crying.'

The other woman sighed. 'You and me both. She'd set her sights on being with her dad this afternoon and ended up stuck with me instead. He's gone to sort out guides and ponies – we're leaving on a trek tomorrow. That's what all this shopping's about – what *do* you take in the way of supplies? Where are you heading? I'm Karen Becker, by the way. And this is Lotus.'

Lotus raised her hand and gave a queenly wave.

'Mair Ellis. Hello, Lotus.' Mair smiled.

The child was extraordinarily beautiful, with a broad forehead and a mouth like a cherub's in a Renaissance painting.

'I was on my way to get a cup of tea,' she added.

Karen nodded across the road. 'Great. We're going to the salon, Lo, aren't we? We have to get ourselves a pedicure before we trek a single step. Come with us, and we can chat. I'm sure they'll give you tea.'

Mair was glad to escape from the staring crowd. The two women stepped over the gutter and picked their way between bullocks and auto-rickshaws to a glass-fronted shop with windows heavily draped in lace. 'Ladies Only Beauty', said the sign in the window.

Inside they found a cracked floor, not noticeably clean, dusty bare shelves, and a row of barber's chairs. There was a smell of old-fashioned perming lotion mingled with incense and boiled laundry. A small flock of women in bright saris instantly surrounded Lotus, lifted her out of Karen's arms and bore her off to the back of the shop. They started combing her white-blonde hair with trills of admiration. Lotus accepted the attention as no more than her due.

A smiling girl with a red-cheeked, perfectly round Tibetan face relieved them of the shopping. A moment later they were installed in adjacent chairs, facing their reflections in a blotchy mirror.

'Go on. You may as well.' Karen grinned.

Mair allowed her Tibetan attendant to unlace her Converse

27

for her, then to steer her feet into a pink plastic foot spa. The motor thrummed under her soles and the water seethed. The whole scene was so incongruous that she couldn't help laughing.

In the mirror Karen's blue eyes met hers. 'Tell me. You must be something like a *capoiera* dancer, right? We saw some of those street performers in Rio. Have you been there? *A*-mazing. I'd so love to be able to move like that. Not in a million years, though.'

Mair laughed again. 'What? No, I'm not any kind of dancer. I worked in a circus years and years ago.'

'In a *circus*? Do you come from a circus family? Go on, your dad was the lion tamer, wasn't he, and your mom was the lady in spangles who did pirouettes on the elephant's back? You were born in a showman's caravan, and as soon as you could walk you were dressed up in a tiny costume for the parade. *Don't* tell any of this to Lotus, please – it'll only give her ideas.'

Karen had plenty of imagination herself, evidently. Mair was fascinated by her spectacular looks and her vivacity, but she wasn't quite sure what to make of her. 'Nothing so glamorous, I'm afraid. My father was a farm-supplies salesman and my mother was a primary-school teacher in North Wales.'

'So, how come?'

Mair might have deflected these questions, but she was the one who had been guilty of exhibitionism and she thought the least she could do was give a straight answer. 'I was a rebellious child, and I'd been threatening for so many years to run away and join a circus that when the time actually came it would have been a loss of face not to do it. Ours was quite a right-on show. No lions. In fact, no animals at all, because that would have been cruel. My friend and I had a trapeze act, and in the kids' show we were the clowns as well. We did that for about four years, and then it was time to grow up.'

'I see.' Karen's eyes narrowed. 'Do I believe all this? Or is it one of those versions of oneself that one does for passing encounters with strangers? If it is, I'll find out, I'm warning you. We're going to be friends. I'm always right about these things.'

A young girl arrived balancing a tin tray of tea glasses. Mair took one and sipped. The tea was milky and thick with sugar, but it was welcome. Her attendant lifted one of her feet out of the bath and dried it in her lap. Then she set to work slathering on handfuls of some gritty potion.

Karen chatted on: 'How could I pass up the chance of making friends with someone who turns somersaults in the air before she's even spoken?'

Across the room, Lotus had a dozen ribbon bows in her hair. Her tiny fingernails were being dabbed with glitter polish.

Mair decided it was time to seize the conversational initiative. 'What are you doing in Leh?' she asked.

Karen's eyes widened. Her face in the mirror became a pale, intent oval. 'We arrived here from Tibet. I'm a Buddhist, you see. It's been a pilgrimage for me.' She began to talk about the monasteries she had visited, and the devotions she had made. She had been blessed by the senior lama after the annual unveiling of a spectacular *thangka* painting, which had been one of the most spiritual experiences of her life. Did Mair practise? Really not? Had she never felt the call to do so? Did she know that one of His Holiness's summer residences was actually here in Leh? Had she seen the huge golden Maitreya out at Thikse *Gompa*?

'Yes,' Mair managed to say to the latter. Brisk massaging of her foot and ankle was showering the floor with dead skin and caked foot cream.

Karen's leg was undergoing the same treatment. She paused in her monologue and turned her glancing attention to the young girl, who had come back with a small selection of polishes on the tea tray. 'Pink or red, do you think?'

'Red,' Mair replied automatically.

'Hmm. Yeah, but I'm going to go for the pink. Don't want to frighten the ponies, do I? Lotus, what colour are your toes?' she called.

'Pink, shiny,' Lotus chirped.

'How pretty. Daddy will love them.'

'And now you're going trekking.'

Karen waved a languid hand. 'That's my husband's partiality. It's a reasonable trade-off, I guess. My monasteries for his mountains. Although we met in New York, we're based in Geneva right now because Bruno is Swiss. These days, he gets to go skiing and mountain climbing pretty regularly from home, but we agreed that this holiday shouldn't be all Buddhist. Lotus would protest about that too, although she's generally pretty easy-going. Not that she looked that way when you saw her this afternoon, I admit, but she doesn't often freak out like that.'

'You'll take her on the trek with you?'

Karen looked surprised, then shrugged. 'Sure. Why not? Bruno carries her in a backpack most of the way. Everywhere we go, Lotus comes along. That way you get a balanced, open-minded kid.'

The child wriggled away from her admirers and came to show off her manicure, spreading her small hands on Mair's knees and beaming up at her. The ribbons fluttered in her ringlets. There was logic in Karen's theory, Mair thought. She remembered her first glimpse of the little family in the bazaar and the intimacy that had impressed her then. Lotus was certainly the most confident two-year-old she had ever met.

'You look lovely,' Mair told her. 'Just like a picture.'

'*Oui – comme Maman*,' Lotus agreed, admiring herself in the mirrors.

The door of the salon opened, setting the lace curtains fluttering. A dark head and shoulders were framed in the doorway. 'Karen?'

Karen glanced up from her scrutiny of her toenails. 'Hi. Did you get everything fixed up already?'

'*Pappy.*' Lotus dashed across and leapt into her father's arms. He swung her off her feet. 'Jumping lady,' she clamoured, pointing at Mair. 'Jumping *high*.'

30

'Bruno, this is Maya,' Karen called. 'My new friend.'

'Hello,' the man said, nodding at her. There was a smile buried in him, Mair thought, but it wasn't close enough to the surface to break through. She started to explain her name, which Karen hadn't quite caught.

Mair was Welsh for Mary. When she was young she had tried to persuade her friends to adopt this more sophisticated version, but it had never caught on. '*Mair, Mair, pants on fire,*' the local kids used to chant. She didn't actually utter any of this, though. Something about Bruno Becker's level, interrogative stare silenced her.

'Mair,' she said quietly. 'Hello.'

The introductions were cut short because the beauty-parlour staff were shooing Bruno out of the door. Ladies Only Beauty clearly meant what it said.

He carried Lotus with him. He indicated to his wife that they would see her back at the hotel when she was ready. 'Nice to meet you,' he said, over his shoulder, to Mair, and was gone. The introduction of a new friend of Karen's was clearly nothing unusual.

Karen stretched out her toes and smiled. 'Peace. That means you and I can go and eat cakes once we're through here. We can have a proper talk.'

Mair felt like a pebble being tumbled along by a tsunami, but Karen Becker was too insistent – and too interesting – for her to make any real attempt at resistance. In any case, what else would she be doing?

Once their toenail polish had dried to Karen's satisfaction they strolled down a nearby alley to the German bakery. Over apple cake and coffee Karen confided that she had wanted to come to this part of the world for years, really ever since she had gotten interested in the Buddhist way in her early twenties. So far it had totally lived up to her expectations. These places were holy – they touched your soul directly. You hardly ever encountered that depth of spirituality in Europe, did you? And never in the US of A. Not that *she* had ever recognised, anyway,

Karen concluded. Did Mair – was she pronouncing it right? – did she know what Karen meant?

Mair thought of the whitewashed hilltop *gompas* she had visited in the last few days. The dark inner rooms with dim wall paintings and statues of the Buddha were thick with the scent of incense and wood ash, their altars heaped with offerings, often touchingly mundane ones like packets of sweet biscuits or posies of plastic flowers. The murmured chanting of monks rose through the old floors, and windows gave startling views of braided rivers and orchards far below. There *was* a divinity here, she reflected, but more than anything it troubled her with its elusiveness.

At one monastery the guide had beckoned her into the kitchen where an old monk was tranquilly preparing the community's dinner. With a wooden ladle he scooped water from a bucket into a blackened pot set on a wood-fired stove. Cold balls of rice were gathered into cloths ready for distribution. Kneeling beside him at a rough table, a boy monk of about ten chopped vegetables from the monastery garden. The old man nodded to indicate that he was satisfied with the effort as successive handfuls of carrot and onion were dropped into the pot. The two worked in silence, and it had occurred to Mair that, apart from her presence, this scene would have been exactly the same two or three hundred years ago. The monks' quiet service to the unending routines of cooking and providing for others had touched her more eloquently than any of the religious rituals.

She tried to describe this tiny epiphany to Karen.

'But I understand *completely*,' Karen interjected. She reached out and covered Mair's fingers with her own. 'There are many paths to recognition, but they are all the same road. You *do* know what I'm talking about. I was sure you would. I felt it in you as soon as I saw you.'

'Even though I was turning somersaults?'

'Because of that, as much as anything else. Why suppress what you wanted to emote? You are the complete you. I endorse that.'

32

Bruno wasn't spiritual in the same sense that she was, Karen continued, but he understood where she was coming from because he related to the mountains. They were his temples, and he made his own pilgrimages among them. 'Take Lotus, for example. I believe in letting her experience the whole world as essentially benign. I want her to grow up as far as possible without fear, without unnecessary restrictions, without petty rules, so she can become her intended self within the stream.'

Mair wondered if Lotus – quite understandably – dealt with excess benignity by having a tantrum or two.

They had finished their coffee and cake. Karen dotted up the last of the crumbs with a fingertip and licked it. She said, 'I must go. What are your plans? We'll be out of town for four or five days.'

'I've got some stuff to look into here. I don't know how long that'll take.'

Karen studied her, her finger still resting against her lips. Mair noticed how the two or three other tourists in the bakery couldn't help gazing at her companion.

'You're very mysterious, you know,' Karen said.

'No, I'm not,' Mair protested.

'But you've never let on why you're in Ladakh. You're not just here for a sightseeing holiday, I can tell that much.'

Mair wasn't going to try to describe the shawl to Karen, or the lock of hair, or the blanks in the family history that had colonised her imagination with such force. Awkwardly, she said, 'My father died recently.'

At once, Karen's face flooded with sympathy. 'I'm sorry,' she said warmly. 'That's sad for you. You were drawn to a Buddhist country for a reason. Have you heard of *punabbhava*? It means "becoming again". That's the belief we have in rebirth. It doesn't annihilate grief or loss, and it isn't meant to, but contemplation of it provides comfort. Sometimes it does, at least.'

Her new friend meant well, Mair realised, and the way she talked might sound alien but it was certainly sincere. 'Thank you.' She smiled.

33

Karen squeezed her hands and stood up. She paid for their tea, waving away Mair's proffered money. 'Where are you staying?'

Mair told her.

'So we'll see you when we get back.'

The next day Mair went to visit the Leh Pashmina Processing Plant. The weather was changing, as if to underline the Beckers' absence. The gilded autumn sunshine Mair had begun to take for granted was filtered out today by low, thin grey clouds as the last leaves were chased down from the poplar trees by an insistent wind.

A small man in a baseball cap emerged from one of the plant's grimy buildings to meet her. 'My name is Tinley. I am assistant manager of production. This way to see the magic, ma'am,' he joked, as he led her across the yard to a concrete shed. Mair followed, not sure what he meant.

Inside, four women squatted in a circle. They had shawls drawn over their heads and across the lower half of their faces. Between them towered a heap of fleece, thick curled clods of raw goat's hair matted with dung, grease and twigs, looking exactly as Mair had seen it when it was stuffed into bags up on the plateau. There was no doubt that this was the untreated *pashm* fibre as it arrived by truck from distant Changthang. The women were teasing out the clumps by hand, removing the worst of the filth and sorting the hair into smaller heaps according to colour, from palest grey-white to dark brown. The air in the bare room seemed almost solid with the rancid odour of goat.

Tinley made a small gesture of regret. 'This is a colour-separating process. It can only be done by the human eyes.' Then he brightened. 'But, as you will see, the rest of our process is modern. Highly mechanised. Come this way, please.'

A metal door slid open on runners and Mair stepped into the next section of the plant. She had been aware of the hum of machinery, but she blinked at the sheer size of what lay beyond the door. The machine must have been fifty yards long, a leviathan of rotating belts and spinning flywheels, vast rubber rollers and steaming tanks. At the end of the line was a drying chamber from which the wool emerged cleaner and softer, but still with thick coarse hairs and fragments of dirt trapped in it.

'What now?' she asked, as she twisted a hank between her fingers.

A second metal door opened ahead. A wave of humid air, heavy with the smell of wet wool, rolled over her.

'Why is it so hot? And so damp?' she choked out.

'It is a humidified chamber,' Tinley said proudly. 'It makes the wool easier to work. This is the dehairing section, see?'

They peered into the machinery. At each stage the remaining wool emerged whiter and softer, as the pure fleece – the goat's innermost insulation against the Himalayan cold – was separated out.

At the end of the line, after another drying chamber, the belt turned back on itself. One man sat in reverent attendance as the cleansed and blow-dried end product billowed from the jaws of the machinery.

Mair couldn't help herself. She stepped forward and plunged her arms up to the elbows into pure *pashm*. It was like handling a cloud, weightless and pure, and exactly the same colour. She remembered that one kilo of the greasy, reeking wool she had seen at the beginning of the line produced a mere three hundred grams of this airy fleece. 'It *is* a kind of magic,' she agreed.

Tinley's eyes glinted. 'Come with me.' He settled his baseball cap squarely on his head and led the way out of the processing plant.

The back lanes were too narrow for two to walk abreast, and were overhung with washing lines, the branches of knotty old trees and the projecting balconies of houses. Tinley walked so fast that Mair had to concentrate on keeping up. At a collapsing set of gates in a whitewashed wall he suddenly stopped and nodded her through. Hens scratched in refuse and the call of the muezzin rose over the housetops.

'*Julley*,' Tinley called, to a man leaning on a broom.

Up four stone steps and through a narrow door, they came into a roomful of women seated at wooden looms. There was a steady creak of floor treadles and the flash of shuttles as they worked. They were weaving plain pashmina lengths, in soft shades of grey and brown. These workers, Tinley told her, were producing shawls for sale through the state-sponsored craft-industry outlets in Leh. 'Very traditional methods preserved, nice work for women here. They can work what hours they can, make some money, and also take care of families.'

'That's good,' Mair acknowledged. But she was puzzled by how different these pieces were from her own.

They passed through the weavers' studio and the women looked up at her and smiled as she passed. The front of the building, to Mair's surprise, opened out on to a view she recognised – the main street, with the minarets of the central mosque rising against the hill crowned with the old palace. Via the backstreet labyrinth they had come into a shawl showroom, lined with the now-familiar shelves. A salesman grinned a flash of gold incisor at her as he began to slide his wares out of their plastic bags.

Leh could sometimes seem like one large wool-based retail opportunity.

There was no question of withholding her custom, though, after Tinley had patiently taken her through the manufacturing processes. Mair obediently picked out three shawls: a pearl-grey one for Eirlys, a toffee-brown one for herself, and a cream one for Hattie, which would suit her friend's dark colouring. She paid twelve thousand rupees in all, and reminded herself that it was not such a great deal of money for all the work that had gone into producing the pashmina fibre.

The salesman took her purchases away to wrap, and on a sudden impulse Mair opened her rucksack and pulled the folded pouch from the innermost recess. Tinley watched curiously as she unfolded her grandmother's shawl and gently spread it on the shop's plain wooden counter. The colours of water and blossom made a pool of brilliance in the subdued light of the shop. The goods on the shelves appeared suddenly drab and coarse in comparison. Tinley gave a sharp sniff as he bent over to examine the shawl more closely, and the salesman swung round to take a look.

'Can you tell me anything about this?' Mair asked.

Tinley picked up a small hand lens from behind the counter and minutely examined the weave, running his fingers over the embroidery before flipping the fabric to examine the reverse. He traced the outlines of the paisley shapes and peered even more closely through his lens at one corner of the piece.

'This is Kashmiri work,' he said. '*Kani* weaving. We don't do this here in Ladakh.'

The salesman said something to him.

'You are selling it?' Tinley casually enquired.

'No. Definitely, no. It belonged to my grandmother. I am . . . just trying to find out something about the shawl's history, and maybe through that a little about my grandmother. I never knew her, you see.'

Tinley put aside his lens and straightened up. 'Then you must go over the mountains to the Vale of Kashmir,' he said.

'I think my grandparents were here in Leh, though. During the 1940s. My grandfather was a Christian missionary.'

'A Catholic? Moravians?'

'No. He was Welsh, a Presbyterian.'

Tinley shook his head, shrugging. This clearly meant nothing to him. 'The Europeans came, not many stayed. They opened some clinics and founded schools for children and for that we owe them a debt.' The unspoken rider was that for other things the missionaries had attempted, presumably the work of religious conversion, less gratitude was due.

Mair said, 'I wanted to take a look at the European graveyard here, but the gates are always locked and I can't find out who has the key.'

Tinley grinned, showing good teeth, and pushed his cap to

37

an angle. He spoke rapidly to the storekeeper and they both laughed.

'That's easy. Tsering, my friend here, his uncle is the caretaker.'

The two men exchanged more information and Tinley told Mair that if she came back to the shop tomorrow, perhaps at three o'clock, the uncle would bring the key and take her to visit the graveyard.

She thanked them both and promised she would be there promptly. She began to fold the shawl again, but Tinley touched her wrist. 'You have seen this?' he asked, pointing to one corner of it. He put the lens into her hand, and she leant over to see what she hadn't noticed before. There was a tiny embroidered symbol, like a stylised butterfly or perhaps the initials BB, with the first letter reversed, and next to it another indecipherable mark. 'What is it?'

'It is the maker's signature, and the numbers "42", which is perhaps the date of completion. It is a fine piece, and it would have taken many months, even years, for the craftsman to weave and then embroider. Probably it was made for a bride, as a wedding shawl for her to take with her to her husband's home.'

For Grandmother Nerys Watkins, as a gift from her husband the Welsh Presbyterian missionary? Mair thought the shawl was far too opulent for that. Nothing she had learnt about her grandparents' circumstances or their restrained faith matched its rarity and value. The mystery seemed only to deepen.

She put the new shawls into her bag with the precious old one, thanked the shopkeeper, and repeated that she would be back at three the next day.

Tinley smiled broadly. 'You must be wearing your new pashmina. The cold weather is coming. Winter is early for us this year.'

As she walked through the old town the next afternoon, she saw how the place was turning in on itself under a bitter wind scything down off the mountain ice fields. She could smell snow in the air, as Tinley had predicted, and she was glad of the warmth of her muted brown shawl round her throat. Most of the house windows were now protected by old wooden shutters, and almost every roof towered with bundles of wood and stored animal fodder. There were fewer people about in the bazaar and she passed only one or two Westerners. In another week or two the last of the cafés and guesthouses would be closed, the summer migrant workers would head down to the beaches and hotels of Goa for the winter season, and Leh would sink into its winter isolation as the snow piled up on the passes. She thought of the Beckers, and wondered how they were coping in their tent in this cold weather.

At the showroom there was, of course, no sign of the uncle with the elusive key. Tsering the shopkeeper waved his hand at her impatience. He wanted to show her a new consignment of shawls, just arrived from the finisher. They drank *masala chai* and nibbled almonds and dried apricots as Mair admired the wares. She was learning that the ritualised exchanges of buyer and seller must take place even though they both knew that money and shawl were not going to change hands today.

After a pleasant half-hour, the door that led to the weavers' studio clicked open. A tiny, ancient man in a fur cap and felt boots bound with strips of leather tottered on the threshold.

'My uncle Sonam.' Tsering beamed, putting a heavy arm over his shoulder. 'My grandmother brother.'

Mair shook hands with the venerable figure, thinking that it was hardly surprising he didn't spend much time caretaking. He looked too old to do anything except sit and doze in an armchair.

'Good afternoon, Sonam-*le*,' she said, giving him what she had learnt was the polite honorific. The old man darted a bright-eyed appraising look at her. He spoke in an undertone to Tsering and jerked his thumb towards the shop door.

With alacrity Tsering pulled on his Adidas jacket. 'We'll go,' he said.

39

'You're going to leave the shop?'

'My uncle does not speak English. Anyway,' he shrugged and spread his hands, his face creasing, 'I do not see any customer.'

He locked the door behind them and the three of them set off, Sonam's long, belted tunic swishing around his ankles and his fur cap bobbing as they crossed the bazaar. He could move surprisingly fast. Within minutes they had reached the familiar locked gates of the European cemetery. Sonam reached inside his layers of clothing, rummaged for a moment, and withdrew a huge key. The gates at last swung open and Mair passed through, under the gaunt trees and between the crosses and headstones. The ground was covered with fallen leaves, their buttery gold already brown and lifeless. The cold stung her cheeks.

'What are you looking for?' Tsering asked.

Mair tried to interpret the German inscription on the nearest stone. 'I don't know,' she confessed.

To her relief, the two men retreated to a small green lean-to placed against a sheltered wall. She wandered along the haphazard rows. There were several tiny graves, one with a stone that read simply 'Josephine, aged 7 months'. She tried to imagine how European women so far from home had struggled to look after their children in this remote place, and how they must often have prayed in vain.

She came to one small group of headstones bearing Welsh names, the Williamses and Thomases and Joneses of her own home valley, who could only have belonged to the Presbyterian mission. She took out her notebook and copied down the names and dates to look up in *Hope and the Glory of God* next time she had access to the Internet. She recognised one line of Welsh that was utterly familiar because she had seen it most recently in the graveyard at home, engraved on a stone just a few feet from her mother and father's. *Hedd perffaith hedd.* Peace, perfect peace.

Homesickness closed on her, unexpected but as tight as a

clenched fist. She experienced a moment's confused longing to be back in the valley. She could see her father at the kitchen table, his head bent over his newspaper and the inevitable cup of tea at his elbow.

She steadied herself by looking towards the white battlements of the Himalayas and the clouds that mounted above them. Evan and Nerys Watkins might well have stood in this same spot and gazed at the same view. Nerys must sometimes have been painfully homesick too, and it would have been further to travel then, and much harder for her to communicate with the people she had left behind. For the first time since she had come to India, Mair felt emotionally connected to her grandmother.

She walked slowly on until she had completed a circuit of the enclosure. It was disappointing, but there was nothing except the three or four Welsh names on gravestones. She was about to cross to the hut, where Tsering and his uncle were huddled out of the wind smoking *bidis*, when she noticed a plaque set into a wall.

She read:

In Memoriam
Matthew Alexander Forbes, St John's College, Cambridge
Lost on Nanga Parbat, August 1938, aged 22

Mair wasn't sure what or where Nanga Parbat was, but she guessed it was a mountain. Twenty-two was very young.

'How are you, ma'am?' Tsering was calling to her. 'Did you find something?'

She shook her head. 'From the names there are some Welsh buried here, but there's nothing to connect them to my family.'

Sonam turned his head and studied her. He looked so old, but he was as alert as his great-nephew. He muttered a question and Tsering shrugged and translated for her: 'He says, why not say first that you are interested in the Welsh people?'

Mair blinked.

Sonam stood up and gestured over the wall. She nodded

agreement and he led the way out of the cemetery and down a lane that meandered behind it, with Mair and Tsering doing their best to keep up. She hadn't explored this quarter of the old town, and she looked with sad interest at crumbling stone walls and gaping potholes. The old buildings were mostly sinking into dereliction. A woman carrying a bundle of kindling on her head greeted Sonam as he sped by.

The lane petered out at a blank wall flanked by two abandoned buildings. One was of plain stone with tall windows veiled in layers of ancient dust, and it struck Mair at once that in its absolute lack of pretension it resembled a Welsh chapel. The one opposite was no more than a wall with a collapsing door in it, but at Sonam's nod Tsering pushed open the door. It gave on to a little paved courtyard surrounded by single-storey buildings. Weeds and saplings tilted the old paving stones, and all the glass in the small-paned windows had gone. A pair of starved dogs appeared in a dark doorway and gave them a yellow-eyed glare.

Tsering and Sonam consulted.

'This is old mission, with school and medical clinic, my uncle remembers well. Across there, that was Welsh church. Then it became Hindu temple, but now there is new one built by them. These days, nothing here.' He gave a shrug without a glimmer of optimism in it. Mair had noticed a similar gesture too often during her conversations in Leh.

Sonam was nodding harder, waving at her to indicate that she should feel free to explore this desolate place.

Avoiding the dogs, she peered into the tiny rooms. The first two were empty, except for weeds poking up through the floors, scattered refuse and torn sacks, but in the third lay some rotten sticks of furniture. One piece was just recognisable as a school-room chair, with a small shelf on the back for books. There had been chairs quite similar to this one in the infants' class at her own school. Mair bent and tried to set it upright but the shelf came away in her hands. At her feet lay the remains of a book, a sad remnant with swollen covers that had been half protected from the damp and cold by the shelf. She picked it up and looked at the ruined pages, and out of the pulpy grey mass two or three words were just distinguishable.

It was a Welsh hymnal.

Mair lifted her head. She had half thought that the two men might have been trying to please her with a visit to a compound that could have belonged to any of the various missions to Ladakh, or might not have had any missionary connection at all. But now she knew for sure.

Seventy years ago Evan Watkins would have preached in the chapel across the lane, and his wife must have tried to teach the children, perhaps in this very room. She tilted her head to listen, as if she could catch the sound of their voices, but all she could hear was dogs barking and the screech and hoot of distant traffic.

'This is what I wanted to find,' she said quietly, to her companions. After a moment she stooped and replaced the hymnal in its resting place.

The three of them retreated into the fresh air. Sonam took hold of Mair's arm. He began to talk with great animation, words pouring out of him as he shook her elbow and peered up into her face. He had no teeth and his face was crosshatched with deep lines, but he suddenly looked much younger than his age.

'Tell me what he's saying?' she begged Tsering.

'He remembers the teacher here, when he was small boy. She was nice. She gave the children apples and they sang songs.'

Nerys Watkins, who had followed her husband to India and brought back the wedding shawl with a lock of hair hidden in its folds.

'That might have been my grandmother. Does he remember her name? What songs did they sing?'

The shake of the old man's head was enough of an answer, but another rush of words immediately followed. His hands measured out a chunk of the air and he grinned as he pretended to totter under the weight of it. Remembering the long-ago

43

was a pleasure for him, she understood, just as it had become for her father. Tsering patted his uncle on the shoulder, telling him to slow down.

'He says there was a wireless here, the first one my uncle had ever listened to. He liked the music that came out of it. The wireless was *this* big, and heavy. It had a battery, and it needed four men and a cart to take that battery all the way down to the river to be charged at the generator. Then the people would come in close and listen with serious faces. The children wanted to laugh, but it was not allowed. That was when there was the war in Europe, and then it came to Asia.'

Evan and Nerys, listening sombrely to the radio news in one of these low rooms, with the oil lamp throwing their shadows on the wall. She could see them so clearly now, at last: Evan in his preacher's black, and Nerys with an apron covering her plain skirt and hand-knitted jersey.

'Yes.' She nodded. 'That was when it was.'

There was nothing more to see in the abandoned compound. Tsering was interested and he made another circuit with her, looking through every doorway, but they made no further discoveries. After his flash of recollection Sonam seemed weary, all his energy spent. Mair gently put her hand on his shoulder. 'Thank you. I'm glad to have come here.'

They made their way back down the lane, Sonam walking much more slowly and with his great-nephew's support. The twilight was deepening and lights shone out of the windows of houses nearer to the cemetery until there was a blink, then another, and the power failed. The single street lamp in the distance went out. Mair and her companions halted under the navy-blue sky as Tsering searched an inner pocket for a flashlight. The old man put out a hand to Mair to steady himself, and she took his arm. Linked together, with the thin torch-beam picking out the deep holes and collapsed walls in their path, they stepped carefully onwards to the road.

At the junction where she turned off towards her hotel, she said goodbye to the two men. The money she gave Sonam disappeared in a flash into a slit in his tunic. He grasped her by the wrist and angled his head to peer at her in the gloom. Tsering translated for the last time.

'In those days, the old times, it was very hard to live here. There was not much, for any people. But it was good, just the same.'

The old man was telling her that Evan Watkins and his wife had not experienced undiluted hardship here in Leh. There had been happiness too.

Mair could understand that.

She shook hands with them.

Tsering grinned, his teeth white in the darkness. 'You are looking for history from your shawl. Now you will be going to Kashmir.'

'I will, yes.'

'Safe journey,' he said.

They wished her goodnight. As she watched them making slow progress down the deserted street, the power came on again. Their moving shadows slid over the old stone walls.

THREE

India, 1941

He had taken their candle behind the screen with him. It was only a hinged wooden frame with brown paper pasted across it, and the light, placed on the hidden washstand, threw his enlarged and distorted shadow on to the paper. Nerys turned to face the other way, in order not to see her husband washing himself. She studied instead the plain wooden crucifix that hung on the wall beside the bed.

The yellow glow of the candle flickered as he carried it from the washstand and placed it on the night table, so she knew it was all right to turn on to her back again. The mattress, stuffed with yak's hair, gave out its familiar rustle as she moved. There was a whiff of carbolic soap with a lingering trace of male sweat as Evan picked up the Bible that always lay next to his pillow. He sank to his knees beside the bed. Nerys at once made a move to push back the blanket and join him in his prayers, but he told her that she should stay where she was.

'The Lord sees everything. He won't frown if you take a few more days' rest, Nerys.'

'I'm perfectly all right,' she murmured, but she lay still because she felt so tired. She listened as he read in Welsh from the Book of Job, one of his favourite resorts. 'Amen,' she said, when she thought he had finished. There was an interval as he prayed in silence, and she attempted the same herself. Among other things, she asked God if He could somehow make a better wife of her.

At last Evan sighed and got to his feet. He took off his thick dressing-gown and hung it on the hook, peeled back the blanket, letting a blade of cold air into the bed, and hovered for a moment in his striped flannel pyjamas, as if to lie down beside her took a positive effort of will.

'Are you ready?' he asked.

'Yes,' she said.

He blew out the candle and got in. The mattress sank under his weight and she tensed her hip and leg muscles in order not to roll against him. Not that she didn't long for the comfort of his arms and the warmth of his skin, because she felt so sad and empty that she craved physical reassurance without any of the pitfalls that words could lead to, but it had been a long day and she didn't want to place even this much of a demand on him.

'Goodnight, my dear,' he said, after a moment.

'Goodnight, Evan,' she said quietly.

It would not be long before he fell asleep. She lay with her fingers interlaced across her breastbone and reviewed the day.

The smaller children gave her the greatest pleasure. She loved the sight of them in class, with school pinafores tied over their ragged clothes, sitting in a neat line with their shining eyes fixed on her as she wrote words and numbers on a blackboard balanced on an easel. One, two, three. Boot, hat, apple, hand. They bore this part of the day patiently, just as they did when she read them stories from the Bible, but what they really enjoyed was singing and dancing and clapping games. They chanted their own words to 'Oranges and Lemons' and 'The Farmer's in His Den', and she tried to copy what they sang because her efforts made them laugh so uproariously. Or with her harmonium and their drums, whistles and tambourines they pounded out made-up songs that filled the room with rhythm and needed no language at all.

The older children were less rewarding. Nerys knew they only came to school because of the mission's free midday meal, soup and rice with a thick stew of lentils. They fidgeted and murmured among themselves as she talked, and as soon as the class finished at three o'clock they raced each other across the yard, happy to be free from her lessons even though the rest of the day would be spent working in the fields, or bent over a weaving loom. She could only hope that the food they ate and the minimal medical attention she could offer, for their racking coughs, gummy eyes and running sores, was a compensation for the two hours of mutual incomprehension they shared with her. By the age of eight or nine, most of them stopped coming altogether. They were too valuable to their parents as extra pairs of hands.

Nerys listened as Evan's breathing slowed and deepened.

However positive she tried to be, it was hard not to feel that they were wasting their time in this place, two ignorant outsiders battling against the primitive conditions, an obscure language and centuries of history.

Of course, Evan wouldn't have agreed that they were ignorant. But Nerys didn't share her husband's absolute conviction that the Word was the only truth, and bringing it to the heathen the only thing that really mattered. She was even afraid that she might be losing her faith altogether, although the mere acknowledgement of this, in silence and under the safe cover of darkness, made her wince with anxiety. How could there be a missionary's wife who didn't believe in the Lord?

Ironically, it was India that had brought her to this precipice of doubt.

Back in Wales, she had first met the Reverend Evan Watkins when he was on home leave from his Indian mission and she was in teacher training, and it had all seemed perfectly straightforward. Their God, the one she and Evan shared, was a daily matter, of course. He was Grace said before meals, prayers at bedtime for family and the sick, the King and Queen and the unfortunate heathen. He was chapel on Sundays, the thick black Bible, Nonconformist hymns, and a whole way of life that she was accustomed to and took comfortably for granted. Even after Evan had proposed (and she had hoped – even *prayed* – that he would ask her), and during their short engagement, the wedding, their honeymoon in Anglesey (she wouldn't dwell on that now) and all the preparations for India that had followed, she had never questioned the basic premise. Evan had heard the call to do missionary work, and she was proud to be accompanying him. She would help him and support him in every way she could, and they would succeed together.

At Shillong, the centre of the Presbyterian outreach mission to India, where they had lived for their first months of married life, it had not been so very difficult. Within the compound there was a large school run by the mission, where the teaching was excellent and the local families seemed prepared to accept the Christian message that accompanied it. As well as the big chapel, with its regular services for mission families and respectable numbers of converts, there was a medical clinic for first aid and minor ailments, classes for local women in domestic skills, hygiene and vegetable-growing that Nerys had enjoyed helping with, and all the support of a small but determined religious community. There was even, at a little distance, a mission hospital, with a resident qualified doctor and three nurses, where women could come to give birth in safer and more sanitary conditions than were available anywhere else in the area. Lepers were treated there too, and TB patients, and sufferers from septicaemia and rabies and all the other shocking ailments of India. Nerys could see that they were doing some good through their work, she and her husband, even though it was in a small, oblique way.

India itself had shocked her. She had only been able to conjure up the most pallid images in advance so the actual vastness, the brutal heat of the plains, so fierce that it flayed her skin and bleached the skies, the swarming people, the solid torrents of monsoon rain, the harsh colours and stink of it all, the flies, the crippled bodies and the raw poverty she saw every day had almost unpinned her. When she tried to confess her dismay to Evan, he had looked annoyed.

'The work is what we are here to do, my dear, with God's help. There is no time for considering ourselves or our misgivings.'

She had begun to retort that she wasn't afraid of work, and she wasn't being self-absorbed, she had only wanted to talk about what they both saw all the time. But she had stopped herself. Evan didn't want to talk about anything except the routine of their days. He had a focus on his work that was so tight, so unwavering, that she began to suspect he was afraid of where speculation might lead him.

In any case, her confusion didn't last. In time she began to see a vitality in this seething country, a kind of dogged appetite that brought babies bawling into the world amid all the desperation, reflected in the eyes of a beggar as he reached up with cupped hands to receive a half-*pice* coin, in the backs of women bent double in the fields, and in the man who sat all day beside the churning traffic with his spirit stove, brewing delicious *chai* to sell to passers-by. Nerys used to stop on her daily walk and drink a cup with this man, sitting on his little three-legged stool while he squatted in the dust. Unfortunately she couldn't see how any of these people might be affected, for either better or worse, by the Christian message that she was supposed to be bringing them. Their situations were nearly all desperate and they had their various religions already. What difference could a merely different one make?

It was a dry, unwelcome seed that took root in her, but its growth was rapid.

Evan worked all the time, preaching, writing, reading and travelling to outlying villages. Even with teaching at the school and trying nervously to deal with the house servants, whose grinning expectation of her orders she found embarrassing, Nerys had plenty of hours to spare. She began helping out at the hospital where the nurses offered much livelier company than the other mission wives.

Her favourite duty was in the labour and delivery room. Her memory of the first baby she saw being born was as vivid as if it had happened that morning. The mother was younger than she was, had borne two children already and had been screaming for two long hours while Nerys sponged her face and struggled to soothe her. But as soon as he was born she reached her arms out for this new infant with a smile that filled the room. Nerys had had to turn aside and wipe her own eyes with a towel.

Her hands slid lower now, an involuntary movement that she tried and failed to suppress, over the corrugated twin arches of her lower ribs, to rest in the slack bowl beneath them. Since her own first pregnancy had miscarried, less than a month ago, she had tried to tell herself that there would soon be another baby on the way. She felt sick and exhausted, and it had taken more than long enough to conceive this one, but still, they would manage, wouldn't they?

Unless this was God's way of punishing her for not believing in Him.

Nerys smiled grimly into the darkness. If she didn't believe, how could miscarriage now or failure to conceive again at some time in the future be a divine punishment for anything?

Think about something else, she advised herself. Her husband sighed in his sleep and curled on his side, facing away from her.

When Evan had been offered the chance to go all the way up to Leh, where the resident Welsh missionary had died of dysentery, he had explained to Nerys that they did not have to go. They should see it as an offer, an opportunity for greater good, not an order. The posting would be a hard one, he warned. Leh was at a considerable altitude; it could be reached by only two possible roads, and those were closed by snow for at least half of each year. They would probably be among only a tiny handful of other Western people, there was no proper hospital, and the local population were likely to be even less receptive to the word of Our Lord than they were down here in Shillong.

Nerys had looked into his eyes.

Evan wanted to go just because the posting would be difficult and uncomfortable. Leh would give him the chance to prove his missionary zeal to God and to his superiors, while providing him with even more opportunities for self-denial. She was beginning to realise that poor Evan secretly had a low opinion of himself. Doubting the value of what he achieved within the mission, all his conscientious work and insistence on taking the hardest route was probably his way of dealing with an absence of self-confidence and self-love. He wouldn't even feed himself properly, however hard she tried to devise meals that would nourish him. He was gaunt, and his face had developed hollows beneath the cheekbones. He was often ill, with fevers or stomach complaints.

I will love you more and better, she silently vowed, *to make up for what you can't do for yourself.*

She had cupped his face between her hands and kissed him on the forehead. 'Of course we must go. I'll be very disappointed if we don't. Even the journey sounds like an adventure.' She had already heard the legends of the road from Manali to Leh.

That night in bed Evan had taken her hand and whispered, 'My dear?'

That was his signal. She had moved closer, her nightdress rucking round her thighs, and murmured, 'Yes.' She made sure that her mouth was almost touching his, so he felt the warmth of her breath.

He probably didn't think that doing it was actually sinful, she reflected. After all, they had been married, in chapel, by Parchedig Geraint Rhys, his friend and teacher, and in front of their two families. It was just – probably – that he didn't think he deserved this much pleasure. Certainly he never tried to prolong the act, or to intensify the sensations for either of them. He submitted to the base urge, as he no doubt thought of it, then detached himself as quickly as possible.

For herself, Nerys didn't care whether she deserved pleasure or not, but she knew from the very first fumbling time her husband came into her that she loved sex. At the beginning she had tried to imagine a marriage where both of you liked it equally and wanted it as much as she did. You'd never get out of bed, she thought. After two years of marriage, she had learnt to keep her imagination under stricter control.

Evan accepted the Leh posting, and the Watkinses made the long journey up into Ladakh. Nerys enjoyed the train journeys to Calcutta and on to Delhi, even though the summer heat of the plains was crushing after the relative airiness of Shillong. At every station food vendors clambered into their carriage with tiffin baskets containing rice and curries, *chai* men rang their little bells, and women imploringly held up cloth slings filled with ripe fruit to the dust-coated windows. She bargained for these goods along with the other train passengers, and arranged little picnic meals in a white napkin to tempt Evan whenever he glanced up from his book. And for hour after hour she gazed out at India as it rolled past the train. Paddy fields, buffalo carts and mud villages gave way to sweltering towns and cities of blistered slum tenements, and ever more hopeless camps where families lived under a tattered canvas awning on one patch of dirt beside the railway lines, with the smoke of countless fires thickening the already viscous air. Then the train would steam out into the countryside again, edging across a vast brown plain as if the acrid city had never existed.

In Delhi they were staying in a missionary house when Nerys finally heard the news of the Dunkirk evacuation on the BBC Overseas Service. Awaiting her were letters from her parents, containing accounts of air raids and food shortages,

53

and of little boys she had known at school who now appeared on lists of men killed in action. It was hard to hear of the terrible changes that her known and loved world was undergoing when she was in such a strange place herself. Anxiety for the people she had left behind filled her thoughts, and India and their work there seemed even more unrelated to anything she understood. She ached to go home; the depth of her longing was physical, almost frightening. Evan came back one afternoon from a mission meeting and found her struggling to breathe at an open window, although the air outside was dense with soot and heat. A woollen sock she was knitting lay on the floor beside her. She had heard that it would be cold crossing the passes on the way up to Leh, and although the notion of chill seemed to have slipped out of the world altogether she was worried in an abstract way that they did not have enough warm clothing.

'I think we are ready to leave.' Evan frowned, choosing either not to see or not to remark on her distress. 'I shall order the tickets for Chandigarh.'

With the advice and help of the Delhi mission they had accumulated a mountain of supplies, ranging from thick felt boots and blankets to tins of butter from the Delhi Dairy Company. Everything had been packed into travelling baskets fastened with leather straps.

Nerys stooped to pick up her knitting. 'Are we doing the right thing, Evan? Do you ever worry that . . . that our efforts might be better expended at home?'

He put down his armful of papers and books. 'Because of the war?'

'Yes.' If they were at home, she supposed, her husband would be a forces' chaplain and she would be school-teaching in the place of men who were away fighting.

'I have been called here, Nerys. I know that I am doing God's will.'

That's all very well for you, she almost retorted, but what

about me? I don't know anything of the kind. What is God's will for *me*?

She had never once actually asked him.

She had always bitten her tongue, knowing that the only safe direction for the conversation to take was for her to agree that she was Evan's wife, and her duty was to be no more or less than that. In any case, all of this, every step that had brought her here, had been her own choice. If she had not chosen to marry him she would be at home in Wales, and tomorrow she would be a spinster schoolteacher making her way to a classroom full of children whose lives she could comprehend, instead of a married woman on her way to Ladakh.

Through the window came the noise of vendors shouting, street children playing in the gutter, a baby's wail, the tinny notes of amplified music. Nerys stood very still, her fingers feeling like melted wax on the knitting needles.

'Are you unwell?' Evan laid his hand on her shoulder. 'Would you like me to call Mrs Griffiths?'

Mrs Griffiths was their hostess, a Delhi missionary wife whom Nerys hardly knew. 'No, thank you, Evan. I'm not ill. I agree with you. We're ready to go, so you should get the train tickets.'

At Chandigarh they left the train and travelled overland by truck, with their luggage roped under canvas on the flat bed of the vehicle, up to a town called Manali. There was another outpost of the mission here and Evan had to arrange the last details connected with their posting to Leh, so they stayed for three days. Manali lay in the foothills of high mountains and the blissfully cool air was crisp and sweet-smelling. The folded ridges that rose above the valley were covered with dark pine trees. The views made Nerys think of Switzerland, although she had never been there. She went for walks beside a crystal stream and watched eagles gliding over high crags. Her spirits lifted like the birds.

On their last evening, she and Evan ate dinner by candlelight in a little wood-panelled room overlooking a garden. When he put down his knife and fork she jumped up and went to him, resting her arms over his shoulders and putting her cheek against his hair. 'I am so glad we're going. I'm sorry I doubted the wisdom of it,' she whispered.

'I prayed you might have a change of heart,' he answered.

Nerys knew that night would be their last in a proper bed until they reached Leh. She had learnt on their honeymoon that she must never make any overtures to her husband, but while he was out of the room she touched a dab of perfume to the nape of her neck and put on her wedding nightdress.

'My dear?' Evan asked, as soon as he blew out the lamp.

At first light the next day, a train of fifteen ponies assembled. It took two hours for all of Nerys and Evan's baggage to be unpacked and redistributed into separate loads that were shared out between the pony men and their animals. A wiry little man called Sethi was in charge of their caravan. It was three hundred miles from here to Leh, over an ancient trading track that crossed the Himalayas. They would ride, and camp each night along the way.

'Come, Memsahib.' Sethi helped Nerys into the saddle of her pony, put the woven bridle with its bells and pompoms of bright wool into her hands, and slapped the animal's rump. It started forwards and their procession wound out of Manali. Thirty miles of steep ascent lay ahead, to the first high pass on their route.

Nerys often thought back with a kind of dizzy disbelief to the rigours of that long journey. The days were a blur of jolting on the back of the pony, or dismounting with aching legs and numb buttocks to trudge in its wake. The track was often no more than a gash leading between tumbled rocks, or a muddy ledge perched over hundreds of feet of empty air with a silver river winding far below. The ponies picked their way along, encouraged by clicks and whistles from the pony men. Their loads rhythmically swayed, sometimes tipping far out over the void. At night Sethi and his men pitched the tent and Nerys and Evan crawled inside and rolled themselves in their blankets. Cold winds battered the canvas and sliced between the tent wall and the groundsheet. The cook-boy lit a fire and in time a tin billycan of mutton stew and another of steaming rice would be passed through the tent flap. Nerys had never felt so hungry in her life. She ate ravenously, devouring everything that was given to her. Evan lay in his blanket cocoon with his eyes closed. He suffered from the high altitude, waking up every morning with a headache and coughing weakly all through the day. Nerys dosed him with aspirin and cough mixture, and coaxed him to eat.

'Just a spoonful of rice, dear. You must have some food, or you won't have strength to do your work when we arrive.'

He raised himself on one elbow, and ate a small amount of his dinner.

They slept fitfully at night, propped up on saddles to ease their breathing, waking to the sound of the wind or the men talking and chuckling round their fire. In the morning the whole process started all over again.

But as the days passed Nerys found that she grew steadily stronger, and with the strength came a new happiness. She gazed at the changing scenery, thinking of how its barren grandeur dwarfed the peaks and valleys of Snowdonia yet reminded her of home. She realised that she felt more at ease in this inhospitable landscape than she had done anywhere in boiling lowland India. She joked with the pony men, using sign language because they had hardly a word in common. Sethi became her ally, riding just ahead of her on his shaggy white pony or patiently leading her mount when her aching body protested too much and she had to climb down and walk for two or three miles.

'Memsahib very strong,' he said meaningfully. He didn't even glance at Evan, drooping over his pony's reins.

Nerys knew that she would never forget the afternoon of the long, gasping climb up to the Baralacha Pass. When at last she staggered up to the highest point, at sixteen thousand feet, it was as if all the oxygen had been sucked out of her brain and her blood, leaving her whole body as limp as string. Evan was grey and gasping, hardly able to sit in his saddle. A man had to walk on either side of his pony to support him.

Then Nerys looked back. Behind her, to the south, stretched the whole of India. She turned in a half-circle. Ahead, to the north, lay the unknown territory of Asia. She straightened up and sucked in a deep breath of the glassy air.

Sethi was watching her. 'Welcome, Memsahib.' He smiled.

The days of riding, camping, sleeping and riding again drew on, and then suddenly they were done. Their little caravan wound up a low hill, and at the crown they found themselves looking out over the Indus valley. There were orchards and walnut trees and cultivated fields stretching along the river-banks. The town of Leh spread over a sunny slope facing a range of high, white-iced mountains.

It was the end of August, and more than a month had gone by since they had left Shillong. As they rode into Leh, passing pony carts loaded with sheaves of dried barley stalks, flocks of goats, and women walking back from the fields, Nerys thought of the cold sliding down the mountains behind them and tightening its grip on the passes they had just crossed. Already there had been snow higher up, melting into slush in the midday sun and refreezing into treacherous ridges as soon as the dark came. Once they had unloaded their ponies the men would set out again for Manali, travelling fast and light against the weather, but the slow journey Evan and Nerys had made couldn't be reversed. Not until winter had come and gone again.

Here we are, Nerys thought, as they passed to the left of a long *mani* wall on the outskirts of town. Thousands of carved stones were piled on it, each one engraved with the mantra

Om mani padme hum. She bowed her head respectfully towards the wall. Here we are, and here we shall stay.

That had been almost a year ago.

Nerys turned to lie in the same position as Evan, but not quite spooned against his body in case she disturbed him. She inhaled his soap-and-sweat smell. Now that he was deeply asleep, she would complete her review of the day by considering this evening.

They had been eating their early dinner. Diskit, the woman who cooked and served their food, had withdrawn to the kitchen. She had been widowed and left with a young family so she was glad to be attached to the mission, whatever religious allegiance it obliged her to demonstrate. They could hear her opening the door to stir the ashes in the iron cooking stove, then piling in more yak-dung fuel to cook tomorrow's stew for the school. The smell of boiling mutton drifted in to them. Evan turned a page of his book. Without even glancing at him, Nerys knew that a shadow had crossed his face. The homely kitchen sounds set up a chain of unwelcome associations in his mind.

The early Moravian missionaries had arrived in Leh in 1853, before the Catholics and long before the fledgling Welsh Presbyterians. They had established themselves successfully. They had introduced the sturdy little stove that was now a fixture in every Ladakhi kitchen, set up the first printing press, and the post office, and had translated the Bible into Tibetan.

Evan felt keenly the precarious position of their own much younger mission, and the pitiful size of his congregation compared with the numbers who made their way to worship at the Moravian church. He condemned himself for his lack of achievements, practical as well as spiritual.

'You don't have to think of it in that way. They are our Christian brothers, and we are doing the same work,' Nerys had once said.

Their fellow missionaries were currently an Englishman, who had spent all his ordained life working for the Moravian church in India and was soon to retire, and a middle-aged Belgian couple. For the endless months of the winter they had been almost the only other European residents in Leh, and Nerys had grown to like all three of them. It had been Madame Gompert, with Diskit, who had nursed and comforted her through the blood and grief of the miscarriage.

She hadn't said anything this evening, and it had been Evan who had put down his knife and fork and closed his book. 'Nerys, I have something to discuss with you.'

'What is it?'

'It will soon be winter again.'

She could hardly be unaware of that. This year, now she knew about the depths of cold and silence, the monotony of eating the same food, the frozen water in their washing jugs, and the isolation of their little world, she thought that she would deal with it better. 'Yes.'

'I can't sit here in the mission all that time. In summer when I go out to villages and the nomad camps, the people are almost all out with the herds. But if I went in the winter, do you see, they would be in the settlements. They will have less work to do and I would have their attention.'

Nerys considered this. There were tracks out to villages in the valley, and hazardous routes over the mountains to outlying *gompas* and clusters of huts surrounding them, but she could only just imagine what it would be like to travel through snow and wind when the temperature fell to nought degrees Fahrenheit.

'I'll come with you,' she said.

Evan was silent.

Look at me, she willed him. At last their eyes met.

He wasn't hostile towards her, neither did he blame her in the least, but the loss of the baby had tipped them over the lip of a divide. As much as he had wanted the child, Evan also needed her to be strong and dependable in the joint enterprise that preoccupied him. Her physical frailty since the miscarriage and the unspoken weighty mass of her sadness suggested that her strength was no longer available for him to draw on. In some recess of his consciousness he resented the withdrawal, and that resentment must loom in his mind as yet another of the personal failings he was obliged to atone for.

They were at an impasse, Nerys wearily concluded. They couldn't talk to each other: it had been his child as well as hers and, of course, Evan grieved for it, but he put up too many defences against her and she had lost the will to try to break through them. She felt the beginnings of anger, too, at his weakness, which was so determinedly masked with stubbornness.

'I couldn't agree to that,' he said, in his most wintry voice. 'You must take better care of yourself than I could undertake to do if we were both out in the field.'

Nerys looked away from him. She closed her mouth, knowing that it made a tight line in her white face. 'You would prefer it if I stayed here alone?'

Evan was surprised. 'You won't be alone. You will have the schoolchildren, the congregation, the Gomperts, Henry Buller and our other neighbours. And the servants will look after you.'

Very slowly Nerys folded up her napkin and replaced it in the wooden ring. She stood up, supporting herself briefly with her hand on the back of her chair. 'Thank you,' she said.

She went across the passage to the kitchen door. Diskit was sluicing plates and cutlery in a tin basin, her pomaded hair wound up in a cloth because Nerys had told her it must always be covered when she was working. The red of the material matched her cheeks. Two men were sitting on a bench against the wall, their yak-skin boots discarded beside the door leading to the yard. Diskit dropped a fistful of forks on to a metal tray and Nerys inwardly winced at the noise. 'Diskit, what's this?'

'Mem, Leh very busy. My cousin brother,' she nodded to one of the two men, 'come from Alchi.'

'*Julley*,' the men murmured.

The girl had learnt a smattering of English from Evan's predecessor, and Nerys had picked up a basic level of Ladakhi. They communicated well, these days, only rarely having to resort to sign language.

Leh was busy. It was trading season and the caravans were in town, from Lhasa, Yarkand and Kashgar in the east and from Punjab in the west. The merchants from Tibet and Turkestan brought carpets, gold and silver to trade with their Indian counterparts for cotton and tea. The local people had wool and woollen goods for sale, every quality from coarse yak fibre to finest *pashm*, and the bazaar seethed all day with different faces and national dresses, and a clamour of languages. The British joint commissioner was also in residence. He was responsible for traffic and trade, and every trader had to apply to him for a passport to enable him to retreat in whichever direction he had come before the winter snows cut off the ancient routes.

The next day the commissioner was holding his annual tea party and entertainment at the Residency, to which Evan and Nerys had been invited along with everyone else of any standing in Leh. They had arrived just too late last year, and Nerys was looking forward to this great event as a rare break from their dutiful and monotonous routine. She had few decent clothes to choose from, but the *dhobi* man had laundered her best blouse and she had ironed it herself, to avoid the creases he invariably pressed into the collar along with a liberal sprinkling of ashes from the iron. She had just finished knitting herself a cardigan. It was soft cream wool, locally spun and the best available, and her job this evening was to add the finishing touch of a dozen pearl buttons.

'Mem, I tell you,' Diskit's cheeks turned even redder, 'my cousin, on road. Sahib and memsahib, English people. Leh tomorrow. Next week Srinagar.'

The two men nodded vigorously. The cousin did some voluble explaining, from which Nerys was able to decipher that a shooting party was returning from the Nubra valley. There were bearers and cooks, a *shikari*, or huntsman, camp-boys, a great bag of game heads, ponies, guns, tents and mounds of luggage, all the trappings of a serious expedition. The shooting party consisted of an English gentleman and lady.

This was real news.

English travellers passing through Leh were a focus of attention whoever they might be, but it was most unusual to hear of any Western woman undertaking the journey out to the remote east. Nerys wondered what she could be like. Curiosity, the prospect of the party, and the hope of some fresh conversation and unusual entertainment revived her to the point that she felt almost herself again. She forgot all about Evan, sitting over his book at the dining-table.

'Mem, I tell you,' Diskit was insisting. There was still more news to impart.

Nerys gathered that the travellers on the way out had stayed in the *dak* bungalow between Leh and Thikse, which was why she had not met them before. This was a small house provided for British government or other officials who were in the area and needed temporary accommodation. She knew that it was a comfortless place with mildewed walls, and drifts of dead flies on the windowsills, and she was not at all surprised to hear that the visitors were looking for alternative accommodation this time. Because of the party tomorrow, the Residency was unfortunately already overcrowded.

She said at once, 'They must stay here.'

The Watkinses had welcomed very few visitors to the mission, because most of the Europeans passing directly through Leh either went to the Residency or stayed with the Gomperts. Henry Buller's house was generally better avoided. She was already running through in her head what needed to be done. Air the sheets, light the fire under the boiler so there would be enough hot water. Jugs and basins. Towels, a posy of flowers for the bedroom table. How to add some elegant touch to their sparse menus for the next few days?

'Diskit, first thing tomorrow you will clean bedroom. Wash floor, all dusting, inside cupboard, everywhere.'

Diskit nodded, serious at the importance of this charge. 'My cousin, tell sahib on road?'

'Yes, yes.' Nerys turned to one of the men on the bench. 'Go back to the camp, say they are welcome here. Can you remember that? *Welcome*.'

When she had finally gone to tell him the latest, Evan had still been sitting at the table with the remains of dinner at his elbow. 'Where is Diskit? What do we pay her for? Am I to do the washing up, or might she find the time?'

'Evan, we're going to have guests tomorrow.'

He had listened with a frown. Nerys's reaction had been curiosity followed by anticipation, but his was defensive. The arrival of strangers in their home meant disruption and threatened worse: exposure, or some unnamed humiliation. His expression had made Nerys want to draw his head against her breasts and stroke his greying hair, telling him that he shouldn't worry or fear so much, but there was no longer any protocol between them for such a move. The weariness that she had felt earlier had descended on her again.

'Diskit will come in a moment. Her cousin brought a message from the road, and I gave her a list of things to do before the morning. I'm going to bed now, Evan. Tomorrow will be a busy day.'

'I won't be more than half an hour,' he had called after her.

Now sleep was a long way off. Nerys battled her rising resentment that Evan had slid so easily into unconsciousness while she lay wide awake and lonely, and increasingly disturbed by the latest disagreement between them.

She wondered if her husband was even aware that they had fallen so far out of sympathy with each other. It was quite possible, she reflected, that she didn't come high enough on his list of considerations to have made any recent impression at all.

Stop it, Nerys warned herself. You will only cause more destruction if you think like that.

Sleep. Just try to sleep.

Her bones ached with the effort of not touching her husband's oblivious body. She was too tired to let herself relax. The hours crawled by until the cocks started crowing.

It was a little past the usual time for lunch when the travellers arrived. Nerys had taught the youngest children's class, and she had told the older ones that they could go home once they had eaten their rice and lentils. The stragglers were still playing and chasing each other in the mission courtyard when laden horses picked their way to the street gate. Nerys and Evan heard the usual confused shouting and barking dogs that meant something out of the usual was happening. The schoolchildren crowded at the stone gateway and Nerys hurried across the cobbles to greet the guests.

She saw a trim man in well-cut riding clothes and a wide-brimmed hat, and a woman holding the bridle of her pony and affectionately rubbing its nose. She was wearing puttees and breeches, and a long muslin veil was tied over her sola topi. A string of bearers and pony men were bringing up mud- and dust-caked bags. The woman looked up and saw Nerys. At once she passed the bridle to a pony man and with one gloved hand she rolled up her veil. She smiled a broad, frank smile, held out both hands and grasped Nerys's. 'Mrs Watkins, thank you so much for rescuing us like this,' she said, in a warm, husky voice. 'I can't tell you what it means to Archie and me. One more night in a tent would have killed me off.'

She was about Nerys's height. Her eyes were the colour of peat, framed by arched black eyebrows. When she took off her sola topi it was a surprise to see that her dark hair was cropped short, like a man's, but even in her riding clothes there was nothing else that was mannish about her. She had a luscious figure, with a narrow waist and long legs that were elegant even in breeches under a rough tweed coat.

'Welcome to the mission.' Nerys smiled back at her. 'It's not the Savoy, but it's better than the *dak* bungalow.'

The man had issued crisp instructions to his servants and now he came to introduce himself. 'Mrs Watkins? How d'you do? I'm Archie McMinn. We're in your debt.' He was sandy-haired, tanned from the sun, with good-humoured blue eyes and a growth of wiry beard. He spoke with a slight Scots accent.

'Myrtle. I'm Myrtle.' His wife laughed.

'Nerys.' As they shook hands Nerys had an odd sense of recognition, as if she knew this woman already. She looked at Myrtle McMinn and she thought distinctly, I knew you must be somewhere. Here you are at last.

She only said, 'Come inside. You'll want hot water, food on china plates, and clean sheets. I remember what it feels like, camping for weeks on end.'

Evan came out into the courtyard, standing like a dark pillar in the sun. He shook hands with the newcomers, telling them that the Presbyterian mission was their home for as long as they needed it. Nerys gave him a quick smile of gratitude. Mission children slid between the four of them, gaping at the McMinns. Myrtle peeled off her gloves and rummaged in the pockets of her coat, bringing out sweets and distributing them between a thicket of hands.

'*Julley*, all of you.' She held the bag upside-down and shook it to show that it was empty. The children fell in behind her and followed her to the door of the house. Nerys firmly told them that it was time to go home, and shooed them away. She led the McMinns to their room.

'You've made it so pretty,' Myrtle cried. 'Look, Archie. What luxury.'

Nerys told them that Diskit would come with hot water

and they were to ask her if there was anything else that they needed. Archie McMinn said that all they required was the pair of canvas holdalls that their bearer would carry in, once the worst of the dust and mud had been brushed off them. Everything else, including his game heads, would be taken with the ponies to camp near the polo ground at the southern edge of town.

'His game bag is really all that matters, you see,' Myrtle teased. 'Two heads of giant mountain sheep with curly horns, two pairs of magnificent antler tops attached to their stags, and every other beast that was included in Archie's permit as well. Otherwise we'd still be out there, you know.'

'It was a shooting expedition, dearest girl,' Archie said calmly. 'What else did you expect?'

The McMinns gave a relaxed impression. They were easy with each other, Nerys thought, happy to have reached civilisation and company after their demanding excursion into the mountains. But she thought they would have been just as happy to find themselves alone together. Diskit brought in the first of a series of hot-water jugs, and Nerys left the guests to change.

Their arrival had lightened the tense atmosphere in the mission house. Diskit was singing as she crossed the passage, and Evan didn't ask how much longer it was going to be before he could have his lunch. Nerys adjusted the spoons and forks on the table, then went across into the kitchen to check on the *thukpa*, the local vegetable stew that was Diskit's most reliable dish.

The guests soon reappeared. Archie had shaved off his beard, exposing a paler crescent of jaw and cheek. Myrtle was still in trousers but they were loose flannels now, worn with a pale shirt and a single strand of pearls. 'I would have put on a frock,' she said apologetically to Nerys, 'but I haven't got one with me. Do you mind?'

Nerys smoothed the front panel of her old tweed skirt. 'Of course not. You look . . . very pretty.'

'No, I look like my brother.'

Even as she ran her fingers through her short shingle with a dismissive shrug, no one would ever have mistaken Myrtle for a boy.

Evan drew out Myrtle's chair for her. Both the McMinns bowed their heads while he said a lengthy grace and the *thukpa* steamed in its bowl. Sun poured in through the small-paned window opposite Nerys, and she was glad to close her eyes for a few seconds and allow its warmth to fall on her eyelids. After her sleepless night she was so tired that she felt not quite real, as if she were missing a physical dimension. When she opened her eyes again, Myrtle was looking at her. Nerys didn't mind her scrutiny. The feeling of recognition seemed to mean that there was nothing to conceal.

It was a cheerful meal. Evan liked Archie McMinn, that was clear, and he almost laughed at Myrtle's tales of their adventures. No remote *nullah* had been left unexplored in Archie's relentless pursuit of game. The McMinns had waded through rivers and crawled over mountain passes, slid down scree walls on the other side, to camp on bleak plains where hailstorms and gales had battered their tent. There was no firewood, no food for sale or barter, no human life for dozens of miles. Archie was up every morning, regardless of weather, eager with his guns and the huntsmen.

'Myrtle's friends are all in Srinagar, playing tennis or drinking cocktails at the club, but she insisted on coming out here with me,' Archie protested. 'What is a man to do? I would sacrifice anything for my wife – except sport, of course – but I cannot make a shooting trip comfortable for her.'

Myrtle looked delighted. 'Do you think I would have missed almost drowning or freezing to death? How many cocktails would it take to create such excitement? I don't mind coming second to your love of stag hunting, darling. And I know *you*'ll understand why I had to come.' She turned to Nerys. 'Because you have accompanied your husband all the way up here.'

'I wouldn't have wanted to be left behind,' Nerys agreed. 'That wouldn't make a marriage, would it?' She couldn't have defined what did, but the McMinns seemed to have discovered the secret.

Evan wore an old-fashioned pocket watch, and Nerys guessed that he was longing to glance at it. He would have a sermon to work on or important letters to write. She was surprised, therefore, that when Archie said he would go outside for a smoke, Evan affably said he would come with him. They strolled into the sunshine and sat in lounge chairs, Evan lighting the pipe he rarely allowed himself.

Myrtle put her plate aside and sat back. 'Well.' She smiled.

Nerys's mind ran on what had to be done in the house before she could be ready to leave for the commissioner's party. Diskit or the house-boy would have to be given very clear instructions about leaving out a cold supper for their guests, in case they were hungry later. Hot-water bottles were to be filled. Then she remembered her new cardigan, still unfinished. 'Oh,' she said.

Myrtle leant forward and touched her hand. 'Is something wrong?'

Nerys would have liked to tell her. What did recognising a potential friend mean, if it didn't include honesty? She said only, 'I forgot a job, that's all. Some sewing I was going to do before the party. Now I'll have to wear something different. It doesn't matter.'

Myrtle regarded her. Her gaze was shrewd. 'There's still time. Let's go and have a look, shall we?'

Nerys didn't try to protest. Myrtle sat on the bed while she showed her the cream cardigan. They agreed that it would be a shame to sew on the buttons in too much of a hurry.

'I've got an idea,' Myrtle said. She went to her bedroom and came back with a brooch. She held it out and Nerys saw a circle of pearls and brilliants backed by a substantial pin. 'You could wear this at the front, so, and it will hold the edges together, and it won't matter if the sleeve buttons are missing for today. Look, you can turn the cuffs like this. It's beautiful knitting. You're very good at making things, aren't you?'

A small cloudy mirror was propped on the dressing-table, and Nerys and Myrtle faced their reflections. Their eyes met as the brooch brilliants sparkled in the sunlight slanting through the shutters.

'May I really borrow it?'

'Of course. You probably think it's insane to have brought jewellery on an expedition like this. It was my mother's, and I like to have it with me. The necklace too.' Myrtle touched the pearls round her neck.

'Thank you.'

'Good. That's solved. Why don't you have a lie-down now? The men are talking, and I should try to write up my journal.'

The recognition extended in both directions, then. Myrtle had seen her weariness. 'The servants . . .' Nerys began.

'. . . will manage quite well, I should think.' Myrtle turned back the coverlet. 'Here.'

Nerys sank down, and found her new friend helping her off with her shoes. The bedclothes were lightly drawn over her shoulders, and the shutters folded to cut out the sunshine. She closed her eyes, and let herself sink.

The Residency garden was packed with a dense crowd of all the people of any importance in Leh, and a large proportion of the travelling merchants who would soon be departing for home. The party marked the last glimmer of summer, and once the decorous tea and sweet pastries phase of the afternoon was over, the talk and music swelled into a tide of noise. Local people and travellers were intent on making the most of the night. The commissioner, a short, jolly man with a scarlet face, had made his speech of welcome from a wooden dais and now circulated among his guests with a whisky-and-soda in one hand. The light turned moth-grey as evening approached, the first stars came out and the white tops of the mountains shone an unearthly apricot in the last gleam of the sun. An area in the centre of the gardens had been roped off, and a huge bonfire in the middle roared into flames as men doused it with kerosene and flung burning torches into its heart. More torches tied on tall poles blazed everywhere in the grounds, licking the passing faces with lurid tongues of colour as plumes of black smoke swirled into the air.

Nerys had slept deeply and she had to drag herself back through layers of dreams and what felt like centuries of time, even though it was less than an hour later that Evan was shaking her awake. Her head was splitting, and she forced two aspirin down her parched throat before trying to get dressed. The effort of putting on her clothes and pinning the cardigan with Myrtle's brooch took almost all the strength she could summon. When she looked briefly in the mirror, her pallor was startling.

They walked the short distance to the Residency with the McMinns. Myrtle scrutinised her. 'Are you sure you want to come?' she whispered.

Nerys nodded. Myrtle accepted the assurance.

She had felt better sitting in the shade of the trees, smiling at people she knew and watching the parade of strangers in different national dress. But now she had to move away from the bonfire's heat, and the coils of kerosene smoke that chased her sent waves of nausea to her stomach. Yarkandi men had performed a Cossack dance against the backdrop of flames, kicking and cartwheeling to the pounding of drums, and now their show was giving way to a procession of monks in traditional masquerade costumes. Two men in grotesque masks swayed in front of the blaze, followed by vultures' heads, towering stags, fluttering peacocks and a paper dragon with thirty human legs, its body lit from within so it glowed like a dancing lava stream. The looming mask faces, all giant eyes and teeth and lolling tongues, seemed more real than reality. The dark mass of trees and prickling sky closed, then receded.

The music pounded in her head. She was going to faint. Gripped by panic Nerys stared round, but she could see no one she recognised. The ground tilted and yawned, a giant bird's head pecked in her direction, and she fell forwards into nowhere.

FOUR

When Nerys came round, it was to see a circle of Ladakhi faces peering down at her. Her head was resting in someone's lap.

'Tell them to step back and give her some air, for God's sake.'

It was a relief to hear Myrtle's voice, and then to see Archie McMinn holding back the onlookers. A bottle of smelling salts was waved under Nerys's nose and she coughed violently. She tried to sit up and Evan's face came into focus. He was kneeling beside her, distress in every line of his body. 'I'm sorry,' she whispered.

'What for?' Myrtle wanted to know. It was Myrtle's lap Nerys was lying in, and Myrtle's hand on her forehead.

'Archie, make all these people go away, can't you?' she ordered.

There were fireworks going off somewhere close at hand, showers of crimson sparks falling out of the sky. The commissioner arrived, his face blooming even redder with embarrassed concern.

'Mr Watkins, we'll organise a stretcher party to carry your wife into the house.'

Nerys fought her way to a sitting position. 'I'm all right now. Please let me get up.'

Several pairs of arms supported her, some urging her upwards and others restraining her. Nerys twisted so she could see Myrtle's face. She looked straight into her eyes. 'Help me,' she begged.

Myrtle understood what was needed. She supported Nerys as she got to her feet and let her lean on her arm. 'I think you can walk, can't you? That's good. Come inside the house with me.'

'Nerys . . .' Evan began.

But she didn't have the strength to reassure him, not at this moment, or to smooth over the acute discomfort her fainting in public would have caused him. 'I'll be all right with Mrs McMinn.' She tried to smile. 'I fainted, that's all. It's nothing.'

'Myrtle will take care of her, old chap,' Archie said, in a tone that implied they shouldn't involve themselves in women's business.

With Nerys still leaning on Myrtle's arm they began to walk slowly, the commissioner sailing ahead of them, like an ice-breaker cutting through the floes of the crowd. When they reached the veranda he explained that every guest bedroom in the house was occupied: would Mrs Watkins mind if he escorted them to his own quarters? He added that a runner had been sent to fetch the Leh doctor, who unfortunately happened not to be at the Residency this evening.

Myrtle put her hand on his arm. 'Won't you go back to your guests now, and let your bearer look after us?'

He looked thoroughly relieved at the suggestion. A moment later a servant showed the two women into a masculine bedroom with the shutters closed against the noise of the party. Nerys saw polo prints on the walls, a brass-framed bed, and a pair of highly polished tall boots with the knobs of boot trees protruding. Luckily there was a day-bed with a plaid rug folded on it, pushed back against a wall. She didn't think she could have made herself comfortable on the commissioner's own bed.

Myrtle shook out the rug. 'Lie down here. Could you drink a glass of water? Or maybe some sweet tea?'

Nerys ran her tongue over dry lips. 'You've been so kind. This afternoon, and now.'

Myrtle sat beside her, took her hands and massaged some warmth into them. 'You need looking after. Is Leh quite the right place for a woman in your condition, even a missionary's wife?'

Nerys couldn't stop herself. She tried, drawing up her shoulders and clenching her jaw, but it was too late. The first sob caught in her chest and then exploded out of her. Tears rushed out of her eyes and poured down her face. She gasped, between sobs, 'I'm not . . . I'm not expecting a . . . baby. I was, but I lost it.' The words were half obliterated and she gave up the attempt to speak. It was a relief to cry. It was the first time she had wept properly since the miscarriage.

The other woman enveloped her in a hug, the warmest embrace Nerys had had for long weeks. Myrtle whispered in her ear, 'Oh, *God*, how clumsy of me, how stupidly clumsy. Please forgive me. I just assumed. Was it bad? It must have been, and you haven't properly recovered, have you? You poor, poor thing. Go on, cry all you can.'

She held on to her and stroked her hair, muttering soothing half-sentences, and Nerys went ahead and cried like a two-year-old.

At last, the sobbing slowed and stopped. Nerys lifted her head, revealing a streaming red face. The collar and yoke of Myrtle's blouse were soaked, but Myrtle only dug in the pockets of her flannel trousers and produced a large linen handkerchief. She dried Nerys's cheeks before putting it into her hands. 'It's one of Archie's. Little lacy things are no good out here, are they? It's camp laundered too, scented with *eau de* kerosene. Go on, blow.'

Nerys blew hard, and then sniffed. She realised she felt distinctly better. 'I've been very feeble today, haven't I? It's not the impression I wanted to give, honestly. It's not what I'm really like.'

'Feeble, eh? Living up here, cut off all winter, the only British woman for a couple of hundred miles, single-handedly running a mission school, tra-la. Yep. I'd say that's as weak as water.' Myrtle was smiling as she thumbed the last tears from Nerys's cheek. 'Take me, by comparison. Lotus-eating half the year on the lake in Srinagar, then venturing out for a dainty hunting trip with just five servants, eleven ponies and my devoted husband. You make me feel feeble, my girl. Feeble and spoilt.' In an automatic gesture she reached with her fingers to twist her pearl necklace.

Nerys's stomach turned over. She realised that, as well as being covered with dust and grass stalks, her cream cardigan was hanging open. Her hands clutched the place where the brooch had been. 'It's gone!' she cried.

Myrtle burrowed in the opposite trouser pocket. She held out the circlet in the palm of her hand. 'It had come undone. You were lucky it didn't skewer you through the heart when you fainted dead away.'

They looked at each other, and then they began to laugh. Myrtle comically scratched her hair so it stood up in a cockscomb, and Nerys rocked back against the buttoned cushion of the day-bed. They were still laughing when the commissioner's bearer knocked at the door. 'Madam, doctor here.'

Dr Tsering bustled in, looking puzzled. He was the only doctor in Leh and, like the commissioner, he spent just a few weeks of the year in town. Nerys knew that he was overwhelmed with sick people clamouring for cures for all their ailments before the snow came – as if leprosy or TB could be cured with a brown bottle of pills – and she regretted that he had been summoned all the way to the Residency to attend to her trivial problem. She collected herself. 'I am much better,' she said.

'Laughter very good treatment, ma'am,' he answered. He

unclipped his bag and uncoiled a stethoscope. 'Now, lying back, please.'

Four days later Dr Tsering paid Nerys another visit, this time at the mission, and declared that she was fit to travel.

In surprise she protested, 'But I'm not planning to travel anywhere.'

Myrtle's company had restored her spirits. They had enjoyed their hours of what Archie McMinn called pincushion time, although the only actual sewing they did was to make simple costumes for a playlet acted by the children. Mostly they had played games with the smallest infants, and walked in the bazaar, and exchanged details of their contrasting histories. Nerys had talked about Wales, and startled herself by describing the low grey crags and mist-filled valleys with a longing she didn't even know she had been feeling.

In turn Myrtle explained that she was the daughter of an Indian Civil Service official, and her childhood had been parcelled out between relatives in England and annual visits to India. 'I didn't see much of my ma and pa,' she said succinctly.

Archie was a railway engineer, and in a few days' time his annual long leave would be over. Myrtle and he were going back to Srinagar, and Nerys already knew how much she would miss her new friend.

Archie had been busy every day, paying off his hunting serv-ants and pony men, making arrangements for the heads he had bagged, engaging more men for the return journey to Kashmir, and visiting the commissioner and the other Leh notables. But one morning, looking grave after returning from the Residency, he strolled from the mission veranda into the room where Evan's predecessor's old wireless stood. 'It would be useful to get the BBC news,' he murmured.

'That wireless has never worked, I'm afraid,' Evan explained stiffly. 'Not in our time.'

Archie nodded, and unscrewed the back to investigate the

innards. Within an hour he had established that there was nothing wrong except that the massive battery was flat. The Residency had a wireless and so did the Gomperts, so the most important news from the outside world reached them quite quickly, but for everything else the Watkinses had to wait for newspapers and letters to make their way overland. Evan agreed that it would be most useful if the mission's wireless could be coaxed back into service. That same day, four coolies and a bullock cart ferried the weighty lead-acid battery down to the Indus, where it was hooked up to the water-powered generator. The next day, accompanied by a parade of dancing children, it made the reverse journey.

With the children still looking on, Archie went to work with pliers and a screwdriver. After a few minutes a sudden torrent of static burst out of the fretwork front panel. The startled audience screeched and fell over each other to get away from it. He twisted the knobs and the static dissolved into a babble of voices, and then the jaunty cadence of an English folk song. The children's eyes widened with amazement.

Archie brushed his palms together. 'There we are.'

That evening after Diskit had cleared the dinner plates, they pulled their chairs close to the dusted and polished set and listened to the news.

German troops had reached Leningrad, and the city would soon be surrounded. The European war was creeping closer. Even Leh no longer felt removed from the threat.

Evan slid a bookmark between the pages of his Bible before he closed it. 'Nerys, I think it would be a good idea if you were to go with Mr and Mrs McMinn to Srinagar. Mr McMinn has kindly offered to escort you.'

Nerys let her knitting drop. Myrtle's eyes met hers, and she read surprise in them. This was an idea the two men had hatched, without reference to their wives. Dr Tsering was evidently in on the plot too. To contain her anger she made herself count five stitches in her work, then asked composedly, 'Why would I do that?'

'You might enjoy a short holiday, and it would consolidate your strength before the winter.'

'And what about you?'

He paused, then said, 'We have spoken about this, my dear. I am going out of Leh to visit a few of the villages, and the more far-flung settlements. I must take the Lord to the people, not sit here expecting the people to come to the Lord.'

Out of the corner of her eye Nerys saw Archie McMinn stretch out his long legs. She resumed her steady knitting. 'I think,' she said, 'we shouldn't bore our guests with this debate. We can talk about it later.'

Myrtle said gently, 'I would love to have your company, Nerys. If it's helpful for you to know that.'

But later, once Evan had brought the shaft of cold air into their bed, enquired if Nerys was ready and blown out the candle, he merely said, 'Goodnight, my dear.'

She turned her head on the pillow and glared at his dark shape. 'Is that all?'

He drew away from her, by no more than half an inch, but she felt it. That small movement told her everything. Evan no longer saw her as his companion and supporter but as yet another source of anxiety. He would feel easier without her, and he would be freer to carry the mission work out of Leh. He didn't want to abandon her altogether, though. To send her off to Srinagar with the McMinns must seem the perfect solution. She could follow his thinking exactly, and all she could really object to was his suggestion that what she needed in order to recover from the loss of their baby was a lakeside holiday without him.

'All?'

'I don't want to go to Srinagar. Thank you for thinking of it, but I don't want to go anywhere if it means leaving you behind.'

'Separation is one of the penalties of the work I do, Nerys.'

He was like a wall, she thought. A blank wall that shut out the view, and endlessly denied that there was anything to be seen.

She tried another tack. 'What about my schoolchildren?'

'I expect they will enjoy a holiday too.' He sighed with the beginnings of exasperation. 'I don't know why you are objecting to the idea. I thought you would be pleased. You like Mrs McMinn, don't you?'

'Yes, very much.'

'Then go and stay with her, enjoy a rest, recuperate. I will cover the ground between here and Kargil more slowly, and investigate the work that might be done in future, if we ever have more people. Then I will come down to Srinagar to meet you, and we shall travel back to Leh together.'

'All this, before the snow comes?'

'It is only the beginning of September, but if the weather happens to be against us the Lord will direct our actions.'

'Do you really want me to go?'

The mattress rustled as he minutely shifted his weight. 'I think it would be a good idea.'

'Very well,' Nerys said, in a cold voice that she didn't want to acknowledge as her own.

Three days later, her bag stood in the mission courtyard beside the McMinns' luggage, waiting to be loaded on to the first relay of ponies. Nerys handed out apples and dried apricots to the scrum of Leh children, not just her pupils, who were staring through the gate at all the activity. Diskit's three grimy offspring were among them, and Diskit herself stood on the house steps in tears. She wasn't wearing her headcloth. Nerys put down the fruit basket and went to her. 'Don't cry. I'll be back in two months' time. Sahib will bring me home.'

Diskit only sobbed more loudly. Nerys put her arm round her shoulders, inhaling the ripe smell of her hair. 'Don't forget your scarf. Always when you are working. Look after Sahib for me.'

Diskit wiped her nose on her sleeve and sniffed. 'Yes, Mem.'

'The ponies are ready,' Archie announced, from beyond the gate, as hoofs rattled on the dried earth. Myrtle had put on her sola topi, with the muslin veil tied around her face, and Nerys had a wide straw hat.

Evan stood to one side, looking unhappy now the moment of parting had finally come. Nerys went to his side and reached up for a kiss. Awkwardly he knocked her hat askew as their dry lips touched. He stood back at once and patted her shoulder. 'It won't be so long. God bless you, my dear.'

She mumbled a goodbye, conscious that Diskit, the house-boys and the schoolchildren were watching, although the McMinns had tactfully busied themselves out in the street. The bolder children flung themselves at her, clasping her knees, and she bent down to hug and kiss each of them, instead of her husband.

Archie and Myrtle were mounted and Nerys's pony was waiting. Archie's bearer helped her to clamber into the padded saddle, then took the reins and turned the pony's head to the road for her. She twisted round to wave goodbye. The procession moved off down the lane, past the chapel and into the street leading to the bazaar, leaving Evan's solitary black silhouette outlined against the stone wall of the mission compound.

It was a cloudless day. As they wound the first miles along the Indus valley, Nerys felt heat strike through her straw hat, and wished she had brought cotton gloves to protect her hands from the blazing sun. After a time, on a high spur of land, she saw the prayer flags and brass spires of Spitok rising above the towering walls. This was the first of the great *gompas* on the route, and it was the furthest point she had travelled from Leh in more than a year.

Myrtle had gone ahead, but now she reined in her pony and waited for Nerys to catch up. Archie and the string of pack ponies were already far in the distance, enveloped in a puff of swirling dust.

'Would you like company?' Myrtle asked. Only her dark eyes were visible between the swathes of veil. 'Or would you rather be left to yourself?'

Nerys looked up at the mountains ahead. The surprising strength that she had discovered on the long ride up from Manali seemed within her grasp again. 'Company, please,' she said.

Myrtle reached out of the saddle to pat her knee. 'Good.'

They faced west, and rode on.

Nerys soon discovered that travelling with the McMinns was a completely different experience from her journey with Evan. At night they stayed in the rest houses set along the route, commandeering the places regardless of who might have arrived ahead of them. As a British sahib and a proper daughter of the Raj, Archie and Myrtle automatically took the precedence they saw as their due. They felt no compunction in ousting Ladakhi or Kashmiri travellers from the shelters, even on one evening a Muslim man, with a hennaed beard, who was accompanied by several veiled wives and half a dozen small children and babies. Evan and Nerys had always been confused and unwilling to impose themselves over other people, even the humblest. Whenever they came to a guesthouse, to sleep beside the road in their draughty tent had often seemed the easier solution.

The rest houses were often no more than two-roomed shacks, a living and sleeping room and an attached kitchen, and they were generally dirty and lacking any but the most basic amenities, but Sahib McMinn and his party were always greeted by the owners with extra civility and efforts to please. It wasn't hard to deduce why, because although Archie demanded a full account of what was owing and didn't overpay by a single *anna*, he invariably understood what the fair rate should be and handed over the money promptly and cheerfully.

Their camp servants always first arrived at the rest house,

and by the time the McMinns rode up, their *yakdan* bags had been untied from the ponies and set in the room for them. Camp beds were erected because Myrtle refused to use the charpoys provided, saying they were alive with bugs. Archie always pretended to be dismayed by his wife's fussy behaviour, but affectionate amusement twinkled out of him. There were plenty of warm blankets, and even linen sheets, which were unpacked and repacked each day. The McMinns' servants bought food locally to supplement the supplies the pack ponies carried, and their cook made the dinners, which were served with plates and cutlery rinsed daily in a solution of potassium permanganate. Sometimes there was even the opportunity to take a bath. A collapsible canvas structure was erected and part-filled, and Nerys was able to sit in it and luxuriously scoop warm water from an enamel jug over her skin and hair.

At the end of each day's journey, sitting in their camp chairs under the cobwebby guesthouse rafters, there was plenty for the three to talk and laugh about. Myrtle gossiped and joked about people they had encountered, or the various foibles of the pony men.

'Do you think they have a rota?' she speculated, about the Muhammadan and his wives.

'No, I should think he favours the prettiest one,' Archie replied. 'I would.'

'How can he tell?' Myrtle wondered.

'They don't go to *bed* in their veils, darling.'

Myrtle hooted with laughter. She smoked thin black cigarettes with opulent gold tips. The first time she lit one, Nerys glanced at her in surprise and Myrtle blew out a long plume of smoke. 'I was on my very best behaviour, you know, when we met. We were staying in the mission house. Will you disapprove hugely when you really get to know me?'

'I shouldn't think so.' Nerys laughed.

Last thing at night, the bearer brought in mugs of hot cocoa. Archie tipped a slug of brandy into his own and Myrtle's, and raised an eyebrow at Nerys.

'Yes, please,' she said. This was a custom to which she had quickly adapted.

There was only ever the one room at the rest houses, but she soon also got used to sharing with Myrtle and Archie. In bed Myrtle wore pearl-grey silk pyjamas with a Parisian label. 'Much better for travelling, you know. The coolies drop lice in the beds when they make them up, but they slither off the silk.'

She was right. Lice had been a feature of the Watkinses' journey up to Leh, clinging snugly in the seams of Nerys's flannel nightgowns.

With Archie's rhythmic snoring and Myrtle's breathing as its accompaniment, Nerys found that she slept better on the Srinagar road than she had done lately in the mission house. Every morning, as soon as it was light, the bearer brought in their bed tea. After they had drunk it Archie went outside in his dressing-gown to shave in daylight while the women got dressed, and then it was time for hot porridge, scrambled eggs and the cook's delicious fresh bread.

They walked or rode all day, through tiny villages with narrow fields of ripe grain winding beside the rutted track, where bedraggled hens pecked at the verges and stray sheep went scudding ahead of the ponies. Banks of tattered rose bushes spread on either side, now hung with orange hips, like jewels sewn on devoré velvet. When the track rose out of the sparse villages, the immense land was rocky and barren. The mountains loomed over them again, shadowed in sepia and purple, the most commanding ridge sometimes crowned with the massive white walls of a *gompa*.

At Lamayuru, a few miles before the Fotu Pass, which was the highest point they would have to cross on the route, they stopped for the night in the shadow of the biggest monastery. It was a lowering, piled-up mass of white walls and red-painted wooden slabs, small-windowed, topped off with the squat domes of a dozen chortens with black and gold twisted spires that glittered like spun sugar. The ponies toiled up hundreds of irregular steps to reach the cluster of buildings clinging to the skirts of the monastery. Prayer flags danced against the blue sky overhead and Nerys was reminded of Spitok *gompa*, past which they had climbed on the road out of Leh. With a prickle of guilt, she realised she had been so busy with the small adventures of the road, and laughing about them with Myrtle and Archie, that Evan had hardly been in her mind. At this distance he seemed a dark, disapproving figure, in contrast to the light-filled days she had been enjoying.

At Lamayuru they were staying in the inevitable rest house, but this one was much bigger than the roadside versions because of the stream of visitors to the monastery. Nerys was shown to a room of her own, no more than a tiny stone slot with a single narrow window. It looked out over a huge drop, with black choughs gliding below the sill.

Their dinner that night was unusually subdued, as if the proximity of the monastery and the columns of red-robed monks quietened even Myrtle.

Afterwards, instead of going back to her cell Nerys went outside and, on an impulse, climbed more steps to the walls of the monastery itself. She tipped back her head to look at the great edifice towering above her, black against the curtain of stars. Patches of faint yellow light glowed like veiled eyes in a few of the windows and she shivered in the wind. She thought she could hear the rise and fall of voices, chanting a prayer. Archie had murmured over dinner that Lamayuru village was a bleak place to live because the tributes and food demanded by the lama to sustain the monks left too little for the villagers themselves. It certainly seemed a desolate place tonight, as she pressed deeper into the angle made by a stone wall to find a scrap of shelter. From somewhere among the tiers of ramshackle houses beneath her rose the sound of a dog howling. She tried to imagine what Evan could achieve in a place like this, offering the promises and threats of a different religion to people who would be better off providing for their families and keeping their rice and mutton for themselves.

All she felt towards her husband was an exasperated tenderness, and she wondered whether this diminished affection, against her own belief that what he did was futile, would be anything like enough to carry her through the years ahead. I could do it, she thought, and anything else he wanted of me, if we had our own children.

She was thoroughly cold now. The monastery loomed so high and dark it was as if it was going to topple over and crush her. She pulled her coat closer around her shoulders and made her way back down the steps. Archie's bearer was waiting at the door of the dingy rest house.

'Come now, ma'am,' he called, and she felt guilty that she had kept him in the draught when he could have been reclining on his blanket with a pipe.

'I'm sorry, Hari.'

He lifted the oil lamp and led the way up the wooden stairs, past curtained doorways to her cubicle. He lit the candle that had been left for her on a little shelf and stood back. 'I bring cocoa, ma'am. Coming now.'

'I won't have cocoa tonight, Hari, thank you. I'll go straight to bed.' She wanted to close her eyes, and for daylight to come quickly. Lamayuru was an oppressive place.

After she had blown out the candle she lay listening to the darkness. There was a series of scraping sounds, probably made by rats in the ceiling. Wind gusted through the cracks between the wall and the tiny window frame. Then she heard another noise. It was no more than a woman's voice giving a low cry, something between a moan and a sigh, followed by a series of rising gasps. And then, as a postscript, a conjoined bubble of laughter followed by a whispered *ssssh*.

Nerys twisted under her blankets and pulled the crackling pillow hard over her ears. She didn't want to have to listen to Myrtle and Archie making love; there seemed too many things tonight that she didn't want to hear or know or think about. Her own life seemed small, solitary and devoid of purpose.

The next day their route led onwards, over the high pass

and through the town of Kargil. With Lamayuru a long way behind them, the travellers were in high spirits. More long but ultimately satisfying days passed, until only the jagged walls of the Greater Himalaya lay between them and the Vale of Kashmir. With the mountains in the distance it seemed impossible that their caravan could find a way to the summit via the Zoji Pass, but as they came closer they were able to pick out the crooked filament of a track zigzagging upwards. In one place there was a dart of brilliance as a mirror ornament or a fragment of polished metal on an ascending pony flashed the rays of the rising sun. Myrtle was reassuring when Nerys reined in her mount to assess the extent of the climb.

'It looks harder than it actually is. Remember, you've already climbed higher than eleven thousand over the Fotu La, and on your way up to Leh last year.'

'I'm not worried. I know we'll do it. I'm just wondering what the view will be like from the top.'

Myrtle's eyes shone between the folds of her veil. 'Like nothing you could imagine. It will be like looking down into Paradise.'

This thought sustained Nerys through the long, baking ascent. Dust clogged her nose and throat and her water-bottle was soon empty. The sun rose higher, beating down on her head and shoulders. While she rode, her pony walked more and more slowly and she felt its shudders when the pony boy whipped its quarters. When she slid to the ground the stones dug up through the soles of her boots and the sun blazed fiercely. The jingle of the ponies' harness set up a rhythm that was only broken by the occasional whistling of marmots from their burrows among the rocks. Black lammergeiers cruised the empty air spaces, lazily turning on their fretted wings.

The pass itself was obscured by intermediate outcrops, and Nerys thought grimly that they would be climbing for ever. Archie was far ahead but Myrtle matched her pace to Nerys's. They exchanged occasional words of encouragement, but most of their energy was taken up with just placing one foot in front of the other.

As they mounted higher, Nerys began counting the number of bends still to be negotiated. There were seven, then five, then only one more.

'Is this it?' she begged Myrtle, dreading a false summit and a concealed cliff still to be negotiated.

Whenever she glanced backwards the wide brown desert of Ladakh had receded further, and she knew that they were crossing into a different country.

'Nearly,' Myrtle puffed. 'Why must Archie dash ahead all the time?'

They came out on to a broad stretch of ground with chortens outlined ahead against the sky. Archie and the forward party were waiting for them. Down the slope Nerys glimpsed the picked-over bones and hide of a dead pony that must have fallen from the line of a caravan. It was a still day, but the air surged around her and she retied the strings of her straw hat.

They crossed the saddle of the pass, thankful for the almost horizontal ground, until they drew level with the chortens. The rough stone mounds were strung with hundreds of flags, faded or still bright, with ragged white streamers festooned between them.

Myrtle and Archie stood with their hands linked, silently looking west. Nerys came up beside them, and stopped short. Spread beneath her feet, unrolled like the most magical of carpets, was the Vale of Kashmir.

The folds of land swept up towards them, lower ridges cloaked with ranks of sombre fir trees and the higher ones bright with silver birches. Long seams of snow lay in the shaded gullies, and waterfalls laced silver threads down purple rock faces. A haze of warmth blurred the great hollow of the Vale, but she could see distant pasture lands, ripe fields, and the curves of a river. After the bare grey and brown landscape she had just crossed, the soft blend of a thousand shades of blue and silver and lavender mingled with pale green and gold seemed too sumptuous to be real. She stared at it for a long time, with the scent of rich earth and sweet water drifting up to her.

Myrtle had not been exaggerating.

It was the most beautiful place Nerys had ever seen.

FIVE

To get across the mountains from Leh to Srinagar, Mair's options were to take the public bus, to find a group of people who were making the trip and needed another passenger to fill their vehicle, or to hire her own car and driver for the two-day journey. The buses ran every day, but they halted briefly over-night in Kargil and left again at one in the morning. Soldiers at the army checkpoints on either side of the Zoji La closed the road at five a.m. in order to leave the hairpin bends clear for army convoys, so official civilian traffic was supposed to be up and over the pass before then. She had seen notices pinned up in some of the Internet cafés offering spare seats for shared expenses in trucks or cars, but when she made her way to a phone office and called one of the numbers, she found herself talking (she was almost certain) to one of the Israeli boys who had been on the Changthang excursion. She made a hurried excuse and rang off. The option of her own car and driver had seemed by far the best until she went into the last travel agency that was still open for business and enquired about the price. She would just have to square up to the legen-dary discomforts and adrenalin shocks of the bus journey. She packed her bag, ready to leave Leh the next morning, and headed out for a last dinner at the best of the *Lonely Planet Guide*'s recommendations.

'Hi there,' a voice called, out of the frosty twilight, as she turned downhill towards the bazaar. 'We were really hoping you were still in town.'

It was Karen Becker, zipped up against the cold in a duvet jacket, her hair bundled under a fleece cap.

'How was the trek?' Mair asked, as they fell into step.

Karen gurgled with dismay. 'Full on, and then some. We went up high and there was snow up to my knees. Everything in the tent froze overnight. Bruno adored every second of it, naturally.'

'And Lotus?'

'She was good. But Lo's always pretty good, and she likes the snow. Look, why don't we meet tomorrow? I'd say come over tonight but Bruno's got some work thing to sort out, endless phone calls to make, and that's not easy around here, *as* you know.'

Mair did know. All foreign mobile phones were automatically blocked and the only way to make calls other than from a phone shop was by buying a Jammu and Kashmir mobile. She hadn't done that, and she was feeling the lack of communication with home. The power supply was too variable to make email a reliable option either.

'I'm leaving on the bus for Srinagar in the morning.'

'*Nooo*,' Karen wailed. 'Don't do that. You mustn't. I've heard it's a terrible ride.'

'Well, it'll be an adventure.'

Karen put her arm through Mair's. 'I've got a much better idea. Stay one more day, and come to Kashmir with us. We've booked a car. There's room if you don't mind sitting in the back with Lo and me.'

Mair hesitated. 'What about Bruno?'

Karen twitched her elegant shoulders. 'He'll be fine with it. He likes meeting new people just as much as I do.'

Mair's first impression of Bruno Becker had suggested otherwise, but she didn't say as much. 'Well . . . it's tempting. I'm not so sure about the bus, if I'm honest.'

'Hey, then it's a deal. We'll pick you up at your hotel, day after tomorrow. It'll be early, I'm warning you. Bruno's a complete fanatic about that sort of thing.'

It seemed that the arrangement was made.

Karen danced along the edge of the dirt road, waiting for a truck to grind by. 'How was your week, by the way?'

Mair began, 'It was interesting. I found out some history . . .'

But Karen was already crossing through the cloud of exhaust fumes. She waved back at Mair. 'Great. See you tomorrow.' An auto-rickshaw driver had spotted her and swerved to a halt. Karen leapt aboard without negotiating the fare. Mair continued in the opposite direction towards the twinkling lights of the bazaar.

With a day to spare, she went back to the Internet café. In an email to Hattie she described the discovery of the chapel and the ruined mission building, but only in the lightest way. Even to Hattie, she wasn't willing to admit quite how intriguing the story of the shawl had become to her. She clicked *send*, while the power held.

Then she checked her inbox. The messages scrolled in, arriving at a pace slower than that of a limping man carrying a cleft stick. She saw one from Dylan and opened it with delight. Her brother wasn't a regular correspondent, but his occasional emails gave her more pleasure than anyone else's.

This time there was only one disappointingly short paragraph, but it promised that she would be interested in the attachment.

Dylan had taken away their father's small collection of photographs, stored over the years in a couple of old shoeboxes in Huw's chaotic study. He had said vaguely to his sisters that he would go through them when he had an hour to spare, and would scan the good ones into an iPhoto album for them both. It was the kind of assignment he excelled at. Eirlys had replied that she was grateful for the offer, because she'd never have time to do it herself. Dylan had smiled covertly at Mair, and she had been struck then by his increasing resemblance to their father. How unwittingly you stepped into your parent's skin, she thought. Probably by now she was more like her mother than she would ever know.

Smiling, Mair set about opening Dylan's jpeg attachment. At first the system refused to co-operate, but she kept trying until she succeeded.

She stared. The photograph was an old black-and-white snapshot, faded and creased. Three women were grouped against a background of water partially covered with lily-pads. The upper left-hand corner of the view was cut off by a diagonal of carved woodwork, so it looked as though the three had been caught on a balcony overlooking a lake. The woman in the middle was posing with her chin up, darting a look of frank amusement straight into the camera's eye. Her wide mouth had full lips that looked black, but must actually have been painted with dark red lipstick. Her wavy dark hair was swept up at the sides and her striking appearance was emphasised by the wide lapels and exaggerated shoulders of her chic jacket. There was a deep shadow in the V of her neckline.

The woman on her left was much more girlish in appearance. She was in three-quarters profile, smiling with her eyes turned to her companions, and she had curled pale hair and a swan-like neck.

The third woman had been captured in a burst of delighted laughter. Her head was thrown back and she looked so alive and full of merriment that it was several seconds before Mair recognised her. It was her grandmother.

Gazing with increasing fascination into the joyful faces, Mair speculated on what Grandpa Evan could have said from behind the lens to make his wife beam with such clear happiness.

Or – perhaps the photographer hadn't been Evan Watkins at all.

Whereabouts was that stretch of dappled water? It didn't look like Leh, that was certain.

Then an idea came to her. There were lakes in Srinagar. Mair referred back to Dylan's message. He had written,

This was loose inside an album of Grandpa's India photographs, mostly very boring. Chapel people standing on steps, looking solemn, etc. So it caught my eye straight away. Who can Grandma's happy friends be?

The longer she looked at it, the more enigmatic and intriguing the photograph became. The three young women seemed so absorbed in their friendship, as well as in the immediate comedy of the moment. Their faces shone with so much life, it was hard to believe that the picture had been taken almost seventy years ago.

Mair badly wanted to find out more about them. The possibility that the picture might have been taken in Srinagar only intensified her desire to get there.

The Chinese woman who ran the Internet shop frowned at her. Over each work station was a laminated sign that read, 'No uploding No downloding'.

Mair pointed from the picture on her screen to the antique printer perched on a bench near the door, and made an imploring gesture to connect them. It wasn't until she took out her wallet and started peeling off notes that any response came. After that there was an interval of button pressing and cable checking and muttering, and finally a five-by-four print emerged from the slot. It was murkier than the original, and the small size reduced the sheer joyous impact, but it was good enough.

Mair carried it back to the hotel and put it safely in the envelope that also contained the lock of dark brown hair.

The Beckers and their driver in the standard-issue white Toyota four-wheel drive drew up in front of Mair's hotel at six thirty the following morning. Karen waved from the back of the car. 'All set?' she called. 'This is going to be fun.'

Lotus was strapped into a child's booster seat. The local

94

driver, clearly already infatuated with the little girl, flashed gold teeth across the seat divide and patted her cheek. Bruno Becker stepped out of the front passenger seat. He looked at Mair with a glimmer of a smile that made him seem slightly more approachable.

'This is very kind of you both,' she said.

'I'm glad you're joining us. Is this everything?' He indicated her holdall. Mair nodded. She carried her rucksack slung over her shoulder, with the shawl, the lock of hair and the photograph secure inside it.

'You travel light. Karen could take a lesson from you.' He swung the holdall into the luggage compartment of the Toyota on top of a sizeable pile of baggage.

'Hey, it's mostly Lotus's stuff.' Karen laughed. 'Come on, jump in.'

Mair took her place next to Lotus. The child's hair was a mass of pale spirals in the steely dawn light.

'Let's go,' the driver said. They headed down the main street, past the prayer wheel and the long *mani* wall. Mair turned to catch a last glimpse of the town. Thick bars of low cloud masked the circle of mountains and the trees were iron-grey scribbles against brown rock. It was very cold, and the streets were deserted.

Karen tilted her chin to the front seats. 'They're worried about the weather,' she announced across Lotus.

'Forecast of snow,' Bruno said briefly, without turning his head. 'We won't be hanging around on the way up.'

Mair settled back in her seat. At first the car ate up the miles of valley road along the bank of the Indus. Karen chatted, and Mair passed Lotus items from the inexhaustible supply of toys and books that surrounded her seat.

Heavy wagons and army trucks moved by in both directions, and as the road began to climb they passed the rough roadside camps of maintenance gangs who worked to keep the route open. Women as well as men carried stones on their backs or shovelled dirt into potholes.

'What a tough life. Look, that woman's got a baby on her back,' Karen breathed. Two more tiny children sat on a rock, watching the steady grind of traffic.

To increase the general bleakness it began to rain, the swollen droplets bouncing steadily off the windscreen. The wipers hummed and the car slewed over deeper and deeper ruts. They came to a police checkpoint and the driver ferried their passports to a hut for scrutiny, while bored soldiers in camouflage swung their guns to marshal loaded trucks. Beyond the checkpoint was a sign that read, 'Border Roads Organisation. The Enemy is Watching You.' The highway ran close to the Line of Control between India and Pakistan, and the heavy Indian Army presence wasn't window-dressing.

They drove on, heading steadily westwards as the road began to climb. It edged past huge precipices, the wheels of the Toyota sometimes seeming to hang over the lip as they bucked round yet another blind bend. Mair averted her eyes from the yawning drops, only to gasp as a truck howled round the corner and headed dead at them. Their driver never seemed to flinch as he steered past the oncoming metal with one inch to spare between solid rock or thin air. The road surface became so rough that the passengers had to hold on to the straps to stop their heads hitting the roof. In the midst of this, seemingly lulled by the relentless jolting, Lotus fell asleep.

'Don't they ever use tarmac around here?' Karen groaned.

Bruno looked over his shoulder. 'It wouldn't last six weeks. This mixture of stone and compacted hardcore is the only thing that stands up to the weather and the trucks, and it takes constant maintenance to keep the road even this usable.' That was the longest remark he had made since leaving Leh.

'Uh-huh. *Ouch.*' They all bounced in their seats. Stones sprayed from under their wheels and pinged out into space. Far below, Mair caught sight of the pewter thread of a river. She offered up a prayer of thanks that she wasn't crammed into a forty-seater public bus with an exhausted driver at the wheel.

'The road between Leh and Srinagar only opened to wheeled traffic in the sixties,' Bruno said. 'Before that it was a track, and the transport was ponies.'

'However long did it take?'

'It's two hundred and fifty miles. A week would have been really good going.'

Mair added, after a moment, 'In the eighteenth century it was impassable even on horseback. Porters carried everything on their backs, all the way from Tibet to Kashmir. Going this way the traffic was mostly wool, for the pashmina trade.'

Bruno turned to look at her. For the first time, their eyes met directly. 'You're interested in the history of the old trading routes?'

'Yes.'

'So am I,' Karen interjected.

Her husband swivelled towards her and smiled. Mair realised that he was a noticeably attractive man, and the unease she had felt in the Beckers' joint presence suddenly lifted. Although at first sight she had envied their intimacy she had begun to suspect that they were actually connected by mutual antagonism as much as shared adoration of their child. But now she thought she must have been mistaken. There was affection as well as amusement in Bruno's smile.

'I know *you* are,' he said warmly.

Mair peered ahead as they swung round yet another corner and saw, through a slash in the clouds, a white wall of snow in the distance.

After an hour, Lotus woke up and began to grizzle. She pulled at her seat straps and turned her face away from the drink Karen offered her. 'We'll have to stop for ten minutes,' she told the driver. 'How far is it now to Lamayuru?'

The men shook their heads.

'Still far,' the driver said.

They pulled in at a roadside tea stall. Rain had turned the road to a wretched ribbon of mud, and sprays of filthy water were flung up by every vehicle that passed. The westbound stream was constant. Mair understood that every driver was under pressure to get up and over the Fotu La before dark or before the snow seriously set in, whichever came first. In the last few minutes the rain had become sleet, hitting the car's windscreen in dismal splotches.

Their little group huddled under the canvas shelter. Lotus cheered up as soon as she saw people. Bruno put her down and she set about making new friends while Karen investigated the contents of the stallholder's saucepans. She chose a thick stew and a ladleful of rice, and fed most of it to Lotus. More cautiously, Mair snacked on a bar of chocolate and a handful of nuts. Their driver stood in the doorway, muttering with the other drivers and surveying the weather.

As soon as they had finished, Bruno hurried them back to the car. Karen sighed. 'What a shame not to be able to see the approach to Lamayuru. In the pictures, it's set right up on the skyline like a fantasy castle, all spires and turrets.'

'Karen, we really can't stop at your monastery,' Bruno said.

'*What?*'

'We need to get over the pass as soon as possible.'

'Oh, come on. An hour won't make any difference.'

The driver was sitting forwards now, his shoulders hunched close to his ears. The oncoming vehicles all had their headlights on and a long line of their little yellow cones was visible, snaking at an improbable angle upwards into the murk.

'It will, darling.'

Karen was angry. 'Listen, what is this? I know it doesn't interest you much but this is the oldest *gompa* in Ladakh. It dates from before the tenth century. There are frescos, *thangkas*, like nowhere else. We've got to see it.'

'Not this time.'

Silence fell, and Mair could feel the silent battle of wills. The wipers smeared away a ruff of sleet that was instantly replaced by another. Lotus quietly sang to her doll.

'It's just a sprinkling of snow, Bruno. Why are you so cautious all of a sudden?'

The driver broke in: 'We go straight to Fotu La. Get down to Kargil.'

That seemed to settle it. Karen's jaw set, but she said no more.

The going got harder but the driver pushed on. Snow was falling now, piling on the heaps of stones at the edge of the road. Fewer vehicles were coming the other way. Mair focused her attention on keeping Lotus occupied, and tried to ignore the precipices that must be only a foot away. It was much more alarming, she discovered, not to be able to see the worst and to be left imagining it.

She glimpsed another quirky Border Roads sign: 'Are you married? Divorce your speed.'

They seemed to have been climbing for a long time. The wheels skidded once, took purchase, and skidded again. Karen's annoyance at missing the monastery had subsided. Bruno and the driver conferred in low voices. They went more slowly, in the lowest gear, following the tyre marks of the vehicle ahead, which quickly faded to nothing more than faint grey ridges in a grey expanse.

'Snow very bad,' the driver said abruptly.

A moment later, on a steep incline, the Toyota's wheels spun and the car began to slither backwards. For a panicky moment Karen and Mair's eyes locked over Lotus's head. Disorientated, Mair tried to work out on which side of them the drop currently yawned.

Bruno was already out of the car. He kicked a rock under one of the rear wheels as the driver leapt out to join him. Karen and Mair sat tensely waiting.

'Get out,' Lotus chirped.

'Not now, honey. Look how hard it's snowing.'

The men shovelled roadside dirt under the tyres but the Toyota edged forward only a few yards before it began to slide backwards again.

'No good,' Bruno shouted through the snow.

'No good,' the driver agreed.

The doors slammed.

'We're not going to make it. We'll have to go back down.'

'Go *back*?' Karen cried. 'After all this?'

'It's five miles or so back to Lamayuru. We'll stay the night there.'

'Really?'

'Yes, really. It's either that or spend the night up here in the car. So you'll get to see your frescos after all.'

Karen scooped up a double handful of red-gold hair and fastened it back from her cheeks. She flashed a grin at Mair, perhaps realising that she had been intransigent. 'Sorry about this. But that's travel, isn't it?'

'It is,' Mair agreed.

The driver made a complicated reverse manoeuvre, slithering in the limited space between rock wall and vanishing road. They began the crawl downhill.

Mair could see nothing except falling snow. She felt a queasy pressure beneath her diaphragm, like a weight of foreboding.

The darkness seemed impenetrable. Mair groped her way along the clammy stone wall, trying to remember which way she had come and wishing she hadn't left her head-torch in the car. She reached a corner, tripped at a shallow step and almost fell, noticing that the air was even icier here. The way to the court-yard must be close at hand.

When her outstretched fingers finally met the door she felt for the iron ring handle and twisted it. The door banged inwards, letting in a blast of wind and snow.

She stumbled outside. The woman who had led her to her room had pointed out the guesthouse kitchen, but with the thick snow now masking all the low doors that enclosed the courtyard she had lost her sense of direction. She didn't glance upwards, aware that the monastery walls loomed so threaten-ingly overhead that they seemed ready to topple and crush the house on its precarious ledge. They would hardly have been visible now, in any case. Gusts of wind drove the snowflakes horizontally and even upwards, half blinding her as she ploughed through the drifts. She ducked under a ledge of snow that blanketed a rough porch, and saw a light.

Another door crashed open and she fell inside, shaking off snow like a dog emerging from water. She put her shoulder to the door and managed to latch it behind her.

'Hello, My,' Lotus called out.

The room was dimly lit by a single kerosene lantern. There were mattresses on the floor against three walls, and in the centre a small stove with a chimney pipe that oozed smoke into the chill, grease-scented air. The woman Mair had seen earlier was stooped in front of the stove, tossing pancakes of dried dung into its cold heart. Several men, probably truck drivers also stranded by the storm, sat hunched on two of the mattresses. They had been smoking and talking in low voices but now they broke off and stared at her. The third mattress was occupied by Bruno and Lotus. The little girl was zipped up in a padded sleep-suit and swathed in a blanket so that only her rosy face was showing. The whole cocoon of her was snugly held inside her father's coat, her head tucked under his chin.

Mair felt distinctly envious.

Any warmth would be welcome in these circumstances, she told herself hastily.

'Do a jump,' Lotus begged. '*S'il vous plaît?*'

'Lotus, it doesn't really work indoors. You have to be outside.'

'Go out,' the child said, and pointed, as if this was so obvious it was hardly worth saying.

'I'll do one for you tomorrow,' Mair promised.

'It's snowing, Lo, remember?' Bruno told her. 'We're all staying right here, inside, where it's warmer.'

He moved aside and indicated a space on the mattress to Mair. She picked her way between a tower of blackened saucepans and a wicker coop containing a dispirited hen to sit down beside him. The men resumed their conversation and the woman slammed the stove door.

Bruno said, 'Karen's got a migraine. She took one look at the bathroom and went straight to bed.'

The bathroom was a couple of yards away, located just to the left of the door. It consisted of a metal drum with a tap, a drain-hole in the floor and a pink plastic soap-dish with a cake of grey soap. The lavatory, Mair had already discovered, was in a lean-to on the edge of the courtyard. It was a long-drop, with several hundred feet of air yawning between the foot-rests. At present, snow was bracingly blowing up through the hole.

The guesthouse attached to the monastery was packed with a large group of German tourists whose bus had failed to get over the pass. The accommodation further down in Lamayuru village also was full of earlier fugitives from the weather, and the Beckers' driver had done well to find this place for them. When they had first arrived, battling the ankle-deep iced mud of the paths, it had looked less like a dwelling than some roughly rectangular deposits of rocks and planks. But there were two slits of rooms in the warren that led off the courtyard, chipped into the rock like hermits' cells. The driver had ushered them into this shelter and gone off to stay with his cousin, who apparently lived nearby. Any further victims of the storm would have to bed down on the mattresses in the kitchen.

Mair asked, 'Can I do anything for her?'

He shook his head. 'But thanks.'

Mair added, 'It's not exactly luxurious but it'll definitely be warmer than spending the night in the Toyota.'

Bruno's arms instinctively tightened round Lotus. 'Yes. That would have been quite difficult.'

Snow as heavy as this would have built up a drift against a stationary vehicle. Overnight the car might have been buried, and escape on foot on a road as isolated as the one they had just travelled would have been dangerous, maybe impossible.

Mair shivered. Despite her show of optimism, she didn't like this place, not for its lack of home comforts but because of the bleakness and the air of indefinable gloom that hung about it. But it was still a safe haven tonight. She glanced at Lotus's pink cheeks. The little girl's thumb was in her mouth. 'We'll be snug as bugs, won't we, Lo?' She smiled.

A square of sacking that masked an inner door was pulled aside and another woman emerged. She was carrying a saucepan with a feeble wisp of steam rising from the contents.

Bruno took the pan and thanked her. He sat upright and said gently, 'Lotus, look, here's your supper.'

He began to feed her spoonfuls of warmed-up baked beans alternating with chunks of flatbread. She wriggled half out of her blanket cocoon and ate with relish, smearing her chin with orangey sauce.

Over her head Bruno said, 'We always carry a couple of cans of beans with us. Lotus will eat them day or night, whatever else goes awry.' He dropped his voice. 'We may find ourselves envying her later.'

A blackened cauldron had been lowered on to the stove. The two women squatted on the earth floor and began to slice onions, tossing them into the pot and exchanging remarks with the group of truck drivers.

'It's only one night.' Mair laughed.

But Bruno didn't laugh with her. 'I hope you're right.'

She thought how forbidding he could look, with his dark face and the black eyebrows drawn together in a thick line. He and Karen seemed so markedly different that she could only conclude theirs was one of those partnerships of opposites.

Lotus finished all the baked beans and caught at the pan to make sure that there wasn't another spoonful in the bottom. Soot coated her hands and Bruno patiently cleaned them with his handkerchief, telling her that she couldn't get into bed with Mummy and leave black handprints all over her, could she? He took an apple from his pocket, peeled and quartered it and fed that to Lotus as well. By the time she was on the fourth slow chunk, her eyelids were drooping.

'Time for bed,' Bruno whispered. He rearranged the child's

103

coverings so that only her eyes and nose were visible, before hoisting her in his arms. Then he slid a glance at the food preparations. 'May I join you later for dinner?' he asked Mair formally, but at the same time his black eyebrows rose in amusement.

'Of course. I'd like some company,' Mair answered.

While he was gone she sat propped against the wall and watched the cooks at work. The stove was heating up and the smell of boiling vegetables hung in the air. Condensation dribbled down the tiny window panes, but the kitchen didn't seem to have got any warmer. She was thinking that she could easily have ended up here with the Israeli boys for company rather than the Beckers, and offered a quick thanks to the gods of Lamayuru for the lucky escape.

Fifteen minutes passed before Bruno returned. After brushing off the snow he took his place beside her on the mattress, watched by the drivers. He waited until they lost interest, then, from his well-stocked pocket, produced a flask. He rummaged again and brought out a pair of collapsible metal beakers, and waved a finger over them. 'Cognac?' he murmured, and poured.

They clinked their beakers. Bruno took a long gulp from his. Mair followed suit and the alcohol instantly glowed through her chilled bones.

'Aaah. How's Karen?'

'She's lying in bed reading one of her Buddhist texts. I put Lotus in beside her – she instantly fell asleep.' He added, after a moment, 'She has great reserves of power and determination, my wife, so she suffers when we have a situation like tonight, when there is nothing even she can do to alter the circumstances. In fact, Karen's brand of Buddhism seems to involve a great deal of determination overall. You might even call it a need for control. I'm not quite sure how that aligns with the teachings. Technically speaking.'

Their eyes met. Bruno's manner was extremely dry but there was a strong reverberation of humour in him. He was Swiss but also quite un-Swiss. That made him interesting as well as

104

attractive, Mair thought. 'Are you religious?' she asked.

He shook his head decisively. 'No. You?'

'Not at all. But my grandfather was a missionary. He and my grandmother were out here in the 1940s, with the Welsh Presbyterian mission outreach to Leh.'

'That's why you're here now?'

'My father died recently. His parents were part of our lives because they lived nearby, but we never knew my maternal grandpa and grandma. My mother died when I was in my early teens so that part of the story was lost. I want to try to uncover some of it.'

Mair rarely talked about her mother, even to Hattie. Her instinct was to protect the bruise that had been left by her death. So it was startling to find herself confiding to Bruno Becker this intimate detail, and to realise that since their first encounter and her explanation of the somersaults she hadn't told Karen one thing about herself.

She had begun to, she remembered, but something else had always intervened.

But Karen was a bright flame, and everyone was drawn to her. It was only the strange circumstances, the snowstorm and their temporary captivity under the shadow of the monastery, that were making Mair talk so unguardedly to Karen's husband.

She took another hasty mouthful of cognac. Her hand was unsteady and the metal rim of the beaker rattled faintly against her teeth.

'Go on,' Bruno murmured.

She told him about the shawl, and her discoveries in Changthang and Leh. He listened attentively, his black head tipped against the stone wall and his eyes on her face. The cook measured some scant handfuls of rice into another pan of water as the scent of mutton swirled through the kitchen.

Bruno enjoyed the story of Tsering's great-uncle, and the old man's early memory of listening in amazement to the mission's wireless set. 'And now you're following the shawl thread onwards to Srinagar,' he said at length.

'Yes. Who knows what I'll find there?' I *will* find out about the photograph, she thought.

He unscrewed the cap of the flask and poured them both another drink. She sipped hers, stretching out her legs and letting her shoulders drop. The long day of bouncing over potholes had left her muscles aching.

Bruno rotated his beaker, thoughtfully examining the reflections in the polished surface. 'I am lucky in that both my parents are still alive. They divorced long ago and my mother remarried. She lives near us in Geneva now – she adores Lotus. My father is still physically strong but his memory has almost gone. My sister and I agreed that he would be safer and happier in a special hospital, which is not nearly as bad as it sounds, by the way.

'When I went to see him just before we came out here, we were sitting on his balcony looking at the mountains and I was talking – I have to talk a lot on these visits. He likes to hear about the rest of the world and everyone's lives, although I'm not sure how much of it he remembers. I was telling him about all the places we'd be visiting, and he seemed to be listening, nodding, the way he does.

'Then he reminded me that an Indian friend of our family was originally from Kashmir. Memory is a strange commodity. He remembered the minute circumstances of the friend and her mother coming to Switzerland after the war, yet sometimes he can't even quite recall who I am. He made me promise that I'd look up the daughter when we get to Delhi.'

Mair nodded, recalling how her father in his last weeks had travelled further and further into the past.

'The mother would have been the same generation as your grandparents. She was a Christian, a Roman Catholic. Perhaps they knew each other.'

'Is that likely? It's a long way from Leh to Srinagar.'

Bruno sighed. 'And that's in good weather. Tonight Srinagar might as well be located in South America.'

'I don't actually know if my grandparents would ever have

106

come this far west. But it's not impossible.' She thought of the photograph again.

'It would do no harm to ask our friend. If we're in Delhi at the same time, perhaps you could come with me to visit her.'

Their eyes met again.

'I'd like that,' Mair said.

They sat back, relaxed by brandy and conversation.

The languid cooking of dinner continued and a small girl made a circuit of the mattress seats, dishing out metal plates and spoons. Bruno got up once and went to look out at the weather, coming back with a grave face. 'Getting out of here is going to be difficult,' he said.

Deep snow would by now be blocking the mountain roads in either direction. Mair could envisage the scale of the work that would be involved in clearing it.

One of the drivers looked across at Bruno. He gave a shrug and an expressive flutter of one hand. 'Very bad. Very early,' he called.

Bruno nodded. 'Very bad,' he agreed. He folded himself on to the mattress again, telling Mair, 'We'd have trouble dealing with a sudden huge snowfall like this in Switzerland, let alone here.'

Remembering what Karen had told her, she asked, 'Are you from Geneva originally?'

Immediately his angular face lost some shadows and he leant closer, almost confidingly. Unwittingly Mair had touched something in him.

'I have to live in horizontal Switzerland, these days, because that's where my work is. I'm an engineer. But my home and my roots are in vertical Switzerland, in the mountains. I come originally from the Bernese Oberland, near Grindelwald. Do you know it?'

'No.' The claustrophobic room, the knowledge that they were all temporarily captive, made Mair long to be transported by a story. In her mind's eye she saw a Heidi-picture of sunlit Alpine meadows and dark fir trees. 'Tell me about it.'

'My people were farmers,' he began. 'In summer they took the cows up to the Alps to pasture. In winter there was snow.'

She listened contentedly. She was warm at last, and Bruno's description of home was familiar, not so much in the precise details but in the way he talked about the rhythms of farming and the small doings of rural valleys. She also clearly heard what he was not saying, in as many words, about his deep-rooted affection for the place and – she was certain – his longing for it. It made her think of her own home. She wasn't homesick, as she had been in Leh, but rather sharply alive to the memories of a place that was lost.

Bruno was telling her how the Swiss mountain farmers in the first half of the nineteenth century had known the hidden ways across the high passes connecting remote valleys. They were poor people, and when the first tourists had begun to arrive in the Alps, the Beckers and their neighbours had discovered they could earn good money by guiding visitors. Until then, he said, no one had ever explored the peaks and glaciers just for pleasure. To travel to the neighbouring valleys to find work or to sell their cheeses or even to make a pilgrimage to a mountain shrine, perhaps, but not for the mere satisfaction of it, or even for the sake of some obscure scientific observation. But then the gentlemen mountaineers and amateur scientists had arrived, and ventured up in the tracks of the local men, and after they had conquered their peaks, they rushed home to describe their triumphs and catalogue their discoveries.

The news spread, and more and more of them flocked to the Alps. Soon the wealthy *messieurs* were arriving in their hundreds from all over Europe, and the Beckers were among the first to offer themselves for hire as professional mountain guides.

'My great-grandfather, for example, he was Edward Whymper's guide,' Bruno said.

Mair had never heard of Whymper, and admitted as much. Bruno raised an eyebrow. 'He was British. He made the first ascent of the Matterhorn, with his Zermatt guides. There was a tragedy on the way down and four men died, but Whymper himself survived. He came regularly to climb in the Oberland and he often took Christian Becker as his guide. In the next generation – that was in the twenties and thirties, my grandfather Victor and another client made an early attempt on the Eiger's north face, only just escaping with their lives from a terrible storm. Victor saved the client's life.'

'You must be proud of that.'

He gave a quick nod. 'We are.'

'I don't know any mountaineers.' But now another memory came to her. 'I saw a memorial in Leh, in the European cemetery. Nanga Parbat.' She could bring to mind the name of the mountain, but not that of the dead man.

Bruno supplied it for her. 'Matthew Forbes. He was a mathematician from Cambridge University, a brilliant young man.'

'You saw the memorial too?'

'I visited it, yes. That Nanga Parbat expedition was led by a Swiss named Rainer Stamm, and he was the man whose life was saved on the Eiger by my grandfather. The two of them were close friends from that day on.'

So she and Bruno both had their reasons for visiting the cemetery. The link between them seemed significantly strengthened by this association of history. What with this and the snow, and the altitude-enhanced effects of the cognac, she could almost imagine how she might let her head tip sideways, gently and slowly, until it came to rest on Bruno Becker's shoulder.

And when she glanced at him she realised, with a faint shock of pleasure as well as a clutch of utter dismay, that he was imagining the same thing.

She levered herself upright and pressed her spine into the cold stone. Bruno shifted his position too.

They were further distracted by the presentation of a vat of mutton stew, the ladle held invitingly above it. Mair hunted for her tin plate and accepted a spoonful, and Bruno did the same. They took a simultaneous taste and Bruno pressed his lips together.

'You were right.' Mair giggled.

The rice that accompanied the stew and a pot of dark brown dhal were slightly closer to being edible.

'We may as well finish this off,' Bruno remarked, unscrewing the cap of the flask once more. 'I've told you more than enough about my people. Now it's your turn.'

By now, it seemed easy to do. She began at the first point that came into her head. 'After my father died, my sister and brother and I decided to sell the old house, the one we grew up in. It was hard to do, but in a way it would have been harder to keep it on. Empty most of the time, just a holiday home, accumulating dust and cobwebs and melancholy. But I can still feel the thread connecting me to the place. It's taut tonight.'

'I understand that,' Bruno said quietly. 'Go on.'

Mair began to tell him about her last morning at the house. She hadn't tried to relate this to anyone else: if she had been asked she'd have said there was nothing to tell, not really.

Eirlys and Dylan had both left early. Eirlys went first, her car loaded to the roof and her clipboard and master-list of lists placed next to her on the passenger seat. Dylan held the yard gate open and he and Mair waved to her as she drove away, leaving the home of her childhood as if she had been crossing off another item on her daily to-do list.

When Dylan was ready, he and Mair stood in the yard. She noticed that a thrush's nest was held in the twigs of the white lilac tree. Dylan took her hand. 'Don't be too sad,' he said.

'It's a positive sort of sad,' she replied. 'It was a happy place, wasn't it?'

'Childhood?'

As they stood there, the yard and the front garden seemed crowded with earlier versions of themselves.

Mair answered her own question: 'Yes, it was. I didn't realise it at the time, though.'

This made them both laugh. As a girl Mair had been blind to the charms of rural life.

Dylan kissed her forehead, then he drove away too.

She was glad to have a last hour alone. She walked through the empty rooms, closing the doors behind her. In the kitchen she rescued a trapped bumble bee, scooping it out to safety in her cupped hands. She followed it outside and leant on the stone wall of the garden. She took in the grey shape of the house, the blots of yellow lichen on the slate roof, the way the windows seemed punched into the thick walls and the whole structure hunkered down against the curve of the hill, so long settled into the ground that it had become as immutable as an outcrop of rock.

There was just one more thing to do.

She scrambled over the wall, using the same footholds she had adopted as soon as she was old enough to follow Dylan out into the fields to play. She walked on a diagonal through the soaking grass, away from the hill crest and the lambless grazing flock, and entered a little wood. The bluebells grew here and in that May week they were at their best, all the ground under the leaf canopy hazed with soft colour. Mair picked a small bunch, the stalks giving a familiar milky snap between her fingers and the scent rising around her. She wrapped the cool stems in a tissue from her pocket.

The bunch of bluebells was the last thing she put into her car, placing it on the passenger seat where Eirlys had stationed her clipboard. She sat for a few moments, looking at the house and the hill behind it. Then she drove away, following her sister and brother down the lane.

When she reached the village she stopped at the gate of the graveyard. On the other side of the street Tal Williams was coming out of the newsagent's. It was his family that had farmed the hills behind the old house for more than a hundred years. He waved his folded paper awkwardly at her, his windburnt face turning redder. Twenty years ago Tal had been Mair's first kiss.

111

She waved back, but he didn't come across the street. He had been at Huw's funeral, scrubbed up in a black suit and a stiff white shirt, and he would guess what her errand must be today.

She went on through the gate and walked along the path past a yew tree. Beside a tap in the wall she found a glass jam-jar and splayed the bluebells in it. Carefully, so as not to spill any of the water, she carried it across and put it on the mound of her parents' grave.

Then she sat on a sunny bench, reading the inscriptions on the nearby headstones although she knew them all by heart.

Bruno was a good listener. When she stopped he ducked his head in a quick gesture of appreciation. By this time they had finished as much of their food as they could manage, and their fellow diners were swaddling themselves in ragged quilts and rolling over, ready to sleep.

He said, 'You could have stayed at home, never left that place – is that what you're thinking? Perhaps you could have married your farmer and lived happily ever after.'

Mair was amused. 'No, I could not. He's not mine and I never wanted him to be. He's getting married to his long-time girlfriend this year. But still there's a yearning for what might have been in all of us, don't you think? There must be times when you think that you could have stayed in the mountains, and taken the cows up to pasture every spring.' And married Heidi, maybe, instead of being drawn to Karen's bright flame.

Bruno's eyes glinted with amusement too. Mair wondered how she had ever thought he was forbidding. 'I do think that – you're right. And, like you, I knew I didn't really want to stay. It wouldn't have suited me. We like the lives we've got, don't we?'

Mair said yes, because it was true.

'Anyway, these days, instead of cows, my family's pastures support several chair lifts and a high-speed gondola. Winter skiing, summer hiking,' he added casually.

Mair understood that the Beckers were therefore not too concerned about money. 'Does Karen have a might-have-been home in her heart too?'

Bruno said, 'Ah, Karen's a free spirit.'

The men across the room had collapsed into a silent jumble of shrouded heads and crooked knees. It was time to brave the cold before trying to sleep. Bruno upended the flask to check that it really was empty, and Mair clambered to her feet.

The floor tilted unexpectedly and she put out her hand to steady herself. Bruno caught it in his. With his free hand he clicked on his head-torch.

'Oh dear.' Mair laughed. 'Good cognac.'

'And good company,' he added.

The force of the blizzard hit them full in the face. The snow in the courtyard had drifted above knee-height and Bruno told her to follow in his footsteps as they battled their way to the opposite corner. The faint yellow cone of torchlight seemed solid with whirling flakes. The door leading to the cell rooms had blown open and a bank of snow was now piled in the freezing stone corridor. Bruno found a shovel in the angle behind the door and he dug furiously to clear a path while Mair directed the light. Working together they managed to force the door shut, and latched it securely with a wooden beam between two iron brackets. Their shadows wobbled on the stone walls.

'Do you have a torch?' he asked.

'In the car,' she confessed.

'Take mine for now. We'll retrieve yours in the morning.'

'But . . .' She stopped. It was obvious that they would be going nowhere tomorrow. She also realised that she didn't mind all that much. Be careful, she warned herself. Don't even *begin* to imagine.

It was the drink affecting her, and the altitude, and the cold, nothing more. Tomorrow she wouldn't even remember these inappropriate yearnings. She wasn't a daydreaming schoolgirl, after all.

'Get some sleep. I hope you won't be too cold.'

'Goodnight,' Mair said firmly.

The torch-beam glimmered on the damp stone wall beside her mattress. She took off the top layer of her clothes but kept everything else on, adding a fleece hat and mittens and a second pair of socks. She crawled under the covers, switched off the torch and closed her eyes, shivering. Immediately an image presented itself, of Karen and Bruno lying together with Lotus between them, the vivid threads of their hair all tangled. She pressed her mittens against her face, obliterating everything except cartwheels of torchlight imprinted in her retinas. She listened to the howling of the wind and eventually, intermittently, she dozed.

She woke to early daylight the colour of lead. All she could see through the tiny window was a patch of featureless grey. Her bones were stiff and her feet and fingers numb. When she tried to move she realised also that she was parched with thirst, and a jagged bolt of pain shot through her head. She stretched out her arm, using extreme care, and found her water-bottle. The contents were frozen solid.

It didn't take long to dress. The courtyard was furrowed with paths dug through the night's snowdrifts. The wind had dropped and in its place there was a blanketing fog, out of which spiralled a few lazy snowflakes. Still moving carefully, Mair plodded through the muffled chill. The kitchen seemed crowded but the figures hunched on the mattresses resolved themselves into the Beckers and last night's drivers, restored once more to sitting positions. Bruno was talking to their own driver, who was gesticulating with his purple mobile phone. Decals glinted all over it. Everyone was grim-faced, except Lotus and Karen, who beamed identically at her.

'Hi, I'm real sorry about last night. I was just laid out. I guess Bruno looked after you,' Karen called. She was pale, but otherwise her usual self.

Mair nodded. All she could think of was finding some water to drink. There was a plastic jug standing on a crate next to the bathroom, and even though she knew this was only filtered, not boiled, she jettisoned all her careful hygiene principles and swallowed two full mugs, straight off.

Lotus was turning the pages of a picture book and telling herself the story in a low voice. Ringlets of pale hair spilt from under her hat and whenever the two indifferent cooks looked her way they smiled at her in spite of themselves.

Mair was hunched over a bowl of warm rice porridge by the time Bruno finished his conference with the driver. He included her in his terse relaying of the latest news.

'Gulam has just spoken to a friend of his down in Kargil. The roads are blocked but the army and the Border Roads crews are working to clear the route in both directions.'

'So what does that actually mean?' Karen sighed.

'It means we wait it out. At least we're safe here, and sheltered. There are some trucks and cars stranded, Gulam says. They'll want to find those people.'

'Have some porridge, honey.' Karen passed Bruno a tin bowl.

'I just wish I'd bought a Jammu and Kashmir mobile,' he fretted. 'Or a satphone.' He turned his BlackBerry over and frowned at the sleek, dead screen. Mair understood his anxiety. The absolute isolation of this place struck her afresh. They were dependent on Gulam's mobile for as long as its battery lasted, unless there was any power supply in Lamayuru with which to charge it. And without that fragile link, they were entirely cut off from the outside world.

'How long does Gulam think it will take to clear the roads?' Karen persisted.

'Unless there's a freak heatwave, it could be several days.'

'Really? That long?' Karen turned to Mair, collecting up her mass of hair as she did so and twisting it into a knot. 'I hope you've got a good book to read,' she said. 'Or you could come with me up to the monastery. The wall paintings are magnificent.'

A silence fell. Lotus found her doll among the damp clothing strewn on the mattress. She began crooning to her in French, her small voice rising into the cold air.

Bruno said that he would go with Gulam and retrieve the rest of their luggage from the Toyota. It would mean digging the car out of the snow, he warned them, so it might take some time. Karen immediately jumped to her feet and Lotus scrambled up too.

'We'll come. We can have a walk in the snow.'

'Make a snowman,' Lotus gurgled. '*Oui*, Pappy?'

Bruno said shortly that this wasn't the park in Geneva.

'Hey, don't be so crabby,' Karen rebuked him.

She wasn't going to be dissuaded. She wanted fresh air and exercise, she insisted – in fact, they all needed some if they were to be cooped up in this place for the rest of the day. She swung round to Mair. 'You'll come too, won't you?'

Mair reckoned that a blast of cold fresh air might help her hangover.

In the end, Bruno agreed that they would all go. Armed with shovels borrowed from the guesthouse they set out into the cavernous mist. Gulam led the way and each step forwards took him deeper into the murk.

The cold was raw and insistent. Keeping close to the wall, they sidestepped in a series of footprints that descended from the ledge. Lotus grasped her mother's hand. She slipped once, her feet skidding from under her, but Karen swung her upright.

'Again,' Lotus chirped, launching herself off the next step. Her pink face shone and she seemed enviably unaffected by the cold.

It was a long descent. A monk came climbing past them, his top half wrapped in an anorak and the hem of his robe soaked and dragging. His shaved head was covered with a bobble hat. An old woman followed, bent under a bundle of firewood almost as big as herself.

Life at Lamayuru would go on, as it always had done, in conditions much worse than today's.

They came to the foot of the steps and reached a steep section of road that curled round the hill. Mair recognised none of this, but Gulam knew the way even in the disorientating mist.

Gingerly they edged their way downwards to a point where the road widened and flattened. With every contour gentled by snow and the mist, a line of tumbledown sheds and a broken cart loomed with the eerie beauty of a winter still-life. Animal pawprints tracked the whiteness here and there. They rounded another corner, and in front of them appeared the mounds of several abandoned vehicles. The snow had been heavily trampled all round them and soiled heaps clogged the road margins where some of the cars had already been partly excavated. Beside the rear door of one were more animal prints and a dismembered bag of rubbish. Shreds of plastic and gnawed vegetable peelings stuck out of the dug-over snow.

The Toyota was the furthest along the line of cars, still a pristine humped dome. Bruno and Gulam swung their shovels at it.

Mair stopped to catch her breath. Something made her glance upwards just as a single gust of wind tore a hole in the mist. Far above, so high up that she had to tilt her head backwards to see them, a cluster of a dozen squat white domes topped with fantastic spirals of black and gold appeared to float in the sky. Ragged flags danced between the pinnacles before vanishing into streams of vapour. It was like a glimpse of another world, and even as she stared at it the mist closed everything out again.

The clink of shovels carried to her, and she could hear voices shouting directions from somewhere below. A generator started up, coughed, and settled into a steady thrum. She stamped her feet and swung her arms to get the blood circulating, but a sense of detachment persisted. She felt that she was standing apart, watching the day unravelling and winding out of her grasp.

The next moments would remain in her memory for ever.

Karen seized a double handful of sticky snow. She compacted it with slaps of her mittened hands, then rolled it on the ground to make the beginnings of a snowman. Lotus scrambled in the churned snow at her mother's feet, and behind them Bruno twisted and stretched with a loaded shovel. Mair's visual memory of him was as a black query-shape printed on blankness. Lotus was darting towards her now, a shining grin showing her small teeth, her button nose runny and her hands lifted in the air.

'Make a jump, My,' she called. 'Jump!'

Mair glanced over her left shoulder. There was enough space, and the snow had been trampled in a rough circle. She gathered her muscles in readiness and took in a breath.

Out of the corner of her eye, she glimpsed an oncoming shadow. It slid from beneath one of the cars and flattened itself among the rubbish. But she was already in the air, the cars and the snow and the blank sky and the shadow itself revolving round her as she executed her back flip. She landed, and heard Lotus's cry of delight.

As she regained her balance the shadow swept in front of her.

It sprang from the ground, straight at Lotus.

The child's cry mutated from delight to a scream of terror, and then there was abrupt silence as she fell to the ground.

The brindled dog straddled the small body, jaws wide to bite, its body shivering and jerking.

Karen screamed and plunged forwards, but it was Bruno who reached the fallen child first. He kicked the dog in the head with such force that it was flung backwards into the air, a rope of saliva twisting from its jaw. Even before it landed Gulam was smashing at its skull with his shovel. The creature snarled and made to attack again, but one more shovel blow sent it skidding through the debris before it vanished into the mist.

Bruno snatched Lotus up and held her in his arms.

Her face was ice-blue and white, her mouth was stretched open but no sound emerged from it and her eyes made huge shocked circles. In the middle of one cheek was the dog's bite. From the margins of torn skin the blood was beginning to spring, pinpricks of shocking crimson in the colourless world.

Her hat had come off and her hair fell in pale threads over her father's shoulder.

Doors opened and people emerged. Where there had been emptiness there were faces and pointing fingers and a clamour of voices.

Bruno was already running. His legs pumped as he raced through the snow, past the staring people, plunging up the steps the way they had come. Karen flung herself after him. Mair snatched up Lotus's fallen hat and clenched her fist on the ball of soft wool. She ran too, hearing Gulam panting beside her and – a long way ahead now – the shiver of Lotus's voice rising in the first thin wail of shock and pain.

Bruno had reached the steps and instantly the mist swallowed him up. Mair had never seen anyone move so fast. She ploughed in his wake, her heart thumping and her breath coming in irregular gulps. Over the rushing of blood in her ears she could hear Lotus's faint cries. At last she came to the top of the steps and the snow-shrouded guesthouse took shape just ten yards away. On collapsing legs she raced across the courtyard with Karen and Gulam at her heels.

In the kitchen a circle of faces gazed down. Bruno had laid Lotus on the nearest mattress. He knelt beside her and battled to keep her still as she writhed and screamed. He poured a trickle of water into the bite, trying to bathe it clean.

Over his shoulder he ordered them, 'Get more water. Soapy water.'

Karen frantically grabbed the arm of one of the cooks. Mair caught sight of Gulam's face as he rattled off a sequence of commands. He looked terrified.

Lotus moaned, 'Mama,' as Karen knelt beside her husband. She reached out her hand and stroked back Lotus's wet hair, murmuring softly, 'It's okay, baby. You'll be all right, everything is all right, Mama's here.'

A basin of water was fumbled through the circle of spectators, and a hand held out the bathroom cake of soap.

'A clean cloth,' Bruno demanded. Karen stared wildly round

the kitchen. There wasn't a shred of anything clean in this house, and their bags were still in the Toyota. Mair quickly peeled off her coat and her fleece. One of her intermediate layers was a fine cotton shirt, put on in Leh yesterday morning. Only *yesterday*? She stripped it off and, with a strength that surprised her, tore it into rags. Bruno soaked the first, lathered it and went on washing the bite while Karen held the child. Mair prepared another strip of cloth with soap and water.

Bruno raised his head to glance at his wife. 'She hasn't had any shots,' he said.

Karen's body stiffened. 'What shots?'

He whispered, out of a mouth that was distorted with anguish, 'You know what shots I mean.'

Mair knew, but she had tried to stop herself thinking it. When she dared to look at her again Karen had aged, and her beauty had tipped into gauntness. Clumsily she wagged her head from side to side, trying to hold back the tide of horrified recognition.

'No,' she insisted. 'No, that can't happen.'

'Will you take over?' Bruno said to Mair. He gave her the cloth and indicated the bowl of water. 'Keep on rinsing. Just keep at it.'

Silently she took his place. Lotus's shock seemed to be subsiding. She cried more normally now, as rage and pain flooded up in its place, clenching her fists and drumming her feet on the mattress.

Bruno gripped Gulam by the shoulder. His knuckles showed white. 'I need your mobile,' he said.

After that, Mair's memories spooled away into darkness.

She remembered hours of Bruno talking, shouting, or abjectly pleading into the borrowed phone. His face was etched with deep lines and there were navy-blue shadows under his eyes.

When the battery went flat, she left Bruno and Karen with the child and scrambled in Gulam's wake, through the mist-thickened lanes, to locate the generator she had heard earlier.

It had gone off for lack of fuel, but with their growing retinue of interested villagers they were directed upwards to the monastery. A monk met them, listened to what they wanted, nodded with an impassive face. Freighted with sick desperation, minutes crawled into hours. Another phone was found. Frustration burnt like acid in Mair. She could see too clearly what Bruno and Karen were suffering.

The phone connections were fragile. Bruno would get through to someone, a doctor or a consular official, or an officer at an Indian Army medical base, and then the signal would break up and he would have to start all over again.

The information was meagre, and it changed with every call. There was rabies vaccine in Kargil. Or else it was available in Srinagar. Or there was none in the entire state, only in Delhi, and the doses Lotus needed would have to be flown up. There was a break coming in the weather. An army helicopter could fly to collect the Beckers, maybe tomorrow. The mist was going to cling for at least a week: no flights could take off. The roads would definitely open again soon; they would stay closed until the spring.

After each reversal Bruno pressed the heels of his hands to his eyes, as if this might obliterate what he dreaded seeing, then grimly resumed the pursuit. Once they had been alerted, his family and Karen's began doing everything they could from Europe and America, but they couldn't relay even what they were able to orchestrate from so far away.

With Lotus in her lap, Karen watched the negotiations out of clouded eyes. Her thin body was tense as a wire.

They all waited in the kitchen, the squalor of it rancidly familiar.

At the end of that first terrible day, there was a clamour in the courtyard. Gulam summoned Bruno outside to see. The dog had been found, and the villagers had circled it and then stoned it to death. Its body was tied up in a sack and deposited in an outhouse. If a way of escaping from Lamayuru ever came, a sample of the dog's brain tissue would be taken for veterinary

121

analysis. In a low voice Gulam told Mair that he didn't doubt what would be found. He had seen this before. A nun had died of rabies here last year. When she sickened she had begged to be taken to hospital, but there was nowhere within reach.

'Many wild dogs now.' He shook his head and then sadly shrugged. 'We try to kill, but . . .'

Mair remembered reading somewhere that the modern veterinary drugs given to livestock poisoned the vultures that had always cleaned up the carcasses of dead animals. With the near-extinction of vulture species, and the abundance of carrion, there had been an explosion in the numbers of feral dogs. And with the dogs came disease. This was what happened.

Acceptance of circumstances and the belief that what would ensue was inevitable was Buddhist, she supposed. Her own response was the opposite. Whatever could be done must be done, and everything beyond that should be attempted. But she fought to suppress all her own urgencies, even a flicker of feeling, beyond what would be immediately helpful to Karen Becker.

Performing grotesque contortions, time alternately crawled and galloped into the second day.

And then the third.

'When?' Bruno pleaded yet again into the phone. 'How long?'

Lotus wore a bright white square of antiseptic dressing taped to her face, but otherwise seemed herself again. She was bored by the enforced confinement, and all three of them did their best to distract and amuse her. Mair saw the separate tenderness that her parents poured on their child, but with each other Bruno and Karen were minutely considerate, and distant. Every exchange about what was to be done, what might happen in the next hour or the following day, was too freighted with importance for them to admit their dread. The fluid intimacy she had envied, long ago in the bazaar in Leh, had solidified into a sheet of clear glass. The two of them moved alongside each other, but not together. Mair couldn't even imagine what their nights must be like.

On the third day of imprisonment, Karen wanted to take Lotus up to the monastery to be blessed by the lama.

'No,' Bruno said. His weary face tightened.

'I want to.'

Bruno turned his head. 'Mair, would you take Lotus outside for a minute?'

She grasped the child's hand and they went out into the courtyard. Filaments of mist twisted over the rough roofs. The sky was nowhere; the world was thick and grey. Lotus was fretful and hung off Mair's hand, refusing to walk another step. Karen came out to join them. Her white face was tinged with grey.

'C'mon, Lo, back to Pappy. Wait for me, Mair?'

When she emerged once more, she begged Mair to come up to the monastery with her.

'My husband,' she began precisely, 'won't let our child be blessed. He calls what I believe in *mumbo-jumbo*.'

Mair remembered the praying.

Inside the inner door of the prayer room, Karen fell to her knees. In smoky lamplight, the rows of monks sat cross-legged in front of their bound texts. Their mumbled chanting was without beginning or end, rising and falling, under the ancient dim wall paintings of pot-bellied gods and beasts and the blank eyes of golden statues. The beams of this hall, at the heart of the monastery, were hung with dozens of mask-faces but all were swathed in blackened muslin because they were too terrible to behold.

Staring straight ahead of her, Karen was weeping. Tears ran down her face and she mouthed a prayer.

Mair cried too, out of impotence.

On the fifth day, the mist broke up. A filmy layer obscured the sky for another hour, and then a tentative blueness appeared.

Bruno rasped hoarsely into the mobile phone and at last he lifted his head. 'A helicopter's coming. We've got to get her down closer to the river where they can land it.'

Lotus was hastily bundled up and her father lifted her in his arms. A procession wound down the steps from Lamayuru village to the appointed place. At last, against the hazy blue, a black dot appeared. Mair pressed a scrap of paper with her email address scribbled on it into Karen's fist. 'Please. Let me know.'

'I will.'

Bruno's eyes were fixed on the sky. The Indian Army helicopter briefly landed, the Beckers ran beneath the rotors, the doors closed on them and they were lifted away.

Mair waited in Lamayuru for another four days, until the Kargil road was cleared for traffic. Then she and Gulam made the long day's drive over the pass, through Kargil and onwards to Srinagar.

SIX

The two women picked their way between tables and parasols, passing busy waiters who swivelled under trays of cocktails. The pontoon rocked gently on the lake water and Nerys put out a hand to steady herself.

'Here we are,' Myrtle announced over her shoulder. 'The Lake Bar, Srinagar Club.' She slipped into a seat at a table for two and indicated its partner to Nerys. When they were settled Myrtle took out her cigarette case and lit one of her gold-tipped cigarettes. She reclined against the cushions, blowing out smoke through clenched teeth and looking at the throng. 'The centre of the universe, to some people.'

'Not to you?' Nerys asked lightly. She felt intimidated. The tables were full of smart women, and men in well-cut riding clothes or the uniforms of the various cavalry regiments. Everyone seemed to know everyone else, and to be extravagantly at ease, laughing a lot as if they were all in on some enormously amusing joke. Myrtle had been greeted by at least a dozen people on their way in.

A white-jacketed waiter bowed in front of them and wished them good afternoon.

'Are you having a cocktail?' Myrtle asked.

Nerys shook her head. 'Just some tea.' Myrtle's eyebrows rose and Nerys hesitated. 'Well, maybe . . .'

'Two gin fizzes,' Myrtle ordered briskly. 'No, it's not the centre of the universe to me.'

'Darling, where have you been?' a voice cried. A woman swooped out of the crowd and pressed her powdered cheek to Myrtle's. 'You've missed a heavenly season. Such fun, honestly. Just look at you! You're so thin – you've gone quite *jungli*. What on earth were you doing up in those mountains? Is Archie with you? Because I'm going to tell him just what I think of him, dragging you off into the wild for weeks and weeks like that. And *did* you hear about Angela Gibson?' She lowered her voice and murmured in Myrtle's ear.

Myrtle gently disengaged herself. 'Frances, let me introduce you. Nerys, this is Mrs Conway-Freeborne. Frances, my friend Mrs Watkins.'

Mrs Conway-Freeborne's glance slid over Nerys's plain linen skirt and home-stitched blouse. Nerys felt even dowdier, if that were possible, under this fashionable person's scrutiny. 'How d'you do?' the woman said perfunctorily. She spoke quietly to Myrtle again, but her avid expression contradicted the discreet murmur. Nerys only caught snatches of the conversation. 'Bolted again,' and 'He won't take her back this time, mark my words.' She tried not to overhear any more and gazed at the view instead. This was only her third day in the Vale of Kashmir. She was still not quite convinced that what she saw could be real.

Behind her lay the windows and flags and awnings of the club, where Europeans in Kashmir gathered to eat and gossip and play. A little distance away was the Bund, the main street of Srinagar's new town. It was lined with shops with strange names like 'Poor John' and 'Suffering Moses', selling silver and beads, papier-mâché and rugs, shawls and silk hangings. In the distance was one of the city's seven bridges spanning the Jhelum river. A horse-drawn *tonga* clopped slowly across it, forcing a lone car heading the other way to a standstill. The river was the old town's central thoroughfare. It wound between wooden frontages and ancient stone *ghats*, and was crowded with barges and water taxis, and lined with markets. Nerys shifted in her chair. There was so much to explore and so much to discover, yet she was sitting here in front of another gin fizz hearing nothing but shrieks of laughter and titbits of gossip about people she didn't know.

A snatch of swing drifted out of the club's french windows as someone turned up the gramophone. She was struck by the incongruity of the juxtaposition – dance music with this dream landscape. Straight ahead of her, beyond the pontoon ropes, lay the lake. The water was shadowed at the margins by tall poplar trees where dragonflies ringed the black mirror surface, and out beyond the moored boats it was a vast sheet of dappled amethyst and silver. A sudden breeze fanned it and the reflections of the high mountains trembled and broke into fragments, their snowy crests scattering into white and pewter ripples. The late-afternoon sun was hot, but as soon as it dipped Nerys knew the evening would be deliciously chill and scented with charcoal smoke.

A pair of Kashmir kingfishers perched on a loop of rope, only a yard away. Their plumage was an intricate marbling of black and white. The birds returned her gaze out of unwinking eyes, rotating their black-crested heads in unison.

'I am so sorry.'

Myrtle's apology broke into Nerys's thoughts. 'Why? What for?'

Mrs Conway-Freeborne had gone away. Myrtle swallowed half her gin fizz and began to pleat the stiff cover of a Srinagar Club matchbook. 'The club chatter, I suppose. Always the same. Always malicious, never charitable.'

Nerys had noticed Myrtle's changed mood since their arrival. On the road she had been humorous, affectionate and curious about their surroundings. Here her manner was more brittle and her impatient attention danced too rapidly from one subject to the next. But there was so much else for Nerys to take in,

Srinagar seeming such a dazzle of sights and scenery after sleepy Leh, that up until now she hadn't given this difference much thought.

She studied Myrtle's face. Vertical frown lines marked her friend's forehead and her wide mouth turned down at the corners. 'You seem to know everyone,' she began cautiously.

Myrtle hitched one shoulder. 'It's rather a small circle. The old faces passing round what they think is new gossip. That's why I'm so pleased to have you here. You are, as they say, a breath of fresh air.'

The McMinns had made Nerys extravagantly welcome. Their home was a houseboat, moored under the shade of trees on the far side of the lake from where they now sat, but it was not the kind of houseboat that Nerys could ever have imagined. The local laws prohibited Europeans from owning property in Kashmir, but the British and others had neatly sidestepped this by buying or building boats to live in. Rows of opulent floating palaces lined the banks of the lake, and whenever the owners fancied a change of scenery, they had only to summon the barge men and have their home poled to a different location.

All the boats had fanciful names: *Cleopatra's Delight*, *Maharajah's Palace*, *Royal Pleasure*. The McMinns' was called the *Garden of Eden*. It was a broad, imposing wooden structure on a flat barge base, painted a soft shade of pale toffee brown. There were twisted pillars and intricate wooden lattices, carvings and pinnacles, a deep veranda at the front, with a sweeping view of the water, and sparkling white awnings all down the sunny side to shade the windows. Within, every surface was lined with carved or inlaid cedarwood. Nerys had never actually seen a cigar box, but she imagined that this polished, sweetly scented interior must be rather like a giant one. Her bedroom contained a huge canopied bed and a miniature chandelier; it was hung with crewel embroidered curtains and lined with rugs. Her bathroom was as elaborately panelled as everywhere else, and pairs of dim mirrors reflected her pale nakedness

128

into infinity. Whenever she wanted a bath or tea – or anything else she could think of, most probably – Myrtle had instructed her to ring the little brass bell that stood on her windowsill. A moment later Majid, the McMinns' chief house-boy, would tap softly on her door. Another much smaller boat, where the cooking was done and where the servants lived, was linked to theirs by a gangplank. All day long smoke rose from its crooked chimney topped with a conical tin hat.

'Yes, ma'am? Hot water for you? *Masala chai*? Small *chota*, maybe?'

Nerys seldom rang. She didn't want to give Majid unnecessary work to do, although she knew that if she even hinted this to Myrtle she would be scolded.

The *Garden of Eden* seemed just that, and it amused her to imagine Evan's reaction to the decadent luxury of it all. But already Nerys was feeling anxious about trespassing for too long on the McMinns' hospitality. She thought vaguely about looking for a room to rent, ready for when Evan arrived, perhaps in one of the tall wooden houses that jutted imposingly over the Jhelum river in the old town.

'You *will* stay, won't you?' Myrtle insisted, as if she were reading her thoughts. 'You're looking slightly less like a ghost, but you're not fit yet, you know.'

Nerys stayed in bed late every morning, where Majid brought her breakfast of rice porridge with delicious Kashmiri honey and fresh bread rolls. When Myrtle went off to pay a call or to shop or to accompany Archie on what she dismissed as some tedious business socialising, Nerys could spend hours reading, choosing books at random from Archie's imposing shelves, or just sitting amid the deep cushions of the veranda, watching the light as it slid over the water. She already felt more robust, as if her body had been remoulded over a firmer set of bones.

'I'm better,' she protested.

Myrtle snapped her fingers at the waiter and pointed to their empty glasses.

Nerys had noticed how she would drink two or three strong cocktails, and then over dinner she would be at first brightly talkative, teasing her and Archie, then argumentative, and finally sleepy. In the argumentative phase Archie would put out his hand to catch his wife's gesticulating one, as if he were trying to net a butterfly, and murmur to her, 'That's enough, old girl. Time for bed.'

Myrtle would snatch hers away. 'It's early. Put on a record, darling. Let's have a little dance.'

Nerys said very firmly, 'I don't want another, thank you.'

Myrtle sighed and her frown deepened. 'Oh dear. I'd forgotten how boring Srinagar can be. Don't you ever get bored, Nerys?'

'Not in the same way as you, I don't think.' You need something useful to do, Myrtle McMinn, she thought. From what she had seen so far, Myrtle's days seemed to consist of telephoning, getting dressed to go out, going out, and then recovering from either the boredom or the alcoholic excesses of going out by undressing and wrapping herself in a silk kimono. What else *did* all these women do, apart from laugh and sip cocktails and paint their nails?

Myrtle scratched a line in the air to indicate that their drinks were to be put on the McMinns' bar tab. She smiled at Nerys, squeezed her arm and let it go. The furrows were erased from her forehead. 'You're quite right. Archie will be home early tonight, and we should go and keep him company. I'm sorry to be so witchy. Frances Thingummy-Thingwig quite got to me, with her evil stories. Poor Angie Gibson wouldn't hurt a fly, and if she's finally left her horrible husband for good then I wish her luck. She deserves better. Now, let's go. Am I forgiven?'

'For nothing,' Nerys insisted. They linked arms and made their way past the emptying tables. It was the soft blue time by the lake that wasn't quite afternoon any longer but hadn't yet become evening. It was the hour when Europeans went home to dress for dinner before meeting yet again later at the club or elsewhere.

A little wooden bridge linked the pontoon to the stretch of close-mown grass in front of the clubhouse. As they crossed it, their heels clicking on the wooden planks, the first bat of the evening flitted from the trees and skimmed overhead. The lights in the club drawing room were on, and a group of people was silhouetted in front of the windows.

Nerys saw a man with a head of curling tawny hair, chopped off anyhow, unlike the tidy military crops of his companions. His face was sunburnt and his clothes looked as if he had shrugged them on without much thought as to whether they were even clean, let alone pressed. He had deep-set eyes, a broad chest, and although he was of only average height he seemed bigger than his companions. He was talking in a resonant voice, in English but with a noticeable foreign accent, and Nerys heard him demand, 'Why not? The answer should be yes. In the mountains no is never an answer, my friends. We must ask again . . .'

As the two women passed by he lifted his head and frankly appraised them. His eyes caught Nerys's and held them for a second. Caught off balance by this she looked straight ahead and followed Myrtle on through the french windows and into the drawing room. They passed out of earshot.

'Did you know them?' Nerys asked, as Myrtle glanced round.

'No – why? Wait a minute. The wild-looking one is called Stamm, I think. He can't be a German, can he? Swiss, or something like that, probably. I don't know the others.'

The room was almost empty. A young woman was sitting alone at the far end.

'Now, here is someone I *do* want to speak to,' Myrtle murmured.

The woman held a magazine intently angled towards the lamp but Nerys could tell she wasn't reading it. A cup of tea sat cold and untouched beside her.

'Caroline?' Myrtle said.

Reluctantly the other put the magazine down. She had very pale skin, so nearly translucent that the blue veins showed in her throat. Her fair curly hair was held back from her temples with a pair of tortoiseshell combs and her full lower lip looked as if it might tremble at any moment. Nerys could see that she was very young, perhaps not much more than twenty, and distinctly pretty in a round-faced, innocent way.

'Caroline,' Myrtle repeated, 'how are you?'

Caroline collected herself. She produced a smile. 'You're back.'

Myrtle made the introductions.

'Caroline, please,' the young woman insisted, when Nerys tried to call her Mrs Bowen. Here, plainly, was someone quite unlike Mrs Conway-Freeborne.

'Nerys,' she offered in return.

'Is Ralph here?' Myrtle wanted to know.

'No. He's gone with the regiment – didn't you hear? I believe it's manoeuvres first and then another posting. There may be one more short leave, or they may have to deploy at once. I don't know anything, though, really. It's only what Mrs Dunkeley and the other wives are saying.'

Caroline's fingers twisted in her lap, and her rings caught the light. Nerys felt a twist of sympathy for this young wife, probably newly married and deeply in love with her handsome officer husband who must now go off to war.

Myrtle sat forwards in her chair. She reached out and caught Caroline's chin, turning her face to the light as she did so. 'And you?'

The girl's skin was so pale and clear that the flush rising from her neck and colouring her cheeks was very noticeable. 'I'm . . .' She tightened her lips and moved away from Myrtle's grasp. 'I'm perfectly fine, thank you.'

She looked warningly towards Nerys, and Myrtle nodded. 'I'll come and call on you,' she told her, in a way that didn't invite contradiction. Nerys wondered whether that was what the girl wanted, because she didn't look as though she did. She was biting her lip, and her long lashes were lowered to conceal the expression in her eyes.

Myrtle and Nerys said their goodbyes, and went on through the club to the jetty where the *shikara* men waited for a fare.

'Here, Memsahib,' called one, out of a row of bobbing heads. 'Cheap fast ride. Where you go?'

They climbed down into his taxi boat as he held it steady for them. Like the others, it was a narrow, elegant craft with a high prow. Under a curtained canopy there was a mattress seat for two, piled with cushions and rugs. Nerys and Myrtle slid into their places as the boatman pushed off from the mooring. He was a Muslim, dressed in a long grey tunic-style shirt and a bright red skullcap. A shawl hung over his shoulders, against the coming chill.

Myrtle told him where they were going and he dipped his leaf-shaped paddle. Water dripped as he lifted it again and they glided forwards through the lotus leaves and ranks of dried seed heads out towards the centre of the lake. The sun was setting and bars of low cloud in the west were flushed with gold and crimson. Mist rose off the water and hung in filmy layers, partly veiling the two low hills of Srinagar, one crowned with a fort and the other with an ancient temple. The Himalayas were dark, two-dimensional masses against an ink-blue sky already pricked with stars. The old town shone with yellow lights, and there were more chains of lights showing on the lake's islands and from the Mogul gardens at the opposite end. The boat seemed suspended in the air, anchored by its mirror reflection. The only sound was the rhythmic dip of the paddle and the boatman singing under his breath. The thought came to Nerys, unformed because it was so unpractised, but still it came, *This is beautiful. I am so happy.*

Then Myrtle's cigarette lighter clicked and the flame briefly lit an ellipse of her face. 'Poor Caroline Bowen,' she said, on an exhaled breath.

'It must be hard for such a young wife, to have her husband going off to fight and not knowing when he will ever come back.'

There was a moment's silence.

'I wish it were that simple,' Myrtle said at last.

'Why?'

She paused. Then she said, 'I'll tell you what everyone knows.'

She described how Miss Caroline Cornwall, as she then was, had come out to Kashmir straight from her secretarial college in London. She was from a good family but her parents were dead – her mother when she was a little girl and her father quite recently, from a heart attack. That had left her stepmother with whom she was on friendly terms without being particularly intimate, because Caroline had been at boarding school since before her father's remarriage.

'A sad story, but not that unusual, I suppose,' Nerys murmured, reflecting at the same time that she had no knowledge of the sort of people who sent their motherless daughters away to school. She couldn't imagine her shy, fond father doing such a thing. 'How do you know her?'

'I met her first at a Residency party. The stepmother has some remote family connection to Mrs Fanshawe.'

Mr Fanshawe was the British Resident in the princely state of Kashmir. In the grand setting of the Srinagar Residency, he and Mrs Fanshawe performed the rituals and elaborate formalities of liaison between the British rulers and the government of India, the maharajah and his court, and directed the complicated strata of military and civilian societies that surrounded them.

'The Fanshawes are very sound on service, and pragmatic on Independence,' Nerys had heard Archie McMinn saying. 'They do an excellent job here, in the old-fashioned way.' She hadn't known what any of that meant; neither did she imagine that she would ever understand precisely because India didn't run in her blood, as it did in Myrtle's and Archie's.

Myrtle was describing how Caroline Cornwall had come

out to join the Resident's household. 'She was appointed a sort of assistant secretary to Mrs F. I think her duties amounted to doing the flowers in the public rooms every day, managing the calls book, sending out invitations and so on. That reminds me, I must take you to sign the book. If you don't leave a card, darling, you won't be invited to lovely gatherings up at the house – cocktails, tea and tennis, that sort of thing.'

Myrtle was laughing and Nerys joined in. 'I don't have a card. And I can't play tennis.'

'My God. Social death. How will you ever meet anyone?'

'I've met you and Archie. That will do for me. Go on with the story, please.'

'Well. Miss Cornwall had been up here barely six months before her engagement was announced to a Captain Ralph Bowen. They met, of course, at the party following a polo game in which she had watched Captain Bowen scoring three goals. Or something of that order anyway – who knows? This was quickly followed by a wedding at the English church, regimental guard of honour, reception at the Residency.'

'All very suitable, by the sound of it.'

'So you might think. This was perhaps a year ago.'

'And now the captain is going off to war.'

That wasn't news. Most of the Indian Army husbands were away, and as the summer season ended, Srinagar was home to a mixture of abandoned wives and the few remaining civilian families whose men, like Archie, were in reserved occupations. Myrtle had remarked more than once that it was a very different place from the pre-war city.

They were in the middle of the lake now. The sun had gone down and the light in the sky faded through lavender to steel grey as the moon rose over the mountains. Nerys watched the silver disc as it sailed through veils of cloud.

'Nerys?'

'Yes?'

'Would you say that you are happily married?'

Her immediate dutiful response was to say yes. Anything less would be a betrayal. And then, with the small start that was becoming almost familiar, she realised once again that she had hardly thought about her husband that day. How could *that* be, for a woman who was laying claim to a happy marriage?

The moment of exultation she had just experienced had been to do with the beauty of the place, and the pleasure of having Myrtle for a friend, but most of all it had arisen from a sense of freedom. For almost the first time in her life, certainly for the first time since her wedding day, she felt like her own person. But then, she reminded herself, if she were not married to Evan she wouldn't be here at all, to be happy or otherwise. She would be at home in Wales, and most probably a spinster. Very few other romantic opportunities had presented themselves. Or – more accurately – none.

Nerys smiled, remembering home and the narrow horizons of chapel and valley. It was true that as a husband Evan was disappointing in some respects: married life wasn't the passionate communion she had dreamt of as a green girl. But she was in no doubt that Evan was a good man, and a kind one in his way, and a human being with much in him for her to admire. She respected him. Theirs wasn't like Myrtle and Archie's partnership, but she reckoned that all marriages were different.

She was also beginning to understand that it was true what people said about absence making the heart grow fonder. She was looking forward to seeing Evan here in Srinagar, even in his stiff black preacher's clothes among the smart club wives. She had a sudden picture in her mind of his hands, long-fingered, as they rested on hers. *My dear?*

Suddenly she was blushing as hotly as Caroline Bowen had done and she was glad of the gathering darkness. 'Yes,' she said deliberately, and with conviction. 'I would say that I am.'

'Yes,' Myrtle echoed. Nerys had no doubt that she was

mentally celebrating her own luck and happiness, not the Watkinses'.

Ahead of them were the lights of the *Garden of Eden* and its neighbours glimmering under the sentinel trees. There was the expected scent of smoke in the air, and of Majid's good cooking. Myrtle cast the butt of her cigarette into the water. 'The trouble for Caroline is that she isn't happy. I don't believe that her captain ever can make her happy, either.'

'I'm sorry for her, then.' Nerys didn't press for more information.

The *shikara* man expertly drew his paddle in a circle, swinging the boat's prow towards the houseboat's steps.

But Myrtle added, in a lower voice, 'She's a very young girl, and her head's full of romantic ideas. She doesn't have many people to confide in. Her husband is always away and she's been looking elsewhere for love and attention, the poor darling. That's not unusual in Srinagar, of course, but unfortunately Caroline has chosen an option that's not just compromising but quite dangerous. As soon as she told me about it I warned her to break it off at once, but from what I saw of her tonight I'm guessing that she has done nothing of the kind.'

The prow of the *shikara* gently grazed the houseboat steps that descended to water level. The boatman caught the mooring post and made fast. At the same moment the double doors leading to the *Garden*'s veranda opened and Archie appeared, yellow lamplight spilling over his head and shoulders.

'Here you are at last,' he called.

Myrtle silently placed a finger to her lips to indicate to Nerys that even Archie wasn't privy to this particular story.

Nerys briefly grasped her hand. 'Mrs Bowen is lucky to have you for a friend,' she murmured. 'And so am I.'

Myrtle threw her head back and hooted with laughter, startling the boatman. The *shikara* rocked as they climbed to their feet, and Archie handed them in turn up the shallow steps before he dropped some coins into the man's uplifted hand.

'Thank you, Sahib. Goodnight, Lady Sahibs.' The boat was already sliding away into the gloom and its ripples lapped sweetly against the *Garden*'s planking.

'You've been having a good time,' Archie observed. 'Who was at the club?'

'The usual tragic figures.' Myrtle sighed. 'I don't think Nerys was impressed.'

'That's not true,' Nerys protested indignantly. 'I was rather overcome by the glamour of it. We met a woman who said Myrtle had gone *jungli*, but I imagine she was actually referring to me.'

Archie rested a hand on each of their shoulders. 'I can't think what she was talking about. You are the two most elegant and beautiful women in Srinagar.'

Laughing, they passed into the houseboat's saloon.

The round table in the centre was laid for dinner, with crystal glasses and silverware on the starched white cloth. The marquetry panels and carved cornicing glowed in the candle-light, and the pervading scent of polished wood mingled with the fragrance of dozens of deep crimson late roses arranged in bowls on the side tables. In silver frames, the faces of Myrtle and Archie's family in England and Scotland crowded the shelves, interspersed with pictures of steam engines and bridges. Archie's Indian Railways work was also his passion, but he complained that his country was at war and he would much rather be in uniform.

He moved towards the drinks tray as Nerys went on down the corridor that ran along one side of the houseboat. The wide floorboards creaked softly under her feet.

In her room, the covers were already turned down on the bed. Her few clothes hung neatly in the sweet-scented ward-robe, each item freshly pressed, with her shoes polished and placed on the shelf beneath. She took off her light jacket and put it on a hanger. How easy it would be, she thought, to grow accustomed to such luxury. It was a good thing therefore that the opportunity wouldn't arise. Soon, in the next few days, she must begin the search for an appropriate home to rent in order to be ready for when Evan arrived. She couldn't trespass on the McMinns' hospitality for ever. Her budget was tiny, but she was sure she would find something.

After a soft knock on her door Majid appeared. 'Are you ready, ma'am? I will send hot water?'

A little procession of Majid's helpers came with tall enamel jugs and filled her bath.

That evening, at dinner, Archie announced, 'My darling, I have to go down to Rawalpindi in two days' time, and then to Delhi. After that I'm not sure, probably east. I don't know how long it will be for, unfortunately. There are some track problems that we must solve in order to cope with troop movements.'

Myrtle put down her knife and fork. 'So soon?' she asked calmly.

Both women knew better than to ask what troop movements, and where.

'I had a telephone call this afternoon. Our holiday's over. We were lucky to get such an extended time off, you know.'

'Yes, of course we were,' Myrtle agreed. She sipped at a glass of water and Majid, who had been silent in the shadow at the far end of the room, came forward to replenish it from a crystal jug. 'I should think Nerys and I will amuse ourselves here for a few more weeks. I don't think I shall go down to Delhi yet. It would mean opening the house up properly, and that seems pointless just for me, don't you think?'

She didn't say as much – because that would have been a complaint, and she made it a firm rule always to defer to the demands of her husband's work – but Myrtle dreaded going back south to their winter home. It was too lonely there, in the quiet rooms, without Archie. This time she was sure he would be away for a long while.

'That sounds a good idea,' Archie concurred.

139

Nerys kept her head bent in order not to intercept the look that passed between them. As soon as she had finished eating she excused herself, saying she had some letters to write, and left the McMinns alone together.

The tailor worked in a tiny shop between the first and second Jhelum bridges.

Archie had driven out of Srinagar the day before, and Nerys was trying hard to be the best possible company for Myrtle. She wasn't finding it particularly easy because she had just received a letter from Evan saying he was detained by mission business near Kargil and wouldn't reach Srinagar until the very end of October. Her own spirits were lower than they had been since leaving Leh. Didn't he *want* to come and join her? Why was his work always so much more important than she was? But, still, she had ignored her own inclination to spend the afternoon moping over a book on the shady veranda of the *Garden of Eden*, and agreed to come shopping with Myrtle.

The tailor sprang up as soon as he saw them. He sat them in the two chairs that took up almost the entire floor space, and began to haul bolts of cloth off the shelves.

'Silk, madam. Finest.' A waterfall of pale eau-de-Nil fabric spilt over Nerys's lap. 'Tussore, linen, pure cotton.' Silver pink, lavender, dove grey, snow white. Nerys couldn't help fingering the folds. She did need clothes, even if they weren't things as lovely as Myrtle's or Mrs Conway-Freeborne's. She even had a little money of her own, the few hundred pounds' worth of capital left to her by her grandparents that she had never touched. She had believed that it might buy a home for Evan and their family some day or – with vague and nowadays seriously diminished piety – perhaps be used to do some good work. But then (the thought made her feel deliciously wanton and self-indulgent) maybe she could spend just a little of it on herself.

'Tweed,' Myrtle said crisply, pushing aside the summer-weight fabrics. 'You will want a *pheran*, Nerys.'

'What's that?'

'A long Kashmiri topcoat with loose sleeves like a cape. Warm, practical. Everyone wears one as soon as the cold weather arrives.'

The tailor came back, tottering under the weight of bolts of heavier fabric. He shook out one length after another and the three began to debate the differences, comparing the thickness of one with the weave of another, considering the subtlest heather-purple check against the green with a thin pimento-red stripe. And then, once Nerys had finally chosen a fine grey-blue tweed the colour of lake mist, there were a dozen details of cut and style to be decided. After that, there was an elaborate series of measurements to be taken, all of this written down in a black notebook with pages as fine as the skin of a brown onion. A samovar was brought in on a heavy brass tray and tea was served, with fresh afternoon bread straight from the oven in the baker's shop a dozen yards away.

The whole process took more than two hours, and Myrtle said that that was really very quick for such an important purchase.

'Seven days, then ready, Memsahib,' promised the tailor.

Eventually they emerged into the late sunshine. Myrtle pushed her fists deep into the pockets of her skirt and looked up and down the narrow street. Her dark hair was growing longer and she had rolled it into loose curls that framed her face. She had also applied red lipstick. Nerys thought how beautiful and bold she looked.

'It's half past four. I have to go to Bandage Club,' Myrtle announced. 'It's not what you'd call fun, I'm afraid, but would you like to come with me? You may get a cup of tea and an iced bun, unless the buns have been withdrawn due to rationing.'

The organisation for military and civilian wives, British and Indian, was actually called Wartime Hospital Supplies. The

141

volunteers sat at long tables sorting and packing bandages and dressings for despatch to the front. Nerys could imagine the club ladies working away while all the time their gossip scorched the antiseptic air. She didn't feel strongly tempted, and the alleys of the old town were beckoning. 'Next time. I think I'll go for a walk now.'

Myrtle looked doubtful. 'A walk? Here? Why not take a *shikara* to the Shalimar Garden instead?'

'I'll take a *tonga* home if it gets too much.' Nerys smiled.

Alone, she wandered past the local baker's tiny niche in the crowded row of shops. The shop consisted of a pit dug in the ground, in which the baker crouched below street level in front of a cylindrical clay oven glowing hot with the wood fire at its base. He leant forward to fan the red embers, and even from where she was standing Nerys could feel the heat on her cheeks and forehead. The vertical walls of the oven were lined with circles of half-cooked dough, the delicious afternoon bread of Kashmir. Three veiled Muslim women brushed past her and the sweating baker half rose from his squatting position to serve them with hot fresh rolls from the highest part of the oven. Even though she had had tea at the tailor's shop the scent of the sesame-crusted bread was too good to resist. Nerys bought a roll for herself and ate it as she strolled on down the alley towards the sliver of canal visible at the far end. On the way she passed one shop selling piles of aluminium pans and kettles, another that specialised in string and rope of every conceivable weight, coiled in pyramids or hung on spools, and others that had nothing but drums of cooking oil, a few sacks of rice, or stacked bundles of firewood to be weighed out on a primitive balance. A man led a donkey swaying under a load of wood that was taller than itself.

When she reached the canal Nerys glanced from left to right. Srinagar was threaded with waterways, an intricate maze of them connecting the lakes and the river, itself much more heavily

142

frequented than the dusty streets. The canal surface here was coated with a bright green scum, broken up in places by the passing boats to reveal the oily blackness beneath. One *shikara* was curtained to protect its passenger from the casual gaze, another boat was loaded with cut greens from the floating gardens out in the lake.

The muddy banks on either side boiled with life. A woman with a bucket was washing plates, and others slapped the suds out of their laundry against convenient rocks. Glistening naked children screamed and splashed in the water as, a little further on, a girl tipped out a bowlful of slops. A miserable goat tethered to a post stood with its stick legs buried in mud as chickens scraped and picked in the filth coating the steps. A raft with raised sides slid across, weighed down with a flock of sheep and a child shepherd. The ferryman propelled it by dragging it along a suspended wire. As soon as the boat scraped the opposite bank the sheep crowded off and poured down an alley, following some ancient route through the depths of the city. Tall wooden buildings jutted over the narrow channel, the top storeys built outwards with their high windows propped open to catch the breeze.

Nerys hesitated as she worked out which way to turn. To her left the route was blocked by the poles and tattered awnings of a busy waterside market, where pierced and blackened oil drums functioned as braziers over which stallholders fried *pakoras* or simmered goat meat; to the right were the brick pillars of a bridge. She retraced a few steps and turned at random into the first alley running parallel to the canal. She had already forgotten where the tailor's shop and the baker's lay in this tangle of walls and crowded niches. Picking her way past heaps of refuse, ripe with the stink of the market, she began to walk towards what she thought was a glimpse of the canal. A cart straddling the way forced her to turn aside again and step in another direction, down an alley so narrow there was room for only one person to walk. A sharp dogleg turned one way, then seemed to double back again, and now the sky was blocked out by a crisscross of overhead lines hung with dyed lengths of fabric, hoisted to dry. A file of bearded men in red skullcaps marched towards her and she flattened herself against the wall to let them by. Nerys knew already that she was lost. She could only keep walking on until she came either to the canal where she could perhaps wave for a *shikara*, or to a road big enough for a *tonga* to ply for hire.

The crowds thinned out as she moved away from the market, and she was sometimes almost alone between stone walls or closed wooden shutters. The few passers-by stared blankly at the lone European woman who had wandered away from the jaunty houseboats and the security of the club.

She began to think that Myrtle's advice to go to the Shalimar Garden instead of here had actually been excellent.

Wondering if she could, after all, go back the way she had come, she stopped to peer behind her. A sudden violent tug at the hem of her skirt made her spin round again, almost over-balancing. The lane seemed deserted but then she looked down and saw a trio of tiny children at her feet. Their faces were dark with dirt, their eyes very bright. The oldest might have been five, and she carried a baby bound in a cloth on her back. Her brother was the one who had grabbed a fistful of her skirt. The girl said a few words and pointed, and all the time the baby stared up at Nerys, unwinking. When Nerys didn't respond, the girl insistently repeated the same phrase, glaring at her as if she must be stupid.

They vividly reminded her of the children at her school in Leh. She missed them all, their clapping and singing and shy laughter – even their resistance to her efforts to teach them anything except games.

Her basic knowledge of Ladakhi was no use here, and she hadn't yet picked up a word of Kashmiri. She tried what Hindustani she knew but the children only shrugged and pulled harder at her. Giving up, Nerys followed as they dragged her along in their wake. Down another twist of the lane, past a mangy dog guarding a doorstep and a beggar who thrust his stick at her, they came to a dark doorway. A piece of sacking was looped to one side and Nerys ducked under the lintel.

Blinking, she looked round.

It was a bare, drab slot of a room that smelt of sour milk and human dirt. A heap of torn covers on some sacks revealed where the family slept. In another corner there were a few pots and pans and a dish covered with a filthy rag. In the middle of the room, on a square cut from what had once been a carpet, sat a young woman. She looked exhausted. Her hair was covered with a strip of cloth for a *dupatta*; her shapeless and soiled cotton tunic only partly concealed her extreme thinness. Her bare feet were filthy and cracked, spread flat on the floor as she leant over a spinning wheel. When the children came in with Nerys she let a spool of spun yarn drop into her lap and dully stared at them. Her daughter launched into what was clearly an explanation of whatever the woman they had captured might be good for. The spinner wearily nodded, attempting a smile for her children's hostage.

More than anything else about the sad sight, that smile touched Nerys's heart.

The little boy started pinching and whining at his mother. Her smile died. She briefly stroked his hair, then twisted a handful of cloudy combed wool and began to work the treadle of her wheel. The gossamer yarn as it was spun was so fine that Nerys, standing not a yard away, could barely see it.

With the baby's head lolling against her back, the little girl rummaged under the sacks and drew out a basket. She unfastened the hemp ties, stooped down and gently lifted out the contents. It was something flat and soft, wrapped in a cloth. When the cloth was folded back, Nerys saw a flash of colours.

With a showman's verve, the child shook out the shawl and twirled it in the air, spinning on her heels so the featherweight wool floated. The little boy, hunched against his mother's flank, clapped his hands and grinned. Even the passive baby chuckled. With care not to let even a corner of the treasure touch the trodden-earth floor, the child caught the folds in her arms and held them out to Nerys. The soft background of the pashmina was a pale rose and at either end there was a broad patterned band, stylised flowers intricately woven in dark red and a dozen shades of green and palest cream. She examined the work closely, intrigued by its fineness. The reverse, she saw, was so like the face as to be almost indistinguishable. How was this beautiful, elegant work done? With Myrtle, she had spent an hour browsing the shops along the Bund but she had seen nothing like this.

'*Kani*,' the exhausted young woman said, as if this explained something. '*Kani*,' she insisted.

The little girl jumped in front of Nerys, bunching the soft wool in her fists. 'Rupees? Rupees?'

The woman touched her fingers to her mouth, all the lines of her face drawn into a plea for money.

In agony, Nerys took out her leather purse. The boy scrambled to his feet and bumped against her shins, trying to catch a glimpse of wealth. She knew what lay inside – just a few coins, and small-denomination notes worn soft in the Indian way. Enough for a *shikara* ride across the wide lake, back home to the *Garden of Eden*.

Nerys shook the little sum out and held it in the palm of her hand for them all to see. With shame, she realised that there was not enough to pay for even a single cocktail at the Srinagar Club.

The little girl turned away. She busied herself with refolding their treasure inside its cloth. The woman nodded, holding up her hand for Nerys's money. She hid it away inside her tunic. She was embarrassed that an honourable potential sale had transformed itself into unvarnished charity, and she wouldn't meet Nerys's eyes. The boy knew exactly what was happening and was already pinching his mother's thin arm again and wheedling for food.

146

Abruptly Nerys turned aside, upset and disturbed by what she saw. In her eagerness to get away she was out in the lane once more, where twilight was gathering, before she recalled that she was hopelessly lost. She had to duck back under the lintel and face the family again. She performed a small mime of confusion, pointing one way and the other, shaking her head and holding up her hands. The mother sighed a brief instruction to the children and bent to her spinning wheel.

Hand in hand with her brother, the little girl led Nerys back past the beggar, who was now sleeping, and the inert dog. The cohort was turning a corner as another, bigger, band of children scuffled out of the shadows. An older boy screeched and began snatching at the clothes of Nerys's tiny guide. She slapped back at him, shouting at the top of her voice as the newcomers set on her and her brother. Their hands were darting all over the children's filthy clothes, searching for the money that Nerys must have given them. Nerys waded in between the two groups, dragging them apart and hustling her friends up the alley towards a glimmer of light.

But now the disturbance had drawn more attention from the warren of dark alleys and passages, and a gang of much older children rushed out at them. These ignored the small fry and jostled Nerys close up against a wall. She tried to slap away their hands as they grabbed at her pockets. The biggest of them, a hulking youth with the dark beginnings of a beard, tore off Myrtle's circlet of pearl and brilliants that she wore pinned at the throat of her blouse.

'Give that back to me,' Nerys screamed.

She was ringed by hostile faces, but she was relieved to see her own threesome retreating under cover of the confusion and melting away. She could give her full attention to her own plight. She stood taller, and pushed the youth in the chest. Instead of stepping back he came closer, thrusting his face into hers. She smelt his breath and the sweat of his body. She was afraid now, and gathered herself to run.

But which way, in this maze of darkness?

Nerys balled her fists and ducked under his arm. She feinted a dash in one direction, the youth followed, then she broke away in the other. But to her horror she saw that a man's misshapen figure loomed ahead, blocking the escape route she had chosen.

Now she was trapped.

The man shot out a hand to catch her wrist and his grip was like a vice. To her amazement he said calmly, in accented English, 'Stand behind me, please.'

The next thing she knew he had interposed himself between her and the mob of children. He said something commanding in Kashmiri and they all fell back a step.

Nerys realised that the man's silhouette appeared distorted because he carried a big bundle of rope over his shoulder. He let the coils drop at his feet and drew out a length to the full width of his outstretched arms. Then, from an inner pocket, he produced a vicious knife and there was a flash of steel as he cut off the length he had measured. Slowly he raised the blade to his lips and kissed it.

Nerys's assailants now watched in reluctant fascination, and she edged to one side in order to gain a better view for herself.

With the knife gripped between his teeth the man took the ends of his yard of rope in each hand and snapped it taut across his chest. Then he quickly doubled the length and snapped that too. He caught up the mid-point in his left fist and, with a flourish, he withdrew the knife from between his lips. The blade flashed once more as he cut the doubled rope in two. The children murmured to each other and pushed closer, and the man let the biggest youth inspect the four ends that were bunched in his fist.

Now, grinning, the man joined the two severed ends in a knot and pulled it tight to test the join. He held the knot up to Nerys. 'Please be kind enough to blow on it for me.'

Intrigued in spite of herself, she did as he asked.

He brandished the knotted rope in front of them. With surgical precision he placed his thumb and forefinger over the knot and slid it down the length of rope.

The knot slipped free, and the magician held up the uncut rope for them to see.

The gang of children gasped. As one body they moved backwards, distancing themselves from this sorcerer. He shook the intact rope at them, giving it a sharp snap in the air and with that they turned and ran, falling over themselves and each other in their anxiety to escape. A second later Nerys was alone with the magician, and the only sounds were of scurrying feet and a dog yelping.

The man bowed. He was of average height but broad-chested and muscular, with a mane of tawny hair. She already knew where she had seen him before.

'Would you like to follow me?' he asked politely. He dropped his rope length into a pocket, sheathed the knife somewhere about himself and shouldered the coils once more. A couple of turns down the alleyway, and a lane thick with weeds brought them out to a wide loop of the Jhelum river. There were lights everywhere, in the tall houses and on the bobbing boats, and music gaily echoed over the water.

The man stopped and bowed again. 'My name is Rainer Stamm,' he said, and held out his hand.

They shook, his huge fist enveloping hers.

'I am Mrs Watkins.' This sounded cold so she added, 'Nerys Watkins.'

'How do you do, Mrs English Watkins?'

He was laughing at her. Nerys withdrew her hand. 'I am Welsh,' she said.

'I apologise for my mistake.'

Swiss, or something, was how Myrtle had dismissed him. He wasn't British, anyway, Nerys was sure of that. He was too confident, too taunting, with his wide smile. Altogether too . . . *leonine*, was that it? 'Thank you for rescuing me.'

Her handsome hero looked at her. 'You didn't need rescuing.

You were looking after yourself. I just provided a moment's diversion.'

'How did you do that, by the way?' Nerys pointed to an end of the rope trailing out of his pocket.

'Ah, it's known as the cut-rope trick. Would you like me to show you? It might come in useful, next time you lose your way in the bazaar. My house is just there. I could offer you a drink with the lesson, perhaps, now that we have introduced ourselves.'

Rainer Stamm pointed a few yards along the *ghat* to one of the fine old Srinagar houses, built of brick and wood and decorated with carvings. Its gabled windows projected over the water.

'Thank you, no.' Nerys smiled politely. 'I must go. My friends will be wondering where I am.'

'Of course. I saw you at the club with Mrs McMinn, I think. Let me call a boatman.' A moment later a *shikara* came gliding to the step where they waited.

'Those little devils didn't rob you, did they?' he asked casually.

Nerys's hand flew to her throat where the neck of her blouse gaped. 'That big one took my brooch.'

'I want you to have it,' Myrtle had insisted. 'It suits you better than it does me.' Her mind was made up and Nerys had known that there was no point in protesting. Since then she had worn the brooch almost every day.

Rainer Stamm bent forward and gently placed his finger in the notch at the base of her throat. 'I'm sorry for that,' he murmured.

Nerys stiffened, but he had withdrawn his hand. The boatman whistled softly between his teeth and she turned to the river.

Rainer offered her his arm, but she made not to see it. She clambered awkwardly into the boat, which rocked violently, causing her almost to lose her balance and the boatman to call a warning from his perch in the stern. Nerys collapsed on to the cushions, irritated by her gaucherie. She would have to borrow the fare money from Archie when she got back to the houseboat. But, as if he had read her thoughts, Rainer gave the man a note.

'Thank you again,' she called, from beneath the awning.

Rainer touched his forehead. He said crisply to the boatman, 'Dal Lake, the *Garden of Eden* boat.'

He wanted her to know that he knew where she lived. It would be difficult, she already sensed, to keep ahead of Rainer Stamm.

The man dipped his paddle and the boat swished forwards.

'Goodnight,' the magician called, across the width of water.

SEVEN

The band struck up and the maharajah himself led out Mrs Fanshawe for the first waltz of the Resident's Autumn Ball.

Nerys watched from the thicket of gold chairs at the side of the ballroom. Mrs Fanshawe in silvery lamé, with feathers nodding in her hair, was entirely outshone by her partner, who wore a jade-green brocade frock coat with a massive emerald fastened among a cluster of lesser gems in his turban. After a respectful interval the floor slowly filled with other couples, European wives and daughters wearing elbow-length white gloves with their ballgowns, as Residency protocol demanded, partnered by a sprinkling of uniformed British and Indian officers, portly dinner-jacketed civilians, handsome men of the maharajah's retinue, and representatives of the various upper echelons of Residency staff. There was a scent of dried lavender, camphor and face powder.

The wives of the Hindu guests didn't dance in public but they had been present at the dinner beforehand, splendid in silk saris that made them look like a flock of exotic birds. Nerys wondered if they had withdrawn to one of the Residency's salons to admire one another's cascades of gold jewellery and privately indulge in unrestricted gossip. Over the silver plate and crystal glasses at dinner the general talk had been of the unseasonably cold weather, the looming probability of war in

152

Asia, the inconvenience of forthcoming rationing and – in whispers – of the latest Srinagar social scandal. Nerys had been in the city for only three weeks but she had already met Angela Gibson, the wife at the centre of the latest murmurings, and her husband had been pointed out to her at several gatherings.

It was odd to realise how quickly you could be drawn into this vortex, even someone as socially marginal as herself.

The thought of the whispers and gossip made her sit up and smooth the skirt of her dance dress, the first she had ever owned. It was rose-pink silk, made up for her by Myrtle's tailor from a pattern in *The Colonial Lady's Fashion Companion*, and she was wearing it tonight with a corsage and a pair of long white gloves borrowed from Myrtle. Myrtle had also rolled up her hair for her, dabbed French perfume behind her ears, and even applied some makeup.

When she had finished, Myrtle had stood back to admire her handiwork. 'Nerys Watkins, you have a mouth like a film star,' she proclaimed. 'If I were a man, I'd want to join the queue to kiss it.'

'*What?*' Nerys examined her own barely recognisable reflection.

Myrtle snapped open her beaded evening bag and stowed away her gold cigarette case and lighter. 'I said *if*, darling. I'm not that way, not even at my hideous boarding school, where such behaviour was not unknown, believe me. But if we all have to do without our men for much longer, who knows?'

Smiling at the memory of this exchange, which until recently would have seemed deeply shocking, Nerys glanced round for her friend. Myrtle was in dull-gold satin, exotic among her powdery British compatriots because of her short black hair and scarlet lips. Naturally enough she was at the animated centre of a circle of interested men, but Nerys would have wagered her grandparents' legacy – or what was left of it, after she had made the substantial payment to the tailor – that Archie McMinn had nothing to worry about.

Rubicund Mr Fanshawe now foxtrotted past, steering a plump woman decked in dowager's purple. Nerys wasn't nearly high up enough in the pecking order to be honoured with a dance herself, but the Resident had greeted her cordially at the reception before dinner. 'Mrs Watkins, welcome to Srinagar. Is Mrs McMinn looking after you? Will your husband be joining us soon?'

She had explained that Evan was still very busy with outreach work in Kargil, but that he hoped to reach Kashmir in good time before the winter closed in. As she said this, she heard the warning of the cold wind, sharp with ice, that rattled the branches of the chinar trees in the Mogul gardens.

'I'll look forward to meeting him,' the Resident said, in his polished way, and the line of guests shuffled forward.

Nerys studied the pearl buttons at the wrist of her glove. What would Evan think if he could see her now, dressed up and lipsticked, slightly dizzy and fond with the Residency's fruit punch?

She told herself that, as he wasn't here, it really didn't matter what he might or might not think.

The gold chair directly in front of her was twirled aside. 'Good evening, Mrs Watkins,' a voice said. 'Our acquaintance did begin in an unorthodox manner, but maybe you will over-look that.'

She looked up to see tawny hair and a wide smile. 'Good evening, Mr Stamm,' she rejoined.

He didn't wear patent-leather dancing pumps, like the other male guests, but a pair of serviceable black oxfords lightly rimmed with riverbank mud. The rest of his evening clothes were unremarkable, except that they were unbrushed, but still he seemed more notable than any other man in the room, including the maharajah.

The band played a little louder, in a faster tempo, and the chandeliers sparkled even more brightly.

'Shall we dance?'

It wasn't like any other dance, in her extremely limited

154

experience of such things. His right hand grasped hers at the proper angle and with the required firmness, and she felt the warmth of his fingers through her white kid glove. His left hand rested precisely in the small of her back and its caress made her sharply conscious of the three discrete layers – in her mind she counted them – of slippery fabric that separated her naked flesh from his.

They skimmed over the floor. When she finally met her partner's eyes, she saw they were bright with pleasure and amusement. He was humming the waltz tune under his breath and he was so close to her that she felt these vibrations pass from his ribcage into her own body, connecting the rhythm of their steps so that they turned as one person, perfectly attuned and with their eyes still locked together. He was a good enough dancer to convince her that she was just as good.

Nerys thought she had better say something. 'Your rope trick was very clever.'

'Thank you. You must let me show you some of my other effects.'

'Are you a magician, then?'

'There's nothing magical about magic, that's the sad secret. It's all practice and presentation.'

'Oh dear. And I believed that my blowing on the knot was what did it.'

'Perhaps it was,' he murmured.

When the waltz ended they stood in a bubble of quiet, hands clasped, until the next began. They chatted now as they danced, like friends.

It was a little while – or perhaps a long time – later that Nerys noticed Myrtle watching them from the edge of the floor, her head cocked to one side and the light catching her diamond dress clips.

'We have attracted the attention of your chaperone,' Rainer Stamm said.

Nerys drew back from him, pretending to be offended.

'Mr Stamm, I'm a married woman. I have no need of a chaperone.'

His laugh rose from the same place as the humming. 'Won't you please call me Rainer?'

'Yes, Rainer.'

'Nerys,' he repeated softly, fitting the syllables to the music. 'So, Nerys . . .'

With a catch on the *r* and a sibilant finish, she thought his pronunciation made her prosaic name sound beautiful. 'May I ask you something?' she began, and he inclined his head even closer. 'The children I was with when you rescued me the other evening, the smallest ones, did you see them?'

'I didn't rescue you. But, yes, I saw them.'

'I'd been at their house because they were trying to sell me a shawl. They're very poor.'

'Many people in Srinagar are very poor.'

'I know that. It just happened that this family found me, and I feel that I let them down.'

In the intervening days, she had thought a good deal about the little family and their one bare room, the girl's sharp-faced persistence and her mother's exhausted smile.

'What is it you want to do for them, Nerys?'

'I'm a missionary's wife,' she began.

Rainer spun her into a turn a little faster than necessary and his hand weighted her spine. 'Are you? So you want to convert them, is that it?'

'No. It's not that I don't support my husband's mission, of course, but I don't have quite the same . . . the same desire to save souls.'

'Assuming that they are not already saved by a different route?'

'Yes, if you like. Last year we lived in Leh.'

He looked at her and she noticed now that his eyes were the colour of barley sugar. 'I know Leh.'

'I taught the school there. I don't have any illusions about the value of what I was doing, but it was better for the children than nothing at all. They were fed a decent meal, and we played games and sang.'

'There are schools in Srinagar.'

She sighed. 'Yes. Of course there are.'

Another dance was ending and there was a drift of people towards the supper room. Nerys caught sight of the girl Myrtle and she had met at the club – Caroline Bowen, that was her name – standing in the centre of the room. There were two bright red patches on her cheekbones. Her partner was a tall, conspicuously handsome and autocratic-looking young Kashmiri man, who now gave her an exaggerated bow and stepped backwards.

Nerys felt the minute disturbance of the air as Rainer's fingers traced her spine without actually touching it. She had to make herself concentrate on his words as his other hand gently released hers.

'It sounds as if these people are pashmina-fibre spinners. The sad truth is that the traditional work they contribute to, *kani* shawl production, is beautiful and slow and no longer much sought after. The mills in England and Scotland can reproduce the old designs much more cheaply, and they turn out Kashmir-look shawls for a fraction of the price. The goods are exported back east, and the local people are squeezed out of the market.'

Kani: that was what the child had kept saying.

Nerys glanced round the room, at the wives, the bold, flirtatious girls and all their conscious displays of fashion, probably not quite the latest thing – even she was aware of that – because of the distance from Europe and the demands of the war but, still, there was so much money here.

'Are you rich, Nerys?' Rainer was asking.

She shook her head. 'The opposite.'

His face softened and she noticed the pale creases around his lips and eyes where the sun hadn't quite reached. 'Maybe there is something you could do for this family. I am too distracted to talk about it now, watching out for the cavalry officer who's going to pounce at any second and claim you for his partner.'

'I don't know any cavalry officers.'

'I am relieved to hear it. May I escort you to supper, madam?'

Nerys took the arm he held out. She felt giddy from the way their connection was racing ahead of her, hurdling the fences of convention and galloping towards – she didn't know where or what. She must tell Rainer that Evan would soon be arriving in Srinagar and make it clear that they planned to return to Leh, most probably now in the spring, to continue the work of the Nonconformist outreach there. That would be quite proper.

There was a sudden disturbance in the centre of the room.

A girl's voice had been raised briefly and now there was a whisper as the crowd parted.

Nerys first saw the aquiline man with the imperious bearing, smiling in his formal long silk coat. Then came Caroline Bowen, her head down to hide her flushed face. She was walking away from him so fast that the heel of her shoe snagged the train of her dress and she almost stumbled. Nerys caught her arm and held her as she passed, and they swayed awkwardly before the girl regained her balance. 'So sorry,' she cried. She looked as if she might burst into tears or into a hoot of laughter, as if she didn't know which way her emotions might swing.

'Are you all right?' Nerys asked.

'Perfectly,' she insisted, with an air of wild gaiety. 'Perfectly. Hot, you know. Fresh air.' She fanned her fingers in front of her face and broke away from them both.

'Let me come with you,' Nerys said. Making her way out of a knot of watching faces, some smirking, some concerned, others flatly curious, came Myrtle. They fell in on either side of Caroline and the three women swept out of the room. Nerys just had time to glance back over her shoulder at Rainer, who calmly nodded.

In the Residency's wide entrance hallway there were fewer

inquisitive onlookers. Myrtle steered Caroline's gloved elbow. 'You know the house. Where can we go that's private?'

The girl hesitated. She looked much closer to tears than hysterical laughter now. 'I can't think. Wait a minute – there's the salon.'

She led the way. A closed door was guarded by a Residency servant in scarlet livery, but he bowed respectfully and opened it for them as soon as he recognised Caroline.

The Residency salon was a replica of an English country-house drawing room. There were sofas with chintz covers, backed by tables piled with books and magazines. A grand piano stood in the curtained window bay and only the flowers, scarlet cannas, puckered cockscombs and vivid gladioli, instead of sweet peas and delphiniums, gave a clue that this was not the home counties. Myrtle steered their charge to one of the sofas and sat her down. At once Caroline's whole body began to shiver. She put her hands up to her face and smothered a sob as tears ran down her cheeks and soaked into her gloves.

Myrtle took hold of her shoulders and briskly shook her. 'Listen to me. You cannot, you *must* not, make a spectacle of yourself like this. Never again. Do you understand me? However bad it is – and you'd better tell us right now just how bad – you have to keep up public appearances. That is your *job*. Your husband is an Indian Army officer, you are a family friend of the Fanshawes. At the very least you owe them all dignified behaviour. You owe yourself much more than that, incidentally.'

The girl's sobs grew louder. 'I can't bear it,' she choked. 'I love him.'

Myrtle sighed. She patted Caroline's silky pale shoulder and waited while the storm of sobbing reached its peak and then showed signs of blowing itself out. She shook a starched hand-kerchief out of her evening bag and handed it to her.

'Should I go?' Nerys murmured.

'Yes,' Caroline gulped.

Myrtle said, 'No. Nerys is a friend and you need more than one, my girl. Are you ready for a glass of water?'

'I'd rather a whisky.'

'I think you've had enough to drink.'

A jug and a pair of cut-crystal glasses stood on a tray. Nerys poured water and put the glass into Caroline's hand. The girl sniffed dolefully and sipped at it with her head down.

'Now then.' Myrtle lit a cigarette. Nerys could hear the music from the ballroom. In the supper interlude, the band was attempting a piece of Debussy, which was less kind to the players' shortcomings than the dance tunes.

'I love him,' Caroline repeated. This time there was a chip of defiance in her voice.

'All right. If you insist. These things happen.'

Over the girl's head, Myrtle caught Nerys's eye. She pulled down the corners of her mouth to underline the seriousness of the situation, but then she countered the effect by winking. 'But you are British, and married. There are ways to deal with affairs like this, and making a public scene is most emphatically not one of them. What were you thinking of? Do you think Ravi Singh is pleased by your discretion and decorum?'

'I didn't mean to make a scene.'

'You succeeded, though.' Myrtle's tone remained frosty, but she took Caroline's hand between hers and squeezed it. 'Tell us what's up, eh? We can work it out between the three of us, you know.'

'I had a letter from . . . from my husband. The regiment has been granted a last-minute forty-eight-hour deployment leave, and he will be here tomorrow. I waited until Ravi asked me to dance, and he did that very properly after dancing first with Rosalind Dunphy and Jean Whittaker, so there was no reason for any of those old witches from the club to notice anything. Then I told him. I thought he would . . . he would . . .'

Two more tears dropped into the lap of Caroline's gown.

'You thought that at the very least he would be jealous, was that it? You dreamt that he might even insist you didn't see your husband. Your gallant knight was going to sweep you over the pommel of his saddle and gallop off with you. But instead he bowed and changed the subject. Did he comment on the band, or the cold weather, or the war news? And so you screeched out your disappointment and desperation in front of everyone?'

'It wasn't like that. You don't understand.' Caroline had gone so pale that Nerys thought she was going to be sick.

Myrtle circled her with her arm now and drew the girl's head down on to her shoulder. 'I'm trying to understand,' she said gently. 'You think this is your only hope of love, your first and last and only hope, and you can't let it go, even though you know somewhere inside you that Ravi Singh isn't really what you want. But he's handsome and virile, and he's whispered to you all kinds of sweet and private things that no one's ever said to you before, hasn't he?'

Mute, Caroline nodded.

'Of course he has. You're very pretty, and you flatter him. But that's all it is. Ravi will marry whoever his mother picks out for him. He's the maharajah's cousin. He has his place here in Kashmir, even though Srinagar is a troubled city. Whatever dream you may have, however much you may be prepared to give up for him, a divorced English woman doesn't fit any part of that picture, darling. He'll take a bride from a Dogra family just like his own, and you two will forget each other.'

'No.' Caroline's head whipped up now. 'Never.'

Myrtle squeezed her hand again. 'I think there are two problems here, and you may be tangling them up.'

'Are there? Am I?' Now it was Caroline's turn to be chilly. From her wide blue eyes and curled blonde hair, right down to the single strand of pearls around her pink neck, she seemed to Nerys to be the perfect English rose in India.

'Yes. One is Ravi, and the crush you have on him. No,

161

wait a minute, just hear what I'm going to say. The other is Ralph. If you can't love your husband, you know, darling, if you can't make it work between the two of you, perhaps you shouldn't waste your young life in trying. Nothing's going to be the same after this war as it was before, not even marriage and thinking of England. If you want to leave him, we'll help you to do it. Won't we, Nerys? But it'll be to achieve your independence, not to look to Ravi Singh to prop you up.'

'*I can't leave Ralph.*' Caroline snatched back her hand. 'That can't happen.'

'I see.' Myrtle chose to overlook the contradiction. 'Well. I'm glad you're so clear on that. But if your intention is to be a good wife in the official way, and to hold up your head in Srinagar or wherever Captain Bowen is posted, then you must be discreet. I won't advise you not to have affairs – you've only got to look about you in this place to recognise that I would be wasting my breath with that – but please be careful who you choose. The unromantic truth about romance is that it's flimsy. Don't make it your sole support because it won't bear your weight. As you are already discovering.'

What a wise woman you are, Myrtle McMinn, Nerys thought.

Myrtle's strong face was filled with compassion now, but there was nothing sentimental about her. She was practical, and if Evan would consider her immoral then she was of the breed that had its own morality.

Caroline gnawed her lip. Then she forced a smile, without a glimmer of it reaching her sad eyes. 'You're kind. Both of you are. I appreciate it, honestly. I think I'll go home now. When you say goodnight to Mrs Fanshawe, would you say that I felt unwell and slipped away so as not to distract her?'

Outside, a long line of guests' cars stretched into the darkness. The Residency's driveway was lined with flaming torches that sent smoke plumes coiling into the wind. Myrtle and Nerys put the now silent girl into a *tonga*, then went back into the house to say their formal goodbyes and to deliver Caroline's message to Mrs Fanshawe.

The Resident's wife graciously accepted their thanks for the evening. 'How very good of you to look after Mrs Bowen. She's such an interesting young woman, but I think she doesn't find life easy.'

Nerys and Myrtle were helped into their evening coats by another liveried servant. There was a primrose-yellow Rolls-Royce purring at the steps; flanked by attendants and lesser members of his entourage, and lit by the lurid light of burning torches, the maharajah swept into his car and was driven away.

The two women sat back under the canopy of their *tonga* as the horse clopped away in the line of cars and other vehicles. They passed under an arch of trees, through the gates and out into the wide streets of the new town. The modern villas of prosperous Pandit and Muslim Kashmiris lay in their secluded gardens, the glow of yellow lanterns showing through autumnal branches. A watchman crouched beside each gate, and as they passed one, the slow beat of a terra-cotta drum held in the folds of a blanket briefly echoed the horse's hoofs.

Myrtle spoke after a long silence. 'You know, if I were married to Ralph Bowen I wouldn't find life easy either.'

'What exactly is so bad about him?'

'He's what Archie calls a three-letter man.'

Nerys had no idea what this meant. She thought that maybe Rainer Stamm could explain it to her.

The following night, the young wife of Captain Ralph Bowen quietly undressed in the bathroom of the small married-quarters bungalow on the rim of the barracks compound. It was separated from its two neighbours by a fence and a pair of identical dusty channels dignified by the name of flowerbeds. The bungalow walls were thin, and Caroline always felt that she had to move carefully so that her neighbours didn't know exactly what she was doing every moment of the day and night.

She brushed her hair so that it lay prettily over her shoulders, and settled the silky ruffle of her honeymoon peignoir. It left exposed a swathe of her throat and chest, and the swell of flesh below. She knew now that she looked beautiful like this. Experience had taught her that much, at least. Her immediate resolve wavered for a moment, but she shut off every thought except those about Ralph, who was lying in their bed on the other side of the door.

Caroline practised a smile at herself, and the mirror reflected a sickly smirk. Not nearly good enough. She pulled at the peignoir so it fell further open, shook back her hair and widened the smile. Then she walked through to her husband.

Ralph Bowen was reading a magazine, in which she caught a glimpse of a hunting picture with couples of hounds in front and a shires backdrop of fields and copses. It was a very old issue – it had been in their house for months. Ralph was wearing his stiff blue pyjamas with piped cuffs. She went slowly round to his side of the bed and stood where he couldn't avoid seeing her.

The silence felt sticky, making her long to shake herself free of it. 'I'm glad you're not asleep,' she said, in a low, teasing voice.

To her relief the words came out of her mouth quite easily. Ralph turned a page. He had drunk two whiskies with soda after their dry little dinner, but he wasn't intoxicated. That might be in her favour, Caroline reckoned, or it could equally go against her.

She had planned all this in advance, but it was harder to put everything into practice when he wouldn't even glance at her. Even so, she slowly untied the belt of her robe, and eased her bare shoulders free. She held the fold of fabric close over her breasts, then gradually allowed it to fall. The air was cool on her back and buttocks. Soon the nights would be icy and everyone would need to carry their fire-pots.

The peignoir now lay in ripples at her feet. Caroline took a shallow breath and stood up straight and naked.

You are exquisite, the other one had breathed.

'Ralph, look at me,' she said.

He let the magazine fall and raised his eyes. He had long, colourless eyelashes, a red face and neck that shaded abruptly into pale skin just revealed by his pyjama coat. 'What are you doing?'

Caroline turned full circle, she hoped voluptuously, letting him see the swell of her bottom, the jut of her hips and the smooth roundness of her belly. 'You're going off to war,' she breathed, 'and I am so proud of you. I want to be yours before you go.'

She swayed towards him, standing now at the mattress edge and looking down. Ralph's eyes travelled over her body. At least he was no longer absorbed in his reading.

'Won't you make love to me?' Caroline implored.

She pulled back the hairy blanket with its scent of mothballs, and a linen sheet from her trousseau that had been imperfectly laundered by their *dhobi-wallah*. She lay down in the narrow space between Ralph and the bed's edge, moulding her body against his. At the same time her fingers worked at the buttons and then the sash of his pyjama trousers. Every inch of him was rigid, except for what counted. This lay in her cupped hand, flaccid.

She closed her eyes, concentrating. She brought her breasts up against his ribs and let her flesh radiate warmth into his. He lay still at first, but then very awkwardly and reluctantly, Ralph rotated towards her so they lay face to face. He kissed her on the lips, his moustache scraping against her mouth.

Encouraged by this response Caroline went on stroking, but nothing happened. She had expected as much, so instead of withdrawing she stretched voluptuously, measuring her full length against him. Then she raised herself on one elbow so she could look down at him. His fine, straw-coloured hair fell back, revealing his rounded and touchingly childish forehead.

His eyes were wide open, the rims reddened by sun and whisky, concentrated with his familiar glare.

'I love you,' Caroline whispered.

Now they were on their way this wasn't so difficult. Everything was going to be all right.

No man could resist you, the other had moaned in her arms. *This is ecstasy itself.*

She couldn't isolate the memories any longer. She gave up the effort and with a shiver let the soft scenes gather in her head, folding like veils between Ralph and herself.

The first time had been the drive out into the country and the picnic. Ravi assured her that other people would be coming with them, but when he picked her up there had been only him in one of his polished cars, with a series of covered baskets stacked in the jump seat and himself full of dangerous teasing as he lifted her hand to his lips.

'So, after all, there will just be the two of us, beautiful Caroline. Will you be safe with me, do you think?'

She was so happy that she hadn't given a thought to her safety. Anyway, what did safe matter?

They had driven out into the countryside, along the dusty road towards the village of Pahalgam, through the slow-moving flocks of sheep and goats. It was a silvery afternoon in midsummer, and once out of the city they flew under the shade of willow and poplar trees, passing terraces of rice paddies where villagers worked doubled up under the shade of conical hats. It was lush and green out here, and when they stopped driving it was silent, except for the crickets whirring in the heat. There was a little pavilion enclosed beside an apple orchard, and Ravi had unlocked it and thrown open the doors. Inside there were cedar floors, greyed with disuse, cushioned divans and an old hookah on a low carved table.

'What is this place?' she had asked, trailing her finger through the dust.

He shrugged, unpacking baskets. 'My family's – just a

summer place to come and enjoy the view. No one uses it, these days, as you can see.'

The view was of mountains, stands of dark conifers running up the ridges to meet steep brown slopes and peaks that rose in two-dimensional serrations against the pearly sky. Caroline already knew that, like all Kashmiris, Ravi loved and revered the mountains.

'Come, sit here,' he ordered. Open windows gave on to an enclosure of sun-dappled grass. Bright yellow butterflies twisted in the air. They were the only two people in the world once Ravi began kissing her. Because he always behaved as if there was infinite time to bestow attention on whatever he did, as if nothing mattered other than what engaged him at that very moment, there was no sense of urgency, let alone of negotiation. She had seen him behave in this way with his horse, rippling the palm of his hand over its flanks, or with elaborate dishes of food as he closed his eyes the better to concentrate on the nuances of spicing, or with the purchase of a jewel from a trader as a gift for his sister, or even in tasting a simple glass of lemonade on a hot afternoon. Now she was the recipient of this extravagant concentration.

He took fifteen minutes to unbutton the cuff of her blouse and roll up the linen sleeve, fold by fold, to expose the crook of her arm. It wasn't the first time he had kissed her: there had been laughing embraces at dances and in gardens and behind the curtains of a *shikara*, but this was the first time he had placed her above everything else. By the time Ravi's mouth moved from hers to the pulse in her throat, and then by infinitely slow downward progression to her breasts, she was melting. He didn't have to ask her: she would have allowed him anything.

No. She would have begged.

With meticulous care, Ravi removed all her clothes. He placed her shoes side by side, as gently if they were made of spun sugar. The warm air drifted over her skin and the buzzing of the crickets filled her ears. He examined her limbs, the incurve

167

of her waist, the matching inner concavities of her thighs and the spring of her toes. Then he raised his liquid dark eyes to hers. 'You intoxicate me,' he breathed.

Intoxicated also by her own beauty, at last, after a whole year of gathering dismay and loneliness, Caroline arched her back against the divan cushions. She noted dreamily the contrast of their skin, cream against caramel. Ravi removed his starched shirt and exposed his muscled chest. She lightly drew her fingers across it and touched the place over his heart. His teeth were very white as he smiled down at her, and then he knelt between her thighs.

When he came into her, with the first quick movement he had made, she gave an involuntary yelp of pain. He froze above her, and she saw that, for the first time in the six months since their meeting, Ravi Singh was surprised. He withdrew again and they both gazed down at a small smear of blood.

'This is your first time?'

Caroline nodded. It was a hideous thing for a wife of a year to have to admit, but it wasn't her fault. She also felt a throb of triumph because it was to Ravi she had given her virginity, not her angry, bewilderingly critical and increasingly absent husband. Love surged through her like a river in flood. Ravi had saved her, and now they belonged to each other. The flower-dotted meadows and green terraces of the Vale had become their private kingdom, now and for ever.

She smiled up at him. 'I'm happy,' she whispered. 'It won't hurt any more.'

Nor did it.

Once he had collected himself, Ravi was even more tender with her. Afterwards she held him in her arms and kissed his eyelids. His black hair was sweat-damp, the lines of his profile had suddenly become familiar and minutely precious instead of merely beautiful.

He pulled his clothing together and helped her to dress, even down to the laces of her shoes. Then they sat back among the cushions and spread out their picnic of fresh Kashmiri fruits and thick yellow cream. Hungry, Caroline ate one-handed, laughing and spilling the food he placed in front of her because Ravi kept her other fingers laced in his.

'Now. Won't you tell me how this state of affairs has come about?' he whispered, putting the dishes aside and playing with the buttons of her blouse.

Caroline blushed. 'My husband is not very interested.'

Ravi raised one black eyebrow. 'I cannot believe it. He is a soldier, a horseman, and also a man of the world. This does not seem quite right to me.'

'I minded about it very much to begin with. I'd imagined – well, all the things girls do imagine and whisper about. My mother's dead, I told you that, and my stepmother before the wedding only helped me with . . . practical matters. Our engagement was quite short. Once we were married, though, Ralph didn't do what husbands are supposed to. Our honeymoon was only a week. Then he was away with the regiment, and then he had a bout of illness. When he recovered he went away again. A year seems to have gone,' she added, in a bleak voice.

'I see,' Ravi said. 'You have been very lonely.'

Caroline nestled closer against him. 'It doesn't matter to me now. I've got you, and it's beautiful. I'm so glad this has happened.' She was thinking that the moment – this very second, with the crickets in the grass and the soft swish of the breeze, the sun spreading its fingers across the old floor, with womanhood, Ravi's love and a life handed back to her – was what every day of her whole existence had been leading up to. It was perfect. She wouldn't have changed a single detail of it.

'My dear,' he said, and she took that to mean that she was his dear.

'I love you,' Caroline whispered, with not a calculating thought in her head.

The contours of his face hardened, just perceptibly. 'Love? Is that what you believe in?'

'Yes, of course I do.'

169

'Even with what you have learnt since your marriage?'

A little beat of dismay drummed in her head, but she ignored it. Caroline looked her lover straight in the eye. 'Yes,' she repeated.

Ravi silently lifted her hand to his lips and kissed each knuckle in turn.

In the four months since that day there had been perhaps a dozen more times. As well as their snatched secret hours together, there had been the routines of tennis parties and rides to the gardens and all the gaiety of a Srinagar season. In these long weeks Caroline had learnt a lot about what to do with a man, and she had also learnt not to blurt out *I love you*. She teased and pouted instead. But Ravi Singh never again favoured her with the full force of his attention the way he had done the first time. Lately, as she had become more dependent on him, he had seemed restless in her company, except for the brief times when they were naked together. Last night at the Resident's ball, when they were dancing and she had told him that Ralph was coming home, he had scrutinised her from under his dark eyelashes.

'So now you will put into practice what you have learnt, eh?' He smiled.

Once she had understood them the shock of his words left her rigid.

Her lover wasn't jealous; her lover was practically a voyeur. He could happily imagine her performing on Ralph the acts she had learnt from him. And in a single flash of perception she understood the truth she had, up till now, ignored: Ravi wasn't biding his time before claiming her, not at all. He was just diverting himself with a married Englishwoman. Exactly as Myrtle McMinn had warned her.

Shock was followed by a jet of boiling outrage. Caroline snapped upright, her hands against his chest, her heels clattering on the dance floor. Ravi immediately stood back and suavely bowed.

170

'Is that it? Is that all you're going to say?' Her voice rose, unintentionally shrill, and the couples dancing nearby slowed to stare at them. Ravi frowned, but her anger and the rising edge of desperation were too powerful.

She drew in a breath. 'I hate you,' she hissed, still too audibly. With a snapshot of Ravi's scowl and the pairs of gaping faces at his back burning into her eyes, she had flung herself away from him, tripped over her train, and almost fallen flat. Myrtle's friend, and then Myrtle herself, had come to her rescue.

What Myrtle had said to her in the private salon only highlighted the truth. The once-absorbing riddle of loving Ravi Singh and being married to Ralph Bowen had in the last month become just that: a Christmas-cracker fragment of paper with a conceit cheaply printed on it that would shrivel into ash and disintegrate as soon as it touched the fire.

Caroline had an even more urgent concern now and it was this that brought her into their bedroom, with the shameful trophy of her experience, to Ralph.

She lowered her head, inch by inch, her cheek brushing her husband's chest and then his belly with its sparse thatch of coppery strands. As if he were being stretched on a rack she felt him tensing, drawing apart and away, his joints minutely creaking beneath her ear. She screwed her eyes shut and lifted her head so that her own blonde hair waved over his groin. Ralph had stopped breathing. Her breath was stuck somewhere inside her ribcage. She took him in her mouth. Briefly, his thing twitched.

Then he shouted, 'In God's name, what are you doing?'

He shoved her backwards and rolled out of their bed as if it were on fire, hopping and grasping with one hand to secure the pyjama trousers that sagged below his hips.

Caroline gaped at him. Ralph was crimson, cheeks wobbling, turkey-faced with anger and embarrassment and indignation.

'That's a whore's trick,' her husband bawled at her.

'Please, don't shout,' she whispered, imagining Major and

Mrs Dunkeley sitting upright in their bedroom in the bungalow next door. She rolled herself in the sheet and sat up.

Ralph had secured his pyjamas. He stood with the bed like a barricade between them, appalled, bristling with righteousness. 'Where did you learn a whore's trick like that? Decent women don't do that sort of thing.'

One of the other skills that Caroline had learnt in the course of her love affair was how to dissemble. She widened her eyes to make pools of innocence. 'How do you know it's what prostitutes do? That's not what it says in my book.'

'What damned book? What the hell are you talking about?'

'The Young Wife's Guide to Married Love,' Caroline improvised. 'I sent home for it. It arrived in a discreet package, don't worry. I thought I needed some advice about how to encourage my husband. I do, don't I?'

'Are you mad? Hand that filth over to me immediately.' Ralph stuck out his fist, but she was ahead of him.

'I read it and burnt it. I couldn't run the risk of letting the servants find it.'

He stared down at her, nose in the air, like a gun dog, trying to sniff out the dimensions of her lie. She met his glare.

'You are disgusting,' he said at last, defeated.

Caroline lifted her chin. 'Why did you marry me, Ralph?'

'Because it's what people like us do. We marry.'

'And then live like this? In sexless, meaningless, endless antipathy?'

He turned abruptly away. 'Yes, probably. Don't be melodramatic.' He gathered up his magazine, took his plaid dressing-gown off the chair beside the bed, collected his cigarette case and lighter from the box on the dressing-table and slipped them into his pocket.

Caroline watched him as he marched to the door. She tried once more, softening her voice: 'I'm sorry. It's your last night. Won't you come back to bed?'

'Goodnight,' he snapped, and the door closed behind him.

She lay back again.

Ravi.

You are exquisite . . .

In a way. But she was not desirable enough or appropriate enough for him to want all of her. Caroline had never felt so lonely, or so afraid, in all her twenty-two years. She lay down and stared up at the ceiling. Tomorrow her husband was going away with his regiment. There was a war on.

Maybe she would be widowed.

Myrtle and Nerys were having breakfast out on the veranda of the *Garden of Eden*. The starry nights were now hollow with cold, but this morning there was still just enough warmth in the sun for them to enjoy sitting outside. A thin layer of low mist hung over the lake water, and the mooring posts were policed by brooding eagles. Boats in the distance slid soundlessly through what looked like horizontal layers of light. Myrtle was reading her letters, briskly slitting the envelopes with an ivory-handled paper knife, scanning the contents and placing them in one of three tidy piles.

Nerys had received just one letter, from Evan. He had written about the work in Kargil, the difficulty of travel to the distant northern valleys, the privations of his daily life – his monkish enjoyment of which was heightened, Nerys was sure, by the imagined contrast with her own sybaritic existence down in the Vale. In the final sentence he announced that he was planning to stay where he was for another two weeks.

She folded the two sheets of paper and replaced them in the envelope. Then she sat back and thoughtfully sipped her tea. Majid came with a fresh jug of water, removed their empty plates and padded away silently on bare feet. Black and white kingfishers dipped at their own reflections as a *shikara* paddled towards the houseboat. The ripples from the prow and paddle rocked the lily-pads, leaving a crystal bead in the centre of each to flash briefly in the subdued sunlight.

'Hello,' Myrtle said, looking up.

The boatman angled his craft to the foot of the steps. It wasn't the flower vendor or the man who brought fresh-caught lake fish wrapped in layers of newspaper, or any other of the familiar traders who plied between the houseboats. He stepped forwards from the stern of his boat, splayed feet balanced against the rocking, and held up a package. 'Delivery, ma'am. Special.'

Myrtle looked at it, then said, 'It's for you.'

Nerys didn't recognise the spiky black script. She gave the boatman a coin and used Myrtle's paper knife to slit open the wrapping. Inside, secured in a twist of paper, was her stolen brooch.

Myrtle knew about the theft. She clapped her hands delightedly. 'That is clever of him. Was the whole episode one of your Mr Stamm's magic tricks, do you think? Performed to impress you?'

'He's not my Mr Stamm. No, it happened exactly as I told you. The brooch was snatched by a gang of children in the old town. I don't see how he could have set it up without recruiting and training the whole lot of them first, and why on earth would he have bothered to do that?'

She scanned the note that came with it. Rainer wondered, following on from their meeting at the Residency, whether Nerys might be free to visit him at home for a drink? Mrs McMinn would also be most welcome. Six o'clock that evening. He gave the address in the old town.

Nerys handed the card to Myrtle to read.

'Hmm. Rather sure of himself, isn't he? What did the two of you talk about?'

Nerys told her about the children from the room behind the bazaar, and her unformed desire to do something to help them.

'So, are you going?' Languidly, Myrtle waved away the smoke from her first cigarette of the day.

'Yes, if you will come with me.'

'It sounds, darling, as if I would be a tiny bit of a gooseberry.

174

I saw the two of you dancing the other night. You were setting the floor on fire.'

Nerys calmly pinned the pearl circlet in its place at the throat of her cardigan. It was the cream one she had worn to the commissioner's party in Leh, which now had its buttons neatly sewn on. 'I am very glad to have our brooch back. I felt so bad about having lost it, because you'd given it to me. I'd like to thank Mr Stamm in person, but there's no more to it than that.'

'If you say so. All right. We'll dress up in our finery and toddle over to see your admirer this evening. What is Evan's news?'

Nerys told her.

'Two more weeks? He'd better get a move on.' Myrtle squinted across at the backdrop of mountains.

'I don't think he wants to come to Srinagar at all.' With a wave of the hand Nerys encompassed the fanciful woodwork of the *Garden of Eden*, the seat cushions with hand-embroidered leaves and flowers, the lake and the Srinagar Club flags in the distance.

Myrtle looked kindly at her. 'How does that make you feel?'

'I married a missionary. I understood what is involved.'

'Yes. Do you want to know what I think?'

'Of course I do.'

Myrtle picked up Rainer Stamm's note from the tablecloth and lightly fanned the air with it. 'I think you should have some fun. You've recovered your health and strength, thank God. I think you should be silly, and enjoy yourself just for a few weeks. I don't believe you'll regret it in the end. Trust me. I'm a wise woman.'

Nerys understood what her friend might be including under the general heading of fun. In spite of this she found herself laughing, and she reflected at the same time on how Srinagar and Mrs McMinn were changing the missionary's wife. 'Yes, I know you are. But that's not what you advised Caroline Bowen.'

'Pfff. You are a grown woman. A very sensible and serious one, who might benefit from an instant's frivolity. Caroline, on the other hand, is hardly more than a schoolgirl.'

'I see. Are you telling me to look at another man?'

Myrtle's eyes widened. 'I'm not advising you to do anything, Mrs Watkins. You have a very good mind of your own.'

EIGHT

Solomon and Sheba was close-moored in a line of other house-boats, in a narrow isthmus of the lake opposite the row of hideous Chinese-designed blue glass hotels that lined the Bund. Tonight this section of the city was suffering one of its regular power failures, so the drumming of dozens of generators competed with the traffic. Headlights swept rhythmically over the dim-lit frontages of shops and cafés.

Mair's *shikara* slid towards the houseboat through a thick tangle of stiff lotus-flower heads that poked up like fists out of the black water. It had been a long and chilly trip up the lake from the Shalimar Garden and she pushed aside the musty blanket with relief as she prepared to disembark.

The boatman paddled to the steps at the lakeside. *Solomon and Sheba* listed noticeably and the timbers of the old structure were unpainted and splintery, but even so it was in a better condition than many of its neighbours. Some of them – still inhabited – had decayed to the point at which they were little more than loose bundles of planking and lopsided poles festooned with tattered curtains.

Farooq, the baroquely obstructive manager of the houseboat, appeared in the veranda doorway and helped her aboard. 'At last, madam. I'm thinking you have left Srinagar. Dinner ready for you.'

Farooq liked to serve the evening meal early and then retire to the kitchen boat. Mair didn't have the energy to protest that it was only six o'clock.

While she ate her curry and dhal she tried to concentrate on her book, but she found herself staring at the dingy tablecloth instead and thinking about the Beckers.

She had checked her emails at least once every day, but there was no news of Lotus. No word from Karen at all.

Farooq came to clear the table and she wandered into her bedroom. The generator only powered a single feeble overhead light, yet somehow the three young Indian couples occupying the next-door boat were managing to amplify their Bollywood film music beyond distortion point.

Images of the snow at Lamayuru filled Mair's head, and of the little girl in her father's arms as the army helicopter descended from the sky.

She decided that she couldn't sit alone in the houseboat for yet another evening.

She put on a warm jacket, arranged the toffee-brown shawl from Leh to cover her hair and slipped the photograph of her grandmother with her two mysterious friends into her inside pocket. From the veranda she beckoned vigorously to one of the row of *shikara* men waiting opposite; he came and ferried her across the narrow neck of water. There was a business centre, little used, in one of the blue-glass hotels and at least she could order a glass of wine. There was no alcohol aboard *Solomon and Sheba*. It wasn't a hedonistic retreat.

There was no message from Karen.

Mair quickly read through the handful of new emails.

Hattie had written in reply to one of hers:

You sound sad, intrepid one. If you aren't enjoying your-self any more, why not come on home? I want to see you! Try not to worry about the little girl. There's nothing you can do, and no news is probably good news. Miss you xxxxx

Try not to worry was much easier said than done. But Mair had no intention of turning for home just because she felt momentarily displaced, and because of her fears for Bruno and his family. Tomorrow she would renew her investigation of the shawl's history.

She wrote back cheerfully to Hattie, then went and sat in the bar, a deserted space manned by an old waiter in a maroon jacket. With her second glass of wine, she ordered a plate of chips. They came with a plastic tub of ketchup and she dipped each pallid, salty chip into the tub as she ate, studying the printout photograph of three women that she had propped against the water jug.

The laughing faces shone out at her.

Framing them was the diagonal of carved wood, and still water patched with lily-pads. It was little enough to go on but now she had seen the lake and the houseboats for herself she was convinced that this must be the backdrop.

Her grandmother *had* been in Srinagar.

The unknown story teased her imagination again, momentarily displacing her anxiety for the Beckers. Mair ate the last of her chips, which were now cold and greasy. She wiped her fingers and slipped the photograph back into her pocket. The envelope containing the lock of silky brown hair was there too.

Tomorrow, she thought.

The street outside was still only minimally lit and the lake beyond was a black expanse with the looming hulks of houseboats. Mair was looking towards the jetty and the handful of boatmen, one of whom crouched beside a spirit stove burning with a coronet of yellow-blue flame. She was peripherally aware of a group of armed Indian Border Security Force paramilitary troopers lounging at the tail of their parked Gipsy pickup, of the traffic having eased, and of the crowds of pedestrian passers-by being mostly men in their long grey or brown shirts topped off with woollen jerkins.

There was a flash of light and the street exploded.

In the millisecond that followed, her retinas burnt by the

white blaze, Mair was conscious of silence in which debris showered through the air, the shock of the detonation that pierced her bones, and then a blast that blew her backwards against a shop wall. She was pinned there for an instant before sliding to a sitting position as her legs gave way beneath her. Grit pattered on her shawled head, and she drew up her knees and arms to protect herself.

She had no idea how long she hunched there, hearing her own rasping breath as the debris stopped falling out of the sky, and screams began to rip through the night.

She was just lifting her head as another explosion came, a sickening *whump* as the BSF Gipsy burst into flame. She heard rather than saw fire engulf it as people came running by, flying in both directions. There was a close-quarters *rat-tat* that Mair had never in her life heard outside a cinema but that she knew was real gunfire. Bullets were zipping through the gravel. She buried her head again, hearing her own whimper of abject terror as a tiny addendum to the shrieks of pain and confused shouting that now filled the street.

A police van skidded down the road in front of her. Against the blazing shell of the Gipsy she saw that all the passers-by had melted into the shelter of shops and hotels, except for two huddled shapes lying prone in the dirt and a cluster of people bent over them. One pair of bloodstained legs wore the khaki of the BSF troopers. An elderly man with a delta of blood covering his face was being helped away by two others.

She realised that the brief bout of shooting was over. Uniformed men eddied between her and the injured.

Mair looked in the other direction and saw that the door of the hotel from which she had emerged only seconds ago was held open. A uniformed bellboy jerkily beckoned to her.

She raised herself on to her hands and knees, straightened up and began running towards him. Whorls of light from the explosion's flash still revolved in the backs of her eyes, making it hard to move in a straight line. The bellboy grasped her wrist and propelled her into the lobby. It was quiet and warm inside, with two or three people standing beside a desk, the receptionist urgently murmuring on the telephone, the same vase of gladioli that she had noticed earlier on her way from the computer terminal in the business centre.

It was hard to believe that the scene she had just witnessed lay only a few yards away.

'Where you stay, madam?' the bellboy asked.

Mair told him.

'You go back soon, soon. Maybe wait here a little while.'

Obediently she crossed to a group of chairs and sat down. Her hands were shaking and the echo of gunfire still popped in her ears. After a few minutes she ordered tea, and drank it while police and army vehicles trundled past the glass door. A thin trickle of pedestrians started up again and, as if to emphasise the rapid return to business, the power came back on. Everything was illuminated, even a yellow and blue neon cola sign that flashed its reflection into the lake. The noise of generators died away, leaving only the buzz of traffic.

Mair called over a waiter and paid for her tea. She shook some of the dust and grit out of her shawl and wrapped it round her head again. Then she walked back into the night. The first person she saw, standing on the jetty, was Farooq. He had come out to look for her.

The Gipsy was now a blackened shell with smoke curling from its melted interior. The injured had been removed, leaving only a dark sticky patch in the dirt. A barrier of white tapes had been strung around the area and a trio of police, weapons clearly on show, guarded the perimeter. Apart from a row of broken windows, some shop walls blackened with smoke and a noticeable thinning of the evening traffic, there was little else to show what had just happened.

Mair crossed to Farooq's side of the road. He waved at her with relief. 'You are not hurt, madam, *inshallah*?'

'No, I'm all right. What about the soldier, and the others? Was it a bomb?'

He folded his hands and bowed in the direction of a waiting

181

shikara. As they were paddled away from the jetty she asked the question again.

Farooq spoke briefly to the boatman. 'I hear it was maybe a grenade, madam. Some soldiers and some people of town were injured. It is very bad for Srinagar.'

'Yes,' she agreed quietly.

In the morning, sitting on the veranda of *Solomon and Sheba* in the eggshell light of a crisp autumn day, she read the report in the English-language newspaper. Bollywood tunes and chatter were drifting from next door and Farooq's white-capped head bobbed at the rear of the kitchen boat. Last evening, she read, five civilians and two BSF troopers had been injured in a grenade attack on a BSF patrol vehicle in the centre of town. The senior superintendent of police, the report continued, stated that a militant of the Hizbul Mujahideen had also been seriously wounded in the subsequent exchange of fire.

The story was told in the barest outline and occupied only the top quarter of the front page, next to the pictures of an outbreak of fire at an hotel in another part of the city. There was no further coverage inside the paper. Mair knew that outbreaks of violence between insurgents and the Indian security forces were so frequent that they caused only a temporary stir, at least for outside observers. The lack of public attention given to them by the authorities was certainly deliberate.

A *shikara* was working its way down the line of houseboats, most of which were empty of guests. It was the flower vendor known – from the painted-tin sign above the canopy of his boat – as Mr Marvellous. He fastened a line at the steps of *Solomon and Sheba* and stood up, rising out of a gaudy sea of cut flowers, his arms full of scarlet, crimson and orange blooms. His smile beamed out at full wattage. 'Madam, for you today very good fortune. Please take all these, just three hundred rupees. Not many customers for me.'

Mair didn't even try to bargain. She reached out for the double armful and buried her face in the cool, dewy petals.

Marvellous paddled away before she could change her mind, and Farooq tutted at such conspicuous over-payment.

'They are so beautiful,' she said.

Something had happened. Until last night Srinagar and its people had seemed sealed away, unfathomable for all the showy beauty of the lakes and mountains. Then she had seen the faces in the street last night, and the way people had got up afterwards and gone on with their lives despite the violence that boiled up around them, and she had begun to interpret the place in a different way. Srinagar was battered, impoverished, decaying into its own arterial waterways, but it was proud. A seed of affection sprouted inside her, fertilised by admiration.

Farooq sidled past, armed with a rag and a tin of polish. He worked with swipes over the table. 'Perhaps, madam, you will be going back to England now.' He eyed her, not wanting to lose his only guest, wishing at the same time to be rid of her anomalous presence.

'No,' Mair said lightly. 'Not just yet.'

Later, in the fourth shop she visited in the neighbourhood of the Bund, the middle-aged shopkeeper took her grandmother's shawl out of her hands. He walked to the window of his shop, screwed a lens into his eye and examined the workmanship. By now, she was used to this procedure. While she waited Mair looked at the display of expensive modern pashminas in tasteful tourist-friendly colours, the highest-priced ones with pleasingly contrasted bands of hand-embroidered paisley design. She remembered the flocks of goats on the sleet-raked Changthang plain, and the processing plant in Leh. This shop on the Bund in Srinagar represented the heart of the final stage of the yarn's journey, although sadly it lacked one essential presence.

There were no customers to purchase the lovely goods.

In each of the four shops, she had been the sole browser. She could only hope that somewhere along the links that radiated from here, in the boutiques of five-star hotels elsewhere in India or the expensive shops of Fifth Avenue and Bond Street, there would be plenty of interested women with money to spend.

At the rear of the shop a bead curtain shivered, even though there was no draught. Mair was being watched, probably by the female members of the shopkeeper's staff or family.

The man returned to the counter. 'Very worn condition.' He sighed inevitably, dropping his lens into a drawer and closing it with a sharp click. He rearranged the shawl folds to expose the yellow stain, and picked at the tiny frayed ends of silk-stitched blossoms. The limpid colours of leaves and flowers revealed themselves as exactly true to nature, now that Mair had seen them in their proper setting. She smiled at the man. It was evident from the most casual glance at her heirloom, alongside the modern versions, that it was an exquisite piece of work. As if she had ever thought otherwise.

'What can you tell me about it?'

The man shrugged. He pointed to the tiny reversed BB signature and the accompanying symbols. 'Seventy years date. It is right in time, but this, this sign, is from very small work-shop of finest quality. Finished since long ago. *Kani* work, yes. To stitch on top, for effect like this, I have seen only once before. Your shawl is nice, you see, but it is copied from real makers. If not, it would be for museum.' He paused, to let his verdict sink in. 'A pity. But I will give you fair price, if you like to sell.'

Mair smiled again. The beads at the back of the shop faintly tinkled in the incense-rich air. 'Thank you. I will keep it.'

'Maybe you look at new shawls. Presents for your friends, you know. Christmas comes soon.'

He was a Kashmiri salesman like every other, already spreading armfuls of merchandise over his counter.

'Maybe next time.'

She had walked a hundred yards along the street, thinking about where she might go to drink tea and eat lunchtime yoghurt when a hand pulled at her sleeve. She whirled round, tightening her grasp on the bag that contained her shawl, to see an old woman, her face covered with a white scarf.

'What is it? What do you want?' Mair blurted, pointlessly in English. The only answer was a scrap of paper that was shoved into her hand before the woman turned and hurried away into the crowd. Mair unscrewed the paper and looked at what was clearly an address.

The place hadn't been easy to find. It was buried in the alleyways of the old town and she had asked a dozen different people for directions, gesturing and signing vigorously all the way. She had walked or been led through refuse-clogged yards where hens clucked between sagging huts, past the open-fronted workshops of dyers and tanners, past windows that gave glimpses of women squatting at carpet looms, and the shanty-shops that sold rice and dried beans from rows of open-mouthed sacks. At every corner there was a thread of waterway, viscid black or blanketed with green weed. But now she was at her destination. A toothless old man sitting in a broken plastic chair in the middle of an alley waved her to an open doorway.

Mair tapped on the doorpost as she peered into a dim passageway. 'Hello?' she called. And then repeated, louder, 'Hello?'

A pair of tracksuited legs appeared at the top of a flight of stairs. A voice asked, 'Excuse me? What do you look for?'

Mair didn't wait for an invitation. Walking in and starting up the stairs, she saw a young man in a Nike hooded top. He would have passed unnoticed in the high street back at home, even with his black beard and skullcap. 'I'm not sure. I was given this address, and I wanted to show this to somebody . . .' She extricated the shawl from her bag as she spoke and held it up like a backstage pass. The young man didn't exactly bar her way, but he didn't stand aside either. 'I was led to believe that someone here might recognise my shawl,' she said, raising her voice.

From the room at the top of the stairs a voice called something and the hoodie youth answered over his shoulder. Mair reached his side and slid past him, smiling politely as she did so. She looked into a room that was empty of furniture but full of men, seated cross-legged against the four walls. It was cold in there with the tall windows on two sides standing wide open.

Everyone looked up at her. There were ripples of soft wool covering every lap. They had all been sewing. 'Excuse me,' she murmured.

'May I help you?' At the far end of the room, a man stood up. He seemed a little older than most of the others, maybe in his mid-twenties. 'Are you here to buy shawl?'

'I'm afraid not.' She explained that she had been sent here, and named the fourth shop in the Bund. The old woman who had given her the address must have been watching and listening from behind the bead curtain. Most of the men bent their heads to their stitching again. One wasn't sewing, she noticed, but his cupped palm was thickly blackened with dye. The only sound was a rhythmic slapping of flesh as he pumped a block into the dye and worked the black print border design on a delicate pink pashmina length.

'Would you like to come with me?' the foreman softly asked.

Mair followed him into a windowless office backing the workshop. There was a neon overhead strip, harsh after the natural light suffusing the other room. The only furniture was a cheap laminate desk and two chairs.

'I am the *karkhanadar*,' he said, in the same soft voice. The workshop chief. 'My name is Mehraan.'

'How do you do?' By this time, Mair knew better than to offer her hand to a Muslim male. She spread out the shawl instead, covering the desk top with glory.

Mehraan had no lens. He took up a fold of fabric and gently stroked it. A minute passed in silence, then another. At last he looked at her. 'I recognise the work.' His English was good.

'Please tell me about it,' she begged.

The man's liquid stare was intelligent, curious, and without a hint of prejudice or hostility. Mair was suddenly convinced

186

that here at last was someone she could talk to. She said, 'I don't want to sell it, or find out what it's worth, nothing like that. But I've come all the way to Srinagar to trace its history. It belonged to my grandmother, my mother's mother, and I think she was here in the city maybe seventy years ago. That's all I know.'

Mehraan nodded. It was obviously his way to consider his words before he spoke. 'It is a beautiful thing. The maker was in the same village as my grandfather.'

Mair's face broke into a wide smile. Through the open windows came the first cry of the muezzin, taken up across the old town.

'Excuse me. I have to go to pray,' he said.

'Wait. Please, you can help me. The shawl meant a lot to my grandmother, I know that. I've followed the story from Changthang to Leh, and on to here. I'm sure you can tell me more.'

Mehraan hesitated. 'You can wait here if you wish. I will not be long.'

He turned and followed the troop of *karkhana* workers down the stairs. They slid their bare feet into the row of plastic flip-flops and muddy trainers ranged by the door. Mair sat listening to the muffled sounds of hooting and dung-heap cocks crowing. Once she got up and looked into the workroom. The shawls lay on the matting in pools of colour, the tiny leaves and petals taking shape in minute stitches of silk.

Within half an hour, the men filed back. The youngest of them couldn't have been fifteen. He ought to be out playing football, she thought. He shot a look at Mair before he bowed his head once more, and she noticed that his eyes were sore and reddened from the close work.

'Come,' Mehraan said to her. 'We will drink tea for ten minutes.'

He led the way to a corner *dhaba*, a workers' place with plastic tables and chairs that was steamy with hot food and crowded after prayers. He exchanged greetings with half a

187

dozen other young men as he passed to the back of the room, and sat down at a table next to the wall. A picture of the Hajj, its shiny surface rippled with heat, hung above them. A waiter brought cups and poured tea from a metal pot.

'Where are you from?'

'England.'

He regarded her over the rim of his cup. 'Why are you in Srinagar?'

'As I said, to follow my grandmother. She was married to a missionary, and they worked here in Kashmir during the Second World War. I never knew her, though. She died before I was born. Is your grandfather still alive?'

'No, nor my father. I have my mother and two younger sisters in my family, that is all.'

'That's a lot of responsibility for you.'

Mehraan acknowledged this with a nod. 'Tell me, you make this journey just to see some goats and a workshop for embroidery? It is unusual.'

'Is it?'

'Most people are concerned with today, and with wishing for better tomorrow.'

At first sight Mair had recognised in Mehraan someone she could talk to. There was no point in making a connection like this and then *not* talking. So she told him about her father's death and the uncovering of the shawl on the last night in the old house. She explained that her sister and brother were married and had young families, but she was single and free to make the journey. 'On behalf of all of us,' she concluded, as if to legitimise what he might consider a self-indulgent as well as an eccentric undertaking.

'I see,' he said. He placed his empty cup neatly on the table.

Mair knew that he didn't completely accept her explanation. She said, 'I needed a quest. All the obvious signposts in my life were pointing down roads leading to places where I didn't particularly want to go, so I chose a footpath. If I've learnt anything from following it, in the last month, it's how much I love the place where I grew up. And how much I value my family. I never did while I was there.'

Now Mehraan smiled. It was the first time he had done so. 'That is good. You are here in Kashmir alone?'

'Yes.'

'You are not a journalist?'

'Of course not.'

'And you are unfortunately also not wholesale buyer of fine Kashmir pashmina to stock your shop in London?'

'I'm sorry, no.'

'That is a shame for me.'

They both laughed. He looked at the clock on the wall above the Hajj picture. 'I must go back.'

The bag with her shawl in it lay in Mair's lap. 'When will you tell me about your grandfather?'

'I can meet you tomorrow. I take a few minutes to eat, before afternoon prayers.'

'Here?'

'Of course.' He stood up to go.

She asked, 'Do those young men I saw enjoy their work?'

'It is work at least. But do you not think they would rather be teachers, or doctors, or even work in a bank? Today there is nothing for them in Kashmir. Nothing.'

Thoughtfully, Mair watched his retreating back.

The next day, she was sitting in the same seat when he reappeared.

'Have you eaten some food?' he asked. A tin plate of chopped onion and sliced limes was placed between them, sprinkled with green chillies.

'Not yet. If you order for both of us, I would like to pay for it.'

He looked as if he might object to this, but he ordered rapidly from one of the men who raced up and down between the tables with steaming plates. 'And so, what would you like to know?'

Many things, Mair had realised overnight. She wanted to know about his life, as much as his grandfather's. She had read in the newspapers about the stone-throwers, groups of militant young men who believed in free Kashmir. They collected rocks and gathered in mobs to pelt the security forces. When the police and army retaliated, sometimes a boy was killed. Riots in protest at a death had led to curfews, increased police and military pressure, a period of uneasy calm, and then the cycle would begin again. How did a man like Mehraan interpret the violence?

Mair began carefully, 'Why is there nothing for your embroidery workers in Kashmir?'

'No money, no jobs, no investment, no prospect. That is nothing.'

'Do you support *azadi*?' Freedom, independence.

This time Mehraan's laugh was bitter. 'Freedom, for a poor man, is an idea only. But, no, I do not myself believe that Kashmir can be independent. It is a matter of economics.'

'Or joined to Pakistan, then?'

'Maybe, after Partition, that could have been a solution. The maharajah, Nehru, your Viceroy of India, they made a different decision. But now, today . . .' Mehraan shrugged and blew out his lips. 'Pakistan has problems enough. Why do you wish to talk about our troubles?'

'Because I'm here. I was out on the Bund the night before last and I saw the grenade attack. Or perhaps I should just be taking photographs of the lakes and shopping for carpets.'

'That would be to be a tourist, yes. A person like you, ma'am . . .'

'Mair.'

'Yes. Naturally you wish to look further than shops. But the difficulties of Kashmir are here for a long time, and they are not easy to understand. I am not even sure myself what I believe. Except in God, and his Prophet, peace be upon him. Of course it is not right to throw stones or worse things at police and soldiers, but young men are angry, and to be without

190

power in our own country makes more anger. On the whole, what you are already doing is wise – I mean, that is to concentrate your attention on your own history. And on shawls.'

Mair looked at her plate. There was a hot, fragrant naan glistening with melted butter and chopped fresh herbs, a dome of rice and a metal pan of vegetable curry. Mehraan wadded a chunk of bread in his right hand and deftly scooped up the thick sauce. She knew that, like Farooq, he was advising her to be careful for her own sake.

'History, then,' she repeated. 'And your grandfather. Tell me about him.'

Mehraan's sombre face brightened. His teeth looked very white within his dense black beard. 'In those days, before Partition, Kashmir was a different country. In Srinagar, out in the villages also, we were Muslims, Sikhs, Hindu, Buddhist, all together. There was of course trouble sometimes, neighbours and disputes, but not so to tear apart a country. My grandfather lived in a village called Kanihama, on the way to Sonamarg. *Hama* means a settlement place, and *kani* you know is shawl-making. There was clear, fresh water there, gardens for vegetables and grazing for animals. Like me he was *karkhanadar* and in his workshop the finest shawls were made, a whole year or more to make one such as yours, in our tradition.'

Mair listened, entranced.

Mehraan painted a picture of a simple life in the idyllic valley, of families working co-operatively as they had done for centuries. The finest items were made in the hope that the completed shawl would find a wealthy buyer, perhaps to be worn for a wedding, or laid in as part of a bride's dowry. In Kashmiri families, he said, shawls of all grades represented the women's security. They could be cut up, sold in pieces to buy food or pay debts, retrieved and pieced together again, stored away in folded linen scattered with bitter herbs to deter moth, and brought out for the great family occasions. Shawls were given as gifts, hoarded as treasure, passed on from mother to daughter. This was still the case, Mehraan said, but the finest examples, the *kani* pieces, like Mair's grandmother's, these were hardly made nowadays and the techniques were all but lost. They were too costly, and the weavers couldn't any longer afford to spend months bent over a loom in the hope of their shawl fetching a good price when it was finally completed. There were copies, of course, machine-woven, but they were nothing.

'Have you seen this work as it is done?' Mehraan asked. The plates of food were empty, although Mair had been so absorbed in his story that she had hardly been aware of clearing hers.

She shook her head.

'If you are interested, there is one place, not far – the *karkhanadar* is one of my friends. He has a buyer for *kani* in Delhi, but that man is a hard, hard bargainer. There is not much profit to make.'

'I would love to see it.'

'I will find out. Come again tomorrow.'

'I will,' she promised. 'Do you have any idea, Mehraan, how my Welsh grandmother might have come to own such a costly piece?'

They walked out into the sunlight. The afternoon was fresh and cool after the steamy *dhaba*.

'She was a Western woman so she would have been rich enough to pay my grandfather for it. Perhaps a gift from her husband.'

What other explanation? But Mair was sure that the Reverend Evan and Mrs Watkins had not been rich, not even well off, and she still couldn't imagine Nerys, the minister's wife, draping the radiant shawl over her modest shoulders.

'Same time tomorrow.' She smiled.

But when she met Mehraan the next afternoon he was in a hurry.

'I do not eat my meal today. I have to go to see a buyer. If you can be quick, we will visit the workroom now.'

They ducked through some narrow lanes to yet another

192

doorway in an old wood and brick façade. Tall windows were designed to admit the maximum amount of daylight for the workers within. Almost all of the space in the small, silent room was taken up by three wooden looms, primitive-looking affairs of beams and knotted string. Three young men sat at the loom benches, intent on what they were doing, but when Mehraan spoke to the nearest he sat back and allowed them to see his work by unpinning the black cloth that protected the shawl length. Laid out in a tidy row across the breadth of it were hundreds of *kani* bobbins, each one wound with a different shade of the hair-fine weft yarn. For each row of the pattern, an intricate design of flowers on a black ground, Mair understood that every one of the bobbins would have to be taken up in order and passed between the warp threads. Each time, the exact number of threads had to be counted before one colour gave way to the next. The pattern-maker's instructions were written out on a rough grid pinned up in front of the weaver, a tumble of scribbled digits that looked like the mathematical calculations of an early astronomer. Next to this was a sketch of the finished design.

Mair let out the breath she had been holding.

It must take fifteen minutes of concentration, she calculated, to weave just one single row of the shawl.

Mehraan asked another question, and the weaver indicated the amount of completed design. It measured less than half a metre.

'Three months,' Mehraan translated.

To keep the finished price down, these designs consisted of two broad bands of *kani* weaving on a plain ground. For an all-over design like hers, Mair could hardly conceive of the amount of work involved. She found that her eyes were stinging, partly in sympathy with the young men who strained over this exacting work all day, every day of their lives, and partly in awe of the legacy that had somehow come into her possession. She felt more than ever determined to pursue the shawl's history and discover how it had come to be in her family.

'Thank you,' she said.

The weaver, who had never once looked directly at her, resumed his counting.

No wonder there was no music in here, no talking, no distractions at all. A single wrong thread would set the pattern awry.

Out in the street, Mehraan said, 'You see?'

'I do see.' She didn't know what else she could say. In a rush, she asked, 'I'd like to visit Kanihama. Would you come with me?'

She thought perhaps he could show her what had once been the workshop, and the houses in which the shawl-makers had worked and lived back in the time when British India still existed.

Mehraan compressed his lips. 'No, I could not do that.'

Evidently she had made an improper suggestion, a single woman to an unmarried young man. 'I see. I'm sorry.' There were tourist guides in Srinagar. She would have to take a Toyota tour to Kanihama instead.

Now Mehraan looked awkward. 'Perhaps . . . perhaps you would like to take some tea tomorrow with my mother and sisters? They speak no English, but I can talk between you.'

'Yes, please. I would like that very much indeed.'

It was a tiny house in a quarter of the city that none of Kashmir's tourists – the few that there were – would have reason to visit. A maze of rambling dirt lanes ran together and branched under the patchy shade of walnut and apricot trees. Open gutters trickled with black water. Between the single-storey houses were rough fences and scrubby patches of garden, barns and carpet workshops, and oily yards where mechanics serviced battered trucks. The lanes were busy with people, while old men looked on from open shops and little boys chalked cricket stumps on concrete walls.

Shadows of dogs prowled the rubbish heaps. Mair looked away whenever she caught sight of one.

Behind their blue-painted front door, separated from the lane by a tiny strip of vegetable garden, Mehraan's mother and sisters were waiting for their visitor. They presented her with a bunch of marigolds and cosmos tied into a posy with a strip of ribbon, and Mair gave them the sweet cakes and chocolates she had bought from a shop on the Bund.

Tea was a ceremony. She took her place on cushions, facing Mehraan's mother across a square of carpet, and the sisters brought in a tall samovar and a tray of china cups. They laid out fresh afternoon breads and honey in the comb, with the sweet cakes arranged on what was clearly the best plate. Mair asked polite questions, and Mehraan dutifully translated. The sisters were fourteen and sixteen, and their mother said it would soon be time to think of finding suitable husbands for them. She gave an expressive shrug. Their marriages were clearly a matter of concern, but the girls just giggled.

Mehraan was only twenty. Mair was surprised to discover he was so much younger than he looked. He had learnt his good English at school; he had been the best student at that. He offered her this last piece of information reluctantly, heavily prompted by his mother. Then he had studied commerce at college in the city, thanks to the generosity of his mother's brother who had a carpet wholesale business. It was Mehraan's job now at the shawl workshop to sell the finished pieces to retailers at prices that would support his workers, and leave a margin for himself and his family to live on.

His father had done the same job. He had been killed twelve years before, caught in the crossfire of a battle between insurgents and the military.

Merhaan relayed all this matter-of-factly, against a background of interjections from his mother and bursts of smothered laughter from his sisters. The older woman's lined face spoke of a hard life. Her bare feet were calloused and her toenails thick and cracked. The two girls were pretty, bareheaded indoors, their sleek hair parted in the centre and worn in a single thick braid that hung down to their narrow waists.

Straining to hear what was not said, Mair guessed that the boy's education had been a way for his uncle to provide for the fatherless family. Mehraan's responsibilities meant that he wouldn't be able to marry until his sisters were settled in their husbands' family homes. Then he would bring home a suitable wife, the family's choice as much as his own, who would eventually care for her mother-in-law in this house.

In turn, Mair answered their questions about England.

It rained a lot, yes. They did not grow rice. Education and medical care were free, although taxes were high. Families didn't all live under one roof, and were often scattered in many different places.

Daringly, between giggles, one of the sisters ventured a question of her own. Mair answered that she was not married, no. Her advanced age was tactfully not remarked upon; obviously she was past the point of being able to hope for a husband, even an apology for one.

The tea was drunk, the bread and cake consumed.

Mair explained why she was visiting Kashmir. When she unwrapped the shawl and shook it out at the mother's feet there was a cry of surprised delight, the afternoon's first expression of spontaneity. It was picked up, held to the light, the maker's mark examined and exclaimed over.

'She says, "My husband's father's workshop,"' Mehraan translated. 'She would know it anywhere.'

There was a spinning wheel in the corner of the room and now the sisters lifted it into place and the mother took out her basket of cloudy raw wool. Her bare foot worked the treadle, the wheel whirred, and she began to spin yarn as fine as a cobweb. Mehraan explained that she sold by the kilo to the dyers and weavers, who then supplied his workshop with plain pashmina lengths.

'I was beginning to think that only men worked in the shawl trade.'

'Spinning is most of the time work for women. Will you tell them how you got this shawl?'

The mother continued her work and the two girls wound finished yarn into hanks. All three listened as Mehraan patiently translated. At the end, Mair reached into her pocket. She took out the envelope and shook the lock of hair into the palm of her hand, and the three women stopped to examine it. The copper lights that glinted in it were quite different from the jet-black Kashmiri heads.

She showed them the photograph too, and they studied that.

The mother tapped her fingernail on the water. 'Srinagar,' she said decisively. She placed the shawl in Mair's hands after one last glance at the maker's mark. Then she sat back and resumed her spinning.

There was nothing they could tell her. Mair had hardly expected that there would be, but she still felt a pang of disappointment. The steady working of the wheel was the only sound. She put the lock of hair away, and the photograph. Then, because the Beckers were always in the back of her mind, a tangential thought slipped suddenly into her head. Bruno had mentioned a family friend he was going to look up in Delhi, a Christian convert whose family had originally come from Srinagar.

Perhaps there were still people living in this city who remembered the war years, and even the missionaries of the day.

'Would you ask your mother one more question? Does she know any old people who might remember the war? The Christian missionaries who were here then, perhaps.'

Mehraan did so, but the only answer was a slow shake of the head. 'No, she knows no one like this. A person would have to be ninety years old.'

'Yes, about that age.'

'Very old,' Mehraan said, with respect.

It was time to leave. Mair thanked the family for their hospitality, and the girls shyly took her hand and smiled at her from beneath their eyelashes. The mother pulled her scarf over her hair and mouth and came to the gate to say goodbye. She pressed Mair's hands between hers and bowed, restrained as she had been throughout the visit, but Mair understood that she had made a friend because of the provenance of her shawl.

Mair and Mehraan were on the other side of the wooden gate before he was beckoned back and his mother murmured something to him. As they walked on again, Mehraan explained that his mother had a good friend who was a nurse who looked after the old people at the European hospital. This nurse might know such an old person.

'Please ask your mother if she could find out,' Mair said, without holding out much hope.

They walked on towards a busy road, where Mehraan summoned a taxi for her.

When it came, the email message was very short.

Mair read it once, then again, staring until the words on the screen blurred but still refused to deny their terrible weight.

Our beloved daughter Lotus died yesterday.
Bruno Becker

She wrote an answer, the hardest few sentences she had ever composed, then made her way back to *Solomon and Sheba*.

Farooq intercepted her. 'Madam, are you ill?'

'No, Farooq. Not ill. I have had some bad news.'

She went into the bedroom and lay down. The lapping of water and birdsong were all around her, but she could see only Lamayuru, the white snow and the shadow of the dog, and Lotus in her father's arms.

'I have some news to tell you,' Mehraan said.

Mair had met him at the *dhaba* once again, and this time he introduced her to two of his friends. They talked in English about independence and political protest, in a fierce but abstract way, glancing at Mair from time to time to check her response. Then the friends left and Mehraan drained his glass of tea.

'What news is that?' she asked. Five more days had trickled

by, and she was beginning to think that it was time to leave Srinagar. Nothing else was going to reveal itself, and the shadow of Lotus's death darkened the perspectives of lake and mountains.

'My mother's friend, you remember. The nurse? She told us she knows an English lady. Her eyesight is very bad. She fell over at her house and needed to be bandaged. She is of the age you say, and she was here in Srinagar many years ago, before the time of Partition.'

There was another single-storey house in the suburbs, this one half hidden in an overgrown garden. Mair stooped to push at the low gate and passed under a tangle of branches. Her knock on the door was answered by an elderly Indian woman, her faded mint-green *kameez* stretched tight over her plump middle. A pair of heavy spectacles was pushed up over her forehead.

'Are you from Dr Ram?' the woman demanded.

'No, I'm afraid not.'

'Then where?'

Mair had prepared her answer. 'I've come to call. I'm looking up a friend of an old family friend. I'm from England.'

The woman looked surprised. 'Are you? You can come in for ten minutes. She is tired today.'

The room at the back of the house was pleasantly sunny. There was a rug on the floor, a large old-fashioned music centre on the table against the wall, and a fireplace with a jug of sunflowers in the grate. In an armchair drawn into a pool of sunlight sat an old woman, white-haired and straight-backed. Her heavily bandaged leg rested on a stool, and a walking-stick was placed against the chair. She turned her head towards Mair. 'Aruna? Are you there? Who is this?'

'I don't know. She says from England.'

Mair moved closer. 'I'm sorry to intrude,' she said.

The old woman's head tilted, giving her the look of an inquisitive bird. Her skin was sallow, deeply lined, the eyes anxiously peering. 'You *are* English. How jolly to hear your voice. Come right over here, my sight's not so good. That's better. Do we know each other? Aruna, can we have some tea? Or would you rather a gin?'

'Actually, we haven't met before. My name is Mair Ellis.'

'Well, how do you do?' She held out her tiny knotted hand for Mair to shake. 'I am Caroline Bowen. What brings you to Srinagar?'

NINE

'It's not too cold,' Rainer insisted.

Rainer never seemed to feel it, but in the last few days the valley weather had become so raw and damp that even indoors Nerys wore her new tweed *pheran* with several cardigans layered beneath. Myrtle had warned her that she would soon have to start carrying an earthenware fire-pot for warmth, as the Kashmiris did. Recently the two women had begun to feel like the forgotten rearguard of an army, as the last of the summer-season residents retreated south to the plains. The mountains were shrouded in mist, the Srinagar Club was empty, except for a couple of subdued tables for bridge, and the Lake Bar was silent, stripped of its lounge chairs and parasols.

Rainer Stamm was one of the few who did remain. Myrtle and Nerys had gone to his party, and instead of the usual faces they had been introduced to a Pandit university professor and his daughter, who was a musician, a Buddhist poet, and two tough-looking young American men whose role had never been fully explained and who, Myrtle later insisted, had been spies. They had had fun at this unusual gathering, and since then Rainer had taken to visiting the *Garden of Eden* for coffee or drinks. In return he invited them to the magic shows he gave to audiences of students.

Today he was explaining to Nerys how a permit he was

waiting for had finally been refused. 'The reason the British are giving me is the war. Tell me, how can it make the smallest difference to the war whether or not one Swiss national climbs Nanga Parbat? On the other hand it does make the greatest difference to me, and to the family of Matthew Forbes.'

'If you climb what?' Nerys asked him. 'And the family of whom?'

This morning they were at Rainer's house in the old town, sitting on the window seat of a casement that projected over a reach of the Jhelum river. There was a magnificent view of a bridge and the stately Hindu temple on the far bank, but the room itself was under-heated and dusty. Rainer's furniture was a collection of battered rejects haphazardly grouped on a once fine but now filthy and threadbare carpet, and his possessions seemed to consist of nothing but books, coils of rope, glittery stage props and hinged boxes painted with occult symbols relating to his magic tricks. Nerys was fascinated by the few glimpses she had been given into Rainer's life, but until today he had offered little real information.

Now he answered, 'You don't know? Nanga Parbat is a mountain. A very fine peak, the ninth highest in the world. It lies just eighty miles north of here. I will be the first person to reach the summit. I decided that years ago. The Germans think it is theirs to claim, but they are mistaken.'

Nerys was beginning to recognise Rainer's brand of bravado and defiance. He made his claims with such intensity and such twinkling humour that it was impossible not to catch his enthusiasm. 'I see.'

His eyes held hers. He didn't often look as serious as he did now.

'Maybe you do. I will capture it by going fast and light. That was always my intention with Matthew.'

'Rainer, I don't understand a word of this,' she protested. 'Are you going to tell me the story or not?'

Rainer was good at telling stories. He liked to exercise command over his audience, just as he did when he performed his magic. He waved his hands now in an *abracadabra* gesture. 'I will tell you on the way. Are you ready to go?'

He had suggested a drive to one of the villages and a picnic. Even the thought of going out into the mist made her shiver, but on the other hand Rainer's company would make up for the cold. Myrtle was attacking her own boredom by volunteering for all the war work that came her way, and today she was on a committee concerned with packing Indian sweets to send home to British children. Nerys didn't belong to the wives' groups, and was quite relieved not to, but solitude and inactivity were a particularly unwelcome prospect today.

She gave in. 'Yes,' she said. 'I'm ready.'

Rainer hoisted an armful of canvas bags and bowed her out into the street. On a patch of derelict ground, with a swarm of children to guard it, stood a red-painted Ford truck. It had a small closed cab and an open back into which Rainer tossed his bags. Two boys capered on the cab roof and others swung on the running-boards. They catcalled and gestured at Rainer until he dropped some coins into the hands of the biggest one, then fought to open the doors for him, like a mob of ragged footmen. Rainer cranked a starting-handle and the engine coughed. Nerys climbed into the passenger seat and they swayed over the ruts, the most daring children clinging to the chassis until the last possible moment.

'I didn't know you had a car,' she remarked, as they accelerated away.

'Of course I do. And for your sake I have even begged a cupful of petrol. Enough to get us where we are going – and who knows? Maybe all the way back again.'

Fuel was reserved for military purposes, and for civilians it was increasingly hard to come by. Nerys laughed. 'I'm impressed. Are you going to tell me exactly where we might not get back from?'

Rainer tapped the side of his nose. 'In good time. First the story.'

They were heading out of town, through quiet streets where

the houses of civil servants and teachers rested in secluded gardens. Nerys settled as comfortably as she could in the truck's rigid seat.

'Did you ever visit the European cemetery in Leh?' Rainer began.

'Of course I did. I used to go and sit there whenever I felt homesick. There's a handful of headstones with Welsh names, belonging to mission families from before our time. It's a sad place because of the little children's graves, but there's a wonderful view.'

'Then you will remember the memorial plaque to Matthew Forbes.'

Nerys did remember. She suddenly saw it in her mind's eye, a simple plate let into the wall of the enclosure.

In Memoriam
Matthew Alexander Forbes, St John's College, Cambridge
Lost on Nanga Parbat, August 1938, aged 22

'Yes, I do,' she said.

Rainer stared ahead over the truck's steering-wheel. They were reaching the outskirts of Srinagar, where the houses and roadside markets gave way to paddy fields and orchards. 'I placed it there, following the wishes of his family. I was with Matthew on the last morning of his life. The very last words he spoke were, "See you in a couple of hours. I'll open a tin of soup."'

'Go on.'

'Fast and light, that was our plan. We were in good shape for the climb. We had a small team of Sherpas, Matthew, two very strong officers of the Indian Army, and me. Matthew and I had camped at twenty thousand feet and were planning to advance the next day to establish a higher camp. Matthew was resting and I had climbed solo to a point on the ridge from which to reconnoitre our route upwards. I was looking towards the summit through my binoculars, when the entire slope above the camp gave way. Matthew, the tent, everything – everything that had been there – was swept away and buried under thousands of tons of ice and snow.'

Rainer's voice remained steady but furrows had appeared in his cheeks. He looked suddenly a decade older. 'I stood in the avalanche debris, and there was nothing around me but the wind. All I could do was climb down to the low camp where the other men were waiting for us to come back. We sent the news home to Matthew's family via Gilgit and Simla.

'His father was a mountaineer, too, and he understood the climber's compulsion to climb, but I don't believe his mother will ever recover. He was her only son, a brilliant mathematician. I had known him and his family for ten years because they came out to Switzerland to ski in winter and to climb in summer, and as soon as he heard about my expedition Matthew begged and begged me again to take him with me. I knew that he was fully capable of it, or of course I would have refused him. We came out from Delhi via Manali and up to Leh, in order to train and to acclimatise, and Matthew loved that place. That was why I placed his memorial in the graveyard there. It would have been a fine achievement for him, you know, to reach the summit. I couldn't have denied him the chance, when he wanted it so badly. But the mountains take away as readily as they give.'

Nerys imagined an eager young Englishman discovering the winding alleyways of sleepy Leh, or climbing to the old palace that stood on a hill overlooking the town to gaze out over the gold and emerald Indus valley.

Understanding that he was revealing a source of deep, private pain, she reached out and put her hand over Rainer's. Her fingers rested on his fist, until she remembered herself and withdrew them again.

'So, you may understand why I must go back. When I stand on the summit, the first man to reach there, Matthew will be with me. I have a book belonging to him that he left in the low camp, with his signature on the inside. I will take that page with me, and I will bury it up there for him.'

205

There was the faintest tremor in Rainer's voice now. Nerys found that her eyes were pricking with tears in response. 'I do understand,' she said.

'Yes. The British authorities do not see it in the same light. There is no permit for me to return. Even though I engineer an invitation and take myself to the Residency party in my evening clothes, such as they are, to speak in person to Mr Fanshawe and dance with his wife, who unfortunately looks like a horse, the answer is no. However . . .' He glanced at Nerys, and the lines in his face softened and disappeared. 'I danced with you, and for that it was worth attending the most tedious British party only to be told I am *not allowed* to climb a high mountain in India.'

'I don't know about mountains or permits, Rainer, but I enjoyed dancing with you too,' she said.

She was remembering some of the words she had heard Myrtle's acquaintances murmur in connection with Rainer Stamm. *Dubious*, *adventurer* and *charlatan* were among them, but Nerys didn't care. He intrigued her and, for all his bad reputation, she thought he was as honest as anyone she had ever met.

Rainer pointed ahead. The road had been climbing north-wards, and the mist that cloaked the valley suddenly fell away in trails of silvery-grey vapour. The foothills emerged with their ribbing of dark pine trees, and the white peaks lifted into the sky behind them. She knew, because she had been watching it for long days, that the snowline dropped by a few hundred feet each morning.

'It's very beautiful,' she said, as lightly as she could manage.

'I would like to take you up there with me, all the way over the passes and up to a place called Astor, from where you can see my Naked Mountain. Nanga Parbat is called that, you know, because it stands alone.' He leant forward and tapped one of the dials on the dust-coated dashboard. 'But we have only just enough petrol to get us to Kanihama and perhaps home again.'

'Kanihama?'

'Wait and see.'

After an hour's driving on a dirt road winding between tall poplar trees and bare paddies, they came to a village of mud-brick houses set in apple orchards. The sun shone over the rumpled blanket of mist that layered the Vale below, and a breeze stirred the trees. Rainer stopped the truck in a small square of houses and Nerys wound down her window. Sweet air flooded into her lungs, bringing with it the loud chirping of crickets, a cock's crow, the splash of running water and the voices of children playing nearby.

'Oh,' she said in surprise.

This place looked and sounded different in a dozen ways but still it strongly reminded her of villages at home that were also caught in the cup of hills and flooded with the scent of woodsmoke and animal manure. She opened the truck door and stepped out, drawing her *pheran* around her.

Kanihama was a lovely place.

Wide-eyed children crept round the corners of houses, followed at a distance by shawled women and men in thick coats and lambskin caps. Rainer swung down from the truck and spoke a few words to a crescent-faced man with a thick black beard.

Rainer turned back to Nerys. 'Your shawl spinner . . .'

He had found out where the woman lived, not far from his own house in the packed alleyways of Srinagar old town, and a few days ago Nerys and he had gone together to visit her. As Nerys had done the first time, they found her in her bare room with her spinning wheel and her children. Nerys gave the family food and some money, and she had tried to make promises about coming back and helping in whatever way she could. The woman only stared up at her, her face dulled by hunger and despair, while the two older children dragged at Nerys's clothes and insinuated their small filthy hands into her pockets. The baby clung to its sister's hair, seeming too listless even to blink. The oldest one had snatched up the family treasure again, and thrust the shawl towards Nerys's face. 'You buy. You *buy*,' she had insisted.

Nerys had gently put the piece aside, asking Rainer to tell the mother that she wanted to help them without taking their single asset.

'Kanihama is the woman's family home,' Rainer continued. 'I heard this much, and I asked for some more information. I discovered that this man is her father.'

The man nodded abruptly to Nerys. She offered the few words of Kashmiri greeting that she had learnt so far and he inclined his head again. A woman joined him, her hair and the lower half of her face covered with folds of plain pashmina.

'They are asking if we want to see their work,' Rainer said.

One of the houses was a little larger than the others, with wooden benches placed against the outside walls to catch the sun. Inside they were shown into a single room, the beamed roof supported by rough wooden pillars. A stove burnt at one side, the fragrant smoke curling up an iron chimney pipe.

There were three looms, looking to Nerys like a dauntingly complicated web of struts and cords. The only sounds were the steady whisper of bobbins as they passed between the threads, and the occasional gentle thump of the heddles.

When the weavers looked up and saw the visitors, the atmosphere of quiet industry changed to a bustle of welcome. The one nearest to them slid smartly off his bench and beckoned Nerys to his side. Watched by the crescent-faced man and two or three of the women, and by a fringe of inquisitive children bobbing in the doorway, he unpinned a protective cotton cloth that had covered his work.

Nerys gazed at the half-completed *kani*-woven shawl that was revealed.

The design was an intricate pattern of peacock feathers within lush borders of floral and paisley shapes, but it was the colours that took her breath away. They captured all the shades of a Kashmiri summer's afternoon, from aquamarine to silver, from the sky's blue to the deep green depths of lake water.

'You like?' the head man asked.

She could only nod.

With a touch of theatre the weaver bounded back on to his seat, and rippled fingers as practised as a concert pianist's over the dozens of bobbins laid out in front of him. He picked out one note, a bobbin wound with pearl-white yarn, and dipped it beneath a single warp thread to create, Nerys realised, a tiny point of light at the heart of a stylised lotus bloom. Then he took up another, this time wound with palest silver, and counted the next five threads before slipping the bobbin beneath them. He was already rapt in concentration, and instinctively she stepped back in order not to distract him.

She realised that she had been holding her breath.

Rainer and Nerys were led outside again and escorted to a sunny bench. Tea was brought and served by one of the dark-eyed girls of the village. She smiled at Nerys but was too shy to linger. Rainer and the head man were deep in a conversation involving more gestures than actual words, so she rested her head against the wall and studied the view. The village seemed far away from Srinagar. She guessed that nothing much had changed here in centuries. Food was grown in the fields and the patches of garden; rice was planted, harvested and sold, and the dry stalks were neatly bound into the sheaves she could see piled in the barn beside her to provide winter fodder for the animals. Two boys drove a small flock of sheep and goats across the other side of the square, rattling their sticks against the house walls and giving low calls of encouragement. A group of little girls crouched together, playing a game of throwing and catching five white pebbles.

Nerys was so absorbed in the scene, and in her thoughts, that she started when Rainer called her name. He was talking now to two of the women who held up enamel jugs and baskets for his inspection.

'We could make up for being too poor to buy the shawl by supplementing our picnic with some of their fruit and yoghurt, don't you think?'

'Yes, I do.'

For a few rupees they chose an earthenware pot full of cool white yoghurt, some small yellow apples, and a square of sacking tied round a generous scoop of walnuts. The villagers were disappointed but evidently not particularly surprised that the visitors hadn't made a more substantial purchase.

'At the price they're asking, they'll have to wait for Vivien Leigh to come calling for that shawl.' Rainer grinned. 'I would have bought it for you, if I had the money.'

'I'm not surprised it costs the earth. It's exquisite.'

The children had crowded in to watch the transaction. Even the two shepherds had penned their animals and come to join the others. Rainer waved his arms and gathered them all into a circle. 'Come on, come and look,' he called.

'Keep them amused for a minute,' he casually instructed Nerys, and strolled away towards the red Ford. Nerys blinked at two dozen expectant faces, and at the men and women who were leaving their work to see what might happen next. Her mind went awkwardly blank until she remembered her little schoolroom at the mission in Leh.

Hoping for the best, she began to sing 'The Grand Old Duke of York'. In her strong, chapel-trained contralto voice she gave the nursery rhyme full volume and emphasis, complete with actions. By the time she got to 'they were neither up nor down' bemused stares had given way to ripples of laughter, and Rainer was back again.

'Not bad. Maybe I will offer you a job as my assistant,' he said.

From the depths of one of his canvas bags he produced four silvery rings, linked in a chain. With a bow he presented the chain to the bearded head man, and indicated that he should give it a good tug and try to pull the rings apart. The man did so, with a great show of strength, but he couldn't break the links. Rainer took them back, turned them once between his thumb and forefinger, and held up four separate rings. There was a hubbub of amazed shouting, which he pretended not to hear, throwing the rings in the air instead and juggling with them. When he caught them again he held them up for everyone to see, and they were linked. This time he passed the chain to the head man's wife, and she giggled within her shawl as she failed to separate the rings.

Nerys loudly clapped, and now the villagers joined in the applause. She and Rainer were hemmed in on all sides as everyone tried to edge in for a closer look. She noticed how he seemed to grow taller and to become more lion-like with the attention of the crowd.

He dropped the rings into his bag and just as casually brought out a flat sheet of plain glass. He held it up towards the sun and the light shone straight through it. He turned the square through every plane, then tapped the surface so that it rang a clear note. Shrugging, he passed the glass to the nearest spectator to hold and began to search through his own pockets. When he didn't find what he was looking for, he pointed to the smallest girl, who had a pocket in her apron front. That was empty, so Rainer made a show of thinking hard. Then he waved his hand over the head of another child, and unravelled a yard of black velvet ribbon from his left ear. The child cupped a hand to the ear and scuttled away sideways like a crab. All the others hooted with delight. Rainer looped the ribbon between his fingers and snapped it taut. Then, with a polite bow, he retrieved his sheet of glass and threaded the ribbon straight through the middle of it.

There was a gasp, and then a collective whispering. The ribbon curled free on the reverse side, and Rainer handed the glass to the head man's wife. She breathed on it, then wiped the mist away with her sleeve. Sunlight flashed off the smooth surface as she examined it. Rainer coiled the ribbon and presented it to her, taking back the glass and stowing it in his bag.

The spectators were too amazed to applaud this time. The children were all dumbstruck, and slightly frightened.

'Ladies and gentlemen, thank you.' Rainer smiled and bowed. In the midst of an astonished silence he took Nerys's arm and they returned to the Ford. They drove out of the little square and down the hill out of the village. He glanced sideways at her as they jolted over the ruts. 'Was that too much?'

'I was impressed.'

He sighed. 'I always mean to offer a little less show, a little more substance. Unfortunately I fail to live up to my good intentions, because illusion is easy and the truth is always so very hard. Shall we have our picnic now?'

'Yes, please. Is the truth so very difficult, Rainer?'

'I know you don't find it to be. That's because you are good, Nerys, as well as beautiful.'

She was good, Nerys decided, because there had so far been very few other options. But no man had ever told her that she was beautiful. With colour rising in her cheeks she stared through the windscreen at the snowy rampart of the Himalayas.

They found a sheltered hollow in the angle of two huge boulders on the lip of a tree-lined ravine. Out of the wind, and with the warmth of thin sunshine held by the stone, it was almost comfortable. Rainer hoisted a rusty drum pierced with rough holes from the back of the truck and set about gathering armfuls of dead wood. In minutes, a fire glowed in the brazier and an old tin kettle was filled from the stream that ran through the ravine. When the water boiled the kettle whistled, the incongruous domesticity of the sound in this wild place making Nerys smile. She made tea while Rainer chopped an onion and unwrapped a chunk of dark red meat. He sliced it into cubes with a pocket knife, and fried it with the onion and a fistful of spices. With the rising scent of cumin and fennel seed, Nerys realised she was ravenous.

'Is there anything you can't do?' she asked him.

'I can't stay in one place,' he answered, without looking up. She understood that this was the truth, and she could take it as a warning if she chose.

They leant back against the rock to eat the curried lamb inside folds of bread, and finished up with rich, thick yoghurt, apples and walnuts. Rainer cracked the shells of the nuts for her and arranged the kernels on his outspread handkerchief.

Nerys made more tea, and poured it into the two tin mugs. 'I want to hear about our spinner now. Why does she live all alone in Srinagar, if she was born up here?'

Rainer sipped his tea. He told her that the girl had grown up in Kanihama's extended families of spinners, dyers, weavers and embroiderers. But then she had fallen in love with a man, one of the pedlars who came through the villages selling oil, aluminium saucepans and trinkets, and she had married him against her father's wishes. The man was from Srinagar and she had gone to the city to live with him in his mother's house, as all the young women did here, because after marriage they no longer belonged to their own family but to the husband's.

The pedlar had turned out to be a bad man, as the father had known all along, although the wife had three children before her husband abandoned her. The mother-in-law then threw the girl out, claiming that she was an adulteress because her son had told her as much, and insisting that the three children must have been fathered by some other man. Left alone, the wife couldn't go back to her own family in the village because they had disowned her on her marriage, so the only option left to her was to try to support her children single-handed. Otherwise they would all starve.

Nerys had seen for herself what that struggle was like.

She had been listening as intently as if to a fable. But now she collected herself, remembering that it was the truth and not a story at all. 'That is brutal, as well as sad.'

'Yes, I am afraid it is.'

'What can we do?'

Rainer shook his head. 'Beyond offering a little money, some food here and there? Nothing. That is the way it is here.'

But *nothing* wasn't any good, Nerys thought. Even the little she had been able to do for the children in Leh was much better than that. Evan wouldn't have accepted *nothing*, either. He would extend a hand, in his pure conviction, to help a sinner, as he saw it.

Nerys closed her eyes for a moment. Evan had been in her mind ever since this morning when the postman had paddled up to the steps of the *Garden of Eden* with the letter.

'There is a good deal of sadness in Kashmir,' Rainer murmured, 'but I don't like seeing it reflected in your face.'

He was looking so hard at her that she had to meet his gaze. In confusion, she thought how recognisable he had become. She knew him, and he knew her.

'Won't you tell me what's wrong?' he whispered.

Nerys squared her shoulders. 'I had a letter this morning from my husband. I was expecting him to join me very soon. But he has decided to spend the winter in Kargil, because his work there has absorbed his attention and he is valuable to the mission. He believes that it would be better and safer for me to spend the winter season here in the Vale, with Myrtle, and then he will travel to meet me after the snows melt again. Then we'll resume our work together.'

This last was what she told herself, but she didn't know for sure. Nor would there be many more mails arriving from Kargil this year. The passes were barely negotiable now, and in another week Ladakh would be cut off within its lines of mountains.

The truth was, Nerys didn't add, that Evan found it simpler to preach and work when she wasn't there to reproach him with her various needs. He could love God's creatures more generally without suffering the daily and specific reminder that he and his wife were not in love at all.

'I don't know your husband,' Rainer answered, 'but he sounds like a fool.'

He took one of her hands and very gently kissed the knuckles. She didn't snatch it away.

Nerys had learnt quite a lot about men and women since meeting Myrtle McMinn. She had seen the way Myrtle wove her way through the parties and tennis games and cocktail hours in Srinagar, flirting and laughing and attracting admiration wherever she went, and she had also seen – and heard – her at home with Archie before he had gone away. Nerys was in no doubt at all that Myrtle did love her husband, but the world wasn't either black or white as far as love went. There were infinite permutations of colour, and a hundred thousand grades of feeling, between loving and not loving. To deny as much, she began to think, was to deny not only the obvious truth but your own humanity.

Nerys wanted Rainer to touch her. She felt dizzy with the force of how much she wanted him to touch her. She was beginning to understand what Myrtle had been talking about when she had advised her to have some fun.

My dear?

But Rainer only touched his finger to the rescued brooch at the neck of her blouse. There was a sudden rustle and snapping of twigs from the line of trees and they looked up to see a bearded goat gazing at them. A goat meant a goatherd not far away.

'I think we should go back now.' Rainer smiled.

The telephone rang in the saloon. A dense scribble of wires slung from wooden posts on the bank brought a telephone line as well as electric power to the houseboat, but its jangling bell always startled Nerys. She had been half reading and half watching the kingfishers out on the lake, and Myrtle was writing letters. Myrtle put down her pen and picked up the phone.

'This is the *Garden of Eden*,' she announced.

Nerys could just hear a woman's voice at the other end. It sounded high and hysterical.

'Not at all. Don't worry,' Myrtle murmured, raising an eyebrow in Nerys's direction.

The voice went on. It was half a minute before Myrtle managed to say, 'I think you should just get into a *shikara* and come straight here . . . Yes, come now . . . Of course . . . Of course . . . See you soon.' She hung up. 'That was Caroline Bowen. It sounds like more trouble.'

'Oh dear. Should I go out somewhere?'

'No, stay here. You could ring the bell for some coffee, perhaps.'

Myrtle went over to the veranda window. She lit a cigarette and leant against the glass, watching for the boat to come gliding over the water.

When she arrived, Caroline was swathed in her *pheran* with the hood pulled down to hide her face. She waited until Majid had served the coffee and withdrawn, and as soon as she showed herself they saw that her eyes were crimson and swollen almost shut from prolonged crying. Myrtle tutted in sympathy, settled her on the sofa and gave her coffee.

'Caroline, dear girl, you have to tell us right now exactly what the real trouble is. Otherwise we can't help. Can we, Nerys?'

Nerys had less confidence in their joint powers than Myrtle. Caroline tried to speak, but at first the girl couldn't find the words and she wouldn't look at either of them. Finally in a low, hoarse voice she managed to say, 'I'm going to have a baby.'

Myrtle nodded, entirely unsurprised. 'Are you? Why is that making you so unhappy?'

Caroline lifted her eyes now. 'It's not my husband's child.'

'Is it Ravi Singh's?'

Her miserable silence was enough of an answer.

'Does Ravi know? Does Ralph know?'

She shook her head. 'No one does, except you two now. Oh, *God*, I'm so glad to have told you. It's such a relief, you wouldn't believe. I've been going mad. I've tried absolutely every single thing I could think of, drinking gin until I threw up, taking hot baths, going riding and putting the horse to fences at a gallop, but nothing worked. I felt terribly ill and tired, and then that sort of passed and now I'm just . . .' she passed her hand over her middle '. . . getting bigger.'

'How many months is it, do you know?' Nerys asked gently.

Caroline bit her lip. 'About four, I should think.'

Myrtle was making calculations. 'What have you heard from Ralph?'

'Just the usual letters. He's . . . not all that good at writing.

Everyone thought they would be going to North Africa, but it's Malaya.'

'Is there likely to be any home leave for the regiment?'

'No. I don't think so.' She took out her handkerchief and blew her nose. 'That's what I hear. Ralph hasn't mentioned anything.'

'All right.' There was a pause before Myrtle went on, 'This is a rather personal question, I know, but we're having no more secrets. How do you know it isn't Ralph's baby? He was here in Srinagar all summer. The timing would be right. And if it were his, he'd be rather pleased, wouldn't he? Especially if it's a boy, I should think. And even if it's not his, with Ravi Singh being so light-skinned . . . It wouldn't be the first time in history such a thing has happened, would it?'

Nerys had said nothing but she tried to flash a warning to Myrtle. Be careful. Don't assume more than you can know.

It was too late. Caroline's face crumpled and her empty coffee cup fell from her fingers and rolled on the rug. Her hands came up to her mouth and her whole body shook.

'What is it?' Myrtle cried. 'What have I said?'

'It can't be Ralph's baby, you see. That's just it.'

'Can't?' Myrtle persisted.

It was Nerys who stood up, retrieved the cup and put it back on the brass tray, then went to sit at Caroline's side. She took the girl's hands and looked into her ravaged face. 'I think I understand,' she murmured. 'You don't have to say any more if you don't want to.'

Caroline seemed reassured by this. She collected herself and firmly shook her head. 'No, I want to – *need* to talk about it. I came over here to Mrs McMinn, I mean Myrtle, and to you, because I knew I must. There hasn't been anyone I could 'fess up to before, and that's what has made it so bad. I mean, my stepmother has been decent enough, but she's at home and I'm here, and we've never had that sort of a motherly conversation. That's to say, before Ralph and I were married I knew I had to arrange matters so when I was in Delhi to buy my wedding

217

dress I saw the doctor there – Mrs Fanshawe gave me an address – and he fixed me up with the hideous rubber thing you're supposed to put in.'

Her eyes held Nerys's.

A three-letter man, Nerys remembered. That was what Archie McMinn had called Captain Bowen.

'I had it in its box on our wedding night, all ready to put in like the doctor told me. But Ralph had drunk too much and he more or less passed out. I wasn't all that surprised, I'd seen him drinking before, so I tried to laugh about it the next day, you know, saying something about making up for lost time. Ralph didn't think it was funny, not at all. He made an excuse that night about feeling ill, and slept on the camp bed. After a few more days I didn't think it was funny either. I'd be putting talcum powder on the rubber thing, and going to bed in my pretty nightdresses, and my husband never did what he was supposed to.'

'Never?' Myrtle whispered. Nerys could see how difficult it was for her friend to imagine such a thing. For herself, it wasn't such a leap.

Caroline held up her head. 'Never.'

'My poor duck.' Myrtle sighed.

'I thought it must be me. Not that I was thinking I might be repulsively deformed or anything like that – I was at boarding school and I'd seen everyone else so I knew I was actually on the decent side of ordinary, if that doesn't sound too conceited. I mean, just not being *alluring* enough. But after a while I started to think, Bloody hell, if I want to and he doesn't, that can't all be my fault, can it? Sometimes we'd get near to it, but I always felt he was closing his eyes so as to be somewhere else while it was happening, and never managing to detach himself quite enough actually to be able to *do* it. Does that make sense?'

'Yes, it makes sense,' Nerys assured her.

'Well, after the honeymoon he was mostly with the regiment anyway. Ralph's a soldier, so was his father, and his father, all the way back to the battle of Waterloo or some such, and soldiering comes first, before everything else. He took the trouble to warn me about that, before we got engaged, and I was keen enough on being married to convince myself I could either change him or live with it. I mean, being realistic, how many other proposals was I going to get? I'd come all the way out here and I couldn't go on living at the Residency for ever. Ralph was quite handsome and he seemed to want me.'

Even Nerys understood that an ambitious soldier would need a wife. The colonel and the colonel's lady. Caroline would have been a very suitable choice.

Caroline looked down at her engagement and wedding rings. 'It was a happy ending, wasn't it? I was going to be Ralph's wife, the mother of his sons. Oh, *God*.'

The tears started up again, running down her smooth pink cheeks. Myrtle passed her a handkerchief and said, 'What about Ravi Singh?'

'I'm sure you can guess. I shouldn't have let him make love to me but I couldn't stop it happening. I felt as if I was in heaven. The glamour, first of all. Everything was such fun and nothing took any effort, not like at my house where even the damned kitchen-boy ignores what I tell him to do and the dust lies an inch thick. Ravi has legions of bowing servants, and a string of sweet ponies, and a chauffeur to take him wherever he wants to go in his big car. The food's all divine, and you should just see the silks and the silver, and he can be more idiotic and funny than any Englishman you've ever met.'

'He has the time to devote to it,' Myrtle said drily.

'I know, I know. And he took ages to seduce me, really he did. It wasn't crude or too insistent, nothing like that. He'd just kiss the inside of my wrist – here – and then quickly cover that precise square inch of skin with my cuff, humbly, as if I'd allowed him a glimpse of the most beautiful treasure in the world. It went on like that for weeks, a tiny bit further each time, and always making me laugh and bringing me heavenly presents and telling me . . . telling me all the things that I had imagined Ralph saying.'

Nerys thought of Rainer and the Kanihama picnic. The only difference was that she was by this time a shade more sceptical about men and sex than Caroline Bowen was. She felt herself redden, and hoped that Myrtle wouldn't notice and wonder why.

Caroline lifted her head. 'When it did happen, it was wonderful,' she insisted. 'I want you to know that I don't regret it, although I'm in such a damned awful mess now.'

Nerys was listening intently.

'It was at his family's summerhouse, in the country. When Ravi took off my clothes the air was like silk over my arms and legs. Nothing was going to spoil that moment – *nothing*. I felt as beautiful as a painting, and as powerful as a queen. He was doing me honour, you know.'

Myrtle and Nerys were silenced. Love had temporarily made a pretty, round-faced, unlucky English girl into something close to a tragic heroine.

Myrtle found her voice first. 'You didn't have your cap with you, of course? The hideous rubber thing in its box?'

'No.'

'And, of course, Ravi didn't make himself responsible for any arrangements of that sort?'

'No.'

Myrtle sighed.

Caroline quickly added, 'The times after that I mostly used it. Well, I did sometimes. The trouble is that it's just not very romantic, is it? If it was with one's husband, I'm sure it would be all right. He'd be used to you going off into the bathroom and fishing around.'

Nerys couldn't help but smile at her.

'Then I began to notice that each time I was with him, Ravi made it less of a ceremony. I wanted him more and more, so much that I actually ached for him. I used to babble stupidly about loving him, I couldn't stop myself, and he edged further and further away. One day when we were alone together, and I was already beginning to guess I might be pregnant, he looked at his watch instead of undressing me and said that he had to go riding.

'At the Residency party I drank some cocktails for courage and when he asked me to dance I tried to talk properly to him. But, oh, the ice of it. I'd never have imagined he could be so cold, while I was just burning up with fury and fear. That was when you two rescued me. Since then, I've been sitting in our dismal empty house, praying for a miracle. But they don't happen. So I'm pretty much in the mire, aren't I?'

'Do you really love Ravi?' Nerys asked. She had seen the man's cold, aquiline face and proud bearing.

'Of course I do. Desperately,' Caroline flung back, but Nerys suspected that she was clinging to love itself rather than Ravi. That was quite a good thing.

'All right. Let's work out what we can do,' Myrtle said. Caroline gave her a grateful look. 'Is it too late for us to find someone who can help, do you think?'

'I'm afraid it is,' Nerys said. She was firm because it was highly unlikely that any proper doctor would agree to perform a late abortion on a healthy woman, and she couldn't bear even the thought of the clumsy unofficial alternatives. The other two regarded her steadily.

'When Evan and I were in Shillong I worked at the mission hospital, in the delivery ward. I saw the results of a couple of botched attempts to get rid of babies. I don't ever want to see another.'

'You are a midwife?' Myrtle gaped. 'I must say, that's jolly useful.'

'No, I'm not. I helped out, that's all.'

'Even so. I've never seen a baby born.'

'Neither have I,' Caroline said. She turned pale at the thought of what lay ahead, but Myrtle was now all briskness.

'Take that woolly thing off, Caroline, and stand up. Turn sideways and let's have a look at you.'

221

She did as she was told, awkwardly smoothing her skirt over a small protuberance. Yes, Nerys thought. Sixteen or seventeen weeks into what was probably a healthy pregnancy. Caroline was slim, but she looked strong and resilient. Even so, she was going to need proper medical care.

Myrtle nodded. She was clearly thinking hard. 'Would you want to keep the baby? I mean, after it's born.'

'I've tried hard enough to stop it, haven't I? There've been weeks and weeks when I've thought of nothing but how to get rid of it. But now . . .' she placed one hand on her belly '. . . I'm confused. It's growing. I can feel it. But it can't be Ralph's, and I know he'll never, never accept what I've done, so if I want to keep my life as it is I've got to hide this from him. I suppose Ravi might have acknowledged the baby as his, at least in some way, but only as a bastard, never as part of his family. He'd never marry me, even if I could get a divorce. I've stopped even dreaming about that,' she concluded.

'I don't think you should let Ravi Singh know anything whatsoever,' Myrtle warned her. 'That wouldn't be helpful.'

'What do you think would be the best outcome for you, Caroline?' Nerys asked.

She gave a small, mirthless laugh. 'Apart from discreetly losing the baby, you mean? I suppose it would be for me to give birth, secretly if possible, and to find a good adoptive home for the baby, perhaps where I could even visit from time to time. Otherwise, I don't know. I suppose for Ralph to come back after the war, and for us to try again, harder, to be married in the way I believe we both hoped for at the outset.' Her lower lip protruded, making her look like a vulnerable child. 'But that's really rather a lot to be wishing for, isn't it?'

Nerys's heart twisted with sympathy. Caroline Bowen was a simple girl who in the end wanted simple things. A husband, love, a family. Was she any different herself?

Myrtle was smiling and her eyes had begun to sparkle. She had lost the bored expression that had marked her more often since Archie had left. She linked a hand with each of the others and drew them into a close circle. 'We're on our own for the rest of the winter. Ralph is in Malaya, Archie's somewhere in the east and Evan isn't coming down from Kargil until the spring thaw. So, united we stand, and this is what we're going to do. We'll *all* be pregnant.'

Nerys said, with a dry catch in her throat, 'I don't know quite how we'll achieve that.'

'Of course you and I won't actually be, unfortunately, but we'll look as if we are. Wrapped up in a *pheran* all winter, with a fire-pot to nurse, who's to know the difference? I've often looked at the Kashmiri ladies and thought as much. Caroline, you'll stay out in the married quarters for just as long as you can hide the pregnancy and convince all those gossiping wives that everything is as usual. Then as soon as that gets too difficult you can claim you're lonely living without Ralph and move in here with me.' She waved a hand. 'There isn't really room for the three of us in the poor old *Garden*, but we'll find a way round that when we need to. At the same time Nerys and I will also be pretending to get plumper and slower, and we'll wrap ourselves up so much that if there is any talk, or any question about where a mysterious baby might actually have come from, no one will be able to point more than the finger of suspicion at anyone.'

She crowed with pleasure at her plan. 'Aren't I a genius? Go on, tell me.'

Nerys said, 'They say madness and genius are closely related. I know which is my verdict.'

Wide-eyed, Caroline was weighing up the idea.

Myrtle swept on: 'You and I, Caroline, can go down to Delhi a couple of times, shopping or visiting. No one will bother us at my house, and you can see a doctor while we're there. Maybe in the last month we'll have to take you to stay somewhere else, away from the watching eyes. Then, when the baby's due, Delhi again. After that, we can look for foster parents, with a view to adoption. There's a war on. Babies are going to be orphaned, aren't they?' Her face was almost feverishly bright now.

Ah, Nerys thought. 'Myrtle?' she prompted gently.

Myrtle and she had never discussed why the McMinns had no children, even when Myrtle had looked after her following her own miscarriage. She had guessed that they had been unable to, for whatever reason, and because her own loss was so often in her mind she had avoided the question.

Myrtle only held up her hand. Her eyes were fixed on Caroline's face. Caroline gnawed her lip. Her situation was desperate enough for her to try anything.

'It might work,' she said at last.

'Nerys? Are you with us?' Myrtle persisted.

They exchanged glances, acknowledging the calculations that they were separately making, and the responsibility for Caroline Bowen and her baby that they would be assuming from now on. 'All right,' she agreed. 'Count on me.'

Caroline's face was brightening. 'You're so good, both of you. I've never in my life had friends like you.' She squeezed their fingers so hard that Nerys feared for the blood flow. 'Friends for ever,' she declared.

'I *am* clever, aren't I?' Myrtle laughed.

That evening, Nerys and Myrtle sat down alone to dinner.

Across the starched tablecloth Nerys said, 'What exactly are you planning? If we're going to be co-conspirators, you know, you'd better tell me everything.'

Myrtle twisted her glass, examining the lights reflected in the depths. 'I want to help Caroline, of course. It's a rotten situation for her.' Then, in a lower voice, she said, 'Archie and I haven't been able to have a child of our own. You'll have guessed that. Archie has always told me that he couldn't countenance adoption. You know, another man's child—' She broke off, sighing in a way that was quite unlike her. But then she lifted her chin and looked straight at Nerys. 'But perhaps if there is a baby, a real one, needing a loving home, he might see it differently. There's a chance, isn't there?'

'I don't know. Perhaps.'

Knowing Archie, who was outwardly the mildest but also the most strong-minded of men, Nerys was doubtful. But seeing the brilliance of Myrtle's eyes she couldn't find it in herself to say so. Her own thoughts were racing on.

A baby, newborn and needing a home. If in the end Myrtle couldn't step in, she could offer to do so herself. An orphan, an Indian baby, how could Evan refuse to help?

'Whatever happens, we've got to look after poor Caroline,' Myrtle said.

'Will you tell me something? What does Archie mean by a three-letter man?'

Myrtle lifted one dark eyebrow. 'It means a queer,' she explained.

'I thought that was probably it.'

'ZAHRA'S SHAWL'

Mair sipped at a glass of warm gin slightly diluted with flat tonic water. Caroline Bowen's eyesight was obviously troubling her because she had to angle her head away from her enviably straight spine just to hold her visitor in partial focus. Mair had begun to explain her mission to Ladakh and Kashmir, but it was too long-winded and she could see that the old lady wasn't following her.

'What did you say? I'm sorry, I don't get many visitors,' she broke in, before Mair had half finished.

The plump attendant had gone away after pouring the gin, but now she shuffled back. She looked discouragingly at Mair. 'I told you. Mrs Bowen is tired today.'

Mair drew her chair closer, taking care not to knock the stool supporting the bandaged leg. 'I'm the one who should be apologising, barging in on you like this.'

Caroline Bowen's smile broke through her confusion. Like a reflection in rippled water, Mair caught a surprising glimpse of the young woman she had once been. A momentary half-recognition snagged in her mind but it was gone as soon as she reached for it.

'Oh, I'm jolly glad to have some company. Aruna and I get pretty bored here on our own, you know. Won't you tell me your name again? My memory's absolutely shocking, I'm afraid.'

'It's Mair.'

'What's that?'

'It's Welsh.'

The white head tipped again as she peered through invisible mists. 'Welsh, eh?'

'Mrs Bowen, do you remember as far back as the 1940s? My maternal grandparents were out in Srinagar in those days, with the Welsh Presbyterian Mission, and I'm trying to trace them. I know it's a very long shot, but I thought you might just remember something . . .'

It was as if the mist thinned to allow Mrs Bowen a glimpse of a familiar view.

'Who were they? Who did you say? I was here, you know – 1941, 1942. Such times, they were. My husband was Indian Army. He was in the defence of Singapore against the Japanese. So many brave men died.'

'Was your husband killed?'

Across the room, Aruna made a move.

The white head turned, the eyes dim and almost sightless again. 'Ralph? No. He was very brave – he won the MC. I'm sorry, dear, I don't know anyone . . . What name did you say? Has our friend got enough to drink, Aruna? Where have you gone?'

'Oh, yes, this is plenty for me,' Mair said quickly. She made a move to gather herself before taking her leave, and Caroline looked up anxiously.

'Don't go just yet. It's heavenly to have a chat like this.'

Mair was uneasy. There was something not quite normal about Caroline Bowen. Perhaps it was just her great age and her apparent isolation in this sunny, ordinary room. 'I don't want to tire you.'

'That's quite all right. I have masses of time to rest, you know. What were we talking about?'

'You mentioned your husband, and the war. Have you been living in Srinagar ever since?'

Again there was a movement from Aruna, this one more definitely an intervention. Caroline lifted her hand.

'No. I went home in 'forty-five. Myrtle and her husband, they stayed on, but most of us went home. After Partition, of course, everything was quite different. The old India was gone. And Kashmir, ah, a sad story. *You* won't remember, Aruna, what it was like in those days. We had such fun. Such marvellous times.' She gave up on the struggle to see the present, and let her head fall back against the chair cushions.

Mair guessed that the images in her mind's eye were much more vivid.

'I was ill for quite a number of years. That was unfortunate, of course. I was in a nursing home in England, and you do lose touch. By the time I was well again, or once they'd decided I was well, I should say, I was widowed, and that's difficult, isn't it?'

They'd decided? Mair wondered. Who might *they* be? 'It must have been.'

'Are you married, dear?'

Mair smiled at her. 'No. It's never happened. Or, strictly speaking, I've never reached a point where it seemed important to make that commitment. I've had boyfriends, but that's what they stayed.'

Caroline was delighted with that. 'How modern. How independent you must be. I'm terribly envious. No widowhood for you, eh?'

'Not without being married first, I suppose.'

'That's marvellous. My advice to you is, stay just the way you are.'

They were both laughing. Once again the younger Caroline shimmered briefly in the old face. This time, Mair almost pinpointed the evasive likeness to someone, but it floated away again. 'So then what happened?' she asked.

'When?'

'After you were widowed?'

'Oh, you don't want to hear about all that. England's a very different place, *quite* different from the country I grew up in.

By the time I had a chance to look about me I realised that India felt more like home to me than England ever would. So I came back out here, and I've stayed ever since. I can manage, even though everything is so expensive.'

'It's time for your medicine,' Aruna said. She picked up a tray, and the almost-empty gin bottle clinked against the empty tonic-water bottle. Mair thought that if Mrs Bowen was living on a small fixed income, her money would certainly stretch much further here in Kashmir than at home in England. Both women watched Aruna as she made her way across the room, evidently on the way to fetch the promised medicine. Mair picked up her rucksack and her brown pashmina.

'I'd better go.' And, as she said it, a face came into sharp focus.

She caught her breath in utter astonishment.

She looked at Mrs Bowen, and immediately she was certain. She burrowed in the bag and brought out the familiar bundle. 'But before I do, may I just show you something?'

She shook out the shawl so that it billowed in the air, then drifted over Caroline Bowen's lap.

The silence deepened in the quiet room. Slowly Caroline gathered a handful of the soft stuff between her fingers and lifted it to her face. She seemed to inhale the scent trapped in its folds, and then, with a great effort, she focused her eyes on the colours of a Kashmiri summer.

A long time seemed to pass.

'Where did you get this?'

'It was with my late grandmother's things.'

There was a beat before Caroline whispered, 'I wish I could see you properly.'

Mair knelt down beside her chair. Caroline's veined claw of a hand reached out and tentatively explored the contours of her cheek and jaw.

She murmured, 'Welsh, didn't you say?'

'Yes. My grandmother's name was Nerys Watkins. I have a photograph of her, with you, here in Srinagar.'

229

'Nerys was my friend. And this,' she held up a bunched handful of soft wool, 'this is Zahra's. Her dowry.'

Caroline's carer came back with the medicine, and found them with the shawl drawn between them like a narrative.

TEN

Winter came. In early December 1941 Japanese troops invaded Malaya. The Indian Army units defending the Malay coast were forced into surrender, and even though they were heavily outnumbered, the Japanese continued their advance down the peninsula towards the Allied stronghold of Singapore. At the same time, almost to the day, Japanese bombs fell on the US Pacific fleet in Pearl Harbor.

The war in Europe had spread to Asia, and in response the Americans began the biggest mobilisation in history.

Far from Srinagar, Captain Ralph Bowen and his company of the Indian 11th Infantry were drawn back to defend the naval base at Sembawang, in the north-east of the island of Singapore. At the same time Archie McMinn, the Indian Railways engineer, at last succeeded in his attempts to get into uniform. Almost at once he found himself co-ordinating rolling stock and personnel to supply the troops in Malaya, and preparing to evacuate thousands of wounded men in the opposite direction.

Across the Himalayas in Kargil, the conscientious objector Parchedig Evan Watkins preached in an almost empty Presbyterian mission hall, and spent his lonely evenings in the mission's tiny, bleak residential quarters tuned in to the war news via the Overseas Service of the BBC. His main

231

consolation, as the cold tightened its grip and the futility of his efforts became harder to deny, was to think of Nerys in the relative comfort and luxury of the Vale of Kashmir. He missed the home she had made for them both in Leh, the noise of small children clapping and singing in her schoolroom, even Diskit's cooking. He prayed humbly for the gift of fortitude, trudged miles through the icy days to small settlements – whose inhabitants received him with frank bewilderment – and realised how intensely he was looking forward to the coming of spring and the reunion with his wife.

For Nerys, Srinagar had a wintry loveliness that the society migrants of the summer season could hardly have imagined.

Smoke from countless wood and charcoal fires curled into the white skies; bare trees were policed by brooding birds; the clopping of *tonga* horses' hoofs was amplified by the frozen silence. When she woke up one morning the lake water was filmy, as if covered by a layer of oil. The next day it had developed a skin of thin, glittering plates, like the markings of some huge reptile, and the one after that it was frozen solid. Moorhens and wagtails left necklaces of spiky prints in the powdery rime, and garlands of icicles festooned the houseboats' carved eaves.

In delight at the beauty of it, she asked Myrtle, 'Does this happen every year?'

'Only about every fourth winter. Before the war, in the years when the lake did freeze, there would be skating parties and sleigh rides. One year the Resident – not this one, his predecessor – held a Jacobean ice fair. It was before I was married, and it was sheer heaven. Everyone wore fancy dress and there was a band playing for the skating and dancing, the Residency cooks roasted kids and a lamb on huge spits on the bank and there were chestnuts on braziers out on the ice. It was the best party of the whole year – people came up from Delhi and Jammu especially for it.'

She sighed for bygone days of glamour. 'There won't be

anything of the kind this time. There isn't a soul here and every damned thing is scarce or rationed or unobtainable.'

'I'm here, and Caroline. We'll just have to devise an ice celebration of our own. Rainer will help.'

'I hope so. We need something to look forward to,' Myrtle agreed. She poured herself some more gin and added a small splash of lime juice.

Rainer had become a regular visitor to the houseboat, appearing at the veranda steps almost as regularly as Caroline did. Myrtle was intrigued by his introductions to Srinagar people on whom she had never set eyes before and who were never going to cross the threshold of the club or pop up at Residency parties.

On the day after Pearl Harbor Rainer took both women to call on his friend the professor. Nerys and Myrtle drank tea with his wife, the musician daughter and other female relatives, while the men sat in another room sharing a pipe and discussing politics and war. Myrtle didn't protest at this automatic segregation, although Nerys had expected her to do so. The professor's women were sharp and surprisingly talkative, as well as slyly funny, and when they got back to the *Garden of Eden* that evening Myrtle declared it was the most interesting time she'd spent in ages.

She had decreed that Caroline should also go out and about as much as possible before her shape became too pronounced. As December passed they took tea or coffee in the echoing confines of the club almost every other day, and were becoming such a familiar sight in their usual corner that the handful of regulars did no more than raise a hand as they shuffled past on their way to the bar or the bridge table. Whenever they left the houseboat the women were slow-moving, shapeless mounds of wool, sheepskin, pashmina and thick tweed. Quite quickly, Nerys recognised that Myrtle's absurd plan was in fact rather a clever one.

However, Rainer had only seen the women together twice before he asked Nerys, the next time they were alone, if she would please tell him what was going on with Mrs Bowen and the *pherans*.

'*Pherans*?' she asked, with what she hoped was wide-eyed innocence.

'That's right. The three of you looked like a row of galleons under sail at the club yesterday afternoon, and I'm sure there will be questions in the book about the heating because lady members seem obliged to wear their outdoor garments in the drawing room. Hmm?'

'I feel the cold,' Nerys offered.

She had acquired a *kangri* and was genuinely glad of it. The fire-pot was a bulbous earthenware container, about the size – well, she admitted to herself, with a flicker of laughter, about the size of a full-term pregnancy – encased in a wicker basket. Every morning Majid filled it with a scoop of glowing embers from the stove in the kitchen boat and brought it to her bedroom. She hugged it against her belly while she summoned up the resolve to slide from under the blankets and dive into her clothes, and once she was dressed she settled it within her various layers before scuttling down the chill planks to the saloon, where the stove was already glowing and Myrtle was huddled beside the coffee pot. Myrtle wore a lambskin hat with flaps that covered her ears, and a pair of fleece-lined gloves with the fingertips cut off so she never had to remove them. Within a radius of three or four feet of the stove it was warm enough to sit and talk, but beyond that lay the realm of ice.

Rainer merely shook his head. He curled a long arm and rubbed his hair so that it stood out like a mane. 'Have I ever listed the four principles of stage magic for you? Please stop me if I have.'

'No, I don't believe so.' Nerys was already laughing. They were always having conversations like this, mock-solemn and formal, yet bubbling under the surface with amusement and flirtation.

'The four principles,' he counted them off on his fingers, 'are misdirection, distraction, disguise and simulation. If, for example, you tell an audience that a jug seemingly full of white liquid is in fact full of milk, that audience will automatically believe you because their collective mind looks no further. I think you three ladies are cleverly employing all four principles to your own ends. As a professional I admire the technique, but as a friend I cannot help feeling somewhat excluded.'

The plaintive note he managed to project made Nerys laugh harder. 'It's not my secret to share,' she protested.

'Ah, well, then. But if I were to offer a fellow illusionist's advice, it would be, ah, that too *much* of a distraction only attracts attention.'

'I see. Thank you,' she said.

That evening she warned Myrtle and Caroline that Rainer had been asking questions. She thought it would be a good idea to tell him what was happening because he might be useful to them in the future.

Caroline was uncertain. 'Is he discreet?' she asked.

Nerys said that she was absolutely sure he was, and Myrtle had something else to add. 'Rainer Stamm is one big secret himself. You remember those two Americans we met at his house, Nerys?'

She did, and Myrtle smiled. 'One of them had had a couple of Scotches, and took rather a shine to me.'

Nerys remembered that, too.

'Well. I thought he might be a spy, but *he* believes that Rainer really is one.'

Nerys was amused. 'Our side or theirs, do you think?'

Caroline looked from one to the other. 'Surely he'd be on our side. He couldn't be a Nazi, could he? Even though he's Swiss?'

Myrtle patted her hand. 'I should think all the best spies have that couldn't-possibly-be quality, darling. But don't worry. I'm inclined to trust Mr Stamm, and Nerys is right – he could be helpful to us.'

It was agreed that Nerys should take him into their confidence.

She was at Rainer's house the next evening, while Myrtle and Caroline were putting in an appearance at a sale of handicrafts and gifts to raise funds to send sweets and cigarettes to the men in Malaya. Myrtle had said that she for one didn't care if she never saw another item of local papier-mâché, and certainly didn't intend to present anyone she knew with a pen tray or a card holder. If she received any such Christmas gift herself, they should take note, she would wait for the lake to thaw and then pitch it in.

Caroline nodded. 'I shall remember that,' she said.

Myrtle and Nerys were sometimes unsure whether she was joking or merely being solemn.

It was very cold in Rainer's room. The sky beyond the uncurtained window was a shower of stars, hollow with frost. They were sitting looking out at the black river water and the yellow points of lamplight showing from houses on the opposite bank. In their wire cage, the pair of white doves he used for some of his tricks were asleep with their heads beneath their wings.

'Who is the father?' Rainer asked, once Nerys had outlined the facts.

'I don't know if I'm supposed to tell you that.'

'I can probably guess.'

'You probably can. You don't miss much.'

There was a small silence. Rainer's mood could dip into sudden melancholy. 'I do miss things,' he said, in a low voice.

'I didn't mean that sort of missing . . .'

'I know what you meant.' He leant forward. Nerys was swathed in blankets as well as all her clothes, and his hand slipped between the outer layers to find hers and then clasp it. 'You are warm.'

'I am. Mine is an exceptionally good *pheran*. I don't even need my *kangri* in here.'

'This plan is Myrtle's, I take it?'

'Yes. But we are all agreed. Any one of us could be pregnant, or all three, or none.'

'Aren't you worried about your reputation, Nerys?'

'No,' she said, after reflection. She didn't care what Srinagar might think.

He came a little closer, his head blotting out the window and the stars. 'Mrs Watkins,' he whispered. Briefly, he lifted her hand to his lips.

'Yes,' she said.

Rainer was looking at her with minute attention. She didn't believe that anyone else had ever looked at her with this degree of precise and steady scrutiny. 'Nerys, you do understand what is happening between the two of us, don't you?'

'Of course. I'm not Caroline Bowen,' she said, with a touch of heat. He couldn't think she was so innocent or so obtuse as *not* to know.

Not rebuffed in the least, he smiled. 'You are a thousand times more desirable than Mrs Bowen, pretty and English and adorably pliant though she is.'

They sat quietly for a moment. Nerys's pulse steadied until she could hear the creak of old wood and the gentle hiss of the fire, not just the pounding of her heart.

Understanding what was happening meant acknowledging the moral dilemma that faced her, but it was also to do with anticipation; the fine control of a serious decision weighed in the balance. To become Rainer's lover – or not – was her choice as much as his, that was what he was indicating, and she was intoxicated by the oxygen of independence that it gave her. She had a sense of the meek selves, the effacing and mildly baffled versions of herself, that had advanced to this point. As if she had been a caterpillar, then a frozen chrysalis, and now was on the brink of becoming a surprising butterfly.

She sat upright. 'I think we both understand quite well,' she said. She held out the small, thick green glass that he had given her and indicated that she would take another half-inch of Rainer's French cognac. Decent drink of any kind was becoming hard to find in Srinagar. Then she settled herself in her cocoon of blankets, her back comfortably against the wormy old panelling. Brandy fumed pleasantly in her head as she sipped it. 'Do you know,' she said, in amusement, 'that various people suspect you of being a spy?'

'Do they, indeed?'

'And are you?'

He enjoyed his reputation, she could see that. He almost tossed his mane.

'No, my darling. I'm a mountaineer, and a magician.'

'In that order?'

'Always in that order. I make my living as a stage illusionist and I have given shows all over Europe. I could mention crowned heads, if I were trying to impress you. But, in my heart, the mountains are always first. I will get to Nanga Parbat whatever the British have to say, and I will claim the peak for my friend Matthew Forbes.'

Images of cruel white peaks as jagged as sharks' teeth glimmered in Nerys's head, and anxiety stirred. She didn't want even to imagine Rainer meeting the same fate as Matthew. 'When?'

He laughed at her, widening his red mouth, pleased to note her concern. 'When I can. But now, with the war so close,' he shrugged, 'I have other concerns. I wish to help the Allies, naturally. The alternative is not to be thought about. I am an expert in camouflage, and in other forms of deception that may have a military value, and I have offered my services to the British. But, as you can see, they have not yet taken me quite seriously.' He waved his hand at the room, and its strange clutter of painted props.

'They ought to,' Nerys said. She wasn't quite sure whether or not she believed Rainer's innocent account of himself.

He lowered his voice. 'Thank you. We shall see. In the meantime . . . I find that Srinagar draws me, and holds my heart in a way that I never expected.'

A small silence fell as they turned their heads in the same arc to gaze over the lights in the labyrinth of the old town.

'I need your help,' Rainer said, after a while.

'Of course I'll help you. Tell me how.'

238

'Wait until you hear. You may change your mind. Because of my various projects I am eager to maintain cordial relations with the Resident, your friend Mr Fanshawe.'

'He's hardly my friend. I'm not even on the social scale,' Nerys protested.

'Mr Fanshawe has asked me to put on a morale-raising magic performance on Christmas night at the Residency. It will be for the entertainment of the staff and their families, what's left of the regimental headquarters, Srinagar society of a certain sort. You will easily imagine.'

Nerys could.

'To manage a show properly, however, I will need a stage assistant. It's usual for the assistant to be female, and preferably of exotic extraction. Mysterious Madame Moth, Miss Soo Ling straight from Shanghai, that sort of thing.'

'I see. Rainer, I've never been on a stage in my life. And Welsh is not exotic.'

'You are not following me. The four principles, remember? Disguise. You will have to remove your *pheran*, I'm afraid, but it can be replaced by flowing robes. Chinese, I think definitely. A little round black hat, a mask. Charming.'

'Will I be sawn in half?'

Their eyes met.

'I haven't devised the programme yet. That may only be the beginning. And I am not an amateur, Mrs Watkins. We shall rehearse, and rehearse, and then rehearse some more. Are you willing?'

'Ready, and more than willing,' she managed to answer.

And later, when she mentioned that Myrtle was nostalgic for the glamorous pre-war ice parties, Rainer said that in return for Nerys's services as stage assistant he would come up with an idea for a Christmas celebration.

Nerys reported all this back to Myrtle and Caroline before they set off for Delhi, avowedly to retreat from the punishing cold and to shop for Christmas, but in fact discreetly to consult a doctor about the progress of Caroline's pregnancy.

239

'You seem very happy,' Myrtle said, looking at her face.

'Yes,' Nerys agreed simply.

'Are you in love with him?'

Nerys glanced round to make sure that Caroline was out of earshot. 'I don't think that would be entirely welcome.'

'That doesn't answer my question. Have fun, remember. Caroline and I will be back in Srinagar on the twenty-third.'

The excursion to Delhi was not enjoyable. The journey, by road and then train, was excruciatingly slow and uncomfortable, and Caroline was anxious and tearful. The Hindu doctor they had found examined her and brusquely informed her that she was quite healthy and could expect to deliver in approximately fourteen weeks' time. He was more interested in where she planned her confinement, and wanted to know why, if her husband was in the army, she was not under the care of the military hospital.

They hurried away, and Caroline declared that whatever else happened she wasn't going anywhere near that doctor ever again. Even worse, on their way back through Connaught Place from his office to Myrtle's bungalow, Caroline stopped to lean against a pillar and catch her breath. Delhi was warm after Srinagar and they had had to put aside their *pherans*, swathing themselves instead in loose silk duster coats and trailing scarves. At that very moment there was a cry of recognition. A woman stepping out of her car at the kerb turned out to be the sister of the major's wife, Caroline's next-door neighbour.

'How divine to see you both. Are you going out to tea? Would you like a lift?'

Caroline told Nerys that she jumped six inches in the air, absolutely certain that she had been resting with her hand on the top of her bulge. The woman was staring at their unconventional turn-out. It was only through Myrtle pretending to be ill, claiming that she was going to be sick or perhaps faint, that they managed to make their escape into the crowds.

'Our driver is waiting. Do give my best wishes to Mrs

Dunkeley,' Caroline called over her shoulder, adding, 'That poisonous witch,' for only Myrtle to hear.

Myrtle told Nerys, 'Delhi's too dangerous. There are too many people with nothing to occupy them but gossip. Unless Caroline spends the next three months in purdah inside the *Garden of Eden*, sooner or later someone we know will catch a glimpse of her and within minutes the entire Empire will hear of it.'

Nerys agreed. 'We'll think of something,' she said.

At eleven o'clock sharp on Christmas Eve, in crackling cold under a colourless sky, two teams assembled on a swept-clean expanse of lake ice directly in front of the *Garden of Eden*. Rainer's idea was a cricket match.

The Residency staff seized on his scheme with enthusiasm, and had in the end taken it over from him.

'After all, I am only Swiss. What do I know of team sports?' Rainer murmured.

The British team was made up of the handful of young men who represented the wartime skeleton of diplomatic staff in the city, some Residency bearers, and the very few army officers who had managed a few hours' Christmas leave. The team captain was Mr Fanshawe. The Srinagar side was captained by Rainer's Pandit friend, the university professor, who was a passionate cricketer. He had assembled an impressive-looking team of colleagues and students, Muslim as well as Hindu. The wicket-keeper was a majestic Sikh.

Stumps and balls had been extracted from the Residency stores and the players warmed up with sprints on the pitch. Most of them wore cricket whites over many layers of woolly insulation, and the effect was of twenty-two very fat men squeezed into small boys' clothes. There had been some difficulty over how to embed the stumps in the ice, but Rainer produced a tool designed for fixing ropes into glaciers and bored six neat holes of the precise depth and diameter required. He filled in the waiting time by juggling with the ball and some apples borrowed from one of the vendors who had eagerly crowded down to the boundary. The Srinagar side won the toss and elected to bowl, and Mr Fanshawe called out to him, 'Now then, none of your magic tricks with that ball, Mr Stamm.'

'For that you will have to wait until tomorrow, sir.'

The veranda of the *Garden of Eden* served as the pavilion, and it was packed with batsmen and spectators. Inside the crowded houseboat Majid and his helpers served hot toddies, fried *pakoras* and plates of mince pies. Under Majid's sceptical eye Nerys had managed to bake the pies in the oven of the kitchen boat, in between the long hours of rehearsal that Rainer insisted upon.

'How is the magic going?' Myrtle enquired.

'Actually, it's hell. Really hard work, mental and physical, and I'm not allowed even a flicker of a mistake.'

'We're all anticipating quite a spectacle.'

Nerys pulled a face of extreme apprehension.

Rainer put on a white coat, oddly matched with a pair of crampons, and crunched out to the umpire's position mid-wicket. He produced a tin whistle out of the air and blew it to signal the start of the game.

The cricket match had drawn a large crowd. The boundary was ringed with food- and *chai*-sellers, their glowing braziers supported on bricks. There was a strong smell of spiced mutton and delicious bread. Men jostled each other to get the best view and a few veiled women strolled in inquisitive groups over the ice from the bank. Children screamed and raced each other until the first ball sailed overhead for a six and everyone scattered. The biggest boys chased the fielder as he skidded after the flying ball.

Some of Mrs Fanshawe's friends and the club wives had persuaded *tonga* drivers to edge their vehicles on to the ice and now they sat under fur wraps beneath the *tonga* canopies, applauding the batsmen as they slithered between the wickets. Mrs Fanshawe herself sat in a large wicker chair like a throne.

In the background the horses blew into their nose-bags,

clouded breath rising as their harnesses jingled. The drivers cheered wildly with everyone else when the Residency third secretary, the star batsman, was clean bowled.

Every single person present was so heavily wrapped and scarved against the cold that they looked like dumplings on legs, taking careful steps over the slippery surface. Caroline's cheeks glowed. The end of her nose and the tips of her earlobes were bright pink. 'What fun,' she called to Nerys.

There was a howl as Mr Fanshawe was spectacularly caught in the slips. The fielder skidded over the ice on his belly, the ball triumphantly held aloft. The Residency team was crumbling under fierce pressure from the professor's eleven. It had been agreed that the match was to consist of just twelve overs each side, and faced with the need to score quickly, the batsmen were risking everything. In rapid succession they pulled on their gloves and descended the steps of the houseboat, striding out to the wicket with bat tucked manfully under one arm. Three minutes later they would make the return journey, raising their caps to the Resident's wife. More familiar than Nerys with the rules of village cricket, Myrtle, Caroline and all the other wives laughed and clapped at this absurd version of the game. More hot toddies and the sherry decanter circulated freely.

Every time another man was out, the players and spectators on the ice leapt and yelled, punching the air and hugging one another with glee.

'Most unsporting,' tutted Mrs Fanshawe.

Small boys glissaded across the wicket and Rainer chased them off. At the end of the twelfth over, the scorer chalked on the blackboard propped against the houseboat steps, *British Resident's XI, 32 for 8.*

By the interval, in which Majid and his helpers served Christmas cake, with the option of tea or more alcohol, the party had become thoroughly festive.

'Such a clever idea. You are a genius,' Myrtle said to Rainer, and Nerys felt the glow of reflected glory. Rainer accepted the praise as his due and went crunching out again to resume his umpiring duties.

The Srinagar opening batsman was out first ball. There was a roar of dismay. Mr Fanshawe, in the deep field, permitted himself a tiny smile. The new batsman, magnificent in an enormous pair of blindingly white pads, was the professor. He made his slow way to the wicket, took his position and hit a six. Three balls later, he did the same again.

Even Nerys found herself edging to the front of the crowd. The sun now emerged as a flat disc of silver, striking rainbow glimmers off the tips of icicles. Myrtle and Caroline excitedly nudged beside her and, shoulder to shoulder, they made an insulated wall of scarves and *pherans*.

The game didn't last much longer. The professor hit his sixth six and a forest of arms shot into the air, with a cheer and a drumming of feet ecstatic enough to be welcoming independence for Kashmir. The players streamed back across the ice, the fielders' cold-nipped faces beaming with pleasure. The vendors immediately closed up their tiny stalls and pushed the braziers to the bank.

'Bad luck,' called the professor, from amid a crowd of supporters.

'Jolly well done,' Mr Fanshawe replied, as the scorer chalked up *Professor Pran's XI, 36 for 1*. 'We must make this a regular event whenever we have ice. Good show, Mr Stamm.'

Rainer bowed, and Nerys wondered how much longer it would be before the Nanga Parbat permit was granted.

Majid was making another circuit with the drinks, but most of the players and guests were beginning to take their leave. Everyone wished each other a very merry Christmas.

'So pleasing to see the men enjoying a game, Hindus and Muslims, Christians and Sikhs all together, don't you think?' Mrs Fanshawe said, as she stepped into the Resident's flagged car.

'If only religious understanding and mutual tolerance were quite as simple as she is,' Rainer murmured, in Nerys's ear.

244

For the last few minutes he had been in an animated conversation with the Sikh wicket-keeper. His eyes glittered. 'Come with me,' he said. He took her arm and steered her towards the bank.

Two of the waiting *tonga* drivers had harnessed up again and drawn their vehicles behind a line gouged in the ice. The wicket-keeper leapt into one as Rainer handed Nerys into the other. The drivers brandished their whips and the horses' breath rose in clouds. The *tongas* creaked and strained and impatient hoofs clattered on the ice. A scowling man in a flat Pathan cap took his place with one foot on either side of the line and raised his arm.

'What's going on?' Nerys demanded. Her voice was sharp with alarm.

Rainer settled back in the creased leather seat. 'A small wager. Look at our horse – he's a fine specimen.'

'*What?*'

The man's arm dropped. The drivers whipped up and the horses started off at such a speed that Nerys was flung backwards. Rainer circled her with one arm.

'You have a ringside seat. It's a race to the other side and back.'

The two horses reached a gallop, their nailed shoes sending up showers of chipped ice. It was incredible that neither of them skidded. The old *tongas* swayed and groaned in protest at the flying speed. Nerys's hands covered her mouth as the wind flayed her cheeks. She didn't know whether to scream or weep with terror. Rainer only slid to the edge of the seat, urging their driver to go even faster. As they reached the far bank the man reined in, and as soon as the pace slackened Rainer jumped out. The instant his feet smashed on to the ice he was running. Reaching the bank, he seized a branch from the old mulberry tree that grew there and raced back again. Waving his own branch, their opponent was only three seconds behind them as they wheeled for the opposite shore.

They were heading back towards the houseboats, following

the arrow of their outbound tracks. The thrill of the race surged through her but at that moment Nerys heard a crack like a pistol shot. She felt their horse check itself and almost stumble. Her eyes were stinging with cold but she saw huge webs of fissures radiating ahead of them as the ice started to give way under the *tonga* wheels.

'Faster,' Rainer howled. He bounded forwards to thump the driver between his shoulder-blades. 'Go faster, man. It's the only way.'

The whip flailed and somehow the horse recovered itself and galloped on. In their wake, icy water welled up and flooded like pools of quicksilver to cover the cracks. Off to one side the other driver had seen their difficulty and veered aside to the safety of thicker ice. Rainer knew that the race was theirs if they could outpace the ice breaking up, and the horse instinctively sensed it too. It was tiring, its head plunging from side to side, but it kept going as the driver's whip stung its lathered flanks. Long seconds later, they floundered to the margin of safer ice and the mirrors of water lay behind them.

The small crowd of remaining guests had been watching, transfixed by horror. Rainer's winning *tonga* drew up and the horse shuddered to a standstill, its hoofs splayed and head hanging piteously. Rainer triumphantly brandished the winner's mulberry branch but everyone was too shocked to applaud. Myrtle came forward and took Nerys's arms as her trembling legs almost gave way on the *tonga* step. 'You're all right now. There was a moment when I was afraid you weren't going to be,' she murmured to her.

'Me too,' Nerys gasped.

'Nothing venture. We won, didn't we?' Rainer returned. He took out a roll of banknotes and began to count money into their driver's outstretched hand. Nerys patted the horse's sweat-blackened side and made her unsteady way back to the *Garden of Eden*.

The other horse trotted up and Rainer beamingly shook hands with his vanquished opponent.

Myrtle was still outside, saying goodbye to the shocked stragglers, when Rainer shouldered his way into the saloon, seeming too large and too elated for the confined space.

Nerys rounded on him, anger making her cheeks blaze. 'What did you think you were doing? We could all have drowned.'

'I know,' he whispered to her, coming so close that his breath was hot on her face. 'But we didn't, and you were excited, weren't you? Don't pretend you're not a hundred times more alive at this moment than you felt an hour ago.'

It was true. She was aware of every square inch of her own skin, and every detail of her surroundings. She was minutely aware of the vivid colours of Myrtle's silk cushions, of the breath flooding her lungs, the sweat of fear that was cooling the nape of her neck.

Life was precious, every gleam in the wood panelling, each tiny pucker of fabric, was exquisitely beautiful, and when she looked up at Rainer he caught her shoulders and drew her even closer. 'You see? You do feel it. You didn't faint or scream or make any female display. You don't need cushions, or allowances made, or a man who will protect and diminish you. I knew it. We have the same spirit, and I recognised you the first time I saw you.'

Their mouths touched for an instant. Longing for him raced through Nerys's veins, flooding after the surges of fear and the sweet thrill of finding herself alive.

It was only Myrtle coming up the steps and the sound of her footsteps kicking the ice off the veranda that forced them apart. Nerys was struggling to breathe as Rainer stepped away.

'I think the match was enjoyable, don't you?' he said smoothly to Myrtle.

'It wouldn't have been an enjoyable day if my best friend had drowned in front of my eyes,' she snapped.

'But I didn't drown. I didn't even get my feet wet,' Nerys said.

Rainer inclined his head to Myrtle. 'I'll leave you both now.

I must go and rehearse for tomorrow evening. I wish you a very happy Christmas.'

Nerys followed him out into the crystalline whiteness.

'Don't forget to run through the routine in your head,' he ordered. 'I don't want a single thing to go wrong with one single trick.'

'Nothing will go wrong,' she answered.

His eyes moved over her face, as explicit as a touch. 'Tomorrow,' he said. He didn't mean the Residency magic show.

She raised her hand to shield her eyes against the light and watched him walk away.

Tomorrow, tomorrow, she repeated. The word and the anticipation expanded to fill her head with wicked gold.

Myrtle had shed her *pheran* and was reclining in her chair next to the stove.

'Don't be disapproving,' Nerys begged.

Myrtle waved her cigarette. 'When have I ever gone in for disapproval? What I am experiencing is jealousy, my girl.'

'You know you said about not wanting to see your best friend drown?'

'Yes.'

'Am I really your best friend?'

Myrtle blew out a calculated smoke-ring. 'Yes, Nerys, you are.'

Nerys had never had a best friend before. There had been the girls at teacher training college and from her grammar school, but none of them was anything like Myrtle McMinn. Even with the glimmer of *tomorrow* meshing her consciousness, Nerys thought that this simple statement was the best Christmas present she would ever receive.

The next morning, Caroline joined them and they walked the short way through thin spirals of blowing snow to the English church. The wooden pews were packed with the hardy remnants of Srinagar Club society. Mr Fanshawe read the lesson, and the congregation sang the familiar carols. The stoves on either side of the nave had been lit in good time, but still they could see their breath clouding the air as they listened to the Christmas sermon. The three women would only have been conspicuous if they had *not* been wrapped from head to foot in their thickest clothes.

Back at the *Garden of Eden*, as they exchanged non-papier-mâché gifts and laughed over Majid's loyal but approximate interpretation of a traditional Christmas dinner, Myrtle warned that they would have to make a new, more ambitious plan for the next three months.

Caroline nodded her agreement. She was biting her lip as she said, 'It's getting harder to hide my shape from the servants.'

Nerys put in, 'At the very least you must move in here with Myrtle in the new year.'

'But where will *you* go?'

'Don't worry about that. I need to find a little place of my own to live. As soon as the passes open, Evan will be here.' She gave the statement deliberate emphasis.

Tomorrow had turned into today.

Caroline said, 'The snow always melts in the end. I wonder, will it ever be the end of the war?'

'That must come too,' Nerys said.

A small silence fell as they looked at one another. The world beyond the fragile, lamplit capsule of the houseboat was rocked by dangers known and unknown, and to imagine what might happen drew the bond between the three women even more tightly. Caroline placed her hand over her stomach, where the baby had begun to kick. Their own future seemed just as uncertain as whatever lay ahead for her unborn child.

Myrtle broke the silence by producing a bottle of champagne that had been immersed in a bucket of lake ice. 'This, my dears, is one of the last bottles of decent bubbly remaining in the entire twenty-one-gun state of Kashmir.' She filled their glasses. 'Happy Christmas, and here's to us and all those we care for.'

Nerys and Caroline echoed her words, but it was a sombre toast.

'This evening, we have Nerys's grand stage début to look forward to,' Myrtle recalled, once she had drained her glass. Nerys covered her face with her hands, because she didn't need reminding, and they were cheerful again.

The ballroom at the Residency was decorated with a huge Christmas tree. Wives of the regiment, with their children who were too young yet to be at school in England, their ayahs, Residency staff and most of the congregation from this morning were sitting in rows of small gilded chairs. There was an atmosphere of festive anticipation.

Nerys peered through a chink in the makeshift curtains rigged up at the back of Rainer's plinth stage, which had been transferred from his house and erected by a team of bearers. Her stomach was a mass of butterflies. In the sea of faces she could see Caroline, wearing a black velvet evening cape with a hood trimmed in ermine, borrowed from Myrtle, and Myrtle in a voluminous empire-line swirl of midnight-blue satin.

Mr Fanshawe made a speech of welcome and Nerys took her place in the wings. She looked across at Rainer, poised on the spot where the curtains would part to reveal him. Unlike his regular evening clothes, his stage costume was spruce and his white tie starched and pristine. She had been intending perhaps to blow him a good-luck kiss, acknowledging their intimacy as well as her stage fright, but then she saw that his eyes were closed and he was completely absorbed in himself.

A mountaineer first, then a magician, she remembered. After that, a man.

The Resident boomed, as if he were a music-hall master of ceremonies, 'Ladies and gentlemen, Mr Rainer Stamm's mysterious medley of magic!'

With two bearers out of sight in the wings hauling on the ropes, the curtains swept aside and the show was on.

For the first segment Rainer ran through a series of tricks

250

with the linked rings, playing cards, billiard balls and scarves. The audience was pleased, and applauded vigorously. Then came the moment. He announced that he would be joined by Miss Soo Ling, just arrived in Srinagar all the way from distant Shanghai.

Wondering if she was actually going to faint from nerves, Nerys pulled down her black carnival mask, patted the black straw hat that hid her hair and swept on stage. She folded her hands inside the sleeves of her flowing Chinese robes and gave a deep bow to acknowledge the storm of clapping.

As she did so, something strange happened. Her fear completely evaporated. She felt calm, clear in the head, and utterly exhilarated.

To start with, the part she had to play in the magic was merely supportive. There was the water trick, in which she passed Rainer the crystal jugs, the trick with the doves that he plucked out of the air, in which she had to make sure their basket was placed in exactly the right spot where it was not visible to any section of the audience, and then the mango tree, where she planted the seed from which – with the aid of mirrors – a mango tree magically grew and fruited. Miss Soo Ling picked the ripe fruit, and ceremoniously presented it to Mrs Fanshawe who was sitting in the middle of the front row. All through this, Nerys played the silent role that she and Rainer had devised. She was pert, sometimes refusing to do what he told her. The children loved the show of disobedience.

By the time it came to the last trick, the show's finale, Nerys knew that nothing could go wrong.

The trick was the magic box. The real responsibility for pulling it off was hers, not Rainer's, but they had rehearsed it so meticulously that she was looking forward to performing it to perfection. Laughter and applause rang in her ears and she soaked it all up; it was as if another of Rainer's tricks had finally hatched this glamorous performer from the chrysalis of a quiet schoolteacher and wife to a Presbyterian minister.

The box, a red-painted structure made in three sections with a series of shuttered portholes painted with silver moons and stars, was carried on by two bearers and positioned on the plinth. As soon as she saw it, Nerys was to drop all her cheeky airs and try to run offstage. Rainer made a show of barring the way and marching her to the box. The audience took sides, cheering either for him or for Soo Ling.

The box was just big enough for her to stand up inside it. He opened the door, demonstrated that it was empty, bundled Nerys in and turned the key in the lock.

Once she was incarcerated, Rainer gave the audience a wink. He lit a cigarette, strolled away to a gramophone placed on a side table and selected a record. The music was Ravel's 'Bolero'. They had rehearsed the precise progress of each phase of the trick to the rising beat of the music.

Rainer cast his cigarette aside. From the wings, he brought out a huge silver sword and polished the blade with a silk handkerchief. With a horizontal sweep of the blade he sliced cleanly between the top and middle sections of the box. The audience gasped. He did the same with the second and third sections. Then he lifted the top third away, and put it down on the plinth. The second box followed.

Flat on her back, sliding on a wheeled trolley in the confined space within the plinth, Nerys heard a child's clear voice call out, 'Chinese lady cut in bits, Mummy.'

There was a muffled gale of laughter, and Ravel was getting louder and faster.

All she had to do was slide very fast between the three trapdoors in the floor of the plinth, get into a crouch and pop her head into one box for Rainer to open the porthole, slide back as he juggled with the boxes, slip her arms into place to wave through the portholes in the second and, as the trick gathered momentum, to stand on her head beneath the third so that her black-stockinged legs and feet in Chinese slippers stuck out upside-down.

She was sliding in the airless space when she felt a sudden jolt and a sideways tilt. Instead of making a smooth glide the trolley jammed at a standstill. At first she couldn't work out what had gone wrong but, gasping for breath, she squeezed her body into place just as Rainer snapped open the next port-hole to reveal her serene masked face. She could hear the laughter and clapping and the relentless crescendo of 'Bolero'. Below, the trolley was now a barrier to her next desperate moves. She scrambled from box to box, losing the sequence in her panic. The inevitable moment came when the shuffle of boxes got ahead of her and a porthole was opened to reveal thin air.

'My God,' Rainer yelled, and there was a burst of laughter. He slammed it shut again.

Recovering herself, Nerys managed to fold her bruised limbs into place. He slammed the door, rapped twice on the box, and when he opened it the second time, there she was.

She made the next position, choking with dust, wildly kicking her slippers in the air to gales of laughter, but as she wrestled for the final place a nail in the floorboards tore a long rent in her sleeve and in the soft flesh of her arm beneath. Biting back a scream of agony she swarmed over the ruined trolley and forced herself upright again in the three boxes that Rainer had now restacked in their original position. Over the last bars of music she heard the tap with the key that indicated he was about to open the door. She pasted a smile on her face.

The door swung open, exactly on the beat.

'She is mended!' shouted the same child.

Rainer took her hand and led her out to take a bow. She smiled harder beneath the mask and held his fingers tight, keeping her arm clamped to her side because she could feel that her sleeve was soaked with blood.

The curtains finally fell to a storm of clapping and stamping.

He spun on her, hot with anger. 'What the hell were you doing? You nearly ruined it.'

'I nearly ruined it? How dare you? The wheel must have come off the blasted trolley. I damn nearly killed myself for your bloody stupid trick.'

Flooded with pain and rage, Nerys swung her good arm at him but he caught her by the wrist before she could slap his face. 'You're a wildcat. I've never heard you swear before.' He was grinning, relishing this unexpected aspect of her.

'I couldn't slide the trolley. It blocked the way. I had to crawl on my stomach, and I've ripped my arm and—'

His smile vanished. 'Let me see.'

There were drops of blood on the stage and her hand was smeared with it. Rainer rolled back the soaked sleeve and saw the wound. He took in a breath. 'I'm so sorry. Forgive me. Here . . .' He whisked a string of knotted handkerchiefs from inside his spotless waistcoat and roughly bound up her arm. Over his shoulder he told the nearest Residency bearer that he was taking Mrs Watkins away to have a cut urgently dressed. Then he lifted her off her feet and ran to the makeshift dressing room, bundled her into her *pheran*, which had been hanging there on a hook, and raced past startled faces to the back of the big house.

'I can walk,' Nerys protested, as they burst out into the navy-blue night. Rainer was staggering a little under her weight, and his heavy footprints wavered in the carpet of silver frost.

'Don't you want to be abducted?' He groaned.

'You can't abduct me. I'm the free spirit, the woman who doesn't need cushions, remember?' She squirmed out of his arms, linking her good hand in his as they raced across the yard past Mr Fanshawe's staring grooms and guards, and through a gate into a lane. By a stroke of luck they came upon a *tonga* making its way to the front driveway in the hope of picking up a fare at the end of the party. A moment later, for the second time in two days, they were under a swaying canopy as the driver whipped his horse into a flying gallop.

As ever, it was cold in the raftered room overlooking the Jhelum river.

'Take this off,' he ordered her. She unbuttoned the Chinese

robe and let it drop at her feet. Rainer kissed her naked shoulders before wrapping her up in a pashmina shawl. Then he lifted her chin and kissed her mouth, holding her against him as if she weighed nothing.

'You are magical,' he murmured, after a long time. With difficulty he stepped back. 'Wait. Sit here. Let me dress your arm.'

He brought a bowl of water and bathed the ragged cut, announcing that it was just a flesh wound and she must be healthy to bleed so freely. Then he flooded it with iodine and she yelped and swore again.

When he had finished bandaging her he gave her a glass of his good cognac.

'I should thank you for rescuing the box trick from disaster,' he said, in a solemn voice.

'I did, didn't I?'

'The trolley wheel must have been damaged when the porters carried it over there.'

'You did your own rescue, when my arms didn't wave out of that box. They loved it, I could hear.'

Rainer clinked his glass against hers. She could see the weatherbeaten furrows of his lion's face. 'We make a good team,' he said. His praise was precious to her.

Then, very gently, he took her hands and helped her to her feet. They looked into one another's eyes.

Rainer said, 'I think now it is the right time. If you agree?'

Nerys inclined her head. She felt like his friend and coeval now, and this touch of intimacy reignited her desire. For all the moral questions and the guilt in anticipation that had plagued her, and despite her emergence as a woman who could make her own choices, now that the moment had come it didn't seem to be a question or even a choice. It was simple, and inevitable.

He lifted her up and carried her to his bed. Then he untied the hangings, so they fell and curtained off the glimmering room.

'This is all the world,' he told her. 'For tonight.'

He knelt over her, and took off her remaining clothing piece by piece. She let him do it, and was surprised at her pleasure in his admiration.

At last he whispered, with a quaint formality that touched her heart, 'If you will permit me?'

She did. She permitted him everything, and she took all the freedom he offered her in return.

She might never have known this, she thought.

She might easily never have learnt this language that in the end came naturally, and the delight would have been locked away for ever, like a wonderful unperformed trick hidden in one of the magician's boxes.

But a long time later, as she drifted into sleep, it was Evan who hovered in her thoughts. She saw him with the eerie clarity of a dream, her husband with his awkward innocence and the anxiety that constantly stalked him. She felt a surge of tenderness towards him, and a prickle of shame at what she had just done. But even so she couldn't regret it. She suspected that she might never do so.

With his arms tightly wound round her, Rainer was already asleep. She listened to his breathing, and in the end she surrendered her drowsy inquisition and slept too.

There was a distant banging, and a voice calling. As Nerys surfaced she had the sense that the noise had persisted for quite a long time. Rainer's arm lay heavy across her chest and she twisted to disengage herself. Opening a chink in the bed's curtains – *This is all the world, for tonight* – she let in a shaft of dim grey light. It was very early, but the day had come.

Someone was hammering on the door downstairs. The voice sounded like a child's. Nerys's clothes were scattered, tangled up in the bedcovers, and she remembered that the bloodstained Chinese robe lay somewhere across the room.

'Rainer, wake up.' She shook his muscled shoulder and he opened his eyes. 'Listen.'

He uncoiled himself, already reaching for his clothes and dragging them on.

'Wait here,' he ordered, but she ignored him. Wrapped in a blanket she was at his heels as he reached the door. Her arm felt stiff and sore, but she forgot it instantly.

On the step was the little girl, the yarn-spinner's daughter. Her dirt-covered face was seamed with the tracks of fresh tears. Her fists pulled at Rainer's legs as she gabbled at him.

'What's she saying?'

'The mother's ill. She wants help, food.'

Nerys stooped and hoisted the child in her arms. Her response was to twist and spit, beating her hands on Nerys's shoulder and howling into her face.

She called to Rainer, 'Tell her we'll come. We've got to get dressed.'

While they scrambled into their clothes the girl darted through the room, snatching fruit off a plate and tying it in the cloth from her head. The desperation of her feral rummaging struck dread as well as pity into Nerys. With the child haring ahead of them, they raced through the icy mud and refuse heaps of the alleyways until they came to the doorway with its shred of protective sacking.

The little boy was sitting in the corner of the bare room with the silent baby in his lap. The whites of their eyes showed in the dim light. The mother was lying stretched out beside her spinning wheel.

It was immediately obvious that she was dead.

The girl crouched beside her and pulled at her arm. Then she gave a low wail like an animal's cry and flung herself across her mother's body.

'Take the children out of here,' Rainer murmured.

Nerys looked round. There was nothing in the bare room except the wheel and the bed of rags. Even the shawl, in its cloth wrapping, had gone. With dry eyes and stiff hands she lifted the baby from its brother's arms and folded it inside her *pheran*. She took the younger child's cold hand, and with

Rainer's help, she detached the now silent girl from the mother's cooling body. There were no more tears and, after that one terrible wail, not a sound.

'Take them to my house. I'm going to find the head man of this quarter and report the death. Then I'll be back,' he said. His face was like a stone.

Nerys led the children back the way they had come. She wasn't sure of the route through the labyrinth of alleys, and she was too angry to try to ask any of the silent men who stood in the shadows to watch them pass. The girl refused to take her hand. She walked in silence, stiff as a small robot.

At last they reached the river and the tall old house. Nerys sat the boy on Rainer's bed and drew the covers across his thin shoulders. The baby was stirring and whimpering and she rocked it as she moved round the room. The girl went to the window and stood with her back to them, staring out at the snow that had begun to fall.

In Rainer's kitchen Nerys unearthed some *roghani* bread and a dish of apple sauce. Unlike everyone else in Srinagar, Rainer employed no servants. She boiled a cup of milk on the bottled-gas ring, and placed it on the windowsill to cool while she fed spoonfuls of bread and apple to the boy. When he had eaten something she was able to persuade the girl to turn away from her sentry position. She snatched some bread and, holding it in two hands, gnawed at it as she returned to her place.

Nerys was holding the mute baby in her arms and feeding it warm milk from a teaspoon when Rainer came back. He brought fresh warm bread and a pot of lentil stew. He set out the food and the girl seized her plate and took it back to the window.

'She had fever,' he said. 'She had been ill for a few days.'

'Why didn't anyone help her?'

'She was an outcast. That's the way it is with them. Maybe it's true – maybe she had been with another man – I don't know. No one will know, now.'

258

Nerys looked from one child to another. They hardly seemed children at all, more like small, carved effigies.

She was aware that a great deal had happened in the last twenty-four hours, and that there was much more to come. Her own concerns, so gripping an hour ago, had become entirely unimportant. 'What can we do for them?' she whispered.

Sombrely he considered the question. 'We'll take them back to the village. To her family, in Kanihama.'

ELEVEN

Two days after Christmas, Nerys and Rainer drove the little trio through the snow from Srinagar to Kanihama. The boy and girl huddled behind the seats of the truck and the baby wailed in Nerys's arms.

The children's grandfather and great-grandfather came out of the village house to meet them.

'We have very little,' the man with the crescent face complained. 'Not enough to feed the mouths already.'

'These are your daughter's children. She is dead, and if you and her family do not care for them they will die too,' Rainer said.

'May the woman rest in peace,' the older man murmured piously. His son's mouth set in a hard line.

The children's teeth were chattering from the cold. In the end a woman came out of the houses and led them away. Nerys would never forget the glance of smouldering accusation, quickly blanked out, that the girl, Farida, shot back over her shoulder. She hadn't uttered a word since her mother had died, and this was the first sign of emotion she had shown. She had grabbed all the food she could lay her hands on, not even waiting to see if her brothers had a share, and the rest of the time she had stood or sat with her face turned away.

'His own child, their flesh and blood,' Nerys whispered to Rainer in disgust.

'Their rules are not the same as yours,' he answered. 'There has been dishonour. The daughter was disowned.'

'We can't leave those children here. Let me take them back to Srinagar. I'll look after them somehow.'

'This is where they belong, Nerys. These are their people, not you and Myrtle and the Srinagar Club ladies with their ideas of charity. Don't let sentiment cloud your judgement.'

'You're so callous. I'm surprised at you.' She was angry with him because she was confused.

In the end money changed hands, and Rainer gave stern instructions to the villagers about how the children were to be cared for.

As they drove away, Nerys wept.

Three days later she insisted that Rainer drive her back to the village to see how they were getting on. What they saw was not reassuring. The baby was silent and limp, even though he was being nursed by an aunt, or perhaps it was a cousin, who had recently given birth herself. The boy, Faisal, cried or rocked himself in a corner and Farida stood in bitter silence.

They had brought more food with them, as well as extra clothing, warm blankets, and a crib for the baby. The villagers stood looking on as Rainer unpacked the supplies, just as fascinated as they had been by his magic tricks. Nerys thought they probably made no distinction between that conjuring and this materialising of desirable food and clothing. The goods were quickly whisked away.

'They're going to take everything for themselves,' she whispered, looking at the ring of dark, unsmiling faces. In the grip of winter Kanihama was a far harsher place than it had seemed on that sunny afternoon back in the autumn.

'Of course they will. Wouldn't you in their place? The idea is to show them that keeping the children in the village brings benefits that wouldn't come their way otherwise. Whoever actually eats this food and sleeps in these blankets, the children will be better off in the end.'

Nerys wasn't convinced, but for the time being she didn't have any other ideas.

Rainer went off to smoke a pipe with the men and she was left among the women. Apart from the *kani* weavers, always bent over their looms, it was the women who seemed to do most of the work. She nodded and smiled at them as they passed and tried not to draw too much attention to herself. Faisal stopped crying, apparently from exhaustion, and she took the opportunity to lift him into her arms. After a moment he fell asleep, and as she rocked him she studied the wet black eyelashes curling against his brown cheek. To her surprise, one of the women brought a wooden stool and pushed it in front of her. Nerys thanked her in Kashmiri and sat down.

Farida didn't even glance in their direction.

From where she sat, Nerys could look out into the square. She noticed that three or four of the little mud-brick structures were empty because the shawl workers had begun to migrate down to the city in search of work. The old, traditional ways of village life were breaking down, the shawl trade was in decline, but the craftsmen's families still had to be fed. Rainer had told her that some of the skilled workers had gone to little factories in the city, set up by Kashmiri middle men to mass-produce cheap approximations of the precious hand-made pieces that took countless hours to weave and gave their makers far too little return for their labour.

Faisal moaned and kicked in his sleep. She wondered how bad his dreams could be. She didn't want to leave him again and go back to lotus-eating down in Srinagar. Thoughtfully she gazed out at the empty houses, and by the time Rainer came back she had made up her mind. He drew up another stool and sat down beside her, and the women glanced covertly at them as they went about their work.

She said, 'If the children are going to live here, I will stay with them. They'll be with their own people but I can make

262

sure they're well and getting what they need. Perhaps I can teach them some games and English words, just like I did over in Leh.'

He looked into her face, grasping her idea but doubting that it was practical. 'It's a harsh life. Can you survive up here, do you think, on your own?'

She lifted her chin, thinking back to her life in Ladakh, to the physical demands of the climb from Manali and after that the relative ease of the journey over the Himalayas with Myrtle and Archie.

'Yes, I can. The *Garden of Eden* and cricket matches aren't exactly what I'm used to. It was fun, but I don't want to live like that all winter. I'm going to have to move out of the houseboat soon anyway, because Caroline needs somewhere more secluded than the married quarters. I'd thought of looking for a room in the old town, maybe near your house, but coming up here and doing something similar to my work in Leh would be much more useful. I won't be alone, either. Look around you. Kanihama is full of people.'

'You don't know their language.' He didn't have to add, 'There are no Europeans here and British ladies, even missionaries' wives, don't live alone in Indian hill villages,' because it was implicit.

'Rainer, I can learn.' Her voice carried an edge of rebuke.

He looked at her for a long moment, and then he touched her cheek. 'You are formidable. All right, Nerys. I'll do whatever I can to help you.'

'Let's start by asking the head man what and who I have to pay to rent one of these houses.'

The negotiations were complex and protracted, but in the end a house – more of a hovel, really, but Nerys was confident that she and Rainer between them could make it habitable – and a steep price were agreed. She handed over a wad of rupees to the village elders, on the understanding that Rainer and she would be coming back very soon, and that this time Nerys would be staying.

'Just a day or so, I promise,' she whispered, to the uncomprehending Faisal. The little boy held on to her leg, then turned away. Farida stared into the distance and didn't acknowledge their departure.

A tight knot of villagers gathered to watch them leave. It was one thing, Nerys thought, to visit Kanihama on an autumn afternoon and to be welcomed as a rich tourist maybe with the money to buy a shawl or two, but quite another to propose a life among the shawl-makers. Apart from what they hoped to get out of her, her intrusion would be entirely unwelcome.

As the Ford bumped over the ruts past the ravine where she and Rainer had picnicked, her resolve temporarily failed. It would be so much easier to stay comfortably in Srinagar until Evan arrived. She reminded herself that she had felt the same anxiety at Shillong, and even more so at Leh, where she had been merely her husband's adjunct, and yet she had been able to make herself useful in both places. And Evan would understand why she wanted to be in Kanihama. The thought brought him oddly close, at the very moment when they had never seemed further apart.

'You are quiet,' Rainer said, over the truck's rattling din.

'I'm making plans,' Nerys told him.

They returned to the house by the river, and the curtained bed.

With Rainer, the physical intricacies and elaborations were turning out to be much as she had imagined them when she had lain awake for the long nights beside Evan, but what did surprise her was the way that two bodies could be ordinary together, and also comical and available without ceremony.

There was no diffident *my dear?* about Rainer, and not a flicker of embarrassment. He could be ardent at one moment and at the next he might break off to talk about the significance of America's entry into the war, or to enquire casually if Nerys was hungry. He could get up from the bed and wander away naked to find a plate of food. If she was eating, or had just dressed herself, he would slide urgent hands inside her clothes or lick the nape of her neck. She realised that, for Rainer, sex was on the same spectrum as eating or arguing, and after Evan's guilt and inhibitions such freedom was a revelation. And it was highly endearing. Yet, oddly, all their physical intimacy didn't seem to bring Rainer closer.

He was massively *there*, a dense slab of muscle under warm skin, but no deeper knowledge of him emerged from their long kisses, or from the way that their limbs twined in an attempt to get closer and deeper. It was like the reverse of a honeymoon, Nerys decided, with amusement. While he had courted her, there had been the promise of a perfect fusion of minds as well as bodies. That had been her romantic dream. Now that they were greedily exploring each other, and she discovered what pleased her as well as him, it was as if the erosion of mystery nudged him further away from her.

She remembered his words, 'I can't stay in one place,' and that warning seemed more intelligible now. She felt it was quite likely that, any minute now, Rainer would step into one of his own painted boxes and disappear.

Nerys tried to explain to Myrtle and Caroline what was happening.

Myrtle caught Nerys's face between two hands and looked hard at her.

'Are you running away from him? Is that what this mad Kanihama scheme is really about?'

'No, I'm not. It's nothing to do with Rainer. I want to be useful, you know that, and I can't do it here, not by going with the wives to charity sales and first-aid demonstrations and committees.'

This came out sounding like a criticism of Myrtle, not just her friends, and Nerys regretted it immediately. 'I'm sorry.'

'Don't be. You're a missionary's wife.'

And now the mistress of a magician, neither of them added.

'I am,' Nerys acknowledged.

It was a time of general uncertainty, so one more area of confusion seemed hardly remarkable.

Myrtle had had no recent news of Archie. 'He'll write when he can,' she said, and always changed the subject.

'You're so brave,' Caroline declared, when she heard about Nerys going to Kanihama. Her round face had grown rounder and was permanently pink these days as the flush of pregnancy deepened. She was worried that her house-boy spied on her and that the *dhobi-wallah* or the woman who did her sewing must have guessed her secret. 'What am I going to do?' she cried.

Myrtle was helping Nerys to pack, and Caroline was sitting in an armchair. Her eyes were shiny with tears and her voice shook with anxiety.

Myrtle told her firmly, 'You are quietly moving in here with me. Majid is discreet, Rainer and I will look after you, and Nerys is only a few miles away.'

There was no definite news of Ralph Bowen, either. With the rest of his Indian Army regiment, he was in the thick of the battle for Singapore.

Nerys was ashamed to catch herself wondering whether it would be for the best if he were killed in action, but then Myrtle confessed to the same dark thought.

'God help us all.' She sighed. 'Nerys, you won't make the same mistake as Caroline did, will you?'

'I will not,' Nerys assured her. She had her own talcum-powdered device in its box, and used it.

'All right. Let's go out and buy what you'll need to set up your home in the hills,' Myrtle said. She brightened up at the prospect of shopping.

On 1 January 1942, a day of heavy frost, Nerys moved into the village house. It consisted of one room with a door that opened straight off the square and a single window, and another room that was hardly more than an alcove leading out of the first. The familiar audience of villagers gathered to watch as she and Rainer staggered from the truck with a charpoy, sheets and blankets, food and clothes, pans and floor coverings and armfuls of rough woven tent fabric to hang against the crumbling walls and keep out the wind.

Rainer hammered the drapes into the old wooden beams, spread out the rugs and got the squat iron stove going for her. It was identical to the one Diskit had tended in the kitchen at Leh, as introduced by the Moravian missionaries. He carried water from the well while Nerys made up her bed and slipped her *kangri* between the blankets. She was so used to carrying it within her *pheran* that she felt light and girlish without its bulk swaying in front of her. She lit the paraffin lamp and a series of candles, and the rough little place looked suddenly homely. Rainer's tin kettle began to whistle on the stove, and she laughed again at the familiar sound. There was only one chair, so he sat on the floor resting his back against her knees while they drank their tea. She knotted her fingers in his tawny hair.

Making a home together that they were not going to share seemed of a piece with the honeymoon that hadn't revealed the man. She watched the candles flicker and wondered, if she were actually married to him, whether the entire marriage would have the same quality. She concluded that it would, but the thought didn't in any way diminish her feeling for him.

Rainer reached up and clasped her hand. 'Shall I stay?' he murmured. The charpoy was inviting and the room hadn't warmed up yet. But this wasn't busy Srinagar. Nothing that she did in Kanihama was going to pass unnoticed. She remembered what had been dealt out to the yarn-spinner. 'Better not.' She smiled, with regret.

'And will you come to Srinagar?'

'When I can.' Even in the depths of winter, farm vehicles and traders made their way up and down the Vale, and she thought it wouldn't be too difficult to pay for a ride.

'I'll bring you food and supplies and news as often as I can.'

'Will you be able to get enough petrol?'

'I have useful contacts,' he answered, tapping the side of his nose with a knowing air.

Nerys assumed that he meant his tough-looking American friends. Since Christmas he had met them several times, and she hadn't asked any questions.

'Are you sure I can leave you here, my sweet girl?'

His words and his concern touched her. She kissed the top of his head and he twisted to scoop her into his arms.

After he had gone, she blew out all the candles except one. She lay down in bed and looked at the shadows. There was no sound except the wind scraping in the branches of the trees, and she realised that she was happy. She wouldn't have gone back to the houseboat on the lake, even if she could.

The days and then the weeks slowly passed.

There were plenty of times during that cold January when she would gladly have run away, but she stayed put. At first it was enough of a battle to eat, keep warm and sleep, and to see Faisal and Farida. The baby turned a corner, began to thrive, and soon became part of the small tribe of infants who were carried or propped up or left to sleep as the village work went on around them. In time Faisal also became less sad. He learnt that Nerys's door led to food and warmth and unfamiliar games, even music and singing, and he came so regularly that he almost lived under her roof. Tentatively at first, and then with more confidence, some other children followed him. They sat in a row on her floor and she told them stories, taught them a clapping song, or drew pictures. Up from Srinagar came Rainer with crayons and paper, sometimes a bag or two of sweets, and once a dozen brightly coloured balloons. That was a day to remember.

Nerys looked up one afternoon and saw one of the mothers peering in at her. They had sold her milk and vegetables and yoghurt, and let her collect wood for her fire, but this was the first time anyone had come to visit. The woman pulled her shawl across her face and drew back as soon as Nerys noticed her, but Nerys insisted she come inside and drink tea. They managed a stilted conversation, with more gestures and smiles than words. After that, some others came with their children. By the beginning of February, Nerys had the beginnings of a classroom set up in a room in one of the bigger houses. She had nothing at all, far less even than in her primitive school-room at the Leh mission, but for a couple of hours each day she did her best to entertain a dozen infants. They sat there, round-eyed, staring or laughing at her, but the next day they remembered what she had done, and if she changed a tune or a story mime there would be an outcry.

There was a school in a village further down the valley, but it was a long walk in midwinter snow and most of the parents preferred to keep their children at hand to watch the animals, or to mind the even tinier ones. Some of the bigger boys went further away to the *madrasah*, but not all the families were able to manage the fee.

Nerys's sketch of a school was regarded with suspicion at first but then, seemingly almost overnight, it was accepted and she was part of the village.

'English,' said Faisal's grandfather, Zafir. 'Please teach some English.'

The British were no longer particularly welcome in Kashmir and it was accepted that soon they would leave the Vale and India itself, but everyone still coveted the passport to prosperity represented by their language. She did what she could, returning to the choruses of *hat, shoe, finger, nose* that reminded her of Leh, and therefore – constantly – of Evan.

He would approve of what she was doing. That, at least.

Only Farida remained aloof and silent. Sometimes she hovered in the doorway, but then she would whirl away and not reappear for a day.

Rainer brought news of the Japanese bombings of Singapore and the fighting in the Libyan desert, messages from Myrtle and Caroline, and a warning that he too might soon be leaving Srinagar.

'Where are you going?' Nerys asked.

'I have some skills that the military can use. Like you, I want to make myself useful,' was all he would say.

269

When she wasn't with the children, she loved to watch the shawl-makers at work. She discovered the dye workshop at the edge of the village where a stream ran between jaws of ice and rock. She saw the spun yarn immersed in copper vats that simmered on wood fires, sending great clouds of mingled steam and smoke into the colourless sky. The dye workers prodded their cauldrons with long sticks, fishing out the hanks of yarn to examine the depth of colour. The pure water and natural dyes gave the rose-pinks, blues and ochres the clarity she had admired in the weaving room back in the village. The dyers were more gregarious than the *kani* craftsmen, who were too intent on their bobbins to take any notice of her coming and going, and she was soon an accepted presence in the steam-filled shed.

It took a little more time before the women tried to show her how to spin, and then there was much hilarity because her efforts were so clumsy.

In all this time the peacock's feather shawl grew by a narrow hand's breadth.

The weaver was a thin young man who always wore a red skullcap. He rubbed his eyes, and looked up at the white mountains to rest them for a precious minute.

One morning in the middle of February Nerys woke up to daylight instead of greyish dawn.

It wasn't late. The boy who drove the goats from their barn to the grazing every morning had just passed – she could hear their bells and his low whistles as the flock streamed uphill. She never needed to look at her clock up here because the time of day was evident from what was going on in the neighbouring houses or out in the fields. The days were lengthening and although the cold seemed just as implacable there was a difference in the light that suggested winter might some day turn to spring. The thought of this gave her a quiet beat of happiness as she got dressed. Through her window she could see the wide-branched chinar tree planted at the centre of the rough

270

square, and it became easier to recall its welcome summer shade.

She stoked the fire in the iron stove, dipped a jug into her water bucket, filled a tin kettle and placed it on the heat. When the water finally boiled she made tea and sat in her chair, wrapped and hooded in her *pheran*, warming her hands on the cup.

Faisal would be here at any moment.

She had no sooner thought of him than she heard the scuffling of small feet and an urgent rattle at the door. The little boy bounded in to crouch next to her and close to the stove's warmth. She solemnly wished him good morning.

'Good *morning*,' he repeated proudly, in his singsong voice. His English words were accumulating fast.

In just two months, he had grown taller and straighter. He didn't rock himself or linger in the shadows at the corner of the room. This morning he was happily rolling a ball, humming to himself and keeping only half an eye on Nerys and the preparation of porridge and eggs.

'Hungry?' she asked him, tapping her hands to her mouth to reinforce the question.

'Yes, please,' he answered, as she had taught him to do, but his attention was still on his game.

Faisal was good company. He was alert, he loved playing and imitating, and he learnt everything she taught him with incredible speed. She missed Myrtle and Caroline, and Rainer's visits were limited by the availability of fuel for the Ford, but it was Faisal's rapid progress that convinced her she had done the right thing in leaving Srinagar.

The rice porridge steamed in what had become a lemon-rind slice of sunlight. She gave Faisal his spoon and they sat down at her plank table to eat.

'Good?'

'Good.' He beamed.

She took a mouthful, and above the voices of two women carrying water and a cock crowing, she heard the approach of a vehicle. Before it turned into the square and rattled to a halt, she already knew that it was the Ford.

'Car,' Faisal said.

Nerys got up and hurried outside. With Rainer in the cab of the truck were Myrtle and Caroline. She ran across to them. Myrtle flashed a warning glance at her and she saw that Caroline's face was as white as chalk. Rainer didn't smile a greeting.

'Come inside,' Nerys murmured, conscious of the eyes that followed every event in the village. They made a protective guard round Caroline as they crossed the few steps to the house. Nerys told Faisal to go and play with the other boys.

'What has happened?' she demanded, as soon as she shut the door.

'Ravi Singh,' Caroline managed to say. It was Myrtle who had to take up the story.

Yesterday afternoon, they had been sitting beside the stove in the *Garden of Eden*. Myrtle was reading and Caroline knitting a matinée jacket. She was sure that the baby would be a boy, and she had chosen pale blue wool from a shop on the Bund.

Majid came from the kitchen boat. He never hurried, so Myrtle knew from the way he bumped into the door that something was wrong.

'What is it, Majid?'

He pointed. 'A boat is coming.'

The lake ice had thawed and now flat grey water stretched from shore to shore. Heading straight for them was a private motor-boat with a uniformed boatman at the helm. The small cabin was curtained but the two women recognised the servants' livery.

Caroline's hands flew to her mouth. 'Oh, God. What does he want?'

Out of consideration to Majid she was wearing a loose embroidered wool coat and Myrtle was similarly dressed, even though the house-boy must have worked out long ago what

272

the situation was. There was no time to run away, or try to disguise matters. All Caroline could think of doing was to hide her knitting in her work bag.

'Perhaps, Memsahib . . .' Majid pointed down the length of the boat to Caroline's bedroom.

'Yes, go,' Myrtle said to her. 'Stay there and don't make a sound.'

The motor-boat's engine cut out and the boatman brought it in a smooth glide to the steps. As soon as he had made fast, the cabin door opened and Ravi Singh's sleek figure emerged. He was wearing riding clothes, impeccably cut in British style, which had the effect of making him look even more haughtily Kashmiri.

Myrtle greeted him at the veranda door.

'Good afternoon, Mrs McMinn,' he said curtly.

'Ravi, I am Myrtle, you know that perfectly well. How lovely of you to drop in, though. What a surprise treat on this grey afternoon. What shall it be? A cup of tea or a cocktail? I rather think a cocktail, don't you? Majid, please.' She clapped her hands and the house-boy bowed his retreat. 'Please sit down, Ravi. You do rather tower over one.'

'I have come to see Mrs Bowen.'

Myrtle widened her eyes. 'You should go to her bungalow, then. Unless she's at the club this afternoon? We sometimes meet there for tea, but I'm a little tired today.'

Ravi slapped his pale kidskin gloves against the palm of his other hand. 'She is not at her house. I think she is here,' he said flatly. He looked at Myrtle's ambiguous silhouette. 'I have heard something.'

Myrtle's voice was sweet and silky. 'What have you heard?'

'That is not for discussion.'

'I see,' she breathed. 'I'm so sorry to disappoint you, Ravi, but Caroline is not here. Maybe she is away. I did hear her mention that she might go down to Delhi, now that the ice is gone. You know, to do some shopping, to see a few people. She is lonely with her husband away, as we all are, and Srinagar

273

is so dismally quiet, these days, what with winter and the war. Don't you agree?'

Majid padded into the room again, carrying the clinking tray and ice-bucket.

'Gin fizz?' Myrtle smiled. She clicked her lighter to one of her gold-tipped cigarettes.

'No, thank you. Please tell Mrs Bowen that she can't conceal anything from me, and it is folly to imagine that a Kashmiri noble family can be held in contempt.'

'If I see her, Ravi, I shall give her your message. I am afraid, though, it will be as baffling to her as it is to me. Unless it's a game. Is it a *clue*?'

'No, Mrs McMinn, it is not.' His manner was frosty enough to ice the lake all over again. 'Good afternoon.'

Majid bowed and opened the veranda door but Ravi swung back. He had caught sight of Caroline's work bag with a loop of pale blue wool trailing from it, and his eyes flicked from it to Myrtle again. 'May I congratulate you, by the way, on an impending happy event?'

Myrtle could do an imperious face too. Her eyebrows rose a fraction but she gave no other sign of having heard his question.

'Good afternoon,' Ravi finally repeated. A moment later his launch was carrying him back across the lake, trailing a furrow of mint-green water.

Caroline shrank in Nerys's chair, her arms crossing over her belly. 'The *dhobi-wallah*, someone, maybe the yard-boy, has told a story to another servant, and the news has passed all the way up to Ravi Singh. Now he's looking for me and the bastard baby that will bring dishonour to his family name.'

Myrtle looked over her head and met Nerys's eyes. 'Don't be afraid of Ravi Singh,' she ordered. 'He can't know anything for certain, and Srinagar servants' talk is no more than that. What we did, Nerys, was to send a message to Rainer and he came straight away.'

'We left this morning at first light,' Rainer said.

'Can I stay here with you?' Caroline implored her. 'No one will guess I've come all the way up here, not even Ravi.'

'Of course you can,' she soothed.

Rainer knelt in front of the stove and deftly blew the embers into a blaze.

Myrtle said, 'Rainer's got another idea, too.'

By Nerys's reckoning it was less than a month to Caroline's due date. Whatever it might be, the idea had better be a good one.

Rainer took his time. When he was satisfied with the fire he sat back on his heels and gave Nerys the warm, half-sleepy smile that immediately made her aware of her skin under the layers of clothes. 'South-west of here, on the road out of the Vale in the direction of Rawalpindi,' he said, 'at a place called Baramulla, there is a Catholic convent. The sisters run a small hospital with the help of a French doctor and his wife. If you agree, Nerys, Caroline will stay here with you out of Ravi Singh's reach – he will naturally assume that if she is not in Srinagar she must be in Delhi.'

Nerys quoted one of the four rules: 'Misdirection.'

'Exactly. Why would she head up into the hills, if she is in the condition that he suspects? I have to go away now to do a small job of work, but when I am back again I will come up to Kanihama and we will take Caroline to the doctor and the nuns at Baramulla. She will be quite safe to deliver there.'

Caroline's head was bent and her fingers constantly pleated the edge of her *pheran*.

'It's a good idea. But couldn't we take her there now?' Nerys asked.

'Baramulla is on the road. There are routes north and west, and therefore all sorts of people passing through. Who knows where Ravi Singh's spies might be? To stay out of sight here is safer, for as long as possible.'

Caroline did look up now. Her blue eyes were full of fear.

275

'I don't want Ravi to find me. I'm afraid of him,' she whispered.

Outside the window there was only the handful of houses and patchy fields and then the mountains. Almost no one came to Kanihama unless it was pedlars bringing essentials to the villagers, and few of the people ever left it, except Zafir and the other head men who took the village products to market further down the valley road or in the city.

'We'll stay here,' Nerys agreed.

Rainer nodded. 'Good. I am leaving this morning, and I will stop at Baramulla convent on my way and tell them to expect us.'

'You have to go so soon?' Nerys gasped.

Myrtle had fallen silent once she had described Ravi Singh's visit, but she jumped up now and said that she would bring Caroline's belongings in from the truck. Rainer took Nerys's arm and led her outside to stand under the chinar tree.

He said, in a low voice, looking round first as though enemy agents might be perched in the branches overhead, 'It is a job I must do. There is an airfield, strategically important. The British and the Americans want me to move it.'

'To *move* it? An airfield? Would that be single-handed?' Nerys asked.

'Not quite. I shall have a small team, carpenters, painters and so on. It will be a trick, of course, an illusion performed with camouflage, dummies, lights – I don't know what else until I see the place from the air. But through my skills the Japanese will bomb an empty patch of jungle instead of an airstrip with thirty fighter planes. There is no one in India or the whole of Asia who can succeed in this job other than me. *I* am the magician.'

She smiled through the chafe of her anxiety. Rainer would never be short of confidence, whatever feat was expected of him. 'Good luck,' was all she said.

He lifted her hand and kissed it. 'I will be back in two weeks.'

She didn't say, 'Promise me,' although she longed to.

She waited under the tree, watching, until the red Ford had jolted out of sight.

In the house, Myrtle and Caroline had unpacked a second charpoy and erected it in the confined space. Caroline stood with her hands to her back, easing the ache. The folds of her *pheran* hardly disguised her bulk.

'It's hard, I know,' Myrtle said softly to Nerys, 'but Rainer will be all right.'

Nerys lifted her chin. 'Of course. Now, let me find us all some breakfast. You can't have had time to eat before you left. There's rice porridge and eggs, and I should think my neighbour will have baked our bread by now. I'll send Faisal for some. It's so good.' She could just see the top of the little boy's head bobbing outside the window.

Myrtle said, 'I've brought my bedroll. Can I stay, too, for a couple of nights? After that I'd better go back and show myself at a Women's Aid meeting or in the club. The story, by the way, is that after a touch of fever Caroline has gone south to recuperate with a nurse cousin of mine.'

'Of course you can stay. What fun,' Nerys smiled.

To have Myrtle and Caroline for company made Kanihama seem a sunny, benign place, and her dusty mud-brick house almost as luxurious as the *Garden of Eden*.

If they sat knee to knee on their stools, there was just room for the three of them at the plank table. After his errand Faisal played with his ball at their feet.

Myrtle took a crust of bread and some spiced apple, but she didn't eat. 'Have you heard the grimmest war news?' she asked.

Nerys gestured briefly at the bare room. There was no news here, except what they could bring her.

'Yesterday Singapore surrendered. The city's occupied by the Japanese.'

Caroline pecked at her food with small, precise movements.

Myrtle added, 'It seems likely that a lot of our men who

survived the battle and the bombing will have been taken prisoner by the Japs. The reports are very confused.'

'Ralph is alive. I know he is,' Caroline said. She seemed unnaturally calm now, almost remote, as if too much was happening for her to be able to deal with it all.

'Have you heard from Archie?' Nerys asked Myrtle quietly.

'One letter. I don't know for sure but he and his men are probably involved with the evacuation of wounded from Malaya. It is . . . Well, we can imagine how it is.'

Caroline put her hand to her belly. She said dreamily, 'This baby kicks all the time. He's like a bull elephant.'

Thin sunlight filtered into the room. The three sat thinking of the child that would soon be born, and the world of uncertainty that would greet him.

For two days they sat by the stove, keeping warm. Caroline knitted blue baby clothes, and they played with Faisal and his brother, the yarn-spinner's baby, now grown almost plump. Farida watched from the margins but if any of them beckoned to her she turned and ran away. Myrtle and Nerys visited two or three of the other houses to drink tea with the women, and as they walked out in their *kangri*-distended *pherans* they told each other that they must look like a pair of little round teapots on legs.

In the weaving house, Myrtle leant over to examine the peacock's feather shawl that the thin weaver hopefully uncovered to show her. The lake blues and shimmering silvers made an iridescent pool in the drab chill of winter's end. 'It is exquisite,' Myrtle agreed, but she shook her head at the man's imploring gesture. 'I haven't got anything like enough money. If I did have, honestly, I would buy it.'

On the third morning, Myrtle said she must go back to Srinagar to listen out for the latest rumours. An old man taking tree trunks down to a wood-carving workshop said that she could ride with him on his bullock cart, as far as a place where it was possible to pick up the public bus onwards to Srinagar.

278

Myrtle climbed on to the seat of the cart, spreading folds of tweed to cover her knees and enclose her *kangri*. 'I shall be heartily glad when this pregnancy finally reaches its natural conclusion,' she murmured to Nerys.

'Try to enjoy the ride,' Nerys advised.

'Life is quite a strange adventure at present, isn't it? Before Rainer whirled us up here, I was looking at those tops of Archie's – you know, the stags and mountain sheep that he shot in Ladakh. Back then, I thought a hunting trip with my husband was very daring. That was before I met you, Nerys Watkins.'

They both laughed, even though there seemed to be little enough that was genuinely funny.

'I'll be back with Rainer,' Myrtle promised. 'Then we'll go to Baramulla and our baby will be born, eh?'

'Two weeks,' Nerys said, and stood back to let the cart pull away.

The days passed very slowly. The villagers were curious about the new arrival, but not overbearingly so. With her usual mixture of sign language and the simple words of Kashmiri she had picked up, Nerys indicated to the friendlier women that Caroline's husband was away at the war, and soon she would be going to the hospital to have her baby. They accepted this with a shrug. In Kanihama babies were born behind a curtain in one of the mud-brick rooms.

Caroline watched the children when they came to play with Nerys. She would join in the singing, or draw pictures for Faisal – *tree, sheep, flower* – but more often she sat with her hand on her stomach, where the protrusion of a tiny heel could often be seen through the stretched muscle wall. Her abstracted air intensified and Nerys put it down to the inner absorption of late pregnancy, remembering how the mothers at Shillong had retreated into themselves in just the same way.

At night they lay side by side on their charpoys. Caroline

slept badly, sighing and shifting under the weight of her belly, and Nerys listened anxiously to her movements. She left a candle burning in a niche, and the draughts sent shadows wavering over the roof beams.

Thoughts of her own lost baby came less oppressively now.

She had chilblains and a cough, but apart from these minor ailments her body felt taut and surprisingly strong from the straitened life at Kanihama, and she took a new, less shy satisfaction in it because of what Rainer had shown her. Putting her own concerns aside, she concentrated her thoughts on what Caroline was likely to need.

The two weeks crept by, but Rainer did not reappear.

Which jungle had taken him? Where was he, who was not even a soldier? It seemed that he had done the disappearing act she had often imagined. Nerys stifled her anxiety, compressing it until it weighed like lead beneath her diaphragm.

'When will they be here?' Caroline asked constantly.

'Don't worry,' Nerys soothed.

The post was delivered only once a week in Kanihama. The postman brought a letter from Myrtle and waited at Nerys's door to see her open it, as eager to hear the contents as they were. She gave him money and he retreated.

Myrtle had scrawled, 'No one knows where Rainer is. Not a word, or even a breath of a rumour. He has simply vanished. Do you want me to come up to Kanihama without him? What can I do to help you?'

Nerys sent a note back: 'He'll come. Stay there, be our ears and eyes. Caroline and I will be all right.'

That night, under the flickering shadows, she reviewed her options. They were limited. It might be possible to borrow a car in Srinagar, with a driver who didn't know either Ravi Singh or the European wives, to take Caroline and herself to the convent hospital in Baramulla. But a journey for a pregnant woman that had seemed a feasible undertaking with Rainer in the Ford became a daunting prospect with a stranger. Alternatively she could convey Caroline back to Srinagar where she could present herself at the military clinic, but that would be to undo all the concealments of the last months.

Or they could stay put.

After sleepless hours, she went out first thing in the morning and asked a series of questions of the Kanihama women. Eventually they led her to a crone with a seamed face and a white headcloth, who was puffing on a pipe beside a smoky fire. This, she learnt, was the village midwife. The old woman listened and nodded, then put out a hand for Nerys's money. In reply, Nerys rocked her empty arms and mimed passing over money. Baby first, then the fee. The old woman laughed, showing a row of blackened teeth, and the laughter spread to the other women. Nerys decided that she liked the midwife, and they shook hands.

Back at the little house, she persuaded Caroline to undress so that she could examine her. As Nerys felt her stomach Caroline's eyes opened so wide that the whites showed all round the blue irises. 'How many babies have you delivered?' she asked, in a tight voice.

'Several,' Nerys answered. The baby's head seemed neatly engaged. If it was a straightforward labour and delivery, all would be well. If not . . . Please, Rainer, she implored within her head. For God's sake, get here before it's too late.

It was a sunny day, and there was even a whisper of warmth in the breeze. Nerys gathered up sheets and cloths and towels and took them in a bundle down to the dyers' shed on the banks of the stream. There she persuaded the men to fill one of their copper vats with crystal stream water, and to boil it. She laundered all the bedclothes and the other pieces, then hung them on the lines that crisscrossed the bank. They dried in the sun and wind, billowing among the brilliantly coloured hanks of pashmina yarn.

Caroline complained of the pain in her back. Nerys filled her *kangri* with embers and gave it to her to rest against. Evening crept up and she lit the candles yet again.

Rainer, where are you?

281

She refused to let her head fill with images of him taken prisoner, or lying wounded in the thick jungle, or worse.

At midnight, Caroline suddenly got up from her charpoy. She went to the window and rested her head against one folded arm, exhaling with a low grunt of pain.

'What do you feel?' Nerys asked.

'It's started.'

'All right. It's going to be all right.' She lit the lamp and stoked the stove.

Caroline lay on the mattress and drew up her knees. She looked terrified, and there were beads of sweat breaking under her hairline. 'Don't leave me,' she almost screamed, as Nerys put on her *pheran*.

'I'll be five minutes. I'm going for the midwife. Try to rest.'

The old woman was fast asleep in her crumbling little house. Nerys shook her awake as gently as she could. 'Come,' she begged.

Grumbling under her breath, she got up and slowly put on her threadbare *pheran*. She picked a battered pail off a shelf, half filled it with a dark brew that was sitting in a pan on the stove top and followed Nerys into the night.

Caroline was gasping with fear and pain as the midwife examined her. There was a dismissive twist to the woman's shoulder as she straightened up again. She pillowed her cheek on her folded hands and pointed to the drink she had brought. Then she marched off again. The message was clear. Caroline should drink some of her herbal brew, and there was still plenty of time for everyone to sleep.

By the time it was light, Caroline was writhing in a twist of laundered sheets. With every contraction she gave a snarl of pain that rose to a scream. In each brief respite Nerys sponged her face with cool water and made her drink a mouthful of the midwife's potion. 'You're doing well,' she kept whispering. As far as she could tell, Caroline was. 'Try to save your strength. Breathe.'

In the middle of the morning the midwife came strolling

back, chewing on a handful of pickled walnuts and spitting out the coarse skins into her cupped palm. Nerys made her wash her hands before she examined Caroline.

'Make it stop,' Caroline screamed. 'Please, God, help me.'

The woman straightened up again, adjusting her headcloth.

'Good,' she said surprisingly, in English, and her face cracked into a rare smile. She took a strip of linen cloth from Nerys's basket and doubled it into a band. Then she put it between Caroline's teeth before the girl's tear-stained face screwed up with the arrival of another contraction. Caroline bit into the cloth as the midwife laid her ear against her belly. There was another scream, choked by the band of linen. With a sudden gush the waters broke.

When Nerys looked between Caroline's legs she could see the wet black oval of the baby's head. 'Can you push?' she asked.

The elemental noises and smells of imminent birth brought the procedures of the delivery room at Shillong flooding back. She felt calm now. She told Caroline how to pant between contractions, and how to push into her pelvis instead of her throat. The midwife perched on a stool between Caroline's knees, and when the baby's head appeared she cupped it in one brown hand and expertly guided the tiny, slippery shoulders with the other.

'One more big push and you'll see him,' Nerys promised. Caroline's crimson face poured with tears, she tore the soaking rag out of her mouth and howled, and the baby was born. It had long, scrawny arms and legs, a thatch of black hair, and it was a healthy girl.

Working together, Nerys and the midwife cleaned the baby's airway, smiled at each other as the first mewing cry erupted, then wrapped her in a pashmina and laid her on Caroline's chest. Caroline was lying back against pillows and blankets. Her eyes were closed and she was shuddering with exhaustion. 'It's not a girl,' she breathed.

'Yes, it is, and she's beautiful.'

It was the same old miracle, Nerys thought, the same and different every time. She tucked a fold of shawl over one minute crimson foot and offered up a jumbled, wordless prayer of thanks. If Evan were here he would have knelt to bless this new life, but as it was, the tiny girl would have to make do with the approximation that was all Nerys could offer, and the mumbled imprecations of the Muslim midwife as she tied off the cord and cut it with a flash of bright blade.

'Let me take her,' Nerys said.

Caroline gave up the baby without protest as the old woman turned her attention to delivering the afterbirth. Nerys remembered how carefully the nurses at Shillong had checked to see that none remained inside the mother, and was relieved that this midwife was equally attentive. With the baby held against her shoulder she stroked Caroline's sweat-soaked hair off her face. 'You're doing so well. You were very brave,' she told her.

'I wasn't,' Caroline sobbed.

There was a scratch at the door, then it creaked open. Farida's small figure stood outlined against the bright light.

'Hello,' Nerys said in surprise.

The little girl sidled into the room, crept closer and tugged at the shawl that swaddled the baby. Nerys glanced at Caroline but her head had fallen to one side and her eyes were closed in exhaustion. She crouched so that Farida could look at the newborn, but the child went further. She deftly scooped the baby into her own arms and sat down cross-legged next to the stove, cradling her in her lap. She began to croon a little song. The midwife nodded in casual approval. As Farida laid a finger against the baby's cheek, Nerys realised it was the first time she had ever seen her smile.

She was relegated to the margins of this ancient tableau, so she made herself busy, putting the kettle on and tidying the bloodstained cloths into a basket.

The midwife finished her work, then she and Farida bathed the baby in a tin basin. The little scrap of flesh kicked and

284

cried, but Caroline was still sunk against her pillows, eyes closed. They dressed her in some of the blue knitted garments and Farida fiercely took possession of her again.

Finally the midwife held out her hand for the money. Nerys counted it into her palm, note by note, and only then would the woman accept some tea with bread and honey. Even Farida took a cup of tea. Caroline's lips were swollen and cracked, so Nerys smoothed Vaseline into them, then made her drink and eat a little.

'Do you want to try to feed her?' she asked, but Caroline only shook her head.

'Zahra,' Farida announced.

She and the midwife debated something, then Farida repeated, 'Zahra,' and adjusted the baby's bonnet.

'Have you thought of a name?' Nerys asked.

Caroline had mentioned that her father's name was Charles, and she had joked once that maybe she should choose Linlithgow, in honour of the viceroy, or even George for the king. That seemed a long time ago, and there had never been any mention of girls' names.

'Zahra sounds pretty,' Nerys added.

'All right,' Caroline answered. Then she added, 'I'm sorry, Nerys. I am so tired.'

'Of course you are. Rest now.'

Somehow, Nerys thought, she must get news to Myrtle.

At the end of the afternoon, when Zahra was asleep in a little box crib with Farida crouched like a shadow beside her, a deputation of women came to the door. Farida's grandmother was among them, and she was carrying an earthenware dish swathed in a cloth. There was a delicious smell.

With stately formality, the women laid out bowls and carved wooden spoons, then ladled out portions of steaming *tahar* rice cooked with turmeric, a dish traditionally made everywhere in Kashmir by Hindus and Muslims alike, to give thanks to God for a lucky escape or a safe delivery from danger.

Nerys and Caroline shared the fragrant food.

'Thank you,' Caroline said humbly. 'Thank you. I have been lucky, I know that. I was afraid that I was going to die.'

Someone knew of a boy who was going down to Srinagar to work with his uncle at the shawl factory. Nerys wrote the note for Myrtle and entrusted it to him.

When everyone had gone, even Farida, she tried again; 'Do you want to hold her?' she murmured. 'She's got such black hair, and big dark eyes.'

'Then she looks like her father. I can't keep her, I can't be her mother, so perhaps I shouldn't even think about her as my baby.'

Nerys stroked her hand. In Caroline's position she wouldn't have been able to stop herself holding Zahra to her heart. Nobody would have been able to tear her away – not without killing Nerys first.

Perhaps in the circumstances Caroline's instinct was wiser than hers.

There was a wet nurse in the village, the same woman who had looked after the yarn-spinner's baby. Zahra could go to her, for now, until Myrtle came and they could discuss what was to be done.

The next afternoon, a car arrived in the square. It was a trader's truck from Srinagar, with a sullen driver who jumped out and flung up the bonnet to examine the engine as if the journey had taken a final toll. Myrtle stepped out from the passenger side. She wore her *pheran* loose over her shoulders, the folds pushed back to reveal her neat waistline.

'I have never been more pleased to see you,' Nerys told her.

Myrtle had brought milk powder and glass feeding bottles, flowers and chocolates, the Srinagar newspaper, but no news of any of the men. 'The talk's all about Japanese atrocities in Singapore, prisoners of war, a hospital massacre. The damned Japs shot the patients and all the doctors. No one has the remotest interest in our little affairs, darling. I saw that woman who lives next to Caroline and told her that Caroline is much better from being in the sun with my dear cousin, and she hardly heard me. How *is* she?'

'Physically she's tired but recovering well. Emotionally, I'm not so sure.'

'And the baby?'

'She's beautiful.'

Myrtle carried her armful of gifts into the house.

'Golly. Look at all this. I feel as if I'm in a smart nursing home,' Caroline called from her bed, and the ghost of her old smile accompanied the words.

Myrtle and Nerys went later to visit Zahra, who was ensconced with Farida and the wet nurse. Faisal was delighted to welcome Myrtle, and danced along with his hand in hers.

Myrtle peered into the box crib, turning back a few layers of blue woollens. 'My God,' she breathed in Nerys's ear. 'It's Ravi Singh.' They both hovered over the tiny baby, gazing at her as if she were a miracle.

After resting for a week, Caroline made the journey with Myrtle back to the *Garden of Eden* where, as far as Srinagar knew or cared, she was still recovering from her bout of fever. She left her daughter in Nerys's care, and both her friends could see that there was more exhausted relief than anguish in the separation. She was unnaturally quiet, except for sudden bouts of weeping that she seemed unable to control, but in Srinagar her distress could be put down to anxiety for Ralph Bowen, whose name had been listed among hundreds of others as a prisoner of war.

Nerys resumed her small routines of songs and word games with the village children, broken up by afternoons of playing with Zahra and her ever-faithful attendant, Farida. It was a lucky accident that the baby's arrival had broken through the girl's shell of isolation, she thought. Farida even began to play with the other children, although she darted away every two or three minutes to make sure that the baby was sleeping or happily watching the patterns woven by the chinar branches over her head. She came every morning now, as reliably as Faisal, to take her breakfast with Nerys.

Nerys began to see how Zahra might even be absorbed into the village. Babies and children didn't seem to require the individual attention of their mothers – they were passed around between grandmothers, aunts and siblings, whoever happened to be at hand. Perhaps, she thought, with Myrtle, Caroline and herself to provide the money, there could be a life for Zahra in Kanihama. At least for her early years. And after that, when the end of the war came, there would be orphans, and displaced families, and children who would need protection in countless different ways. Who could predict what might happen to this particular orphan?

That was how Nerys reasoned, with even more secret hope and longing now that Zahra was born.

At the beginning of April, when buds had begun to swell on the thorn bushes and chinar twigs, and the fields and vegetable patches were green with new shoots, Nerys heard the sound of another car approaching. In her anxiety for Rainer she had conjured the same sound a hundred times, only to be as regularly disappointed, but now, once she let herself listen properly, it was unmistakable. She dropped the saucepan she was holding and ran outside.

It was the truck, driven by Rainer. The door swung open but he seemed unable to climb out.

She cried, 'What's happened? You're hurt. Let me help you.'

His face contorted. 'Not that side. Come round here. If I could lean on you . . .'

With his weight supported on her shoulder they shuffled to the house and she helped him to the chair by the stove. His face was haggard and his torso seemed twisted, like a tree struck by lightning.

'Where's Caroline?'

So wherever Rainer had come from, it was not the city.

She said quickly, 'In Srinagar, with Myrtle. She's recovering, and the baby is here. It's a girl.'

Rainer passed his tongue over parched lips. 'I am so sorry,' he murmured, 'to have let you down.'

She put her cheek to his. 'You didn't. Drink some of this.'

She had heated up a cupful of the midwife's latest brew. She still didn't know what the mixture contained, but she was impressed by its restorative effects. Rainer tasted and spat. 'Dear God. What's this poison?'

She relaxed a little. 'Rainer, what's happened to you?'

He took her hand and held it against him. After a moment he said, 'I was lucky. I didn't quite walk away, but I survived. Some others didn't.'

Nerys sat down beside him on the stool usually occupied by Faisal or Farida. His hand was badly scabbed and at the edges the renewed skin was puckered as if it had been burnt. To be bombarded with questions wasn't what he needed, she thought. He would tell her when he was ready.

He wasn't ready until he had slept for two hours. Nerys helped him to undress before he lay down. Under the tunic that he was wearing over loose trousers, his arm and shoulder and the upper part of his chest were covered with stained, yellow-soaked burn dressings.

'Would you like me to change these for you?' she asked matter-of-factly.

'Later,' he said. As soon as his eyes closed he fell asleep.

Nerys left him in her bed and went outside to play catch and hide-and-seek with the children. The piercing mountain air was scented with woodsmoke and animal dung, just as it had been on the afternoon when Rainer had first brought her here, and now in the sheltered places the sun felt hot on her shoulders.

Later she tiptoed inside and began to prepare some food, but when she turned to look at him she realised that his eyes were open and resting on her.

'Tell me I'm not dreaming,' he said.

'You're not, unless I'm dreaming the same thing.'

He reached out his good arm. 'Come here.'

Carefully, so as not to jostle him, she lay down in the narrow space. He put his lips against her forehead. 'That's better.'

Her heart was thumping so hard, she wondered if he could feel it against his scarred ribs.

At last, he began. 'I got myself out of a military clearing hospital. I'm only a civilian, and one with dubious national status at that, so they didn't try too hard to hang on to me. I managed to get on a flight to Delhi, and I'd left the truck with a friend of mine there so I was able to pick it up and drive straight here.'

She could see what this effort had cost him.

'All the time I was lying there I was thinking that I'd promised to take Caroline and you to Baramulla. If I could have got word to you, I would have done.'

She smiled at him. 'I knew that. I admit that I was worried when you didn't come, but the anticipation was much worse than the reality. Babies are born all the time in Kanihama, you know.'

'I am sure you were magnificent. As always.'

'Not at all.' Nerys laughed. 'The village midwife was the heroine. That was her special healing potion you were drinking.'

'I hope it will work,' he said, with a touch of grimness.

She waited.

'So, I did my conjuring trick. That's all it was, just an illusion on a grand scale. The British were reluctant to give me what I needed at first, because it was a top-secret mission and I had no security clearance. As far as the brass are concerned, I'm German-sounding enough to be an enemy agent. But they had to let me work it in the end, because there was no one else with the skill to do what they needed.'

It was good, Nerys thought, to hear the old Rainer talking.

'As you know, I had to move the airstrip so the Japs would bomb the wrong place. Against a dense jungle backdrop it's very difficult to judge scale from the air, especially at night, so on a similar site two miles up the coast we cleared an area one third the size of the actual landing area and constructed a scaled-down version of the real thing. I was given a team of British sappers. We built and painted balsa-wood planes, huts, storage dumps, dummy fuel stores, everything. I flew over it in a reconnaissance plane, just a few hundred feet up, and it was superb. The real site was invisible under camouflage netting, the other looked identical. Of course, part of the mission was to convince the Japs that they'd taken out the fuel dumps as well as the planes. Fuel's crucial in any battle. If the enemy thinks you've got none when you have plenty, that's a tactical advantage.'

There was a small silence while Nerys considered this. The trick would have involved staging a huge blaze, she thought.

'We had explosives, enough to create a big bang. We constructed a pyre that would burn well and doused it with fuel. There was a system of detonators that I was controlling, so as soon as there was a direct hit on the dump I could make the whole works explode in flame, just like a cache of aviation fuel going up.'

Rainer paused, searching for words.

'This took a certain amount of trial and error. Difficult to do, without smoke plumes giving our position away to enemy spotter planes. So we built a kind of tunnel within a tunnel, in which to test the detonator systems. I had two of the sappers inside, setting up the lines.'

He put a hand over his eyes. Then he said in a level voice, 'Something went wrong. A dropped light, a stray spark. I don't know. The tunnels caught fire. Within a second, they were ablaze. I went in, but I couldn't reach the men.'

Nerys imagined the thick, smothering humidity of the remote jungle, the black smoke in an enclosed place, the stench of burning.

'That happened the day before the operation. I wasn't there to see it, but when the time came the fake airstrip was lit up in place of the real one and sure enough the Japs came over. I understand that the explosion and burning of the false fuel dumps was most effective.'

He paused, shifting to ease the pain from his burns. 'I'm glad of that, for the sake of those two men.'

'Yes,' was all she could say.

Rainer wiped his mouth with the back of his good hand. 'You were kind enough to offer to change these dressings? There is a box in the truck.'

She went out again into the sunshine, and saw Farida patiently standing near the door with Zahra swathed in a shawl on her back. Nerys held out a hand and led her into the house.

'Look, here's Farida,' she told Rainer. 'And this is Zahra.'

He propped himself up. Nerys and Farida turned back the shawl to reveal the baby's wide dark eyes, olive skin and crest of jet-black hair. Hesitantly, he put a scarred finger to the tiny cheek. 'Hello,' he said. Then he looked up and met Nerys's eyes. 'I'm glad to see that there are beginnings as well as endings,' he said.

As she walked to the Ford, Nerys looked up at the mountain-tops. The snow was melting fast, filling the stream that dashed past the dyers' sheds in an icy flood. Very soon, the high passes would open and the road from Kargil would be clear again.

TWELVE

A startling crash in the undergrowth, then a long rattle of stones rolling downhill made Mair jump. She swung round and glimpsed a goat's scrawny hindquarters as it dashed away. A second later its stink swept over her and she was instantly transported back to Changthang, where all the weeks of exploration had begun. And here, in the abandoned village, was where her unravelling of the shawl's history finally ended.

Mehraan's father's and grandfather's families and the other *kani* craftsmen had lived and worked in this huddle of cottages, now little more than broken walls surrendered to the weeds and thorn bushes. In the middle of the rough square stood a gaunt tree trunk, the scorched and splintered wood indicating that it had been struck by lightning. She picked her way past it and stood in the doorway of the biggest house. Looking upwards through the bare rafters she could see a lammergeier riding on the upward draughts of air.

There were a few scraps of abandoned furniture on the earth floor of the house, an old aluminium pot among the mud-brick rubble, the chimney pipe of a cooking stove tilted in one corner. It was like the old mission house in Leh. The people who had lived here were gone, and they were never coming back. The links were broken.

Shivering a little, Mair went outside again and wandered

away to the edge of the village where the river rushed down through a rocky ravine. There were more derelict buildings here, roofs of rusted corrugated iron hanging at dangerous angles, a corner of one sheet creaking in the wind as a counter-point to the splash of water. Downhill, across a bend in the river, Mair could pick out a red dot. It was the Coca-Cola baseball cap worn by the driver from the Srinagar travel agency, who had brought her up here on a half-day excursion in the inevitable white Toyota.

She sat down on a flat rock and looked over at the remains of Kanihama.

Mehraan's grandfather, the weaver who had signed his work with a double BB, was dead, his son too, and the villagers had moved elsewhere. Fine shawls were still made in Kashmir, and were bought for weddings and stored as precious currency, or else they went to Delhi and from there to the expensive shops of the West, but they were not woven in this village. This place belonged to the shepherds and their animals.

Abruptly Mair jumped up again. The scent of the wind, the smell of animal dung, even the patches of hardy turf between grey rocks reminded her of home and the old house in Wales. As longing for the valley swept over her, she heard her father's voice. 'Had enough of your travels? Come on, come back to us.'

She blinked. He was gone, but what he had said was right. It was time to go home. She wanted to see Hattie and her other friends, her brother and sister.

There was one more visit to make in Srinagar, and after that she was ready to leave. Mair put her hands in the pockets of her coat and began to skip downhill.

'Here you are again. How jolly,' Caroline called out, as soon as Aruna showed her into the room.

There was sitar music quietly playing but Aruna switched it off and ostentatiously tidied the handful of CD cases. Caroline's bandaged leg was still propped up and there was a smell of antiseptic. She began talking as if no time at all had elapsed since Mair's first visit.

'I'm so glad you dropped in. Seeing the shawl again brought it all back, you know, such marvellous memories. They were dear, loyal chums to me, Myrtle and Nerys were. I remember it all perfectly. The *Garden of Eden*. How we used to laugh about that.'

'Srinagar was like the Garden of Eden?'

Caroline gave a long peal of laughter. 'No, I mean the house-boat. Myrtle's – on the lake.'

'Oh, I see. The names. The one I'm staying in is called *Solomon and Sheba*.'

'What fun. It's terribly good of you to take time to visit an old crock like me. There must be masses of things you'd rather be doing on your holiday.'

'No,' Mair said. 'Really, there aren't.'

'Do have some gin. I'm not supposed to drink, the doctor now tells me. But I can give you some – don't suppose that will do me any harm, eh? Aruna, where are you?'

Remembering the last time, Mair insisted that she would much prefer tea. Aruna was despatched to make it. 'I've brought a photograph to show you,' she said, as soon as they were alone together.

Caroline's white head turned. 'Have you, dear?'

Mair knelt by her chair and held up the picture. 'If I turn this light on, and hold it towards the window as well, do you think you could see it?'

Slowly, stiffly, Caroline took it and drew it so close that it touched her nose. She screwed up her eyes so that they were almost swallowed in loose skin crosshatched with wrinkles. Her other hand patted the folds of her clothing and retrieved a pair of glasses on a cord. By setting these in place and angling her neck to one side, she seemed able to bring it into focus.

She studied it for a long time.

'Yes, that was the *Garden of Eden*.' She pointed with a knobbly finger. 'That's Myrtle McMinn, with your grandmother,

295

Nerys, the dear creature. Look at us. We were girls, weren't we? Hardly more than children ourselves.'

She let the picture drop on to her chest. Without warning, tears ran down her cheeks. She took a handkerchief from her sleeve and dried her eyes.

Mair whispered, 'I'm sorry. I didn't mean to upset you.'

'Not at all. I'm just being silly. So long ago, you know. So long I can hardly believe I was once that girl.'

'Can you remember who took the picture? Was it your husband? Or Mr McMinn? Or maybe my grandfather?'

'Evan Watkins? Such a stern, sweet man he was. No, it wasn't him.'

'Who, then?'

Caroline shook her head. She smiled through her tears, a very old person's wily, secretive smile. 'It was the magician. My goodness, he was the pin-up. Whatever was his name? I can't have forgotten.' Her face clouded, then cleared again. 'I remember. His name was Rainer,' she said.

Mair actually heard a click, like a key fitting a lock.

At Lamayuru, the night before the terrible day, Bruno Becker had told her that his mountain-guide grandfather had worked for Rainer Stamm, the mountaineer. The two of them had almost died in an attempt to climb the north face of the Eiger. She could precisely recall the cadences of Bruno's voice, and she could almost taste the cognac on her tongue. 'Rainer Stamm?'

Caroline nodded in surprise. 'Why, yes. That's right. Do you know him?'

'I don't. His name was mentioned to me by someone else, when we were on our way from Leh to Srinagar.'

'Who would that be?'

'Bruno Becker. He's Swiss, and he's married to an American woman called Karen.' She thought that the names just might mean something to Mrs Bowen. She added, 'They had a beautiful little daughter called Lotus.'

'They *had*?'

296

The forensic sharpness of the question took Mair aback. She said quickly, regretting her lack of foresight, 'It's a very sad story. I'm sorry, I didn't want to bring you bad news.'

Aruna carried in the tea tray. There was a homely patchwork tea cosy, china cups and a battered silver bowl containing sugar cubes with a pair of clawed tongs. It all looked much more appealing than warm gin.

'I don't know these people,' Caroline said. 'Do you take milk and sugar? Please go on.'

Mair hesitated. 'I met the Beckers by chance in Leh and we set out from there together. We were cut off on the way by a heavy snowstorm, and at the place where we were staying the little girl was bitten by a rabid dog. I heard a few days ago from her father. I'm afraid she didn't survive.'

Caroline put down the milk jug. Her hand shook and china clinked on the tray. 'I am so very sorry to hear that. How painful for her family. The death of a child is a great tragedy.'

Aruna took the filled teacup from her and passed it to Mair. 'Don't be tired,' she warned the old woman. Over Caroline's head she glowered at Mair.

'I am so pleased you brought me the photograph,' Caroline murmured, and sweetly smiled. She's slipping into forgetfulness, Mair thought. The old lady didn't really have any idea who her visitor was. The photograph represented a tiny piece in the mosaic of her memories, the pattern still bright and sharp in places but rubbed into a featureless monochrome in others.

Caroline seemed to be talking to herself now more than to Mair. She nodded. 'Yes, it must have been precious to Nerys. The picture, and the shawl too.'

Mair took it out of her bag one last time and shook it out so it floated on the air between them. 'When I showed it to you the other day, you said something like, "This was Zahra's."'

'Did I?'

'So . . . I wondered if you would like to have it? To give back to Zahra, perhaps?'

It was a stab in the dark, no more than that. But the

reaction was startling. Caroline threw up her hands. 'Oh, no, no, thank you. Poor little Zahra. It was a way of paying for her, you see. Yes, that was what it was. Oh dear. Now I am going to cry.'

Appalled, Mair saw how Mrs Bowen crumpled like a winter leaf. She was completely at sea now.

Aruna marched forward and put her hand under Mair's arm, propelling her to her feet. 'Mrs Bowen must not be upset so much. I ask you to leave her in peace, not to come with these old things.'

'I'm s-sorry, so sorry,' Mair stammered.

Aruna almost frogmarched her to the door. Caroline's face was hidden in her hands.

'Please forgive me for upsetting you,' Mair called to her.

Outside the room Aruna rounded on her. 'Why do you come here to talk of these hurts? She lose her own little girl. You know so much but not this? Long time ago, but she spend many, many years in England in asylum. She come back here to Srinagar and life is quiet for her. Please respect.'

'Of course. Of course I will. I didn't know.'

Caroline called loudly, 'The letters, Aruna. From Nerys. They are in a box. I want the young woman to have the *letters*. She is my friend Nerys Watkins's granddaughter, you know . . .' Her cracked old voice shook with urgency, but Aruna almost bundled Mair into the street. The door closed firmly on her. Mair waited for a moment or two and knocked again, but she knew there would be no answer.

The blue mountains were doubled in the flat lake water, and a twinned reflection turned every passing *shikara* into a strange insect suspended in glassy air. In the shallows beside the *Garden of Eden*, lotus flowers turned their creamy petals into the sunshine. Sighing with satisfaction at the view and the day's springtime perfection, Myrtle drained her glass and held it up to let Majid know she needed a refill.

She had curled her hair, applied her favourite dark red

298

lipstick, and there was a determined gaiety in her manner. Nerys noticed how many drinks she had had, but she well knew that this was how Myrtle dealt with a low mood. The latest news of Archie was that he had been posted nearer to the front line but Myrtle would never express anxiety, even to Nerys and Caroline. She sparkled today as she always did, although there was a metallic glint in her brilliance.

'Do you realise what we have here?' she cried. 'Three mothers and one daughter. That's rather lovely, don't you think?'

Nerys had brought Zahra down from Kanihama. The baby lay in her red and green woven wicker basket under the shade of an awning. She was a tranquil little creature, accepting her bottle from whoever was on hand to give it and gravely eyeing the world from Nerys's arms or from her sling on Farida's back. Sometimes Caroline could be encouraged to hold her, but the tense lines of her shoulders and her shadowed smile betrayed her uncertainty. The other two women didn't try to force the issue. Ever since she had given birth, Caroline had been in a delicate mental state. Some days, Myrtle reported, she lacked the will even to get out of her bed in the houseboat. Myrtle didn't think she was fit to go back to her bungalow in the compound, but Caroline had numbly insisted that this was what she must do.

'Otherwise what will people think?' she said. 'I've completely recovered from my so-called fever. I told Mrs Dunkeley so. You have both been so kind to me. If only I knew what was going to happen to Zahra . . .'

Her eyes filled with tears all over again. Caroline cried too often these days, at a dead bird glimpsed by the roadside, a crippled child begging in the bazaar. Nerys and Myrtle hurried to reassure her. 'Zahra is well and happy. As far as the world is concerned, she will be a mission orphan, just like Farida and her brothers. There's nothing to link her to you or to Ravi Singh,' Nerys said, for the hundredth time.

Myrtle adored the baby. She swept her up and rubbed her firm nose against Zahra's soft button one, and covered her olive skin with lipsticked kisses.

'Divine, so divine,' she crooned. 'I could eat you all up, ears to toes. Oh, God, Nerys, do you think Archie might let us adopt her when this bloody war ends?'

Nerys hesitated. She said carefully, 'Srinagar will whisper that she's yours and not Archie's. We've given them every reason to jump to that conclusion.'

Myrtle cackled. 'Who gives a damn about whispers? I don't. When Archie comes home and sees her, I'm sure he'll fall in love with her too. Don't you think?' Then she looked up from her contemplation of the baby and her eyes met Nerys's. 'But are you and Evan going to fight me for her?'

It was a joke, with a shiver of painful truth in it.

Nerys loved Zahra too. Sometimes she felt afraid of how much she adored the dark eyes and tiny curling fingers. But she could only shake her head. She hadn't seen Evan since the previous autumn, and he was beginning to feel like a stranger to her. Who could predict what her husband might allow, or might refuse even to consider?

Zahra's future was just one of the legion of uncertainties facing them all.

Majid brought Myrtle another drink. Picking up the basket, he announced, 'Time for baby feeding.'

He had fallen for Zahra too, and whenever he could he spirited her away to the dim recesses of the kitchen boat to be cooed over by the cook and the boys and their retinue of aunts and sisters. As he took her off he said, 'Visitor coming, ma'am.'

They looked up to see a gold-painted *shikara* gliding over the water. Against the gaudy cushions Rainer lay back and smoked his pipe. He waved and called to them, 'Summer is here.'

In Kashmir May was the most beautiful month of all. The almond, apple and cherry trees were in bloom and falling petals blew in the breeze, like the antithesis of snow.

The boatman made fast and Rainer hopped up the steps to the shade of the veranda. He was strong and his burns had healed quickly, but he never spoke about his excursion to Malaya.

He kissed Caroline and Myrtle twice on each cheek, then lifted Nerys's hand and touched it to his lips. She blushed at the sudden tenderness in him. 'I have come to take Nerys away,' he announced. 'It's a day for a picnic in the Shalimar Garden.'

'Off you go, then,' Myrtle waved a hand. 'Caroline and I will have tea and maybe a cocktail or two at the club.'

'Won't you let me try out my new toy first?' Rainer had brought an elaborate new Leica camera with him, complete with tripod and a set of lenses. He lifted the camera body out of its brown leather case and fiddled with the settings. Then he pointed to the corner of the veranda framed by the carved-wood canopy. 'Sit over there, perhaps, with the lake behind you.'

'Whatever you say, Mr Stamm.'

Myrtle took her natural place in the middle, tipped up her chin and looked straight into the camera. Caroline edged beside her, smiling but looking to the other two for her cue as she and Nerys hooked their arms around Myrtle's waist.

He said, 'That's very pretty. I shall name this portrait "Summer in the *Garden of Eden*".'

Nerys always remembered Myrtle's scent and the waft of cigarette smoke, the light catching the diamond in Caroline's engagement ring and Rainer clowning behind the lens. He put a black cloth over his head and muttered inside its folds, then shouted, '*Hey presto!*' As they laughed at him, the shutter clicked.

'You haven't disappeared in a puff of smoke,' Myrtle pointed out. 'And neither have we.'

'I must be out of practice,' he said.

A cloud licked over the sun, and for a second the shimmer faded out of the day. Nerys drew her cardigan over her shoulders and checked that Myrtle's circlet brooch was safe.

'Have you time for a drink?' Myrtle asked. 'Do just have

301

one, won't you? Caroline and I might be quite blue once we're left on our own.'

'Please forgive me this time. I want to talk to Nerys,' Rainer said.

The *shikara* man was waiting for them at the steps, idly dipping his paddle and watching the insects skimming over the water. Ripples briefly fractured the reflected mountains. Myrtle clapped her hands and her smile widened.

'Of course. Have fun!' she cried.

A moment later Nerys and Rainer were gliding towards the trees at the far end of the lake. Nerys was quiet because the afternoon's loveliness seemed intensified by its fragility. Rainer's arm rested over her shoulders, but she was thinking how opaque he had become. Or perhaps he always had been. She had learnt the shape and weight of him, his scent and taste and the various timbres of his voice, but he had given away so little.

In the great Mogul garden the fountains splashed between the beds of crimson peonies. They walked under the dappled shade of unfurling chinar leaves and Rainer talked of a new trick he was devising and an invitation he had received to perform magic to entertain British and American troops.

'But *where* will you be going?' Nerys asked, out of dread of his leaving and fear that he might stay. 'And when?' She had her own urgent reason for wanting to talk to him today.

They came to the top of the garden's series of steps and turned to look back at the view.

'Let's have our picnic,' he said.

As always, Rainer took pleasure in the precision of practical arrangements. From a canvas rucksack he produced a white cloth and spread it in the shade of a huge old tree. There was a metal flask of fresh sweet buttermilk laced with mint, and afternoon bread just an hour old, fragrant and crusted with sesame.

Below them rolled the flowers and geometric water courses, sparkling with fountains, and beyond that the lake with its blue islands, the haze of smoke over the old town and the two

Srinagar hills crowned with a fort and a temple. Perhaps he had brought her here to lay all this at her feet, like a Mogul emperor with his latest concubine. She turned abruptly to him but he stopped her with a finger to her mouth.

'I have to leave Srinagar, Nerys. I would have gone already, if every hour with you didn't make me wish for two more.'

It would be so easy to believe him.

Then he whispered, 'Come with me. Stay with me.'

Briefly, the world contracted until it was no more than the twin points of light reflected in his barley-sugar eyes. His finger moved to rest in the notch at the base of her throat and, giddily, Nerys imagined the cities she would never see unless she followed Rainer, the journeys they might take, and the mountains he had promised to show her.

But when she tried to picture their homecomings, a home refused to materialise. There was no such place. Not even Rainer's particular magic could frame one for the two of them.

It took the greatest effort she had ever made to clasp his warm hand and draw it away from her, but she managed to do it. His response was to move even closer so that their mouths almost touched. 'Nerys, will you marry me? I want you to be my woman.'

She let the words run through her like Kashmiri honey. But then she straightened her back and looked into his eyes. 'I am married already. We have been trying to pretend I'm not, that's all.'

Rainer batted the objection away. 'Divorce him. Or if we can't marry, come and live with me. You are not a woman to be hedged by conventions. I know you better than that.'

And that proved he did *not* know her.

In her pocket was this morning's letter from Evan, filled with the fussy details of the work he was obliged to leave in order to travel to Srinagar, details that he wished her to investigate in connection with the possible establishment of another mission in Kashmir, and all the silent, fretful constructions of her husband's fear and anxiety.

303

She *was* a woman to be hedged by conventions, because those conventions were what she had pledged to uphold. It was only now that she was presented with the real possibility of flouting them that she understood how firmly she intended to stand.

Her stomach turned over at the thought of what lay ahead. There was a single flicker of brightness in the vista, and that was pride in making – at last – the hardest decision of her life.

'No,' she said. 'Evan will arrive in Srinagar later this week. He is bringing the mission to Kashmir, and I will support his work.'

Disbelief kindled in Rainer's eyes.

She studied the creases in his skin, the humorous twist of his mouth, and realised that of all the times she had desired him in the months since Christmas she longed for him most urgently now.

He said, 'Don't give away your own happiness for another person's sake. Don't abandon your own life.'

And in her raw state she was suddenly angry with him. The uncertainties that had swamped her in the past weeks fell away. Whatever lay in store, she would be living her life by her own principles, not Rainer Stamm's.

'Abandoning my life? That's an arrogant assumption. I am doing no such thing.'

A motor launch inched its way across the lake, spinning a silver thread behind it. Perhaps it was Ravi Singh's, she thought.

'I love you,' Rainer said quietly.

He had never told her this before. She tried out the response in her head. *I love you too. I'll always love you.* But she said nothing. The afternoon was loud with birdsong and the chirp of crickets yet silence bled between them, cutting them off from each other and sealing their separation.

'I leave Srinagar tomorrow,' he warned her.

She lifted her head. 'Did you believe I'd follow you?'

He met her eyes. 'I let myself hope.'

304

'I am so sorry.'

As she studied his face, his expression changed. In a single second he became a different person. He smiled at her, a performer's smile that he might have flashed at an audience before some feat of disguise or misdirection. 'What a shame. But why are we so serious? Life is for enjoying, and that's what we should do. If we can't, *pfffff*.' He shrugged and exhaled, and his foreignness struck her as it had never done before.

Scrambling to his feet, he held out his hand. 'Come on. Why don't we finish our walk? It's a beautiful evening.'

They descended the long series of steps and crossed the terraces between fountains and water channels. On the lowest level of the garden there were great beds of scarlet tulips. To Nerys's burning eyes, they looked like pools of blood.

Outside the walls they fought their way through the insistent crowds of beggars and trinket-sellers and *chai*-vendors brought out by the promise of summer, and she felt exhausted by the sheer hourly effort it took just to exist in India.

I want to go *home*, she thought, for almost the first time since she had come to Srinagar. The longing for Wales, for her own place and people and that other green valley threaded with streams, almost overpowered her.

At the jetty, the gold-painted *shikara* was waiting for them. The boatman handed her aboard and saw to it that she was comfortable on the mattress cushions. Instead of taking the place next to her Rainer sat opposite with his back to the boat's prow.

'So I can look at you,' he said. The sun was slipping down the sky and the light had changed from blue to gold. When they reached the middle of the lake, where veils of mist were beginning to lift off the water, Rainer picked up the boatman's spare paddle that was stowed beside his feet. He studied the familiar leaf-shaped blade and then inverted it. Pressed against his chest, it formed a heart.

They reached the *Garden of Eden*. There was nobody at

home, but they heard voices from the kitchen boat. Rainer stood up, balancing against the *shikara*'s gentle rocking, and helped Nerys to the steps. Then he released her hand. 'Goodnight,' he said.

'Goodnight, Rainer. I hope you have a safe journey.'

Wherever you are going.

She stood on the veranda under the carved-wood awning and watched the *shikara* glide away. Rainer still stood upright, with the inverted paddle close to his side. This was the image of him that she would carry with her: his shadow laid over the still water, cupped in the reflections of the boat's high stern and prow, and the leaf-heart placed over his own, a shield as well as a declaration.

'Good evening, ma'am.'

Nerys spun round. It was Majid in his white tunic, hands pressed together.

'Majid, where is Mrs McMinn?'

'I think club, ma'am.'

'And the baby?'

'She is here, ma'am.'

When Zahra woke up, Nerys gave her a bottle, bathed and changed her. The scrawny limbs had grown rounded and dimpled. When the sudden darkness fell she stood on the veranda and rocked the baby in her arms, her lips pressed to her black hair.

When Myrtle climbed out of the *shikara* that had brought her back from the club she stumbled on the steps and almost fell into the water. 'Damn, blast it. That's my last pair of decent stockings in tatters,' she cried.

Nerys took her arm and tried to steer her to a chair. Myrtle resisted, and folded into the sofa instead. She put her head into her hands and massaged her forehead. 'My wretched, dazed brain.'

'I'll get you some water.'

'Have you heard the news?'

306

Nerys waited, her breath catching.

'A poor boy has been knifed to death. They found his body in one of those brick alleys in the bazaar.'

She didn't even have to ask the question, because Myrtle was already answering it. 'A Muslim boy.'

Set upon in the dark by Hindu youths, themselves avenging some earlier attack by Muslims: the latest episode in the religious hatred that swelled under Kashmir's smooth skin.

'There's rioting,' Myrtle said. 'At the club, just now, they were advising everyone to go home and stay inside until the morning. *Otherwise* I'd still be there.'

Nerys listened, and in the stillness she thought she could just hear the distant sound of shouts and stone-throwing.

'I don't understand India any more. It's all I know, but I can hardly recognise the country where I grew up, or understand what's happening to beautiful Kashmir. They want us to leave, and we will do, but what will happen after that? There'll be nothing left, nothing but blood and destruction.'

Myrtle groped in her handbag and found her cigarette case. She lit one of her gold-tipped cigarettes and exhaled a blue cloud. As Nerys watched her, she lost her poise and her powdered face crumpled. 'Everything is ending. What's going to happen to us all?'

Nerys had never seen Myrtle cry. She held her in her arms and smoothed the tears that chased blackened streaks down her face.

'God, I'm *drunk*. Pie-eyed. Archie doesn't let me do it, you know. But he's not here, and everything is so dismal, and I'm an apology without him.'

Nerys insisted, 'No, you're not. You're a brave, strong, admirable woman, and the best friend I've ever had. I've learnt so much from you and that's the honest truth.'

They gripped each other's hands. The clamour in the distance seemed to be subsiding, leaving only the night noises of lapping water and owls hooting.

Myrtle sniffed and blew her nose. 'Damn. So sorry. Stupid of me. It's the drink and the news of a senseless murder. How was the Shalimar picnic? Where's Rainer?'

'He wanted to tell me that he's leaving Srinagar tomorrow. Today was a goodbye.'

'Oh, my darling. And here's me with *my* tale of woe. To hell with it all. Come on, let's have a nightcap. Don't you think so? Mmm?'

'No, Myrtle. No more to drink. Come on, let's get you to bed.'

'You sound like Archie. I rather like it.' Myrtle stood up and made her unsteady way to Zahra's basket. She leant down and turned back an inch of coverlet. '*You* are the future, aren't you, little girl? Thank God we have you here to remind us there's some point to this wicked world.'

Then she let Nerys help her to her room, where she submitted to having her shoes removed and her dress unbuttoned. With some difficulty, Nerys settled her in her bed among the starched pillowcases, embroidered hangings and silk quilts. There was face powder scattered on the dressing-table's glass top, a clutter of scent jars, discarded clothes piled on a carved wooden chair.

'Stay with me,' Myrtle begged. 'Talk. Tell me, I don't know . . . Tell me about you and Rainer.'

Nerys thought about it. 'I shall miss him,' she said in the end. She loved him, she might have added, but there was no sentence or suggestion that followed on from that admission. The mountaineer-magician and the missionary's wife? She smiled. The end of their affair had been there all along, sewn up in its beginning.

'When does Evan get to Srinagar?'

'He said in his letter that there were two or three days' work he wanted to finish in Kargil, then he'll be on his way. So in a week's time, at most.'

'Rainer knows that, of course?'

'Of course.'

'Hah. He's making a tactical exit, then.'

'He asked me to go with him. He asked me to marry him.'

Myrtle drew in a breath and turned her head on the pillow. 'And?'

There is no *and*.

'I reminded him that I'm already married.'

'And you'll do your duty,' Myrtle agreed. 'All right. Tell me one thing, and please be honest. Do you feel guilty about last winter?'

Nerys looked at her. Myrtle's eyes were growing heavy with sleep.

'No,' she said.

'That's good to hear. Because nothing corrodes a marriage like guilt, my girl.'

'Evan and I will have to find a way to live. But I won't be doing so as an apology, or an act of atonement for having committed adultery.'

Myrtle gave a spurt of drowsy laughter. 'I *like* that. I'm impressed. Caroline should take a lesson from you.'

'Caroline will find her own solution. But d'you think that's what we're really about, the three of us? Doing our duty?'

'Of course. That's what we do. We're wives of the Raj.'

There was another faint bubble of laughter before Myrtle drifted into sleep. Nerys waited until she was breathing steadily, a puff of a snore with each exhalation, then slid off the bed. She adjusted the covers over Myrtle's shoulders and only hesitated for a second before kissing her damp forehead. She could smell the gin in her pores.

From Kargil, Evan had taken a guide and horses over the Zoji La as far as the Hindu shrine to Shiva at Amarnath, and from there he joined the stream of religious pilgrims returning to the city. For the last nine miles of the journey the Srinagar road was passable to vehicles, so he crowded with the other travellers into a public bus.

Nerys was waiting for him at the depot on the dusty outskirts of the city. One bus had already pulled in and discharged its passengers. There were farmers coming to market, pilgrims, labourers and several vast families running to three or four generations, but Evan hadn't been among them. She returned to her seat on a low stone wall and watched the seething crowds. There was a din of traffic, and the thick smell of exhaust fumes and kerosene. An emaciated dog with open sores on its back nosed in rubbish scattered at the roadside. A second bus rounded the corner and stopped at the far side of the road. A throng of men burst out and began to drag their bundles from the interior. The cacophony of shouting and hooting grew even louder, and in the midst of it she caught sight of Evan. He climbed slowly down the steps of the bus and awkwardly retrieved two shabby grips from the cascade of bags being tossed off the roof by the baggage men. Then he stood stiffly in the full heat of the sun, one bag in either hand, a sombre figure in his dusty black clerical clothes.

Nerys jumped up and slipped through the crowd. She touched her hand to his sleeve and he swung round. His eyes widened as he gazed at her. 'Nerys, you look beautiful,' he stammered.

She was startled and pleased. Evan never commented on her appearance. 'Do I?'

'You do. You look like . . . one of the colonial ladies.'

'Well, I'm *not* one. I'm Mrs Watkins of the Welsh Presbyterian Mission to Northern India, just the same as ever. Hello, Evan.'

'Hello, my dear,' he said. He was shy of this new version of his wife with her hair prettily arranged and her floral-print dress.

'Welcome to Srinagar.' She stood on tiptoe and kissed him, her lips just catching the corner of his cheek as he turned his head.

'It's busy. So many people. I'm not used to crowds,' he said.

'I know. But it's a beautiful city, once you get to know it.' She took one of his bags and linked her other hand in his.

'Where are we going?' Evan asked.

'First of all to the *Garden of Eden*,' she answered. 'Myrtle is there, and I want you to meet Caroline. After that we can go home. To Kanihama, I mean.'

Zahra was back with the extended families up in the village. Nerys had decided that this would be the best context in which to introduce their shared orphan baby to Evan.

They stayed in the city for two days as Myrtle's guests. Nerys was not surprised that Evan was suspicious of Srinagar. He loomed uncomfortably among the cushions and framed photographs in the houseboat, and he refused altogether to make the *shikara* ride across to the Srinagar Club. The summer season's round of parties and polo matches had started up again, although in a more muted way since most of the men were away with their Indian or British Army regiments, but Evan would have no part of it. It was only under duress that he accepted his invitation to that week's cocktail reception on the lawn at the Residency, and took his turn to shake Mr Fanshawe's hand. He misunderstood the protocol of the receiving line and began a lengthy account of the Presbyterian Mission in India.

'There is good work going on in Kargil, I am pleased to say. We have a growing congregation and I have recently left the mission under the highly competent supervision of one of my fellow ministers,' he explained. 'We are now bringing the message into Kashmir.'

'Jolly good,' Mr Fanshawe said pleasantly, and one of his aides manoeuvred Evan away. In wartime, missionaries of any creed or nationality came very low down on the British government's scale of importance.

Caroline came to tea on the houseboat, wearing a duck-egg blue crêpe de Chine blouse and her pearl necklace. She looked pale but held herself steady. In a low voice she explained to Evan that she had been unwell recently and her husband was in Malaya, a prisoner of war of the Japanese.

'I shall pray for you both and for his safe return,' Evan said.

'Thank you.' Caroline touched his hand, seeming genuinely comforted.

311

That night, Nerys and Evan lay side by side under the cigar-box panelling. Her husband's presence seemed to amplify the houseboat's creaking and the rippling of water, and because they were conscious of the way that the sound travelled they spoke in whispers.

'Your friend Mrs Bowen is highly strung.'

'Yes, she is.'

'I feel sorry for her,' he said.

Nerys thought he must recognise a fellow sufferer. She could feel the tension that ran through Evan as if there were steel wires under the seams and buttons of his flannel pyjamas.

'Mrs McMinn has been kind, all these months.'

'Yes,' Nerys agreed.

'I was a little afraid that your head might be turned, you know.'

The darkness masked her smile. 'By kindness?'

'Of course not. By this way of life. The *Garden of Eden*, indeed. We can't afford legions of servants in white jackets. We don't drink gin, or smoke cigarettes.'

'I am your wife, Evan. I understand what our way of life must be.'

Nerys thought of Rainer and the way that he regarded his body as a useful instrument, not an adversary either to be tortured by or to be guilty about. And then, with precise determination, she moved on from the memories of Rainer and what they had done together in order to concentrate on the knowledge she had gained from them. She curled herself against Evan's rigid hip, and fitted her chin in the nook of his shoulder. She listened to the way their breathing snagged and then almost imperceptibly synchronised. Gently she hooked her arm over his ribs and warmth spread between their bodies.

He cleared his throat and turned on to his side, facing away from her.

Once, Nerys reflected, she would have taken this as a rejection and she would have drawn back to lie staring miserably into darkness.

Instead she nestled closer, fitting her curve against his. His spine was a string of bony knobs. Her lips touched the most prominent one at the base of his neck. 'It's all going to be all right,' she whispered.

She had to believe that it would be.

They fell asleep still curled together.

Two days later they reached Kanihama.

Evan strode into the ramshackle square and surveyed the old men sitting under the shade of the chinar tree, the wandering goats and the mud-brick houses. A pack of children, led by Faisal, broke out of their game and clamoured at Nerys's knees. Farida appeared in the shadow of a wall, with Zahra asleep in the sling on her back. She lifted her hand and let it fall as soon as Nerys saw her. Thin spirals of smoke rose against the blue sky and the air was cool after the city's heat.

The tight set of Evan's shoulders seemed to loosen. He looked round with less certainty, but with kindled interest. Perhaps, Nerys thought, this place brought their real home to mind in the same way as it did for her.

She led him into her house. He took in the brick walls with their rough hangings, the bedroom that was little more than a smoky alcove, her *kangri* in its storage niche beside the iron stove. 'You spent the winter *here*?' he asked.

'From January, yes.'

There was a silence. Inquisitive children had gathered in the doorway and an outer circle of villagers was assembling to watch the latest spectacle.

Evan put his hand on her shoulder, then shifted it so that his fingers traced the stalk of her neck. 'I admire you.'

'It wasn't so bad. It gets quite warm when the stove is lit.'

'I shouldn't have said what I did, about your head being turned. I'm sorry.'

'There's no need to be.' She smiled.

Faisal slid into the room. 'Hello, sir.' Pointing with a sharp, filthy forefinger he recited, 'Head, arm, knee, foot.'

313

'Very good, well done.' Evan nodded. 'Who is this boy?'

'Faisal. He's very clever. He was my first pupil.'

'And how many do you have now?'

'A dozen. It's a barter system. They learn a few words of English, and I am occasionally paid in eggs, some onions and carrots.' She laughed. 'It works rather well.'

'What about their families?'

'They are weavers, dyers, embroiderers. It's a Muslim village. They don't have a mosque here, but there is a prayer room. The women work very hard, growing the vegetables, tending the animals, raising the children. Most of the men are in the shawl trade. The pieces they make are exquisite but they have become too expensive to sell and make a profit.'

Evan went outside, ducking his head just in time to avoid the low door lintel. Farida detached herself from the wall and stepped backwards.

'This is Farida, and the baby is Zahra,' Nerys murmured, with her heart knocking.

He glanced at them and nodded. 'I can begin our work here,' he said. 'I will start with the villagers, then visit the outlying settlements. I noticed on the way up that the area is fairly heavily populated, given the altitude.'

She smiled. 'There's plenty of water, fertile soil, sunshine for four months of the summer. The Kashmiris believe their valley is a small paradise.'

Evan frowned. 'Do they?'

It was hot under the midday sun. He removed his black clerical coat and turned back frayed shirt cuffs to expose his thin wrists, as if to indicate that he was ready to start work at that very moment. At the head of a small group of village men, Nerys saw Zafir making his way towards them. He bowed to her, his dark crescent face unsmiling.

'Your husband, ma'am?'

Nerys made the simple introductions, praying that at least Evan would not launch into being the Christian preacher. To her relief, he quietly accepted the men's scrutiny and finally

Zafir gave him a nod that indicated a qualified welcome. That was a good beginning, she thought. The only way for Westerners to be accepted in Kanihama was to accept its ways, and she guessed that Evan must have come to a similar – perhaps belated – conclusion in Kargil.

They made their way back to the house. The kettle boiled and Nerys brewed tea Kashmir-style, laced with spices. It was strange to see Evan seated opposite with his clerical collar off and the top shirt stud undone, his watch chain glinting across the concave front of his waistcoat. She smiled at him, and his watchful face broke into a faint answering smile.

'I think I shall buy a bicycle,' he announced. 'It will be useful to get about on.'

Later she took her pupils across to her makeshift schoolroom. He looked in on a singing game, and said that perhaps he would use the room for Bible readings and a discussion group.

'Was that how you began in Kargil?'

'It was. Not many came. I think our prayer meetings and services at Leh were well attended only because of the excellent *thukpa* dinners you and Diskit served afterwards.'

'Poor Diskit.' Nerys laughed to cover the pressure of her sympathy for Evan, for the patient, unshakeable depths of his belief and his willingness to go on working against all the odds of India. 'I'll see what I can do here, without her invaluable assistance.'

'Thank you, my dear. I owe you perhaps more than I had realised.'

The little group of children looked from one to the other.

'Shall we sing our song for Mr Watkins?' she suggested. With the accompaniment of their rattles and drums and carved pipes, they joined in a chorus. Evan listened to the end, then said he really must go and write his report for Shillong.

If it had been strange to see him sitting opposite her in this little house, it was stranger still to have him lying beside her that night. When she blew out the candle the darkness seemed so solid that it weighed on the bedclothes. She was thankful that Rainer had never once slept in this bed with her.

It will get easier not to think about him, she told herself. Time will pass.

'You seem very fond of that baby,' Evan remarked. Nerys lay with her head on his shoulder, her arm lightly curved over his chest. She thought a little of the tension had melted out of his limbs.

'Zahra? Yes, I am. And of Faisal too, and his sister and brother.'

She had told Evan nothing of Zahra's history, except that her mother had left her in the village because to own her would be to bring dishonour to her family. Evan had seen too many orphans in India to be inconveniently curious about this one.

He said firmly, 'I hope we will have a child of our own before too long.'

He turned on his side, but this time it was to face her. 'I'm sorry. I have been a poor husband to you. I thought about it a good deal when I was alone in Kargil. I intend to do better in future.'

When his mouth met hers, she tasted his sincerity. Evan was utterly incapable of dissembling.

Unlike me, unlike me.

'I haven't been the best wife, either.'

Evan gave this his consideration. 'Shall we agree to leave our unsatisfactory beginning behind us?'

In that lies the only hope for our future.

'Yes, I would like that very much.'

His hand moved. She let her knees fall apart and then her thighs, and he tentatively explored her. Now, at least, she understood what the explorer might discover. Slowly, by tiny stages, she led him into new territory.

There was no need for him to ask, *My dear?*

They fell into a routine at Kanihama. Evan did acquire a bicycle, and his dark, spindly figure urgently pedalling up the steep tracks

316

was at first a comic spectacle for the villagers and just as quickly became a familiar sight that people hardly noticed. He started his Bible classes, attended by none of the men, except some inquisitive youths and the village simpleton, who tried to add his voice to Evan's. Not one of the women came, of course. Then Nerys began to offer a simple dinner of rice and vegetable stew and a few of the poorest people ventured in. Evan said he would relay this promising news to Shillong and Delhi.

Nerys taught her little children, and in the afternoons she played with Faisal and the others or took Zahra for a walk along the winding tracks above the village where the resin scent of pine trees filled the air. In the evenings they ate their simple dinner, and read together by the light of a kerosene lantern. The war news from Europe, North Africa and Burma filtered up to them in days-old newspapers, in letters from home, and bulletins from Myrtle and Caroline in Srinagar.

It was the end of June when Nerys received a letter from Myrtle.

She slit open the envelope and a half-sheet of paper fell out. The few lines had been scribbled so quickly that they were hardly legible.

> Archie has been seriously wounded. He's been brought back on a troop ship and is in a military hospital in Chittagong. I'm leaving at once. Don't know how I'll get across there, but I'll do it somehow. D. Fanshawe is helping. Look after Caroline a little, if you can.
> Ask Evan to pray for A.
> Always your friend, M

With numb fingers Nerys refolded the note. In her basket, Zahra kicked her bare feet at a bar of sunlight.

Mair was in her bedroom on *Solomon and Sheba*, packing to go home. She was rolling up the last T-shirts and stuffing them into the crevices of her rucksack when Farooq knocked on the

317

door. He had already been twice on different pretexts, his hennaed beard twitching with curiosity, so she sighed and told him to come in.

'Very much luggage,' he said, peering into her open bags.

'Really? I call this travelling light.'

'Visitor to see you. It is one young man.'

She made her way down the creaking passageway, nodding to the male half of the Australian pair of aid workers who had recently arrived, and stepped along the gangplank to the lake shore. Mehraan was sitting astride a mosquito-sized motorbike, cradling his helmet in his lap.

'Mehraan, is this machine yours?'

'I have just bought it. It is useful.'

'It must be. I'm glad to see you. I'm leaving Srinagar tomorrow and I thought I'd come to the workshop later to say goodbye.'

'So I save you the trouble.' He smiled. 'Also I have done some small pieces of work for your friend, the English lady who has hurt her leg.'

'That's very kind of you.'

'Srinagar is not all bombing and throwing stones, you see. The lady's house is old, and some parts will fall down if we do not help to prop it. Yesterday I am there and her nurse gives me this package for you.'

'What is it?' Mair asked.

'*I* do not know,' he said.

Inside a folded piece of sacking tied with string was an ancient cardboard box with collapsing walls. Mair lifted one of the flaps and saw a bundle of old letters. There was a note attached, written in an almost indecipherable looped hand-writing on lined paper.

My eyesight is now too poor to reread your grandmother's letters. Perhaps you would like to see them. Please do not trouble to return them.
Sincerely yours,
Caroline C. Bowen

'Oh,' Mair said aloud.

'Something is wrong?'

'No, nothing at all.' She was astonished that Caroline had remembered their conversation and then actually hunted out the cache of letters. She was trying to decide now whether she should go across town now to thank her in person for this treasure, but quickly concluded that it would be better not. She didn't think Mrs Bowen was being confined by Aruna, but her carer obviously preferred her not to be upset. The way she had been hustled out at the end of her last visit made her reluctant to risk causing another disturbance.

'Can you wait here for five minutes, Mehraan?'

She raced back to her room and found a large picture postcard of the Shalimar Garden. On the back she wrote a message of thanks for the loan of the letters, and promised that she would make sure they were returned safely even if she couldn't deliver them in person. 'I hope, though, to hand them back to you myself,' she promised, and signed her name.

Then she put the card into a big envelope, addressed it and gave it to Mehraan. 'Next time you visit her, will you give her this from me?'

Aruna would read it to Caroline, at worst.

'I will,' he said. He put on the enormous helmet and pressed the bike's starter button.

Mair would have liked to give him a hug, or at least shake his hand, but she limited herself to a warm smile and a nod. 'I hope we'll see each other again, Mehraan, next time I come to Srinagar.'

'*Inshallah*.' He kicked off the stand and zoomed away towards the Bund.

Early the next morning, Farooq waved her off in a taxi to the airport.

'Soon safe back with family in England,' he said gleefully, palming her generous tip and slipping it into the pocket of his shirt.

When the Delhi flight took off at last, Mair peered out of the window to watch as the lovely valley dropped out of sight and the brown plains opened beyond. Now that she was actually on her way, she was profoundly sad to be leaving Kashmir and all of India behind. She reminded herself that she was going home, and at the other end of her journey, Hattie would be waiting at the airport to meet her. Her spirits immediately lifted.

She would come back to Srinagar. She had already half promised Caroline Bowen that she would.

On her lap, still in its brittle envelope, lay the single letter that she had taken out of the box to read on the flight.

THIRTEEN

The chapel was small, austere and brown-varnished. The windows were clear glass with a view of grey hillside through the drizzle. As she took her black hymnal out of the slot in front of her, Mair thought of the abandoned chapel in Leh. She touched the folds of the brown pashmina tucked inside the collar of her best coat.

The minister took his place, the organist brought a meandering voluntary to a close and the congregation rustled to its feet. The bride came down the aisle on her father's arm, and Mair's old friend Tal turned to look at his Annie. His red face was anxious and, just as it had done since he was a boy, his stiff shirt collar looked as if it was half an inch too tight for his neck.

All weddings are the same, Mair thought, however different the superficial trappings. Anxiety and eagerness and the fizz of happiness popping just like a bottle of champagne.

The minister welcomed them all in Welsh, and her thoughts turned again to Nerys and Evan Watkins.

Afterwards, in the hotel receiving line, they shook hands with Annie's parents and then Tal's, and Mair batted away their well-meaning questions with 'Oh, I'll have to meet Mr Right first.' The bride and groom smiled, acknowledging their rightness for each other.

Dylan, Eirlys and Mair moved into the crowd of guests.

321

Weatherbeaten faces nodded over best suits and farmers' meaty hands gripped thin-stemmed glasses. Huw Ellis would have enjoyed this gathering of neighbours at the highly suitable joining together of two local families. He had always mildly regretted that not one of his three children had chosen to stay at home in Wales, although he had never complained. He had never even really objected to Mair and the circus.

'I wish the old man could have been here,' Dylan said, speaking for them all.

The reception was followed by the early meal and then long speeches, by which time a dozen exhausted children were chasing each other between the tables. Eirlys's husband Graeme rose from his place next to Annie's aunt, the headmistress from Liverpool, and announced that he would remove his boys and Dylan and Jackie's little girl, and put all three of them into bed at the holiday cottages where they were staying.

'No, really, I don't mind,' he insisted. The tables were being cleared and in a corner of the room a deejay was setting up his decks under a row of coloured lights. Mair withdrew with Dylan, Jackie and Eirlys to the bar.

From somewhere near waist-level, a voice chirped to Mair, 'Hello, dear. You're the image of your mother, aren't you?'

She looked down. The corner table was occupied by a little old lady wearing blue brocade and a spray of white carnation with maidenhair fern. Her rakish fascinator looked all the more so for having tipped forwards over one eye. Mair slipped into the empty chair beside her.

'I'm Mair Ellis,' she said, not certain that she hadn't been mistaken for someone else.

'I know that. I said, you look like your mother. I'm old enough to remember when *she* was born. Not long back from India, were they, your *nain* and *taid* Watkins? Gwen must have come as a surprise to them.'

Nerys had been forty-one – Mair knew that because she had verified the dates. She had half hoped that her mother and therefore she herself might have had a closer connection to

322

India, but when she consulted *Hope and the Glory of God* again she had been reminded that the minister and his wife finally left the missionary service in 1947 and Gwen hadn't been born until 1950.

'You're a proper Watkins in your looks,' said her new friend. 'Your brother, now, he favours your dad's side.'

'And me?' Eirlys wanted to know. Of course, she had missed none of the exchange even though she had also been negotiating a drinks order and a simultaneous conversation with Tal's brother.

The old lady pursed her lips. 'Well. Very proud of *you*, Gwen was. Always top of the class, she'd say. Doctor now, isn't it?'

Dylan put his arm round his sister. 'Consultant.'

Eirlys smiled, turning slightly pink. With her abrasiveness melted by a few glasses of wine she looked younger and – almost – carefree. 'Were you a friend of our mother's?'

The explanation, involving several farms, intermarriages and cousins on Tal's mother's side, was far too complicated for Mair and Eirlys to follow, although they nodded politely. Mrs Parry told them she had gone to chapel as a girl to hear Parchedig Watkins preach; that was before Gwen was born. Then in the school holidays she used to push the new baby out in her pram, while Nerys was doing her housework. When her own husband died, twenty-five years ago now, she had moved down to live with her sister near Caernarfon. 'But the old place, I still think of it as home.'

That was how it was, Mair reflected. Holiday homes pocked the hillsides and caravan parks scurfed the coast, but if you belonged here you didn't distinguish those as much as the fields and stone walls and valley lanes that hardly changed in a lifetime.

When her eyes met Eirlys's she saw that she was occupied with the same thought.

The house was sold but they hadn't lost their place, because they shared the root familiarity. Mair was happy that they had all made the journey back to Tal's wedding. Eirlys had been quite right to insist they did.

Through the open door Mair could see a slice of the dance floor. Tal led his wife into the centre of the empty space and they began the first dance together.

'Tell us about Mum,' Eirlys said.

Dylan joined them now. The Ellis children were like fledglings with their beaks open, always eager for any new crumb of information about their mother.

Mrs Parry nodded her white perm and the fascinator feathers bobbed. She evidently liked an audience. 'She was a precious gift, that girl. Into his fifties, your grandfather was, by the time Gwen came along. They both worshipped her, of course. I remember seeing Mr Watkins in his black coat, coming along the road with Gwen toddling beside him holding his hand. She was all dressed up in a coat and hat too, like one of the little princesses. Talking away to each other they were, no need for another soul. You always knew they were a happy family, the Watkinses. Lovely to see, it was.'

Eirlys stroked the knuckle of one finger across the corner of her eye. Then she squared her shoulders. In the next room the music was loud and the dancing was getting under way.

Mrs Parry sipped her drink. 'Of course, they'd seen the world together, hadn't they? It seemed really exotic to all of us, I can tell you, Mr and Mrs Watkins having lived all that time in India. It must have been nice for them to look back on it together, while the reverend was still alive.'

Mair thought of the photograph, her grandmother's laughter, and the backdrop of lake water and lotus blooms. Caroline had said that Rainer Stamm took the picture, and he was the pin-up. She realised that she very much wanted to see Bruno Becker again.

Bruno knew the Swiss side of the story, but she wasn't sure how to ask him about that. *I'm so sorry your daughter died. Now, tell me about long ago.* But it wasn't just for the information he could maybe provide that she wanted to see him: it was for himself.

Mrs Parry leant forward and tugged the knotted fringe of

324

Mair's shawl. 'It was the best time of her life, Nerys used to say. Kashmir, you know.'

'Did she? Did she really?'

'Mair's just been out there for three months. Visiting the places where they worked,' Dylan put in.

The old lady wasn't impressed. 'I expect it's all changed, like everywhere. Mind you, most of them are over here anyway, aren't they?'

Mrs Parry was the opposite of Caroline Bowen, Mair decided.

Tal came into the bar. His tie was undone and he looked hot and ridiculously happy. To Mair, he said, 'Do I get a dance, then?'

He took her hand in his huge fist and they worked their way into the thick of the dancing. Crimson faces and sweating bodies bobbed all around them. Mair could see Annie in the middle of the mob. She had removed her veil and tiara and the sausage ringlets set in her hair were gently unravelling.

Tal still danced the same way he always had done, with wild arm swings and pumping legs. He caught Mair's eye and smiled like a shy boy, and she was taken straight back to her sixteenth birthday party when Tal was the nearest thing she had had to a boyfriend.

It was quite possible that the record had been 'Love Is All Around' then as well as now.

Her talk with Bruno at Lamayuru was loud in her mind and, as if to amplify it, the one-time possibility of her parallel life was humming and judging, gossiping and letting its hair down all round her. 'We can't jive to this, Tal,' she shouted, and he hollered back, wiping his forehead and grinning, 'Why not?' His legs somehow kicked sideways, defying his knee joints.

Mair was sixteen, and thirty, and her imagination was like a warp thread in the Kashmir shawl, holding its pattern on the way to sixty and beyond.

All this afternoon and evening she had been sifting memories, pasting scenes and conversations on top of each other: her childhood and adolescence, the ruined mission at Leh, Dylan and Eirlys through all the years, Srinagar, Hattie, Tal, her father and mother, the Changthang plain, Nerys, chapel, mountains, her nephews and niece. Lotus.

Giddily she steered her thoughts again. Maybe this was what getting older meant: more and more you are aware that everything that happens overlays another memory, sets up more ripples of association, until each event seems as much a resonance of something else as fresh reality. She guessed that this was what life was like for Caroline Bowen in her quiet room in Srinagar, and for Mrs Parry nodding and reminiscing in the corner of the bar.

Mair's feet tangled with Tal's so that she tripped and fell into his arms. He caught her by both elbows and swept her upright again. 'Thanks for coming,' he shouted in her ear.

'I wouldn't have missed it. I hope you'll both be very happy.'

'I'm pretty confident,' he said. 'We know what we like, don't we, Annie and me?'

Much later, sated with obscure valley gossip, warm wine and eighties disco, the Ellises made their way back to the holiday cottages.

Jackie slipped away to bed and Eirlys, Dylan and Mair sat down together with the whisky bottle. They were taking pleasure in being together tonight precisely because they knew that modern lives would make this harder to achieve in future.

'Didn't we have a good time? I was right to make you both come, wasn't I?' Eirlys said.

Dylan snorted over his glass and wiped his chin with the end of his tie. 'You're always right, snowdrop. And we love you.' He tilted what was left in his glass. 'Here's to us, my sisters.'

A year went by, and it was at the beginning of another Kashmir spring that Myrtle and Archie finally came back to the *Garden of Eden*. The pieces of Archie's body had been put back together by the doctors in the military hospital. 'But, unfortunately, not in exactly the same order,' he joked.

Artificial limbs might have been fitted eventually, to replace his crushed lower legs, but the spinal injuries that had resulted from being buried under a toppled railway freight car during the bombing raid were too serious ever to mend.

His wheelchair was carried on to the houseboat by Majid and half a dozen other helpers. The passage inside was just wide enough to allow them to roll him out on to the veranda where he could sit all day with a rug draped over his shoulders to watch the changing light on the water and the mountains.

Myrtle confided to Nerys that it was this one objective, getting her husband back to the tonic air and the loveliness of Srinagar, that had kept her going through all the weeks and months in the hospital. Wounded men had arrived in their hundreds and had either died or recovered sufficiently to be moved to recuperation centres, only to be replaced by new casualties in the seemingly endless tide of bloodied bodies, but Archie had stayed. His injuries were so serious that for weeks he was not expected to survive, yet he clung on and, in the end, almost imperceptibly, he began to improve.

Myrtle lived by his bed. She talked to him, read to him from his favourite books, or simply held his hand. 'He never gave up. He was braver than any human being should ever have to be,' she told Nerys.

Archie said, in one of the few moments when Myrtle was not within earshot, 'Without her I would have closed my eyes and given up. It would have been much easier. But somehow she convinced me that we'd come back here one day.'

He lifted a hand and pointed at the glimmering water and the reflections of passing boats. The flower-seller's *shikara* glided towards them, loaded with buckets of spring blooms; Nerys leant down and bought an armful of splashy peonies. Archie buried his gaunt face in their damp furled petals. 'I would never have come home without Myrtle. I'd never have left that hospital. I owe her this view, these flowers, every day that we have together now. I can't feel sorry for myself, can I, when so many poor fellows died? And while so many more, like Ralph Bowen, are in the Jap camps?'

She smiled at him. Mounted on the wall behind his head were the magnificent antlers that he had brought back from his shoot in Ladakh. Archie would never walk again, let alone ride or shoot or play cricket or any of the sports he loved. Within her smile, Nerys was biting the insides of her cheeks to suppress her tears.

Myrtle came back with Majid and the samovar. She put a cup of tea into Archie's hand and spread a napkin over his chest in case he spilt it.

She was thin, with bony pockets showing at the base of her throat and deep, dark circles under her eyes. She didn't drink cocktails any more. 'What if he needed me in the night and I was pie-eyed?' She had shrugged. She smoked instead, snapping her gold lighter to a new cigarette as soon as she had stubbed out the old one. Now that she had achieved her objective of getting Archie home, their problems were multiplying.

He was almost completely confined to the *Garden of Eden* because it took so many pairs of hands to lift him on and off the boat. They had tried once to carry him into a *shikara*, but the craft had rocked so much that he had almost fallen into the lake. The path along the bank was narrow and bumpy and when it rained it became clogged with heavy mud. In their old life, as the McMinns hopped to and fro, the mud had been no more than an inconvenience. Even on the houseboat the floors were uneven and the panelled bathroom was unsuitable for a man who couldn't walk. Once the summer was over it would be far too cold for him. The English doctor came regularly to visit Archie, but he had explained to Myrtle that if her husband were to develop any serious lung or circulatory complication Srinagar's little military hospital would not be the best place to treat him.

'I don't know what to do for the best,' Myrtle finally confessed to Nerys. All her energy, the formidable power that

Nerys had once worried about because it had no direction, was taken up with looking after her husband. But not even Myrtle could solve everything.

'I think maybe you'll have to move,' Nerys said gently. 'Perhaps you could rent a bungalow in the new town. You can have a garden, grow flowers, even some vegetables.'

'The doctor thinks I should take him to Delhi. But the *heat*.'

'Couldn't you go just for the winter?'

The lighter snapped and its little flame doubled in Myrtle's eyes. She blew out a column of smoke. 'This winter, yes. After that, I don't know. Money is the problem. Our Delhi house belongs to the company so we can't keep it for ever. We'll have Archie's disability pension, but that won't run to keeping two places. I don't know what the old *Garden* might fetch nowadays. Who would buy her?'

They didn't talk about it because they didn't need to, but Srinagar was changing. The evidence of it was everywhere, visible in the way that Hindus and Muslims moved past each other in the narrow alleys of the bazaar without exchanging a greeting, audible in the outbreaks of violence under the cover of darkness, embodied in a mysterious fire that consumed an ancient Hindu temple on the Jhelum bank. Conflict flared in the gardens and under the chinar trees. Some of the Pandits, Hindus who had been teachers and government officials, were quietly leaving Kashmir. Professor Pran, the cricketer whose batting had won the Christmas match on the ice, mentioned that he might move south because it would be better for his wife and daughters even though it would break all their hearts to leave Kashmir. The old British echelons were disintegrating too. The Quit India movement gathered force on all sides against the Raj, and as the conflict intensified Nerys remembered what Rainer used to say. 'Hindu against Muslim. Divide and rule, that's the motto of you British.'

As much as she could, Nerys helped Myrtle to nurse Archie. It was hard work for Myrtle and it left her little time for anything else. But they agreed together that the McMinns would

329

stay on the *Garden of Eden* until Myrtle could find a buyer for the old houseboat. Archie spent these days out on the veranda with his pipe and the newspapers. He claimed to be the happiest man in Srinagar.

'What about Zahra?' Myrtle privately fretted to Nerys.

'Do you think you could look after her now, as well as Archie?' she asked.

Myrtle sighed.

Nerys said firmly, 'Don't worry about Zahra. She's well and happy.'

Up in the village Faisal and his little brother had been fully absorbed into the tribe who played under the big tree or went out into the fields with the sheep. They were wiry, dirty, exuberant children, and therefore indistinguishable from most of the others, but Farida still held herself apart. That same spring, Evan had decided he must move back to Srinagar. A new missionary had arrived to help him, and the young man needed a home, as well as training in a setting less stark and – although Evan would never have said so – more rewarding than Kanihama. Nerys divided her time between the village and helping Myrtle to look after Archie. Whenever she left Kanihama, she paid the village women as much as she could afford to take care of Zahra in her absence. She would have been anxious even about this had she not known that Farida would be the baby's faithful guardian.

Just once, after Archie had come back to Srinagar and it was becoming clear that caring for his physical needs was going to be all that Myrtle could cope with, Nerys tried to talk to Evan about adopting a child themselves. She thought she managed to keep the edge of longing out of her voice, but her husband looked curiously at her. 'What child?'

'Zahra, perhaps.'

'Which one is that? There are so many infants, Nerys, and the Lord has called us to care for all, not to single one out. As for a child of our own, we must accept His will.'

He spoke in his most aloof and implacable tone, and Nerys turned away in silence.

Zahra was still carried everywhere in the sling on Farida's back, and at night the two children shared the same mattress and blanket. Farida never ate a mouthful herself until Zahra had been fed, and she preferred sitting with her in her lap to running about with the children of her own age. The headscarf she wore covered her mouth as well as her hair, but her black eyes were always solemn and watchful. The only time a smile seemed to glimmer in them was when Zahra did something new and clever.

Farida was old beyond her years, but Nerys had to accept that there was nothing she could do to change this. She watched the two children together with a sharp mixture of pleasure and sorrow.

In Srinagar Nerys had acquired a sort of schoolroom on a street that led down to a reedy canal because she and Evan were living in the rooms above it. Evan's recently arrived assistant missionary was called Ianto Jones, a myopic young man with an Adam's apple that bobbed up and down whenever he spoke. Together they rode their bicycles into the city or took a bus up to the villages on the Kanihama road.

In the schoolroom, once she had cleared out the lumber and put down rat poison, Nerys gathered some of the bazaar children. Just as she had done in Leh and Kanihama, she played games and sang songs with them, and afterwards fed them a simple meal. The numbers grew. And as soon as their living rooms were habitable, she asked Evan if he would mind if the two little orphan girls from Kanihama came down to stay with them.

'Those village orphans again? Why?' He frowned. 'Haven't you got enough to do?'

'I miss them,' she said.

It was more than a year, but Nerys was still not pregnant. Evan was more considerate of her feelings than he had been at the beginning of their life together, and he squeezed her hand now with an air of resigned indulgence.

'All right, my dear. If that's what you want, by all means bring them down here for a visit.'

Farida enjoyed a truck ride and then a bus journey to the city. She sat upright at the back of the bus with the handful of shawled women and their babies, just as if she were the same age as them.

Zahra was walking now, even though Farida still preferred to carry her. When she was put down she tottered through the unfamiliar spaces, starfish hands outstretched, on plump bare legs that were as smooth as pale brown hens' eggs. Her eyes were the colour of dark jade, and there were threads of gilt in her toffee-brown hair.

'She is an unusual-looking baby,' Evan said, before he stuffed a pile of pamphlets into his knapsack and bicycled off with Ianto. He was too busy and too preoccupied to be curious about anything beyond what directly concerned him.

Archie was different. He was much more broadminded, and by the first time the three women gathered on the *Garden of Eden* with the two little girls he already knew the full story. He had hooted with laughter at the account of the *kangri* winter, and listened in amazement as Caroline shyly mentioned the winter birth up in Kanihama.

'My good girl, how very brave you were,' he said.

'I had the two best friends in the world – you can do a lot with friends to help you. Nerys took good care of me when the baby was born.'

'And you had a cup or two of herbal potion,' Nerys put in. 'We never found out what was in it.'

Archie gestured with the stem of his pipe. 'We were both lucky. And just think, I've got the two of them to nurse me now.' He caught his wife's arm as she passed, and she kissed the top of his head where a bald patch had appeared in his sandy hair.

Shadowed by Farida, Zahra toddled from the *Garden of Eden*'s veranda to the saloon and back again. She pulled silver-framed pictures off low shelves, smeared glass doors and polished tables with her tiny hands, and everyone beamed as they watched her.

'She's certainly going to be a beauty,' Archie said. No one spoke of it, but there was still a pronounced look of Ravi Singh about her.

Caroline's eyes followed every move she made. Tentatively, as if she hardly trusted herself, she had begun to hold her daughter, curling her hair around her fingers and stroking her cheek with a fingertip. Zahra impartially beamed at her, showing a row of tiny white teeth as Farida looked on, waiting until Zahra would be hers again.

Nerys and Myrtle observed this growing tenderness.

'Maybe, some day, there'll be a way after all,' Myrtle whispered.

Neither of them tried to speculate further. Nerys kept her own longings to herself. For now, the baby belonged to all of them and it was enough to see her growing and flourishing. Zahra represented hope in a dark time.

Evan regularly came to smoke a pipe with Archie and discuss the war news. One midsummer afternoon, leaving the two men in the veranda's shade, the three women took a *shikara* ride across to the Shalimar Garden. Zahra was firmly held by Farida but she wriggled and laughed, stretching her hands out to birds overhead and the droplets of water scattered by the boatman's paddle.

The garden was busy with families picnicking in the shade of the huge trees, with strolling soldiers on leave, and vendors of fruit and drinks. Zahra's eyes and mouth widened when she saw the glitter of fountains and the glaring brilliance of the flowerbeds. She fought to be put down and as soon as her feet touched the grass she swayed ahead, in and out of pools of shade, her head rotating as her attention was caught by dancing yellow butterflies, a waddling lapdog, a child's pram being wheeled by an ayah.

'She looks so happy, doesn't she?' Caroline said. She couldn't quite let herself be proud, but relief and gratitude for this afternoon were clear in her eyes.

Nerys bought an ice-cream from the vendor on the first terrace and gave it to Farida. The girl let a fold of her headscarf fall in her eagerness to lick it, but then hesitated and looked to Zahra as if she ought to give her the first taste. 'No, it's all for you,' Nerys assured her. 'Zahra is too little.'

Farida closed her eyes to concentrate on this treat. They climbed a broad flight of steps, at Zahra's slow pace, with Zahra just deigning to hold on to Caroline's finger for balance. At the top of the steps they all turned to look back at the mirror of the lake, shimmering with heat at the centre of its ring of mountains. Srinagar seemed more beautiful today than it had ever been.

'This is almost like old times,' Myrtle said. Nerys slipped her arm around her friend's thin frame as they turned to climb higher, with Caroline a few paces ahead. To their left an elaborate picnic was taking place under the stateliest chinar tree. There were ladies in folding chairs, some holding parasols, several men sitting on the grass, and servants standing at a discreet distance.

Zahra chased after a butterfly. Moving too fast she overbalanced and fell, hitting the grass and knocking off her sunhat. Farida was busy with her ice-cream and it was Caroline who dashed to pick her up. In the two seconds of silence while Zahra sucked in her breath and prepared a scream of shock and outrage, Caroline swept her into her arms and kissed her bare forehead.

A man stood up and slowly strolled towards her from the picnic group. He was immaculate in a white *kurta* under a sleeveless coat of pale cream linen.

'I hope the child is not hurt?' Ravi Singh said.

Zahra howled and Farida threw aside her ice-cream.

Caroline's eyes met Ravi's. 'It was only a little tumble.'

She let Farida take the baby out of her arms. Farida whispered and soothed, and the crying quickly stopped. Ravi's gaze didn't move from Caroline's face.

She looked much older than the girl who had married Ralph

Bowen. The two years she had lived through had faded the pink English rose, but the more pronounced cheekbones and the shadowed eyes gave her a sombre kind of beauty.

'Who are these children?' Ravi Singh asked. His voice was like ripples in silk.

'You remember my friends, Mrs McMinn and Mrs Watkins?'

Ravi's manners were formally perfect as always. He bowed to both of them. 'Of course. Good afternoon. A beautiful day for the Shalimar Garden.'

'Hello, Ravi,' Myrtle nodded. She placed a cigarette between her crimson lips.

Nerys said, 'I teach some children in one of the districts of the old town. These two are staying with my husband and me at the mission. They are both orphans, unfortunately. We do what we can to help them.'

Ravi did shift his gaze now. Zahra's long black eyelashes made a damp curl against her honey-gold cheek. One plump foot dangled in a tiny kidskin shoe. Farida glared at him. 'I see,' he said.

'Please don't let us keep you from your party,' Myrtle drawled.

'I am grateful for the reminder, Mrs McMinn.' He bowed lower, his handsome face taut. 'Good afternoon.'

He turned, but at the same time he put his hand to Caroline's elbow and drew her aside. She couldn't do anything but follow him. His mouth softened at once into a smile and he lowered his head to murmur into her ear. 'I have missed you, dear Caroline.'

'Have you? Why is that?' A pink flush spread up her throat and coloured her cheeks.

'I would like very much to see you again. You can tell me what has happened to you since we last met. Whatever it is . . .' he paused and examined her again '. . . it has changed you from a girl into a beautiful woman.'

Caroline pulled herself upright. She detached her arm from his grasp and took a step away from him. The colour in her face was darkened by outrage. 'That would be impossible. My husband is a prisoner of the Japanese in Burma. Like many other army wives, I am waiting, praying, for him to come home.'

'Your husband's absence was never an obstacle in the past.' He smiled.

'That was my mistake.'

Ravi was displeased. His mouth set in a line and he lifted one black eyebrow. 'Then I am sorry to have reminded you. I hope the memories of that other time don't trouble you too much.' A cold glance flicked over Zahra, now happily stumbling towards the flowers.

'Goodbye,' Caroline said. Ravi was already striding back to his friends.

Myrtle and Nerys swept up the girls and all three women hurried back down the steps towards the lake.

'He – he asked to see me,' Caroline managed to stammer, once they were out of sight.

'That man certainly has sexual confidence,' Myrtle said.

'I'm afraid of him.' Caroline's heart was thudding in her chest, and she was horrified to realise that half of her discomfort was caused by a physical longing to see Ravi again. Wanting to glide through the marble corridors to his private rooms, where the pale silk hangings fluttered in the breeze and rose petals floated in silver water basins.

'Don't be afraid.' Nerys was beside her, and Farida, with Zahra's tired head lolling on her small shoulder. 'You're safe with us.'

'What if he guessed?' Caroline breathed.

'He didn't. And he won't,' Myrtle insisted.

Nerys was not so sure, but she didn't say anything. She thought of Rainer and how all her instincts, whenever there was a threat, were to turn to him for help. But Rainer had disappeared from Srinagar and there was no word of him. She had heard one rumour that he had gone back to Switzerland for good, another that he was involved in a secret mission

336

somewhere in the south Pacific, and yet another that he was with a magic show, touring the Allied troops' rearguard posts. But she had no way of knowing if any of these had a grain of truth in them.

Myrtle led the way. 'Let's go back home, to the *Garden*.'

Their *shikara* was waiting for them at the landing stage.

FOURTEEN

August 1944

'Do you know for certain?' Myrtle asked. A plume of cigarette smoke drifted over her head, offering her a small degree of protection from the flies that troubled Nerys and Caroline. There was a dung-heap on the other side of the garden wall. The afternoon was stiflingly hot, and a thick haze blotted out the sky.

Caroline's eyes were so wide that the whites were visible all the way round the blue irises. Her fingers knotted in her lap as she twisted her wedding and engagement rings. 'Oh, yes, I think so. I mean, it's not official yet. Mrs Dunkeley says that as soon as there is definite confirmation of names and ranks, Division HQ will formally notify wives and families. But I think it must be true.'

Nerys leant back on a wobbly bench seat, her ankle brushing a bed of coriander that loaded the air with its scent. She had been watching Caroline with deepening concern.

Archie took his pipe out of his mouth. 'Good show. Brave fellows,' he said. His wheelchair was drawn up in its usual spot under the shade of an almond tree.

The bungalow in the outer sprawl of Srinagar's new town had a small fenced garden. With the help of a bent old man, who laboured in the sun with a battered straw hat perched on top of his red skullcap, Myrtle had been growing squash and spinach and a bed of fist-sized kohlrabi. 'Look at this one, I'd win first prize with it in any village show in England,' she had claimed, as she brandished the dirt-coated object. 'The question is, why would anyone want to eat such a thing?'

The McMinns had retreated to Delhi for the previous winter, leaving the *Garden of Eden* locked and empty because Myrtle had been unable to find anyone who wanted to buy it. But just as the heat of the summer had begun to build yet again, an American civilian couple had taken it for the season, with a vague promise that they might consider a purchase if all went well. Bob Flanner was in import-export, Myrtle reported, and seemed to have plenty of dollars to throw around. Mrs Flanner had employed Majid and the rest of the staff, which Myrtle said was a great relief because even paying them a much-reduced retainer wage was more than she and Archie could afford. As a short-term solution, the McMinns had made the difficult journey back up from Delhi and had had their furniture moved into the little rented place. It was a long way from the lake and there was no view of water or mountains, or of anything much, except a brick wall and the tops of trees in the nearby gardens, but Archie had insisted that it was ideal. 'So quiet. Our neighbours are all charming people. And I love to sit in a garden in the cool breeze.'

'After this summer, I just don't know,' Myrtle confided to Nerys.

There was nothing Nerys could suggest, no prediction she might make that would carry any more weight than a hundred others, let alone offer Myrtle grounds for optimism. Uncertainty was still the daily reality, not just for themselves but for the war and what the end of it might bring.

At the end of March the Japanese had marched from occupied Burma into India via the remote Naga hills. Their commanding general's intention was to cut the road between Imphal, the

339

capital of the Indian state of Manipur, which lay just seventy miles from the Burmese border, and the sleepy garrison town of Kohima. They failed to take Imphal but Kohima was besieged. The fighting in and around the town continued into April as a scratch force of mixed British and Indian regiments struggled to defend it.

The Allied forces grimly battled on as casualties mounted. Reinforcements slowly trickled up the road from the Allied supply base at Dimapur and the siege was finally lifted. On 22 June, twenty miles outside Imphal, British troops from Kohima met men from the 5th Indian Division who were moving up to meet them. The Japanese advance into India was halted. Their troops were increasingly short of ammunition, air cover and food supplies, and the Allied forces began slowly to clear them from the hills, driving them back the way they had come into Burma.

Through all this time only Evan and Ianto Jones had carried on as normal. Against all the odds, a big shipment of Bibles had arrived from Wales, and the two men cycled every day to hand them out to their tiny congregation and whoever else seemed inclined to accept the Word. But to Nerys it seemed that they had all been holding their breath for weeks and were now able to let out a gasp of relief. One evening she came back unexpectedly to the little whitewashed room that served for a chapel at the mission to find Evan on his knees in prayer. She whispered an apology for disturbing him and prepared to tiptoe away but Evan caught her hand. 'Stay here with me, Nerys.'

She fumbled into a kneeling position beside him.

'I am praying for our men in battle, of course, in Burma and wherever they are,' he said, 'but I am praying also for you and me and our future family, my dear. If the Almighty will just be good enough not to take that as a selfish supplication.'

Her heart squeezed with sympathy for him. Evan longed for a child as much as she did. He regularly reached out for her under the cover of darkness, embracing her without saying a

word – as if to speak would be to open floodgates of embarrassment – but in spite of his inarticulacy she thought they
understood each other a little better nowadays. She tried to
reassure him. 'I'm sure He won't.'

In the silence that followed she even tried out a halting,
unpractised version of a prayer herself. It was a very long time
since she had tried to pray. Children's voices rose from the
enclosed yard under the windows where her mission pupils
played and chased each other. She humbly prayed that Evan
might relent and consent to their adopting Zahra. Once she
had done that she ventured to say, 'We could still have a family.
There's more than one way . . .'

There wasn't even a beat of hesitation. 'I don't believe I
could do it,' he said. 'Not take on someone else's child and
raise it as our own.' There was a note of pure desolation in
his voice.

Nerys knelt for a moment longer, then stiffly got to her feet.
She patted Evan on the shoulder and he bent his head without
speaking. His hair was now almost entirely grey.

Down in the schoolroom yard Zahra, aged two years and
three months, came running to greet Nerys. Not one of the
children there was plump but Zahra still had soft dimples in
her pale-brown knees and elbows. She had two rows of perfect
white teeth and her brown-gilt hair had grown long. 'Ness,
Ness,' she called in delight.

By the end of July the 15,000 Japanese soldiers who had
marched into India were struggling back towards Rangoon.
Half of them were to die along the way, starved and exhausted
and crippled by dysentery.

Then at the beginning of August, extraordinary news had
filtered through to Srinagar.

A detachment of British prisoners of war had been found in
the remote hills inside Burma. Following the fall of Singapore
the men had originally been held at Changi prison, but then
they had been moved northwards to labour on the roads that
were being hastily constructed in the attempt to supply infantry

advances over the border into India. These men, fortunate not to have been butchered by their retreating Japanese captors, had been discovered by an advancing unit of the Indian Infantry. When the soldiers stumbled upon them they were hiding in a makeshift camp on the outskirts of a hill village, uncertain of the progress of the Allied advance and starved almost to death. Captain Ralph Bowen was one of those men.

This was the news that Caroline brought to Myrtle and Archie's bungalow on that hot afternoon.

'Do you know for certain?' Myrtle repeated.

'No, but if it's true, if it really is him, he might be here in a few weeks' time. I'll be able to look after him, won't I? I'll be a wife again, like you are to Archie.'

Archie rarely spoke of his own war experience, and he didn't look directly at any of them now. But he said, from under the shade of the tree, 'It won't be easy for him, you know, getting back to Srinagar. His old life will seem to belong to another chap entirely. None of us can conceive of what he's likely to have seen and suffered.'

He looked away at the fence and the treetops, then recovered himself. 'He's damned lucky, though. We're all lucky. We're going to win this war, quite soon now, and then there will be a life again. A new world.'

He pounded his clenched fist into the palm of the other hand and his hollow face brightened in anticipation. Nerys marvelled at Archie's spirit in genuinely counting himself as fortunate, and in looking forward to a new world in which the British India the McMinns had known all their lives would almost certainly no longer exist.

'Yes.' Caroline nodded. Her hands were shaking.

It was Myrtle who voiced the question, but each of the women had it in their minds. 'And what about Zahra?'

Caroline seemed to quiver with fear.

Since Archie and Myrtle's return the question had been in abeyance, because the odd circumstances had developed their

342

own rhythm and there had seemed no reason to intervene. Between them, they had become an extended family to the little girl. Caroline played with her or took her for walks, always with Farida to accompany them, yet for all the originally promising signs it seemed that she had never properly learnt to love her daughter. Her face was shadowed when she looked at her, her arms always stiff when she held her. It was the McMinns and Nerys who freely deluged Zahra with affection and pointed out her latest achievements to each other with open pride. Archie adored watching her running and playing, and he could spend hours chatting to her and telling her stories. But Myrtle had finally admitted to Nerys that she doubted she could care for another dependant as well as her crippled husband.

'I'm afraid that I don't do even that properly,' she said. 'How could I be a mother as well, when everything in my world is already dedicated to Archie?'

'I know, I understand. Maybe Evan and I, in the end . . .' There's always hope, Nerys believed.

Nerys insisted that the two girls spent a good proportion of their time up in Kanihama, with the weavers' families. It was important not to cut them off from their background and likely future, she believed. But it was easy for them to come often to Srinagar, especially during the golden Kashmir summer.

'Caroline's afraid to love her,' Myrtle had said once, when she and Nerys were alone.

'She had a breakdown after the birth. That's what happened,' Nerys had answered. 'Zahra's bound up with that, and it's the illness coming back that Caroline's afraid of.'

A sudden breath of wind tinkled the clay bells of a cheap temple ornament that Myrtle had hung from the veranda beam. The gardener appeared between his vegetable beds, his straw hat nodding in time with his movements as he lifted and lowered his watering-can.

Archie gestured towards the house with his pipe stem. 'Shall I trundle inside and let you girls talk together?'

Caroline shook her head. 'No, please. You know all about

343

everything. Just tell me what I must do. I can't let Ralph know about what I did with . . . what I did, especially now when he has been through so much and is coming home to be taken care of. I can't, can I?' Panic made her voice rise.

'So, don't say or do anything,' Myrtle concluded.

Nerys tried to be reassuring. 'We can all go on taking care of Zahra, just like we do now, always have done, as discreetly as need be. Kanihama's far enough away, and in the city we've got the umbrella of the mission. She's an orphan, one child among many others. No one has asked any questions about her, have they?'

Caroline numbly shook her head. It was a year and more since the afternoon in the Shalimar Garden.

'It's not going to be so difficult,' Nerys said. She was making calculations. Zahra and Farida must spend more time secluded at Kanihama, but that would happen naturally as autumn and winter came round again. Maybe she could move back to the village herself. How might she explain that to Evan?

'You're right, I shouldn't do anything. I want to see Ralph come back safely, I want to see if . . . if we can, you know, make a life together, somehow. Why not?' Caroline faltered.

If only you could, Nerys thought. She tried to look on the positive side. Maybe Ralph would have softened in the three years that he had been away. Maybe having an exhausted and starved survivor to care for might give Caroline the backbone of confidence she needed. Maybe a solution to the Zahra problem would eventually present itself. Maybe Evan would indeed change his mind. 'There's no reason why not,' she said.

Caroline bit the corner of her lip. 'I need to find a way . . . to provide for her, don't I? With money, I mean. To make sure that even if she hasn't got a mother . . . that is, a proper mother who can . . . So that some day she'll at least have a dowry. She'd be able to marry then and have her own daughter.' Caroline's face crumpled and she began to cry.

Archie scratched the side of his jaw with the stem of his cold pipe, still enough of a British officer to feel uncomfortable at the sight of a woman's tears. Caroline somehow collected herself. With a watery smile through her distress, she muttered, 'Sorry. I'm stupid. Zahra's better off than Farida and the others, for a start, isn't she? There's always the hope of a windfall. Or, I know, a legacy. My godmother, maybe.'

'Exactly,' Myrtle agreed.

Money was now a problem for all of them. Nerys had almost used up her inheritance from her grandparents, the mission outreach and school funds were minutely accounted for, and the McMinns were no longer comfortably off.

'The Lord will provide,' Nerys said. That was what Evan believed, and Ianto.

'In the meantime I'm going to make some tea.' Myrtle went off into the house, clapping her hands and calling out for the heavy-footed girl who helped in the kitchen. Myrtle and Nerys often laughed nowadays about her similarities to Diskit, all the way back in Leh.

The samovar and the tray of heavy Benares brass were familiar from the *Garden of Eden*, as were the delicate china cups and saucers with their pattern of pale blue harebells.

'Thank you, darling girl,' Archie said, and patted her hand when she passed him his cup. 'I love tea-time.'

'Could that possibly be because of its proximity to *chota* hour?'

There were no more cocktails, but Archie's bottle of whisky made its regular evening appearance.

'No, I don't believe so. Tea has its own limpid charm.'

The McMinns still teased and joked, and Nerys was the only one who knew how hard for Myrtle the work of nursing him was, and how deeply she missed the vigorous man she had married. She looked at both of them now with the greatest affection.

After tea, Caroline said that she must make her way home to the married-quarters bungalow in case there was any more news. Nerys said that she would walk with her as far as the *tonga* stand. They left Myrtle at Archie's side, her arms resting on his shoulders. The sinking sun cast a long, conjoined shadow on the ground, as if they were one person.

Caroline and Nerys went out of the back gate into the lane. The sky had cleared and a black cloud of flies rose from the neighbour's dung-heap, and a beggar who had been squatting beside the fence gathered up his ragged *dhoti* and ran away ahead of them on legs as thin as a stork's.

'Will you be all right?' Nerys asked. A bony old nag raised its head and the driver scrambled out of the back seat of the *tonga* where he had been dozing.

'Of course I will. I should be happy. My husband's coming home to me. Plenty of other women's aren't.'

Nerys stood back and the old carriage creaked away.

It was uncomfortable to remember their half-hope that Ralph Bowen might not return, as if more problems might be solved than posed by a man's death.

Poor Ralph, she thought. As much poor him as poor Caroline: at least as much.

She began the walk back to the mission. It was a long way but she loved slipping through the streets and along the reedy paths that lined the waterways. The Srinagar smells of dung and fragrant cooking and smoke clung around her; shouts, a snatch of music and the clang of metal-beating gave way to the hooting of traffic as she ducked across a busy road and plunged into a maze of tiny streets that had become almost as familiar as the lanes in Wales. Close to home, she came from under a bridge and saw long lines of cloth hung to dry outside a dye works. Reflected strips of crimson and pink and saffron and violet wavered between green temple domes in the silver river water. The city was beautiful and impervious, and its conflicts made her small concerns seem even smaller. By the time she reached home she was calm, and as ready as Evan himself to accept whatever befell them all.

Caroline paid off the *tonga* man and unlatched the garden gate. It creaked and stuck on its hinges as it always did and she gave up the attempt to open it, squeezing through the narrow gap instead, as she usually ended up doing. Julia Dunkeley was gardening next door – Caroline could hear the snap of secateurs as the woman tended her struggling roses. Caroline ducked her head and hurried up the path, past a bed of thirsty marigolds, hoping that for once her neighbour wouldn't poke her head over the fence.

It was hot inside the little box of a house. The new house-boy had forgotten to close the blinds before he left and the sun had been pouring in all afternoon. The early-evening light was still bright enough to show up the dust coating the bureau and dimming the glass of the framed wedding photograph. Caroline went quickly through to the bedroom. She undid the buttons of her sundress and let it drop at her feet. She stretched her neck in an attempt to ease the thumping pain in her head, then twisted her hair and pinned it up off the nape where the skin was damp and sweaty.

The bed was smooth and flat under a striped cotton cover. The bolster was in place, two pillows placed side by side on top of it, just as always. Caroline closed her eyes. In a few weeks, perhaps as little as two or three, Ralph's head would rest on the left-hand pillow. One of his military-history books from the little row in the sitting-room bookcase would be waiting for him on the bamboo night-table.

She was shaking from head to foot. A trickle of sweat ran between her bare shoulder-blades.

She turned away from the bed and ran out of the room.

In her underwear, she sat down at the bureau and lowered the lid. From a musty drawer she took a sheet of writing paper and rummaged in one of the wooden niches for a bottle of Quink ink and a fountain pen. *Dear Ravi*, she wrote.

She stopped and bit the end of the pen, then rushed on.

I'm sorry it has taken such a very long time to reply to
your note. Maybe everything has changed for you since
you wrote it. If so, please disregard this. Otherwise I
should like to come and see you, as you suggested.
Sincerely, Caroline

347

She didn't need to unfold the letter that he had written to her over a year ago because she knew it by heart, but she did take the thick sheet of heavy cream paper from its hiding place. Thoughtfully, she ran the tip of her index finger over the embossing. Ravi's handwriting was black, fluent, with strong downstrokes.

He had written to ask her to come and visit him in private, saying that he missed her, and also that he believed they had certain matters to discuss. The last line of the brief note seemed to have been written with more speed, less calculation:

Please come, dearest girl. Ever yours, Ravi

What matters, precisely, did he want to discuss?

Sometimes, during the long months that had elapsed, Caroline had let herself believe that he did love her, and that the only obstacle keeping the two of them apart was her own determination. Most of the time, though, she had been able to hold the conviction that Ravi Singh was only interested in his own pleasures, and that he was a man to be feared.

The threat in this letter was so gossamer that it was hardly identifiable. But now that Ralph was coming back she had to find out what Ravi really intended, or else live in perpetual uncertainty.

There was another reason for wanting to see him. It was for Zahra's sake. Somehow, if she could only find a way to do it, she intended to exploit the fact that Ravi Singh was so carelessly, thoughtlessly rich.

Caroline found an envelope for her note, sealed and addressed it. Then she went into the bedroom for the box of matches that stood beside the candlestick on her night-table. She struck a match and put the flame to one corner of Ravi's letter. She held the curling paper until her fingers burnt, then dropped the last cream fragment into the tin wastepaper bin.

Sweat had dried on her skin and she felt cold.

*   *   *

Sitar music was playing as Caroline followed the soft-footed servant across a paved inner courtyard. At the centre of the enclosed space was a pool lined with turquoise and gold tiles, where plump fish caught the shafts of sunlight. A trickle of water struck a cool note in the heat of the afternoon.

Ravi was reclining in a low chair in a vaulted room off the courtyard. The musician was seated cross-legged on some cushions in the corner, head bowed over his instrument. Ravi stood up as soon as the servant showed her in. 'How beautiful you are looking.' He kissed the back of her hand.

Caroline ran the palm of the other one over the full skirt of her summer dress. Ravi had grown plumper, she thought, with a soft pad of flesh under his jawline that lent a touch of corruption to his boyish profile.

Ravi nodded to the sitar player and gave a curt order to the servant. Both of them withdrew and Caroline looked around her with intentional coolness. She had often been alone with Ravi in other rooms of his house, but this one was new to her. There was a carved desk with a high-backed chair, almost throne-like in its grandeur. The green leather desk was piled with papers, locked boxes, soft felt pouches, printed documents. Opposite it was a recess where a divan stood, heaped with silk and embroidered cushions. Otherwise there was only the chair and a low table with a neat pile of leather-bound books. The windows were tall, narrow slits that barred the Kashmir rugs with shafts of gold. It seemed that Ravi wasn't so much the lazy playboy any longer. This was the room of a busy man who was doing important business – or who wanted to give the impression that he was.

Caroline was disconcerted by the atmosphere of austere opulence. Already Ravi was getting the upper hand. She turned away from him for a second, pretending to look through one of the window slits to a view of the garden.

'Where shall I sit?' she asked, over her shoulder.

'Come.'

He put his arm round her waist and guided her to the divan.

It was big enough to allow two clear feet of space between them as they sat back among the cushions. Caroline drew her feet up beneath her and studied Ravi's face. The extra flesh made him look older, but he was still extraordinarily handsome. She suppressed an inconvenient wish that he would kiss her, and more.

'What would you like? Some tea? A cocktail? Iced lemonade?'

'Perhaps some lemonade, thank you.'

He clapped his hands and the servant reappeared. They were always there, invisible but within earshot, she remembered that. Seconds later a tray was brought with frosted glasses, a jug in a holder of silver filigree, a dish of sliced lemons and limes, starched white napkins and a basin of water with floating rose petals. Ravi dipped his fingers and dried them, Caroline followed suit. The lemonade was poured.

'Leave us now,' he said, and the servant bowed himself out. Ravi unhooked a silk hanging and let it fall over the doorway. They were alone, as far as they ever would be.

'Do you know, it is more than a year since we have seen each other?'

'Yes, it is.'

'In the Shalimar Garden. You were with Mrs McMinn and the missionary's wife. And the orphan children, of course.'

'Yes, that's right. Your memory is good.'

The lemonade was icily refreshing. Ravi's dark eyes didn't flicker. He knows, Caroline thought. Of course he knows. She smiled at him.

'The missionaries do very good work,' she said.

Ravi circled her wrist with his thumb and forefinger, drew her hand closer. He studied the fine network of blue veins under the skin before touching the hot pulse that beat there. 'You are nervous.'

'No.'

He smiled, mocking her with raised eyebrows. 'What have you been doing for a whole year, little Caroline?'

'I don't know that an account of my time would interest

350

you. I live a quiet life. There is a war on, and my husband has been a prisoner of the Japanese all this time. But I have recently heard that he has been found alive in Burma, and will be returning to Srinagar as soon as he is fit enough.'

'I'm happy to hear that. Are you happy, Caroline?'

'Thank you for asking. Yes, I am.'

He's playing with me, she thought. Like a cat with a mouse.

Ravi nodded. He said, 'I have some news too. I am to be married next month.'

She paused. 'How wonderful. Congratulations. Do I know her?' Her mind was working at the possible significance. It would be safer for her, surely, if Ravi was a married man with a reputation to protect and his own intimate concerns to distract him.

'I don't think so. She is from Jammu. It is a very satisfactory match for both families, but the details have taken some time to finalise.'

He gestured at the documents on his desk. Caroline understood that this would not just be a marriage between two individuals. How absurd that she had ever even dreamt of any different outcome.

'Perhaps you can help me. I have a serious decision to make,' he said. He crossed to the desk and picked up the pouches, then dropped them on the divan in front of Caroline. They were fastened with threads of woven silk. She untied one and tipped the contents into her lap, swallowing a gasp. They were rubies, cut and uncut, magnificent and blood-dark.

'A bridal gift, a necklace. What do you think? Or these sapphires, perhaps?'

Another cascade of stones, lake-blue to deepest ultramarine, spilt into her cupped hand. Ravi picked out one the size of a thumbnail, angled it towards a shaft of sunlight, then tossed it back into the heap. Some of the stones slipped between Caroline's fingers and he scooped them up as casually as if they were pebbles.

'Azmeena has pale skin. I think the sapphires will flatter her. Would you agree?'

'I don't know your fiancée, Ravi. I can't possibly advise you as to what jewellery you should choose for her.'

He smiled again, took the stones back to his desk and dropped them in a little heap on the blotter. He tossed the empty pouches after them and sat down again, much closer now. 'Her skin isn't as pale as yours. Yours is the whitest I have ever seen. Here.' He leant closer still and touched her breast. 'And here.' His fingers brushed the folds of her skirt where they draped over her inner thigh.

Caroline felt the blood swirl inside her head, leaving her lips as dry as sandpaper. She opened her mouth with difficulty. 'Please. Don't do that.'

He raised an eyebrow, as if to ask, *Why have you come here, if not for this?* He put his head on one side, frankly examining her. 'Circumstances are changing for us both,' he said.

'That's true.'

'We have known each other well, darling Caroline . . .' Now he lifted a strand of her hair and twisted it round his finger, stopping only just short of pulling it. He was close enough for her to feel his breath on her cheek.

'. . . and we must be particularly careful of our shared history. In order to protect each other as well as ourselves, don't you agree?'

The words themselves were neutral but there was something so delicately insinuating in his tone, so implicitly threatening, that she shifted herself away from him.

'I will never breathe a syllable about the way you seduced me, Ravi, if that's what you fear. I'm not a tart, or a trouble-maker, or even a chatterbox. You took advantage of me when I was much more innocent than I am now, but you can trust me to be discreet about it.'

Caroline's mouth was so dry that the inner folds stuck to her teeth. She worked her lips and tongue to make the saliva flow and he stared at her, his features crimping with faint distaste. 'Seduction? Is that how you remember it? My recollection is that you needed very little persuasion.'

Her head dully pounded as some of the scenes flashed past her, vivid as on a cinema screen. Rose petals, riding out on horseback in the flushed dawn, grass and perfume, Ravi's lips and hands. She didn't answer.

'I suppose,' Ravi said, 'we should also note that at the time you were married to a serving British officer, and I was a mere bachelor, promised to no one at all.'

She lifted her chin. 'I have already said that you have nothing to fear about my discretion, and you are right that I have more to lose than you do. That's how it usually is, isn't it, between men and women in these matters?'

'Men of one sort and women of another, yes.'

She wouldn't rise to that. She concentrated on swallowing, her throat working hard. He looked down his fine nose at her, as if he thought she might be slightly mad. In the silence she could just hear the pleasant trickling of water in the courtyard outside.

'Is there anything else you would like to mention, dearest girl, while we are having this affectionate talk?'

She didn't hesitate even for a second. 'No. Nothing whatsoever.'

He waited, and she let him wait. The seconds ticked by. In the end he sighed and gently stroked her forearm.

'So we have made a pact, Caroline, haven't we? Trust in exchange for trust.'

'If you like.'

'I do like,' he breathed. 'But if I find that my trust has been betrayed . . .'

'It will not be. Tell me, Ravi, are you making a similar pact with every one of your mistresses? It must be very time-consuming for you, if you are.'

He threw his head back and laughed, apparently delighted with this. 'No, my dear, I'm not going to so much trouble. But you and I, we have something very particular between us, don't we?'

He knows, she thought again. He knows everything. 'I am flattered that you think so.'

He studied her again, still openly amused. 'Very well. We'll leave it there. And now that we have made our pact, don't you think we should seal it?'

His hand suddenly tightened on her arm. He pressed her back against the cushions and shifted his weight so he rolled on top of her. He was heavy nowadays, and very strong. His smiling mouth came down on hers, and as Caroline wrenched her head to one side, her lip smashed against his teeth. Only an hour ago she had dreamt a girlish version of this. *Was* she mad, perhaps, or just stupid? She writhed beneath him, broke from under his shoulder and bit as hard as she could into the starched cotton of his *kurta* sleeve.

'Little bitch,' Ravi snarled, but her resistance only excited him. He tried to cover her mouth with his hand but she managed to fight free. She remembered the flocks of silent servants, out of sight but never out of earshot. 'Help. *Help me,*' she screamed.

Ravi dropped her arm. He muttered under his breath and stood up, straightening his clothes. He walked to the nearest window slit and stood with his back to her, regaining control of himself. Caroline jumped off the divan and backed away as far as she could, coming hard up against the desk. He was between her and the door – otherwise she would have run for it. As the carved desk edge dug into her buttocks, the jewels flashed into her mind. Quicker than she could even think of it, one hand shot out, snatched a gem from the little heap and whisked back again. Praying that it wasn't the biggest of the lot, she slid it into the seam pocket of her skirt. The tailor and dressmaker, introduced to her by Myrtle, had insisted on placing it there. 'Memsahib always need pocket. Handkerchief, letter, some little thing.'

When Ravi slowly turned back from the window, she was a yard away from the desk and staring at the door.

'You are like a lioness,' he said, almost tenderly. 'And your lip is bleeding. Let me . . .'

His handkerchief was starched and scented. He dipped one corner in the bowl of water, cupped her chin and gently dabbed her lip. Caroline closed her eyes, submitting to his care. She was breathless, her heart jumping.

'There. That's much better,' he said.

'I want to go home.'

'Of course you shall go home. Are you ready?'

He opened the door. Across the courtyard, Caroline just glimpsed the movement as one of the servants stepped out of sight. She would never know if anyone would have responded to another scream.

Extravagantly, she had ordered her *tonga* man to wait for her. She hadn't wanted to run the risk of finding herself stranded out here, on the rural far side of the lake, and she was thoroughly glad of the decision.

'But I would have sent you home in the car,' Ravi protested.

'There is no need.'

He folded down the rickety step himself, before the grovelling driver could reach it, and handed Caroline up into the seat.

'Goodbye,' she said.

Ravi told the driver to take her home, and handed him a note that made the man's eyes revolve. 'I hope not altogether goodbye.' He smiled. 'Please give my regards, won't you, to your friends Mrs McMinn and the missionary's little wife?'

The *tonga* man whipped up his horse and Caroline sank back under the hood. Her hand was buried in her pocket. She sat shaking until Ravi's house was a mile behind them, then leant forward and ordered the driver to take her to a different address.

The dealer was in the old town, a street or two from the dressmaker's shop, which was why she had noticed it in the first place. She stepped down at the junction of two roads and waited there until the *tonga* had jingled away, then hurried past a row of old brick houses. The stone slid between her sweaty fingers and the realisation of what she was doing made her head pound with fear. When she reached the doorway she was panting and her heartbeat drummed in her ears. The window was dusty and a ginger dog lay stretched over the hollow wooden step. The small sign read *Dealer in Gemstones*.

The trader sat inside, reading a newspaper. He folded it away and slowly stood up. On his counter was a polished brass till, a glass case containing some shoddily ornate necklaces and rings, and a jeweller's loupe.

'Good afternoon, Memsahib.'

To Caroline's heightened awareness he seemed both suspicious and ingratiating. She placed her clenched fist on the counter and opened her palm. She saw that the stone was a cut ruby, a decent size but not so big as to be startling. She was in luck. So far. 'I wish to sell this.'

The man inclined his head, then took the jewel. He pinched it in a pair of metal tweezers and unfolded the magnifying glass in order to study it. What if, Caroline thought, this man was Ravi's own dealer and he recognised the stone?

No, this place was far too shabby. That was why she had thought of it.

The man breathed harder and turned the ruby to inspect it from another angle. Caroline's legs were trembling so much she was afraid they might give way beneath her. She gripped the edge of the counter for support and told herself that all this was for Zahra. The stifling feelings of longing and fear and inadequacy that she always felt in connection with her daughter – *her daughter* – instantly swept over her.

The man put down his loupe. 'Not a fine stone.'

'How much?'

He turned down his mouth, dismissive. 'Two hundred rupees.'

Too quick, much too little. Caroline's sharpened senses told her that it was worth far more. She held out her hand for the ruby.

'Three hundred,' he snapped.

She stared. 'Three thousand.'

'Five hundred. Last word.'

After that it was only a matter of bargaining. Finally the man gave a surly nod. He went into the back of the shop and

Caroline guessed that he was opening a safe. A moment later he was laying out a pair of thousand-rupee notes, pink and crisp instead of the ragged and filthy low-denomination notes in general circulation. Two little oval profiles of the king. Caroline tucked them away in her skirt pocket as the dealer dropped the ruby into a tiny bag.

Outside the shop she took a deep gulp of air. The sky had turned the colour of lead and a sinister breeze blew up the alley, presaging a storm. Ten yards off a thin-legged beggar sat on a step, his head hanging. Caroline edged by him and followed the familiar route past the tailor's shop.

When she reached home she locked the bungalow doors. She hid the rupees in the camphor-scented drawer where she stored the folded items of her trousseau, including the nightgown she had worn on her wedding night. Just a glimpse of it was enough to make her slam the drawer shut. She crawled under the bedclothes and lay there, shuddering and listening to the roll of thunder. The thought of what she had just pulled off drew a gasp of wild laughter, but as soon as the laughter petered out she began to cry.

Nerys was surprised and pleased when Caroline asked if she might come with her to visit the girls in Kanihama. They took the bus as far up the valley as it went, and from there one of Nerys's friends from an outlying farm gave them a lift in his old van. The back was piled with sacks of rice, a chicken coop lashed on top. The two women squeezed into the passenger seat, gripping its sticky sides to keep their balance as the truck swayed through the slides of mud and rock created by the recent rain. Nerys chatted to the driver, laughing and resorting to sign language whenever her vocabulary failed her. Caroline sat and seemed to listen, but her body was tense.

The square at Kanihama was decorated with fallen leaves, and clouds hid the brown folds of the mountains. The house where Nerys had lived and where Zahra had been born was occupied now by some of the dye-workers. Nearby a billy-goat tethered to a pole browsed a bare circle of earth.

'Ness!'

Farida and Zahra came running at her, followed by Faisal and the others. Caroline stood a little to one side, fixedly smiling as the children pulled at Nerys's hands and searched her pockets for treats. Nerys hugged Farida, then swung Zahra off her feet. She kissed the child's sweet-scented neck and tried to pass her straight to Caroline, but Zahra recoiled and hid her face against Nerys's shoulder.

'It's all right. I don't want to hold her,' Caroline insisted.

Most of the women were out in the fields, but a small deputation of men led by Farida's grandfather, Zafir, came out of the prayer room to receive the visitors. They were led into one of the houses and seated on the best rug while tea was prepared. Nerys and Zafir exchanged polite remarks about the approach of winter.

'Do they remember me?' Caroline whispered to Nerys, as the tea was poured.

'Yes. But your relationship to Zahra is not discussed, even if they bring to mind the connection between you. That's because they're not very interested. These are simple people, and their immediate family structures are far looser than ours. The weather and the crops, tending the animals, enough money to feed themselves, that's what concerns them.'

At the word *money* Zafir pointed his black beard towards them.

'The shawl,' Caroline said distinctly. 'The beautiful shawl, do you remember? I saw it being woven. It must be finished by now.'

The word *shawl* provoked an instant response. Zafir gave an order and a man left the room. Nerys sipped her tea in the ensuing silence.

Three minutes later the man came back, accompanied by the pale-faced weaver and two other young men. They brought a folded linen cloth, carried on the weaver's outstretched

358

forearms as if it were a religious relic. When he stooped at the women's feet and began to unfold the cloth, Nerys shot a warning glance at Caroline.

The last fold of linen was turned back.

Even in the dimness of the room, the shawl shimmered like light on water. The weaver shook it out so the colours danced in the air. The other two young men caught the corners and brought the piece closer to show off the design. These were the embroiderers who had sat for a whole year, one end apiece, to work over the woven blossoms with their intricate stitches. The shawl wasn't just their work, though. It also belonged to the spinners and dyers, and the *talim* man who had drawn up the intricate pattern for the weaver to follow. It was the prize possession of the entire village, their collective investment in the *kani* tradition that was steadily fading away. Nerys saw the weaver's pitifully thin shoulders and his eager eyes, and she had to blink away the tears from her own.

The head man thrust a corner of the shawl towards them, pointing with his blackened fingernail at a mark stitched there, like a double BB with one B reversed.

'This man. Fingers like butterfly wing. So light,' Zafir said.

'I want to buy it.'

'Caroline, you can't possibly, it'll cost the earth,' Nerys whispered. 'It's years and years of their work.'

'How much?'

The weaver and the two embroiderers drew in a huddle behind Zafir. There was a fierce muttering between them. Stony-faced, Zafir turned back to the two women. 'One thousand five hundred rupees.'

Nerys did the mental arithmetic. 'That's nearly a hundred and twenty pounds. We'll never be able to bargain . . .'

'Here,' Caroline said. From the pocket of her blue tweed coat she brought out an envelope, opened it and produced the two crisp notes. The men stared, but Zafir's hand was already outstretched. Nerys was sure that in all their lives they had never seen so much money.

'Tell them to keep the rest. Tell them it's for taking care of Zahra. I want her to stay here with them, where she'll be safe.'

Caroline stumbled to her feet. She made her way to the door, leaving behind her the shawl, the money and Nerys.

When Nerys finally emerged she had the shawl with her, wrapped once more in its protective linen. Caroline was looking towards the stream as it splashed down through the rocky gorge. Under the chinar tree the children were playing a game with sticks and stones.

'When does the snow come?'

It was October. 'In a month or so.' After that the roads would be difficult or impossible to negotiate until the spring thaw.

Caroline nodded, as if her attention was far away. 'It's beautiful here, isn't it? I always thought so.'

Their van driver had finished his delivery of chickens and had collected a row of baskets filled with red apples. She put her hands into the empty pockets of her tweed coat and began to pick her way through the drifts of leaves towards him. As she passed the children she stopped for a long moment, but Zahra was gurgling with laughter as Farida rolled pebbles at her. She picked up the roundest, whitest one and threw it at the tree trunk, never even glancing at Caroline.

Nerys was treated differently. As soon as they saw she was leaving they ran at her full tilt, and she had a word and a sweet for all of them. They knew that Nerys always came back, so there was no serious outcry when she left.

The van swayed down the track. Nerys tried to pass the wrapped-up shawl to Caroline, but she shook her head. 'That's Zahra's dowry. I want you to keep it safe for her.'

'Of course I will. Caroline, the money . . .'

'Let's just say it was a legacy. That's it. A legacy. From my fairy godmother.'

Nerys didn't like the wild sound of Caroline's laughter.

*　　*　　*

360

By early November, the mountains were cloaked in snow once more and the old brown city creaked with frost. There were already predictions that this year the lake would freeze for the first time since the Christmas cricket match.

One afternoon Caroline came home to the bungalow after visiting Myrtle and Archie and found the house-boy kneeling on a folded rice sack beside the blackened bed of marigold stalks. He was polishing a pair of army boots as if he wanted to rub the leather away. Shivering, she clicked open the front door. 'Ralph? *Ralph?*'

There was an army cap on the rickety hat stand.

The man looking up at her from the armchair was almost unrecognisable.

His face was little more than a death's head with eyes bulging out of purple sockets. His head was almost bald, except for a few colourless strands, and the exposed scalp was raked with livid scars. Caroline ran to him but the spectre raised his crossed arms. She wasn't sure if it was to fend her off or an automatic reaction to protect his brittle body from potential assault.

She stopped short and dropped to her knees on the hearthrug. She put one hand out to touch his knee and felt the raw bone through the khaki.

He said, in a voice that was not much more than a whisper, 'I'm sorry not to give you any warning. There was a plane coming up with a spare seat at the last moment, so they put me in it.'

'They told me you were still too weak to travel. I can't believe you're here. Thank God you're alive.'

His mouth opened in a version of a smile, revealing that he had lost several teeth. 'Just about. You look well, Caroline. You look . . . pretty.' Ralph lifted a strand of her hair, as if he couldn't quite believe in its bright blondeness. He twisted it round his forefinger, stopping just short of pulling it, and she remembered that Ravi had done exactly the same thing.

Her face instantly boiled scarlet. She jerked backwards and gave a gasp as the hair tore from her scalp. She fell back on her heels and Ralph stared at her.

'Let me – let me get you something to eat,' she stammered. 'There's . . . chocolate. Or honey, Kashmiri honey, you like that.'

She saw that already she irritated him.

'I can't eat very much,' he snapped.

Caroline bit her lip. 'Tell me what I can do for you. Please, Ralph.'

His head fell back and his eyes closed. That single exhausted movement told her that what he had been through, the darkness she could only guess at, had opened a chasm between them. She knew with sudden and absolute certainty that, whatever she might do and however hard she tried, she would never be able to please him now.

All right, she thought. But I'll try. I'll make that my penance.

'Nothing. Nothing at all,' he said.

FIFTEEN

March 1945

He was as handsome as always, and as secretive. She could
hardly believe that he was really here in Srinagar. He had
materialised in the flesh, just like Miss Soo Ling in the sliding
box or the doves in one of his stage tricks.

Nerys let Rainer lead her through the streets near Lal Chowk
until they reached an ordinary little *dhaba*, a place where
tradesmen from the nearby workshops came to swallow a
plateful of cheap food. He pulled out a metal chair for her at
a plywood table.

'What would you like?' he asked. 'Champagne? *Pâté de foie
gras?*'

She laughed. 'Yes, please. And then strawberries and cream.
Rainer, I can hardly believe it. Are you really here?'

He extended his hand so she could check its solid warmth.
She clasped it between both of hers, just for one second, which
was as much as she could allow herself.

He looked fit, windburnt and as tightly coiled as a spring.
'Thank you for coming so quickly,' he said.

She had received a scribbled note, delivered by one of the
urchins from the bazaar. Without stopping even to look in the
mirror she had set out to Lal Chowk. He was waiting for her
in the middle of the teeming square at the centre of the city,

as if to underline physically what she already knew – that their weeks together had been the very heart of her time in Kashmir.

'As if I was going to choose not to, perhaps.'

He looked into her eyes. 'It might have been difficult for you. Is your husband in Srinagar?'

'Yes. He's very busy.'

There had been no need to lie to Evan about where she was going because he hadn't asked. She hesitated and then added, 'Rainer . . . nothing has changed. I'm doing what I always intended to do. I am the missionary's wife and helper. Now and always.'

'I know. I know, I know, I know. But I can still love you, can't I? I went away because it would have been impossible to stay and watch you being Evan's wife, and all I learnt was that wherever I am I feel the same. I do try to look upon loving you as a blessing, you know. It makes me a better person, probably.'

They laughed at the *probably*.

Rainer wasn't unhappy, she could see that. It wasn't his way.

The simple joy of seeing and being with him swelled inside her, making her feel light and easy as she hadn't done for months.

A dish of onions and limes was placed in front of them, followed by a bowl of *dhal makhani* and a basket of hot *naan* bread. Rainer demolished the food without looking at it, as if finishing it off were a task that must be completed. Nerys sipped cardamom tea.

'Tell me about everything,' he demanded. 'How are you? I want the truth, too.'

Nerys's smile faded a little. It had been a hard winter.

'No, wait a minute. I've got something for you,' he said. He opened the inside pocket of his coat and slipped a small brown-paper folder across the table.

The three women on the houseboat veranda were laughing at a forgotten joke, with lotus leaves and a stretch of lake water spread behind them. It was a charming photograph, capturing the happy glamour of the old days on the *Garden of Eden*. Nerys looked across the table. 'Is it mine? To keep?' she asked.

'Of course. I'm only sorry that it has taken me so long to come and give it to you in person.'

'Thank you.' She put the photograph away in her handbag. 'I am all right,' she told him. But I miss you. Every day.

He heard the unspoken words. 'And Myrtle and Caroline?'

Myrtle and Archie were down in Delhi, and Mr and Mrs Flanner had finally bought the old houseboat. Nerys had bumped into Laura Flanner at a WVS fund-raising housie-housie party, where the new owner complained that the McMinns hadn't told them the half of what was decrepit about the boat. Nerys protested that to her it had always seemed the lap of luxury.

Laura Flanner had raised one Bostonian eyebrow. 'Is that so?'

'But, then, I'm from Wales.'

Myrtle had written to say that it was terribly sad and a bore but she didn't think they would be coming up to Srinagar for this summer. After the war – suddenly everyone had started to talk about *after the war* as a real time, rather than just a prayer for the remote future – Archie was hoping to find a peacetime job with the railways again. Office-based, of course. He stood a better chance of that by staying in Delhi, Myrtle said, and wheeling himself off to see everyone he could think of. 'You know Archie,' she had written. 'He never gets despondent, and he'll never give up.'

Nerys found Srinagar a much duller place without the McMinns.

Caroline and Ralph Bowen appeared together at the Residency cocktail parties that the Fanshawes still occasionally hosted, or Nerys would sometimes catch sight of them at a regimental concert or among the spectators at a tennis match. Everyone said how encouraging it was that poor Captain Bowen was recovering so well and how fortunate it was that he had his wife to look after him. Nerys wondered if she was the only

365

one to notice that as Ralph got physically stronger Caroline seemed to grow paler and more silent. Sometimes she came alone to tea with Nerys at the mission. She had developed a nervous habit of twisting the rings that were now loose on her third finger.

'I'm quite all right,' she insisted. 'I don't sleep very well these days, that's all. Ralph has terrible nightmares. He won't ever tell me what he's dreaming about, but I think it helps him to wake up and find that I'm there. That's something, isn't it?'

Nerys told Rainer the outline of this.

'And Zahra?' he asked.

The two girls had been in Kanihama all winter, and Nerys had visited them as often as the road was open. Zahra was well looked after, and the precious shawl was safely folded away with Nerys's best clothes in a chest at the mission.

'There's not much news in Srinagar.' She smiled at Rainer. 'Tell me yours. Where have you been, all these months? I know I probably shouldn't ask. But I thought of you very often.'

How odd it is, she thought, that two people can have one spoken conversation while conducting another in their hearts.

'Did you? I like that. I've been devising a new trick. It's a good one, you'll enjoy it. I put on a few little magic shows for the troops – it was a cover for some camouflage advisory work. Covering troop movements, supply depots.' He added, 'Nothing at all heroic. I'm only a Swiss civilian. I'm not a friend because your people can't be completely certain I'm not an enemy. It doesn't matter now. The war will be over in a few weeks.'

Evan was saying the same thing, and he had begun to talk about the mission recalling him to Shillong or even their eventual return to Wales. Nerys had more than once tried to bring up the subject of adoption, but he had been adamant that God's will was either to give them a child of their own or that they should remain childless. She tried to devise plans for Zahra, but she knew that realistically all she could do was wait and hope.

'And so, now what?' she asked Rainer.

366

He hooked one shoulder. 'I have something important to do.'

There was no point in asking what that might be.

By now he had polished off all the food. He pushed the dishes aside and said abruptly. 'I asked you to meet me here because I want to introduce you to someone. Will you come with me now?'

Nerys looked at him in surprise. 'Of course.'

They left the *dhaba* and walked through the crowds. There were more people about, drawn out of their houses by the thin March sunshine, but the wind was still cold and Nerys wrapped her faithful *pheran* tightly around her.

The house was built of soft red brick framed by thick wooden beams, an old Srinagar home in a quiet street. The door was opened by an elderly woman in a sari. Rainer was obviously a regular visitor. He spoke quietly to her and the door inched wider. They slipped inside and were led up the shallow wooden stairs.

In the upstairs room another woman, much younger, was sitting on a window-seat staring down through slatted shutters into the street. As soon as she saw Rainer she jumped up and hurried to him. Glancing away as they greeted each other, Nerys noticed a crucifix on the wall. On a shelf below, with a candle burning in front of it, stood a framed photograph of a child. A rosary hung over the frame.

The servant closed the door.

'Nerys, this is my friend Prita.'

Nerys took her hand. Prita's face was drawn and her eyes were full of shadows. She was dressed all in white, the colour of mourning.

'I am glad to meet you,' the woman said, in a low voice. 'Rainer has told me about you, that you are a good woman and a good friend.'

Nerys knew that the link between these two was something more than simple friendship. The air in the room seemed to shiver.

'He has been very kind to me in my sad times,' Prita continued. 'See, over here? This is a picture of my son. God rest his innocent soul.'

The boy was perhaps three, a solemn-faced infant in a white shirt.

'Arjun's father was killed in 1942. My husband was for Free Kashmir, this is what he and his fellows dreamt of, and his idea was not welcome to the British or to the maharajah. Many men died in the uprising at that time, but there was no end to it then and there will be much more killing to come. I sadly believe that the time of death in Kashmir is only now beginning.'

Nerys still held the woman's hand. It was light and dry, the sinews prominent under the thin skin.

'I am staying here after that for the sake of our son, even though the enemies of my husband are mine too. Our child was Kashmiri first, before any religion, and if he did not grow up in Srinagar, what life would he know? But now . . .'

Rainer came to Prita's other side. He took her in his arms and kissed the top of her head where the smooth black hair parted. His solid bulk made Prita seem tiny. For a moment the three of them were drawn together as tightly by her grief as by any history.

'Arjun was quite well, you know, a baby like any other. Then he was ill, one month, two, worse, and then he died. Rainer told me, you are a nurse. You will understand what I cannot.'

'Not a proper nurse. Only a missionary's wife,' Nerys whispered. She was thinking: rheumatic fever, diphtheria, tetanus, measles, infant diarrhoea – there were so many diseases that carried off the children.

Her arms ached with longing to hold Zahra.

'It's only two weeks since Arjun died,' Rainer said.

'I am so sorry.' There was nothing else Nerys could say.

Prita's ravaged face turned. 'I am not behaving well to my guest, to Rainer's good friend,' she managed to whisper. 'Perhaps you would like some tea.'

Nerys hugged her and then stepped back. 'Thank you, not now. But I will see you again,' she promised.

'Thank you,' Prita said, and Rainer's face flashed his gratitude.

'I'll see you home, Nerys.'

He told Prita that he would be back soon.

Nerys and Rainer walked towards the mission. After the shadows of the widow's house the day seemed bright and noisy.

He said, 'I wanted very much to introduce her to you. I am going to marry her, you see.'

The street clamour rang in Nerys's ears.

You asked me to marry you. And my answer was that I am already married.

A group of American soldiers on leave flooded out of a bar and blocked their way. Nerys threaded her way past. One of them saw her face and apologised. 'Excuse me, ma'am.'

She found her voice. 'Do you . . . love her?'

Rainer stopped walking. He didn't touch her, but it was as if he did. 'I think you know the answer to that.'

'Then . . .'

'I am going to take her back to Europe. Her husband was one of the leaders of the Kashmiri independence movement, and even before 1942 he made many enemies. He paid for that, but his death also left his family in an impossible position. Prita has a few friends, but they will be as vulnerable as she is once the war ends and you British leave India. This state will be cruelly divided and it won't be safe for her to stay here, a widow without anyone to defend her. Prita's husband was a Sikh but she is a Christian convert. A Catholic, like me.'

They were close to the Jhelum river and Nerys stood gazing at the *shikaras* loaded with local goods on their way downriver to be traded or sold in Baramulla and as far away as Rawalpindi. She thought of the floating vegetable gardens out on the lakes, the apple orchards and rice paddies, the shops along the Bund, and the shawl-makers up in Kanihama. Srinagar and the whole of Kashmir were outwardly calm in the lemon-yellow spring sunshine, but she knew how deep were the rifts that lay beneath the surface. Evan and Ianto still went out every day to try to convert lower-caste Muslims and Hindus, and they reported that the two sides hated each other even more than they hated the British. Nerys heard that a radical Sikh leader had threatened, 'If the Muslim League wants to establish Pakistan they will have to pass through an ocean of Sikh blood.'

The fragile, exquisite Kashmiri summer was coming, and she shivered at the prospect of what darkness might lie ahead.

Of course Rainer would do whatever he could to help one woman, who had lost her child as well as her husband. She imagined how he would take his wife back to Switzerland, where they would perhaps live in another lush valley with the white mountain-tops looking down on them. 'I understand,' she said. 'It's a good thing you're doing.'

She had also been in India long enough to know that many marriages were arranged between near-strangers and became strong, successful and affectionate unions. 'I hope you will be happy,' she added, with most of her heart.

They reached the bank of the river and looked along the steps at the familiar scenes of people washing their clothes, cooking, rinsing pans and soaping children.

'Will you come to my wedding?' Rainer asked.

'Of course I will.'

'Thank you.' He touched her hand.

She had once thought he was inscrutable, but now she suddenly saw him in all his strength. She also knew that she loved him. 'You'll be going to Switzerland?'

There was a pause. 'Eventually. My father is there, and I have friends in the mountains. But I shall miss Kashmir.'

He didn't add *and you*, and she was in a way relieved. They had said enough to each other.

They reached the door of the mission. Two bazaar children were sitting on the step even though Nerys's schoolroom had closed hours ago. One tapped her mouth and reached out her cupped hand. Rainer took a coin from his pocket, the other child snatched it and they ran away.

'I'll let you know the day and time of the wedding,' he told Nerys. 'It'll be very soon.'

'I will be there,' she promised. She stood with her hand on the door's iron latch and watched him go, walking back to Prita through the oblivious crowds.

She was already awake, knowing that he was in the grip of the dream again. Ralph writhed, his arms cradled over his head and his legs kicking as he tried to fend off whatever it was that stalked and terrorised him. Sweat had soaked his pyjamas and the bed-sheet. Caroline tried to hold him but he tore himself away from her. He muttered and thrashed and then screamed, just once, but loudly enough for her to imagine Julia Dunkeley waking up next door.

'Ralph, please, hush. It's all right. I'm here, you're safe. It was a nightmare, just a bad dream again.'

He struggled blindly upright, twisting as he tried to escape the horror in his head. She caught his arm and fought to steady him, but panic lent him strength. He brushed her off and pounced. His hands closed round her neck and squeezed, thumbs like steel digging into her windpipe, heavy limbs pinning her down. Caroline's breath gargled and then stopped. She never knew how close she came to losing consciousness, only that the pressure of his fingers suddenly slackened and air rushed into her lungs. She gasped and shuddered, too shocked to move. In the darkness she sensed that Ralph drew back, his hands in the air, confusion gathering in him as he jolted into consciousness.

'Caroline?'

She managed a sound, no more than a rasp in her throat.

Ralph fell back against the bolster. He groaned and panted as she eased herself upright and slid to the edge of the bed. She groped for the box and struck a match, then lit the candle. The electricity was on, she could hear the distant hum of the barracks generator, but she knew from experience that a bright

371

light could frighten him before he was fully awake. The candle flame wavered and steadied behind her cupped palm.

'Caroline?'

She found that she could speak, although her neck and throat throbbed agonisingly. 'I'm here. You were having a nightmare.'

His face and skull glistened with sweat. He nodded, eyes searching the long shadows in the room as the night terrors receded.

'Shall I make you some tea?' she asked.

'No. Not tea.'

He sat up, pyjamas pasted to his body, and swung his legs out of bed. He put on his dressing-gown and shuffled to the door.

'Ralph, please, won't you tell me about the dream? Maybe if you talked about it, it would help to make it stop.'

He shook his head. His fingers twisted the doorknob and she knew that he was longing for the whisky bottle.

'All right, not to me, perhaps, but what about one of the other men? Men who will have seen . . . some of the same things?'

'No. It's a bloody dream, that's all.'

She followed him into the sitting room. He snatched the bottle of cheap Indian whisky off the engraved silver tray that had been their wedding present from the Fanshawes and poured three inches into a tumbler. His hands were shaking and the rim rattled against his teeth as he drank. He didn't even put the glass down as he refilled it, but his hands were already steadier.

'Ralph, don't drink so much. It doesn't help.'

'Yes, it does,' he said flatly. 'Believe me.'

After the nightmares he would drink until he anaesthetised himself and then fall into snoring oblivion. When he woke up the next day he would be as pale as death, angry as a trapped bear, and she would have to tread around him as if in a minefield.

372

Caroline was afraid of her husband and of his barely contained violence, and however much she sympathised with him, it seemed that she was helpless in the aftermath of what he had seen and suffered. Ralph could go out to the club, or to the regimental mess with the other officers he counted as friends, and outwardly appear almost his old self. Only she knew how haunted he was, and how fragile the shell that contained him.

Involuntarily her fingers crept up to explore her bruised throat. She saw that he was looking oddly at her and drew them away again.

'Was I trying to throttle *you*?'

'Yes.'

'Christ. It wasn't you in my sleep, you must know that. There was a Jap, one of the jailers. Sadistic bastard. He . . .' Ralph's eyes closed, then snapped open as if he couldn't bear to contemplate what lay behind his eyelids.

Caroline waited, holding her breath. She was imagining how another man (the same *sort* of man, perhaps) might have recognised his prisoner's weakness – Ralph's particular vulnerability, which he kept concealed at such cost and had hoped to hide even from his wife – and worked on it in ways that were quite possibly cruel beyond her understanding.

'Go on,' she said softly, hoping to encourage him.

She shouldn't have spoken. Ralph gulped back the second whisky and the glass clattered on the tray. 'For Christ's sake, no. I didn't mean to hurt you. I was dreaming.' He came towards her and she had to resist the impulse to shield herself. But he only touched his hand to her shoulder before withdrawing it. 'It's a bloody rotten life for you too, isn't it?' he muttered.

A slow flush crept up her face, and the blood hammered painfully through the bruises. Ralph stared down at her until his mouth puckered, the way it did when he was forced into anything more than a routine exchange with her. He turned sharply away, muttering, 'Almighty God, what is the *matter* with you?'

He didn't expect or wait for an answer. He picked up the bottle, saying in a harsh voice, 'Go to bed. I'm going to sit up and read.'

In the morning, she would find him sprawled and unconscious in the armchair.

The Catholic church was a little red-brick structure with a miniature steeple and a roof of corrugated iron painted pea-green. Nerys and Caroline sat in the front pew beside Professor Pran's daughter. They were the only guests. Prita came down the aisle on the professor's arm, wearing her white sari and a white *dupatta* woven with a tiny thread of gold covering her hair. Rainer waited for her at the altar rail, his coat brushed and a dark red rose in his buttonhole.

The priest who conducted the service was Father Kennedy of the Catholic Mission. Nerys knew him slightly, and Evan had once told her that he was a fine missionary. As Rainer and Prita exchanged their vows, she looked up at the plain glass in the church's tiny trefoil windows and thought about the various contracts that a marriage entailed. It was more compli-cated, much more, than honouring and obeying suggested.

And as for love – how many versions of that were there?

Beside her, Caroline sat with her head bent, turning the rings on her wedding finger. The chafed skin beneath was raw and flaking. She wore a gauzy scarf round her neck to hide blue-purple thumbprint bruises.

After the bride and groom had signed the register in the miniature vestry, with the professor and Nerys as their witnesses, Rainer took them all to his favourite *dhaba* for the wedding breakfast. Father Kennedy came too, and told some good stories about the early days of the mission in Kashmir. It was a happy party. Prita said very little, but she smiled sometimes and rested her hand with the new gold band on her husband's arm.

The next day Nerys went up to Kanihama to see Zahra and the loyal Farida. She stayed in the village for a few nights, singing songs and playing games with Faisal, his little brother and the other children from her old schoolroom. She had taken with her some simple medicines and dressings, and treated the villagers' numerous winter ailments as best she could. She assured Zafir that Zahra's precious shawl was in her safe keeping, and at the same time discreetly made sure that the other side of the bargain was being honoured. She was in no real doubt that the little girl was well looked after, particularly by Farida – life up in the village was hard, but she could see that Zahra was healthy and full of laughter.

When she returned to Srinagar she brought the two girls with her for a spring visit to the city, the first of that new year. When they arrived the pair scampered ahead, down the lane to the mission door, past a beggar who sometimes crouched in a niche in the wall. Inside the house Evan absently stroked the girls' heads and Ianto beamed through his spectacles. The children who regularly came to the schoolroom took them back into their games.

Nerys was disconcerted by Caroline's response when she told her about the girls' arrival. Her hands flew to her mouth and her face drained of colour. 'I can't see her. I really cannot, not now that Ralph's here.'

Nerys's heart sank. 'But as far as Ralph and everyone else is concerned she's a mission orphan.'

'I *can't*. You don't understand.'

Ralph saw everything, Caroline believed. Guilty, she flushed under his scrutiny and heard in her head, *What is the matter with you?*

'All right.' Nerys sighed. 'If you feel you really can't. But it seems a shame.'

April came. Rainer was packing boxes, preparing to leave his apartment overlooking the Jhelum river. The coils of rope, mountaineer's hardware and the paraphernalia of magic tricks were all gathered up, heavy drums sealed and labelled for collection by various freight agents.

In Europe, the US Army Air Force and RAF Mosquitos had taken it in turns to bomb Berlin as the Red Army closed in on the city overland.

'It's almost over,' Ralph said, listening to the news. Caroline turned aside.

After the war. After the war. What would that *mean*? She felt increasingly as if she were in one of Rainer Stamm's magical boxes, where the roof and walls squeezed closer and closer together. She was trapped. Out of the corner of her eye she saw the flash of metal and even felt the kiss of steel on her skin as a blade sliced through the wall. She flinched, and realised that Ralph was glaring at her.

Evan opened a letter from the Welsh Presbyterian Mission, postmarked Shillong. He put it aside until Nerys had seen that Zahra and Farida were asleep in their shared bed and Ianto had eaten his supper with them and gone off to his rented room beyond the bazaar. Then he said, 'My dear, I have something to tell you. We are recalled to Shillong.'

'What? When?'

'In a month or so, probably. Of course, much depends on the war news. But I'd say it would be something of that order. You'll be pleased to hear that Ianto is to stay on to continue our work here. I hope very much that we shall be able to travel back through Kargil and Leh, to revisit my earlier converts. I am going to write and ask if that might be possible.'

'It's very soon,' Nerys managed to say.

Evan had taken a sheet of writing paper to begin his letter. 'We have been in the field for quite a respectable amount of time,' he said.

I shall have to take Zahra with us, Nerys decided. Somehow, it will have to be done. Perhaps Farida belongs in Kanihama with Faisal and the others, but I cannot leave Zahra behind.

Ralph went to a dinner at the mess. The few of his brother officers who remained in Srinagar HQ were invariably polite to him, even deferential, but the cordiality they showed him had not increased since his return. If anything, he was more of an outcast. They were aware of what he had been through, but the effects were not discussed. They were not articulate men.

Tonight, however, the atmosphere was different.

They had listened to the latest news bulletin. Yesterday the Russians had reached Vienna. Major Dunkeley thumped his clenched fist on the table. The bloody Boche were finally done for, he declared. It wouldn't be long before Berlin and Hitler himself fell into Allied hands. It was a damned shame that it was the Reds and not the British who were to have that honour, but even so – it was not too premature to have a small celebration, between friends, was it?

There was a ragged cheer, and the port decanter was called for.

As it circulated and the cigar smoke thickened, Ralph briefly became just another officer among soldiers who at last had victory in their sights. He drank and joked and sang the regimental ditties, and his glass was filled and refilled.

Since Changi and Burma, Ralph Bowen's liver had never functioned properly. There were several other parts of his body that let him down too, so he didn't take particular notice even when the MO ordered him to go easy on the old bottle. He drank to get drunk in any case, and that point came more and more quickly.

Too soon, he slipped beyond the self-imposed barriers. In the press of warmth and brotherhood, he let his arm fall from the back of the chair where it had been resting on to the broad shoulders of Lieutenant Ormsby. Under the revolving fans the room was swimming but this was a safe place, even a beloved one.

Ormsby shook himself free and leapt to his feet. 'For Christ's sake, Bowen.'

A glass of port skidded off the polished table and smashed to the floor.

'That's enough,' growled Dunkeley. 'Captain Bowen, please return to your quarters.'

In a capsule of silence, Ralph reeled out of the room.

A voice called after him, 'Off you go to that pretty little wife of yours,' and someone else tittered.

The cool air outside made him stagger. He leant against the door frame and a passing servant said respectfully, 'May I help you, sir?'

'No. Leave me alone,' he muttered.

He tried to take one more step but his legs gave way. He collapsed into the gaudy bushes that bloomed under the windows of the mess. He instantly fell into a doze, but he thought he could only have been asleep for a second or two. When he surfaced again he could hear voices, and the sound of two men relieving themselves on the lawn a few yards away.

'Julia's sister ran into her in Delhi a couple of years back. She was coming out of a doctor's office with McMinn's wife.'

'I wish *I*'d been in Delhi with Myrtle McMinn.' The other one laughed.

'They were both mightily uncomfortable to be spotted. Alice said she was certain she was pregnant.'

'Who – Caroline Bowen?'

'The same.'

Ralph felt the grit and dirt under his cheek. He lay as still as he could.

There was a loud guffaw. 'Not by her husband?'

'This is the interesting part. Bowen was in Burma, wasn't he? No – it was that unspeakable Ravi Singh fellow, apparently. That's how the story goes. Of course, it could be just Srinagar gossip, but they were pretty thick at one time, the two of them.'

Somebody belched and excused himself, and then footsteps swished across the grass towards the bungalows. The voices were swallowed by the darkness.

When he was sure that he was alone Ralph hauled himself painfully to a sitting position. He rested his head in his hands and tried to think.

Caroline? His wife – who seemed more like a white mouse than a woman – his wife and Ravi Singh?

It seemed utterly unlikely, and as he tried to pursue the notion he realised that it didn't hold much significance anyway. A woman in bed with the wrong man? A miserable little by-blow, done away with by a doctor in Delhi or even delivered and then hidden away? What did it matter?

Worse things had happened – far, far worse.

Ralph manoeuvred himself on to hands and knees and, by hauling on the bushes, achieved a standing position. Frowning hard and repeating the words *one, two, one, two*, he found that he could march very acceptably. He swung his arms smartly, and even though the ground shifted and tilted he made it all the way to the lane that ran past the married-quarters bungalows. Here was the gate. No, not that one. Further. Wouldn't do to step into the wrong house.

Next but one. Almost there. Sleep, that was the thing.

A patch of deeper shadow lay in the long grass beside the fence. His blurred eyes settled on it and in the same instant the shadow stirred. It became a man, hunkered on the ground, lying in wait for him.

Ralph staggered, but the enemy's threat almost sobered him. Bayonet or pistol, which would it be? He wouldn't stop to find out. Kill him first.

He kicked out hard, into the man's legs. The figure recoiled and scrambled to his feet. Ralph caught him by the arm and punched at his head. The pain from his knuckles shot up his arm and he cursed and almost overbalanced. It wasn't a Japanese soldier at all, just a beggar. He had seen the wretch here before. He landed another more satisfactory punch. 'Get out, damn you. Don't let me catch you near my house again.'

The beggar broke free. To Ralph's amazement the man seized his arm and twisted it up behind his back. Pressing his mouth close to Ralph's ear he hissed two or three words that Ralph didn't understand. Then he flung him aside and loped away up the alley, barefoot, silent as a cat.

Drink swirled in Ralph's head again as he hung against the fence.

Had there really been a man or was he in a dream?

He was gone, anyway.

He opened the door of the bungalow and the familiar smell of brass polish and insect powder and curry spice enveloped him. He wanted a nightcap, but what he had heard on the mess lawn nagged in his mind. Ask Caroline, ask his little wife for the truth, that was the thing to do . . .

Their bedroom was pitch dark, but he sensed that she was awake.

'I heard a funny story at the mess tonight,' he shouted.

The lamp clicked on. Caroline sat up and stared at him, her eyes wide. 'Did you have a nice dinner?'

'I heard a funny story,' he repeated. 'I heard you had a baby. My dear wife. What do you think of that?'

Her hand shot up to her mouth. 'What do you mean? Who said . . .?'

So it was true.

She looked shocked and utterly terrified, but not *surprised*.

Ralph was breathing hard. At first it hadn't struck him as particularly important, whatever Caroline had done while he was fighting to stay alive in Changi and Burma. Their marriage was a sham in any case, and what did any of it matter? But now the humiliation of the night in the mess, the treatment he had just received from a bloody beggar in the street, the fog of drink and the incessant pain in his body all rolled together. He wanted to howl like a dog. He wanted to lay his head down and for everything to stop hurting. He wanted his wife to stop whispering, and being afraid whenever he glanced at her, and act like a man.

'Ra-vi Singh,' he said, drawing out each syllable.

Fear leapt in her eyes.

Ralph had met him only a handful of times, years ago, but he had a sudden vision of the man's dark, sneering, dismissive face. Ravi Singh was a native, even if he was the maharajah's relative. Anger ballooned in him. He clenched his fists and swayed towards the bed. Caroline whimpered and threw up her arms to fend him off, and as she did so, he understood that what he hated most of all in her was her lack of spirit.

He wasn't going to hit her. He wasn't ever going to strike a woman.

'Don't be so bloody feeble. You can tell your lover I'm going to kill him.'

'Ralph, he's not . . . he's not my lover. I was stupid and lonely. He's a wicked man. Don't go near him. Please, I beg you not to.'

'I am going to kill him,' Ralph repeated. The idea made him feel much better. He remembered the way the butt of his service revolver fitted his hand.

And so, a nightcap. That was what he needed now – now the decision was made.

He swung away from the bed and made an unsteady diagonal to the door. In the sitting room the bottle stood ready on the tray. He hoisted it in a fist and collapsed into the armchair. No bed. Sleep here.

Caroline lay rigid under the sheet.

She had pledged secrecy, hoped and believed that she had kept it. Yet it seemed that her infidelity was the subject of mess gossip and, far, far worse than that, somehow the whole world knew all about her child.

After a while her heart slowed a little. Disconnected thoughts ricocheted through her head. Trying to hide her pregnancy had been utterly foolish. It was what Myrtle would have done, if she had ever been stupid enough to make such a mistake in the first place, but Myrtle would have carried it off with *élan*.

Her friendship with Nerys and Myrtle, the days on the *Garden of Eden*, the cricket match on the frozen lake, even Kanihama, all seemed to belong to another age. Caroline felt frozen, but blades of self-hatred stabbed through the ice.

The only thing she could do was go to Ravi, tell him the whole truth and ask for his understanding.

If he were to kill *her*, that wouldn't matter. She thought she would even be glad of it. She couldn't let Ralph go anywhere near him, though, because it was Ralph who would be hurt, or slaughtered.

From that, at the very least, she would try to protect him.

And then there was Zahra.

She rolled on to her side, drawing up her knees. Cold. Good, keep the coldness, that was protective.

She must ask Nerys to take care of Zahra. Nerys would do it much better than she ever could.

Tomorrow: Ravi, and then Nerys.

She lay and waited for the hours to crawl by.

SIXTEEN

The launch drew closer, its bow pennant drawn taut by the wind and a fresh green wake churning behind it.

Caroline stood at the end of the jetty not far from the Shalimar Garden. The powerful engine throttled back and the boat made a semi-circle, stirring up the reek of lake-water as it slid to the mooring post. Two liveried servants stepped ashore and made fast and she saw Ravi waiting for her under the white awning. She let the nearest servant hand her on board, and stepped down on to the scrubbed-teak deck. Immediately the engine roared and the launch curved away again, heading out into the lake.

Ravi bowed suavely. But this was better than she could have hoped for. He couldn't do much to her out here, in full sight of passing *shikaras*, with two of his servants close at hand.

They sat down in canvas chairs at a brass-cornered table. One of the servants was at the wheel; the other retreated below to the little covered cabin. The thrum of the engine and the swish of water would make what she had to say inaudible to anyone but Ravi.

'This is an unlooked-for pleasure,' he said, glancing at his jewelled watch. 'Unfortunately I have to meet someone at precisely eleven o'clock.'

When at last the long, terrible night had ended, she had

scrawled a note and sent it by a messenger. Once she was dressed, Ralph had lurched past her and fallen into the bed she had just vacated. She had left him there, yellow and snoring, after giving instructions to the house-boy that he was to take Sahib his coffee immediately he woke up. Ravi's reply had reached her within the hour and she had hurried out of the house to meet the launch at the place he indicated.

'I have something to tell you,' she said.

'Please go ahead.'

She drew air into her lungs. Her mouth felt stiff, dry as paper, but she got out the plain words she had rehearsed. 'After our time together I had a child. It was your child, Ravi. I didn't want my husband to find out, so I concealed the whole thing.'

'Mine?' His voice cut like a knife.

'Yes.' She shifted her gaze from the tabletop, upwards to meet his. 'You are the only man I have ever had relations with. I was a virgin, remember?'

'Yes. And is this what you wanted to say to me?'

'Not everything. My husband heard about the baby last night, from an officer in the mess. I thought I had kept everything secret, even from you, which was what I originally decided was for the best, but now it seems that I have failed. So naturally I have come straight to see you, to tell you everything and to ask for your understanding.'

Ravi pondered, the corners of his mouth turning down. At last he spoke. 'I see. Tell me, Caroline, did you really imagine that I didn't know?'

Caroline shrank. 'I hoped not.'

'I have had you watched, my dear. You – and your friends running about with their *kangris*.'

'You knew about Zahra all along?'

He gestured impatiently. 'Your weavers' village is not exactly beyond my reach.'

So at least one of the people up there must have been in Ravi's pay. Caroline shivered at the thought of Zahra innocently playing under the tree with eyes always upon her, ready to report her movements back to Srinagar. Yet it had somehow suited Ravi to leave her alone. Maybe all he wanted was to keep her at a safe distance from his family.

She lifted her head. 'I am here to warn you, Ravi. My husband is very angry. He was drunk last night . . .'

Again the impatient gesture. 'I know that too.'

It didn't matter how. She would have to come to terms later with the extent to which she and everyone she knew had been spied upon. 'He told me that he is going to kill you.'

Ravi threw back his head and laughed, as if this were the most comical thing he had ever heard. 'Is that all you've come to say?'

She said, 'I don't want Ralph to be hurt. I know he won't come off best if he does try to injure you.'

Ravi's amusement vanished. In a voice so low that it hardly reached her, he murmured, 'And I thought you might have come to explain why you stole my ruby.'

The launch passed between the wooden pillars that marked the beginning of the river channel. Over to their right Caroline saw a line of houseboats, the *Garden of Eden* at the end of the row. The flower-seller's *shikara* was making its way towards his customers, the packed blooms a dash of brilliant colour against the rippled water.

Her voice almost failed her, but there was nothing she could do except try to brazen this out. 'As you seem to know every-thing else, you probably also know that I sold the stone to a dealer. I had to have money to take care of the child.'

Ravi nodded, as if this satisfied him. They slid past the Lake Bar of the Srinagar Club, its tables and sunshades newly set out for the approach of summer. A white-coated waiter stood ready to take cocktail orders and a little clutch of *shikaras* for hire bobbed at the side.

'I shall have to leave you here.' He pointed to the steps that led towards the Bund. Sunlight glinted on a car making its way over the first Jhelum bridge. 'By the way, my wife expects to be confined later this summer. I shall have a son.'

385

'How wonderful for you,' Caroline said. 'I do hope it will be a boy. I hope all will go well.'

Ravi laughed again, plump and handsome under the awning. Her hopes were utterly meaningless to him and her good wishes meant nothing. Over his shoulder he gave a curt order to the boatman and the prow swung towards the steps. The boat was briefly secured and Ravi stood up to help her ashore. Caroline had achieved nothing at all by seeing him.

She stepped out on to dry land.

Unable to stop herself she asked, 'What are you going to do?'

'About?'

'About my child.'

'I am going to protect my family's interests, of course.'

Another command to the boatman, the ropes were unlooped, and the launch sped away.

Nerys listened in horror as Caroline spilt out the story.

Outside in the mission yard, half a dozen children played with a ball and a set of wooden crates. Their noise floated in through the open windows, Zahra's happy voice audible among them.

'What did he mean, do you think, about protecting his family's interests?'

Helplessly, Caroline shook her head. 'He's ruthless. He does what he wants, gets what he wants. What can we do?'

Nerys was at a loss, and a sense of deep foreboding took hold of her. 'I don't know. But somehow we'll have to hide Zahra so Ravi Singh can't find her.'

Evan was out, but Ianto Jones was in the chapel room laying out service sheets for a prayer meeting. Nerys made a rapid decision. 'Ianto? Please stay and watch the children until three o'clock. Then lock the yard gate when they've all gone.'

He blinked behind his thick glasses, Adam's apple bobbing. 'But—'

'Please.'

With Caroline at her heels, Nerys ran down the stairs and scooped Zahra out of the little group of infants. Farida threw the ball aside and attached herself to Nerys's heels. At the gate they stopped and scanned the alley. The beggar wasn't there. Nerys asked Farida if she had seen the hands-out man today and the child nodded. He had been there earlier, but she had seen him going away again.

They dashed along the canal bank to the river, past smoky food stalls and *chai*-vendors and gossiping boatmen. Nerys clasped Zahra in her arms and the little girl laughed and wriggled in pleasure at this new game. They were gasping for breath by the time they reached Rainer's door. Nerys thumped on it, even in the heat of this moment remembering the night when Farida had come to fetch them out of Rainer's bed, only to find her mother dead.

Rainer opened the door. 'Is the city on fire?'

Nerys and Caroline ducked inside. Farida plumped herself down on the step, refusing to come in with them. She gathered up her skirt and pulled her shawl over her head, apparently settling down to watch the street.

In the upstairs room, cooled by the breeze off the water, Prita was sitting sewing amid the last of Rainer's myriad boxes. She put her work aside and stood up, wordlessly greeting them with a bow over her folded hands.

Zahra was heavy. Gratefully, Nerys let her slide to the floor. The child's attention was caught by the bright silks in Prita's work basket and she ran straight to them. Then she saw a pair of small pointed scissors and made a grab for those too. Prita caught her hand and told her in Kashmiri, 'No, those are too sharp. You will cut your fingers.' She put the scissors out of reach on top of one of the boxes.

'What has happened?' Rainer asked.

Caroline stammered out her story again. Taken by a stranger's attention, especially one who spoke the village language so well, Zahra started chattering to Prita. Nerys was watching Caroline and then looking for Rainer's reaction, but out of the corner of her eye she saw Prita reach out and awkwardly, longingly, stroke Zahra's hair.

Without quite knowing why she did it, Nerys took up the embroidery scissors, stooped down to separate out a single thick lock of the same brown-gilt hair, and snipped it off.

Rainer frowned. 'Yes. We must take her away from here.'

Zahra broke away from Prita and Nerys, heading now for the white wicker cage where Rainer's stage doves shared a perch.

'Birds,' the child cried in delight. 'Zahra birds.'

Rainer opened a painted box and took out his tailcoat. He slipped it on, covered the cage with the red silk handkerchief from the top pocket, and invited Zahra to search the others. As soon as she had made sure that one was empty he produced the four interlinked metal rings from it, and spun the chain round her throat, like a huge necklace. She tugged at it, puzzled but smiling, before he whipped it away and threw four separate rings in the air. While she was still captivated by the juggling, he lifted a corner of the red handkerchief to show her that the cage was empty.

Zahra's eyes rounded. 'Gone,' she breathed, staring at the perch and then the empty air.

The three women looked on. Prita was fondly smiling and even Caroline's pale, tense face had briefly softened and coloured.

Rainer beckoned to Zahra and she went straight to him. He touched his finger to his lips before blindfolding her with the red handkerchief.

Nerys remembered afterwards how Zahra had laughed, showing no fear, and stretched out her hands to try to grab Rainer as he gently turned her three times in a circle.

Off came the blindfold again. The cage was still empty. Rainer mimed perplexity, but then his hand shot into the same pocket of the tailcoat and, with a flourish, he tossed into the air first one white dove and then the other. The birds flew up over Zahra's head and settled on an open shutter.

Nerys clapped, and Caroline and Prita joined in.

Zahra was too delighted to move. She gazed at Rainer in awe. He held out his arm and the birds obligingly came back to roost.

'More,' Zahra whispered.

'Rainer . . .' Nerys began, intending to say that there were important things to discuss. He was rummaging through the box. Out came his magician's cape, embroidered with occult symbols. '*Rainer . . .*'

They all heard the slap of bare feet on the stairs. Farida burst into the room. 'Hands-out man.' She held up four fingers. Four men.

Nerys ran to the window that looked away from the river. Through a crack in the shutters she saw them, and recognised one of the faces. It was the beggar who frequented the alley behind the mission, only he didn't look like a beggar any more. And at the end of the narrow street she could just see the polished silver radiator grille and shiny black bonnet of an opulent motor-car.

'Ravi Singh's here.'

There was a thunderous knocking at the door. Caroline backed up against the wall, hands to her mouth. 'Oh, God. Don't let them in.'

Rainer didn't hesitate. Smiling, he held up the red blindfold. Ready for another trick, Zahra jumped into his arms. He signalled her to silence, wrapping the blindfold again. The knocking at the door grew more insistent. Rainer enveloped himself and Zahra in the swirling cape. Prita was at his side too, hanging on his arm. He muttered one sentence to her and she slid behind his back.

Downstairs there was a crash as the door burst inwards. Shadowed by Prita, Rainer picked up the box of tricks with his free hand and calmly walked to the head of the stairs. Ravi Singh's men clattered up to him and he waved them on into the room overlooking the river. Caroline stood frozen, but Nerys had crossed to Prita's chair and taken up her discarded sewing. As the four men tipped into the room she put in a careful stitch and glanced up at them in surprise.

'Good day,' she said in Kashmiri. And in English, 'This is a private house, you know. How can we help you?'

Ravi Singh stood framed in sunlight in the street doorway, his dark shadow thrown on the old wooden floorboards. He wore dazzling white *kurta pyjama* and a high-buttoned coat of pale buff linen, every inch the haughty Kashmiri aristocrat.

'Hello there,' Rainer cheerily called down to him. 'What's all this?' Not waiting for Ravi's answer he skipped down the stairs to meet him.

As his foot touched the bottom step he seemed to trip and almost overbalance. The box of tricks flew open and a shower of glittering rings, metal cups, scarves, coloured balls and gewgaws cascaded at Ravi's feet. Rainer's extravagant cape, the opposite of a muted *pheran*, swirled about him as Ravi stepped backwards with an exclamation of startled annoyance. He was scowling in distaste at this display of heathen arcana.

'How clumsy of me.' Rainer sighed. One-sidedly he bent to scoop up a coloured ball, but at the same instant two doves escaped from within his cape. Their wingbeats were loud in the confined space. Ravi leapt further backwards, crashing against the door edge, his arms flailing to beat off the birds. Prita's white pashmina shawl fluttered as she enveloped herself within it and drew a fold over her bowed head. She slipped past Ravi Singh and out into the street.

'So sorry.' Rainer laughed. 'I am training the birds. You see we have some way to go.'

Casually he unhooked his cape and let it drop from his shoulders. He folded it neatly and placed it inside the box, then piled the fallen items on top. Finally he took off the tail-coat and closed the lid of the box on everything. In his shirt-sleeves he stretched out his arms and the doves flew back to him.

'Is this a social call?' he asked the glowering Ravi.

'It is not. I have come for the child.'

'For this five men burst into my house? Child? Which child is this?'

With a growl of impatience Ravi pushed him aside and took the stairs two at a time. Nerys still sat with the sewing in her lap, but when Ravi appeared she got up and went composedly to meet him. Caroline stood like a ghost against the window as the four men hunted through the room.

'What are you doing?' Nerys demanded.

Ravi strode to Caroline. 'Where is the child?' he shouted.

Rainer came back and put the doves into their cage. 'Would our guests like some refreshments?' he asked.

Nerys slid to his side. Rainer flicked a glance at Ravi's half-turned back, then cupped Nerys's face in his hands. He whispered to her, 'She will be safe. Don't worry if you hear nothing for a while. And I will come back, I promise you.'

His lips brushed her forehead. Before Ravi angrily swung away from the trembling Caroline, Rainer had melted away.

Vanished, as if into thin air. Nerys inwardly smiled.

'Search the house,' Ravi ordered. 'Where has the Swiss gone? Bring him back.'

His furious expression indicated that he knew he was already outwitted. The men ran to do as they were told and Ravi confronted the two women again.

'The girl was here an hour ago,' he said. 'Where is she now?'

'She?' Nerys innocently asked. She had trouble not smiling, and she realised that she was actually enjoying herself. She took Caroline's cold hand and drew it under her arm so they presented a solid front against Ravi. 'We have had some mission children to visit. They love the magic, you know. But they have all gone home now. Is it one of them you mean?'

Ravi came one step closer but Nerys only raised her chin and held on to Caroline. Nerys's look said plainly, I may be only a woman but I am British, a missionary's wife. You are a powerful man, but what do you think will happen if you lay a single finger on either of us?

He stopped short, with his hands clenched at his sides.

'Who was the Indian woman?'

'I think you must be referring to Mrs Stamm. I am sorry you didn't give me the chance to introduce you. Perhaps there will be another opportunity.'

Ravi's handsome face was contused with anger, but he managed to speak coolly enough. 'As you well know, Mrs Watkins, the child I am looking for is actually my own daughter. I have decided that neither Mrs Bowen, nor her husband, nor your little Christian mission is fit to care for her. I am going to take her into my own household.'

Perhaps as a slave to one of your sisters – or quite probably much worse than that, Nerys mentally supplied. 'I'm afraid you are too late. The child is no longer in Srinagar, and will soon be leaving India.'

'You cannot remove an Indian native from her own country and people.'

Her level gaze retorted, It's still wartime. India has thousands of orphans, starving or abandoned. Do you think one child will be missed among so many?

But she didn't make the attempt to contradict him.

Two of the men came back. The house was empty and their search hadn't taken long. Presumably the other two were combing the streets for Rainer and Prita. Nerys felt no anxiety on that score.

Ravi flung a last glance at Caroline. 'Do you still imagine that you can outwit me?'

Only Nerys could feel how violently Caroline trembled.

With his men at his heels, Ravi left them.

As soon as they were sure he had gone, Nerys took the distraught Caroline in her arms. 'Don't worry. Zahra will be safe. Rainer will see to that.'

But she thought that Caroline's mental state had slipped beyond anxiety for Zahra or even for herself. She was shaking, and biting her lips so hard that toothmarks showed in the thin skin. She seemed eaten up by a black terror that had no rational

392

roots in her real difficulties, and by deep unhappiness that flooded all her being. All Nerys could do was hold her tight, murmur disjointed words that did not comfort, and hope that her despair might eventually lighten.

'Sit down,' she murmured to her. 'I am going to make you some tea, and then take you home.' She guided Caroline to Prita's chair.

Farida appeared in the doorway. The girl marched straight to Nerys, her eyes burning. Nerys gripped her shoulders. 'You did very well, Farida. Zahra will be safe from bad men now.'

But Farida only swung out at Nerys with two fists. She beat them on Nerys's body. 'Zahra. I want Zahra.' She wouldn't ever give way to tears, but the depth of her distress was plain.

Nerys could only catch at her wrists to restrain her, and say, 'I know, I know you do, but she has had to go away. I hope she'll come back, Farida, but I don't know when it will be.'

The girl tore herself free and ran to the door. With a heavy heart, Nerys watched her go. It would be hard for all of them until they knew what Zahra's future was likely to be, but hardest of all for poor, loyal Farida.

Outside in the bright afternoon, a woman in a plain white sari walked quickly through the streets with a child on her hip. The child was crying but no one paid the slightest attention to such a commonplace sight. At a sufficient distance, a tough-looking European man in shirtsleeves took the same route. A series of detours through enclosed alleyways and across weedy patches of derelict ground brought the people to the gate of Professor Pran, the Pandit university teacher who was shortly to move away for ever from the beloved city of his birth.

When Caroline and Nerys returned to the Bowens' bungalow, the worried house-boy was waiting on the step for them. 'Madam, quick now. Very sorry, Sahib sick. Hospital.'

Julia Dunkeley's head popped up beyond the hedge. It was her husband who had sent for the doctor while Caroline was

393

out. She said she would come with Caroline to the hospital, but Nerys told her very firmly that there was no need for that because she would accompany Caroline herself.

The army hospital was a series of single-storey buildings set in scrubby gardens, and in the past weeks Ralph had spent plenty of time there. Now a nurse led the two women to a curtained-off corner of a long ward in which wounded men lay propped in their beds and convalescents read or played cards at a centre table.

Ralph was asleep. His skin was a dark yellow colour and he was breathing in thick gasps through his open mouth. A metal kidney dish stood on the locker. Caroline sank down on the edge of the bedside chair and Nerys told her that she would wait outside. There was a loggia opening off the ward and she went out there where the air was less redolent of clogged dressings and sickness. Small groups of men sat smoking in bamboo chairs. She found an empty seat and sank down, gratefully closing her eyes.

She needed time to assimilate the events of the day.

Later, Caroline made her way towards her. She looked as if she were sleep-walking, even though her eyes were unnaturally wide. 'The doctor says his liver is failing. He is very ill.'

The bluff MO had made a tent of his fingertips, not quite looking Captain Bowen's wife in the eye. He had talked about the severe damage her husband's bodily systems had sustained while he was a captive of the Japanese, and how his life was in the balance.

'We must hope fervently that he will recover from this crisis,' he said, and added that for the next few days the outcome was unpredictable. But if and when Ralph was finally out of danger, his life from now on would always have to be highly regulated.

'You understand me, I'm sure,' the doctor said. 'He must keep quiet, watch his diet, drink absolutely no alcohol. There will be a disabled discharge, of course. He is fortunate to have a young wife to care for him.' Then he had touched Caroline lightly on the shoulder. 'This is another shock for you, my dear. But if we do manage to pull him through, the two of you will have your life together. I promise you, we will do our very best for him.'

Nerys led her between the flowerbeds. Caroline's head hung as she concentrated on the effort of walking. They were almost at the hospital gates when she suddenly jerked upright and began to laugh. 'He won't be able to shoot Ravi Singh now, will he? But just to make sure, I'm going to throw his guns in the lake.'

'It's all right, Caroline. I'll speak to Major Dunkeley about the guns,' Nerys soothed.

She wished very much that Myrtle and Archie were here today.

At the bottom of a narrow ravine choked with rocks and twisted tree roots lay the wreckage of a red Ford truck. Broken glass covered the stones, shards of it glittering in the sunshine.

An Indian Army troop carrier had drawn up at the roadside thirty feet above, and a trio of soldiers scrambled through the chutes of torn earth and uprooted saplings that marked the truck's descent. As they reached the mangled vehicle the buzzing of flies was the only sound. One of the men stooped and peered into the upside-down cab. A pool of blood had collected in the roof felt and the flies swarmed there. There was much more blood on the grey metal dashboard, and the torn ribbons of a white *dupatta* scarf hung from the twisted wing mirror.

The men searched through the cab and the truck body, picking through open boxes that spilt a few clothes, some metal cups, a bright-coloured ball squashed and dented by the impact. From the twigs of a thorn bush one man retrieved a child's plaited leather sandal.

There were no bodies to be found, no valuables, only the rifled luggage. The soldiers conferred in low voices and then began the steep ascent back to the road where their companions smoked and waited. This was an under-populated area, too rocky and barren for any farming, even for grazing animals. There were caves at the upper end of some of these ravines, used as hiding places by Azad Kashmir rebels or other desperate men, and the rocky ground was also home to packs of wild dogs. One of the men said that there were wolves hereabouts too. Further down the mountainside, where shepherds spent the summer months, there were stone-lined pits that had been dug as wolf traps. The others shrugged. Whether this was an accident followed by looting, a roadside hold-up or a murder scene was not their concern, and they had seen plenty of sights more disturbing. The wireless operator reported the incident to their base and gave the map co-ordinates. Then the troop carrier resumed its journey.

There were six berths in the cabin and a single small porthole. The woman and child had been assigned a middle and lower left, each with a cretonne curtain that could be drawn for privacy. The porter deposited their cabin bags and the man gave him his tip. As soon as they were alone the three of them inspected the little space and peered into the miniature bathroom.

'I wonder who you'll be sharing with?' the man said.

They would be women, of course, whoever they were, and most probably also Indian. Perhaps they would be nuns, or scholarship students heading for England.

The child clung to the woman's hand. His hair was cut short and he wore an everyday *kurta pyjama*.

'Why can you not come with us now?' the woman demanded.

'I can't, because I have a promise to fulfil. You don't want me to break a promise, do you?'

It was a discussion they had been over many, many times.

'Who will meet us in England? How will I know who they are?'

'My friend will be at the docks, that is another promise. You have his photograph safe so you will recognise him?'

She held it up. It showed a smiling elderly man in leather

boots and knee breeches, his hat pushed to the back of his head and a pipe in his mouth.

'Edward will take care of you both. And very soon, a matter of weeks, I will join you and we will go to my home in Switzerland. You'll be happy there, I know. That's promise number three, isn't it?'

She smiled, at last. 'You are very good.'

He took her face between his hands and kissed her forehead. 'Remember, as soon as the ship leaves the dock you are safe. You can put her in her proper clothes again, and she will no longer be Arjun but the orphan daughter of friends you are taking to her father's cousins in London.'

The woman nodded obediently.

'Don't worry so much.' He kissed her again, then lifted the child off its feet and swung it to the top bunk. 'You are the king of the castle up there, aren't you?'

Later, with the klaxons sounding to warn those who were not sailing that they must leave the ship immediately, they reached the head of the gangway. Everywhere friends and relatives were hugging and weeping as the moment of parting approached.

'I'll see you soon,' the man breathed. He kissed the two of them once more and ran down the sloping gangway. He stood on the dockside as the giant hawsers were released and the ship's hooter gave three long blasts. Craning his neck upwards, he could just see the woman at the ship's rail, the child held tightly in her arms. He waved until his arms ached, and watched the white *dupatta* fluttering in response. When finally he couldn't see it any more across the breadth of water, he turned and threaded his way through the cacophony of porters and baggage carts. Ahead of him, towering over the Bombay docks, stood the giant arch known as the Gateway to India. The man began to hurry. He had to catch the Frontier Mail to Rawalpindi, where his American companions and their sherpas, recruited from Darjeeling, were waiting for him. Then they would begin the long journey north to the mountain. It was already much later in the season than he had intended.

Ralph was still in the hospital, but the chief MO believed that he had turned a corner. The doctor told Caroline that she should be proud of her husband because he had an unquenchable will to live. She turned her eyes down to her hands, picking at the rags of skin until her sore fingers bled. A voice in her head, louder and more insistent than ever, continued to tell her that she wasn't worth anything, couldn't be, because she didn't have the will to do a single thing, even to put an end to herself.

If you had an ounce of courage, you would do it, if you had an ounce of courage, you would . . .

When she was not at the hospital, she spent most of her time alone in the stifling bungalow. Nerys tried to persuade to come and stay at the mission, but Caroline was finding it harder and harder to be with other people, even Nerys.

'I'm just tired,' she whispered. 'Tired and worried. When will there be any news from Rainer?'

'I don't know. We just have to trust him to do the right thing,' was the only answer.

On 9 May, news of the unconditional German surrender was announced and Victory in Europe was declared. Srinagar broke into celebrations, although India still looked eastwards to the Pacific war. Multi-coloured lights dappled the black lake, and in the early hours of the morning, dance music still drifted out of the club.

Mr Fanshawe let the diminished British military and civilian population know that on the night of 10 May an impromptu VE Day party would be held in the gardens of the Residency.

'Please come – come with Evan and Ianto and me. Just for an hour,' Nerys begged Caroline.

'All right,' she finally agreed.

Making a huge effort, she had the *dhobi-wallah* air and press her silk dress, she put curlers in her hair, and even searched the tin cupboard in the bathroom for the lipstick Myrtle had once declared was just the right shade for her skin. An hour before the party was due to start she sat down on the veranda chair to gather her strength. The air was hot and seemed thick enough to choke her. She rested her head against a cushion and fanned herself with an old magazine.

The clink of the gate latch woke her from a doze. A man stood just inside the fence, holding out an envelope. 'Madam, for you,' he said softly.

On legs that felt like tubes of jelly, Caroline tottered down the step to the path and held out her hand to take the letter. Worrying vaguely that she didn't have a suitable coin, she asked him to wait, but the man had already closed the gate. His shadow passed behind the bushes and Caroline glanced down at the handwriting on the envelope. A cold hand clutched at her stomach.

Standing in the veranda shade she tore it open.

Ravi wrote that the child was dead.

The Swiss man's ruined vehicle had been found in a ravine. No bodies had been recovered as yet but there was enough evidence to make it certain that the deaths had taken place.

A tragedy, of course. Ravi was sure that she would want to hear about it before the news became generally known. He conveyed his sympathy and good wishes.

Caroline dropped the letter. Soundlessly, she drifted through the bungalow's cramped rooms, her eyes travelling over the familiar furnishings, the faded covers, Ralph's books of military history and their framed wedding photograph.

In the bathroom she searched until she found Ralph's old razor. Carefully she unfolded the blade and stared at the dull blue steel. There was a rime of dried soap near the handle and when she inspected it more closely she saw a speckle of dark stubble. Nausea swelled inside her but she fought it down and repeated the word *courage*. Courage, courage. Then she swiped the blade, first one wrist and then the other.

Hours later, in the garden of the British Residency, lanterns were glimmering in huge trees as the bandleader held up his baton and bowed to the revellers crowding the lawns. An expectant silence fell, and then there was a huge *whoooosh* as the first firework streaked up into starry blackness. Scarlet sparks cascaded downwards as the victory cheers roared out.

Nerys broke away and murmured to Evan, 'She said she was definitely coming. I'm going to the bungalow to find her.'

Evan didn't care for parties and was glad to leave this one. 'I'll come with you,' he said.

The adjoining bungalows were in darkness. Everyone was out at the victory celebrations, at the Residency or the mess, depending on rank, and all the house-boys had taken the opportunity to gather for a smoke and gossip in the cabin near the compound entrance. Nerys and Evan made their way along the lane, the sweet scent of stocks from some lady's garden heavy in the night air. They were still yards away from the Bowens' gate when they heard the noise.

The front door was locked but Evan threw his weight against it and the lock splintered away from the frame.

The bathroom was sticky with blood, the floor and white-washed walls and enamel bowls and thin towels, and Caroline's arms were rusty and caked as she cradled her head in them. Her blonde hair was matted, and congealing blood smeared the protruding knobs of her spine, which was all they could see of her as she lay curled in the corner, screaming and screaming.

Evan's face was as white as paper.

'Go to the compound gate. Get help,' Nerys ordered him. Then she knelt down in the blood and tried to draw Caroline's arms away from her head. The razor she had been clutching dropped to the floor with a clatter.

'It was good of you to come all this way. Thank you,' Ralph Bowen said stiffly.

Myrtle and Nerys picked their way along the dock in the Bowens' shuffling wake, as the homebound passengers for the SS *Euphemia* flowed on to the ship amid a river of trunks and cases borne by hundreds of coolies. A detachment of khaki-clad soldiers filed up the gangplank to the sound of a military band playing on the aft deck. Ladies in afternoon dresses and shady hats stepped out of cars, and the hooting and shouts and police whistles and all the cacophony of embarkation was stricken by the hammer blow of midsummer heat. Caroline hardly lifted her head.

The Bowens' cabin was on an upper deck with a tiny port-hole, giving a view of the davits of a lifeboat a couple of feet away. The cramped space was too small for the oversized bouquet the McMinns had sent in advance.

'Thank you for these too,' Ralph said, after he had read the card, briefly fingering one of the dark red Kashmiri cockscombs. He was spectrally thin, and what remained of his hair was pasted to his blotched cranium, but his colour was almost back to normal. As promised, he had been given an early military discharge, with a Military Cross to mark his conspicuous bravery, and now the Bowens were on their way back to England.

'Why don't you sit down?' he said to his wife.

Without raising her head, she let him steer her to one of a pair of miniature armchairs separated by a round table with the same circumference as a modest hatbox. The only other place to sit was on one of the two berths. Caroline's wrists were bandaged but she kept the dressings hidden by clutching the cuffs of her cardigan. Her uncurled hair fell in a thick mat over her eyes.

Nerys and Myrtle stood awkwardly.

'We could perhaps find somewhere to have a cup of tea? There's time before we sail, I should think,' Ralph offered.

Myrtle refused, politely, and his relief was evident.

'Caroline?' Nerys said.

She lifted her head in response, but her blue eyes were clouded. The sedation she was under made her confused and lethargic. It could have been worse, was Nerys's mordant thought. Ralph and the doctors could have put her in a strait-jacket. But maybe then the ship's authorities would have refused to accept her on board.

There seemed not to be a healing word any of them could say.

'You'll be home soon. Just rest and enjoy the sea air,' Nerys said. 'You promise you will write to us, won't you?'

'Of course I will,' Caroline answered, in the voice of a dutiful child.

'Goodbye, darling. *Bon voyage*,' Myrtle said. Her scent, when she hugged Caroline, must have stirred a happier memory. Caroline smiled uncertainly, and her eyes brightened. Nerys had Rainer's photograph in her handbag, and for that brief moment Caroline could almost have been the girl in the picture again.

They left her sitting in the little armchair, staring at the Kashmiri blooms.

Ralph followed them out of the cabin, carefully closing the door behind him. All along the passageway there were glimpses of festive scenes in the other cabins and there was a bustle of porters and baggage. The three of them made their way to a vestibule at the end where a door leading to the deck let in some humid air.

'You have been very kind to Caroline since . . . ah, since her illness, both of you,' he said abruptly.

'It was all Nerys's doing. I've been in Delhi the whole time,' Myrtle demurred.

'Of course it is very sad that the poor child died and set all this off,' he added. 'I hope Caroline will recover in time. It may even be for the best, in the circumstances. She is so very fragile, the slightest thing . . .'

Nerys began a retort, but Myrtle's fingers rested lightly on her arm.

'Take care of her,' was all she did say.

Ralph nodded. 'Her stepmother and I are in complete agreement. Once we are back in England she will go into a nursing home for a complete rest.'

'Perhaps that won't be necessary, after the sea air on the voyage. And it will be so good for her to see England in summer,' Nerys hazarded.

The newsreel pictures of bomb-damaged cities and exhausted people queuing for food were not sunny in the least, but in India everyone clung to the pre-war images of home.

Silently Ralph pressed his hands together.

Myrtle assured him there was no need to come with them to the gangway, and Ralph agreed that Caroline should not be left alone for too long. He shook both women's hands and thanked them once again.

Then he strode away towards the closed cabin door.

Nerys and Myrtle didn't speak much until they were in the dusty taxi heading back to their hotel. They made a circuit of India Gate in the honking traffic.

'Zahra isn't dead, we all know that,' Nerys burst out.

Myrtle went on staring out at the solid press of rickshaws and bullock carts as their driver forced a route.

Nerys insisted, as she had done a dozen times, 'It's one of his tricks. He set it all up, the accident with the Ford, to convince Ravi Singh not to pursue them. I *know* he did. Rainer promised me she would be safe and I trust him absolutely to keep his word.'

For a month, ever since the discovery of the crashed Ford had been made public, she had been telling herself that the accident was no more than classic misdirection, or disguise, or distraction. But day after day had passed, and there had been no word from Rainer.

'I don't know,' Myrtle murmured. 'Perhaps we should just begin to get used to the possibility that it's true.'

'No,' Nerys said. It was a stony monosyllable.

No bodies had ever been discovered, but the police – so the gossip went, although no one knew anything for certain, even Mr Fanshawe, since no British subject was involved – were prepared to accept that in a wild and lawless area, any one of a number of things could have happened to them. In the face

403

of all the blood, the ransacked luggage and the absence of any other evidence, the authorities were ready to reach the convenient conclusion that there had been three fatalities.

'*No,*' Nerys reiterated.

Somewhere, Zahra and Prita and Rainer were alive and safe. She was used to Rainer's prolonged absences. He came and went according to his own devices. He had done ever since she had known him, and he would never change. She had never wanted to change him and – even if she had been free – to marry or even live with him would have been to do just that. Their beginning would have contained the end, and although she missed him in every waking moment, she understood that much.

The reason why there was no news would become clear. He *would* come. He had struggled back up to Kanihama, hadn't he, as soon as he could travel, even with serious burns, because he had made a promise?

The last time she had seen him Rainer had touched her forehead with his lips. *Don't worry if you don't hear anything. She will be safe, I promise you. And I will come back.*

They reached the little hotel, and rather than retreat to their room, where a sluggish fan did nothing but stir up the heat, they went into a cavernous bar off the lobby. Palms drooped in brass pots and there was a grey smell of stale smoke. As soon as he saw them a solitary young waiter sprang up from his post, switching on a wide smile of welcome.

Nerys would very much have liked a stiff gin but nowadays Myrtle would only ever touch lemonade, so she ordered the same for herself.

The waiter's vigil obliquely reminded her of Farida, who would be sitting as she did every day on her accustomed step outside a village house in Kanihama. She kept watch on the sparse traffic up and down the mountain tracks, and she raced to meet every new arrival, in case Zahra was coming.

This thought made Nerys so sad that she was ashamed of her own selfish, mute yearning for the missing child.

404

Myrtle lit a cigarette and clinked her tall glass against Nerys's as if they were drinking cocktails at the Lake Bar of the Srinagar Club. She blew out a plume of smoke and leant back with a sigh. 'That was a fairly dismal farewell,' she said. 'But we had to come, didn't we?'

Nerys could only agree. 'We did. I'll go and see her as soon as Evan and I get home. She'll be better, I'm sure. And, of course, there'll be news of Zahra to tell her by then.'

Myrtle turned her speculative gaze on her friend. She was much thinner now and her cheeks were almost hollow, but she still laughed all the time. Men still turned to look at her as she passed.

'Maybe. What have you heard from Shillong?'

Nerys told her that she and Evan would be leaving Srinagar for Shillong in the next month. With the agreement of the central mission they would travel, as Evan had wished, over the mountains to Kargil and Leh to revisit his handful of converts, and then, by the mountain passes that they had first traversed, back to Manali. The privations of the journey that had seemed so notable then would be much less striking now, Nerys thought. They were all used to the absence of comforts.

'Do you remember our great journey across to Srinagar?' Myrtle smiled.

'I'll always remember it. I don't think I knew how to be me until I met you,' Nerys told her. She knew how much she owed to the McMinns.

Archie now held a part-time administrative post with the Indian Railways, and had used his engineering skills to adapt a car in which he could drive himself. It made a big difference, he cheerfully reported. His tops, the fine sets of antlers that he had bagged on his Ladakh shooting holiday, had found a permanent place on the wall in their Delhi house. Neither shooting excursions nor lakeside seasons in Srinagar were a possibility any longer.

'Everything changes,' Myrtle said, looking away again. 'I wish you weren't leaving India.'

'Will you and Archie stay on?'

'We don't know anything or anywhere else,' she said.

From her chair Nerys could see across the lobby to the main door, guarded by a man in a dark red turban and long coat, and a slice of the open street that lay beyond. Dust-heavy air shimmered in the heat, and throngs of Indians crowded the road, all classes and religions, mixed up with servicemen of a dozen nationalities, who had poured in as demobilisation began, the pedestrians diving between packed buses and shiny cars and carts pulled by coolies. All of this busy humanity streamed every hour of the day past the *chai-wallah*, who sat on the kerb with his spirit lamp and tin cups, staring into infinity with an unfathomable smile.

Only a few hundred yards from here was Bombay's Victoria Terminus, with its soaring arches as grand as any cathedral. Tomorrow Nerys would take a train north and Myrtle would return to Delhi.

Nerys understood that she loved India, and she would miss every brutal and beautiful fragment of it.

She shook herself, and dug into her bag for a linen-wrapped package. She turned back a corner of the wrapping to show Myrtle the shawl. 'I was going to give it back to Caroline before they sailed. But the moment never seemed right.'

'No,' Myrtle agreed.

Caroline believed that her daughter was dead, and the Kashmir shawl was woven with guilt as well as loss.

'I'll keep it safe for Zahra myself,' Nerys decided.

'All right.'

Myrtle had been trying gently to persuade her friend that all three of them were dead – why else had there been no word from Rainer? – but she had had no success, and had lately decided that it was kindest to let Nerys come to terms with that truth in her own time. She said, 'Shall we go crazy and order ourselves another lemonade, perhaps?'

Nerys smiled. 'Let's do that.'

In a brown envelope in her bag was the gilt-threaded lock

of Zahra's hair. She didn't tell even Myrtle about that. It was her talisman, her remaining link to the laughing little girl who had run at her and shouted, 'Ness, Ness.'

The lake lay as flat as a mirror. Evan and Nerys had taken a *shikara* ride across to the Shalimar Garden, because this was their last evening in the Vale of Kashmir.

At the mission Evan's books and their few significant pieces of furniture and kitchenware stood packed and prepared eventually to be freighted home to Wales. Their travelling bags and baskets of supplies were ready for the bus that would take them to the end of the Srinagar road, and from there they would pick up the pony men and their animals and begin the long ascent out of the Vale, up to the heights of the Zoji La and beyond that across into Ladakh.

Early August was already frilling the chinar leaves with ochre, and over the old town lay the familiar autumnal veils of lavender-coloured smoke. When the two of them reached the uppermost terrace, they turned to look at the spreading view. The water was criss-crossed with tiny boats that from this distance looked no bigger than water beetles, the floating gardens were ripe with vegetables and fruit, and over everything the mountains rose in pleats of purple and grey.

Evan was coughing almost absent-mindedly, like a tired sheep in a pen. This year he had fallen victim to a series of chest infections and Nerys was worried that his health and strength might not be up to the long journey ahead.

'Don't fuss about me, Nerys, please,' was all he said, when she tried to talk to him about it. She glanced sideways at his profile now, familiar as always in his abstracted contemplation of his work, the mission, and the ways of the Almighty. He was gaunt, suntanned from bicycling in and above Srinagar, shy and awkward as he always had been, and dear to her.

He felt her gaze on him and turned abruptly. He said that he would have to get back soon, because there were two or three final matters that he needed to discuss with Ianto Jones.

Nerys nodded her acceptance and they fell into step as they began the descent. She took his arm and slid her hand beneath it and he held it there, gently pressed against his body.

For the sake of economy they had paid off their first *shikara* man, but there was a small flotilla of them waiting near the jetty and one soon came gliding towards them in the hope of a fare. Within the little sanctuary of flower-printed curtains looped back with raffia strings, they sat back against the cushions as the lake scent rose and caught in their throats. The boatman pushed away from the mooring and, glancing back at him, Nerys saw that he was holding his paddle close to his chest. The inverted leaf made a heart shape, and the memory pierced her like a blade.

Almost three months.

Rainer, with Prita and Zahra.

Vanished, as if into thin air.

Her grief was like a stone, but she contained it within herself. It was only for tonight, her last in this lovely place, that it seemed too much to bear.

She turned her head so that Evan might not see her face, and kept her eyes fixed on the fringe of houseboats that clung to the lake shore.

SEVENTEEN

The tiny coronet of blue flame seemed too fragile to survive in this place of howling wind. One of the men grimly hung over it, steadying the rim of the pan on the burner as the rough scoops of snow refused to melt. His companion lay huddled in his bag, his eyes closed as the storm hammered and roared at the canvas walls. The tent swelled like a pair of lungs labouring to suck in a breath of thin air, and then, with a bang and a shriek, collapsed inwards again. Trying to shout above the din took more energy than either of them had to spare.

After an hour, just enough snow had melted to allow them to mix a cup of powdered soup apiece. One man held the two precious warm drinks because the other insisted on laboriously unzipping the tent opening before he drank. Snow drove in at them and the tent pegs only just kept the flimsy capsule anchored. It was absurd, the watcher belatedly realised, to have imagined that he might see anyone coming – or, indeed, that any living thing could move in the thick of this storm. Altitude and exhaustion were eroding his judgement. He struggled to close the flap again.

They hunched over their soup.

'What time is it?'

'Quarter after six.'

It was thirty-two hours since the man they referred to as

Martin Brunner and his companion had set off from their tiny camp. At 20,000 feet, they were more than five thousand feet above the base camp established at the foot of the Rakhiot icefall. Since they had left their base the three mountaineers and Pasang Pemba, the strongest and most experienced of their sherpas, had been carrying loads and leapfrogging their slow and painful way up the mountain to this point. It was now mid-July and the weather had been atrocious. Snow had fallen every day and filled in their laboriously cut steps, and in places it had swept away their fixed ropes.

On the morning of the previous day, Martin and Pasang Pemba had left camp to reconnoitre the rock formation they called the Moor's Head. This ugly and threatening rock wall blocked their access to the high saddle of the mountain and the summit beyond, although the summit itself had been almost constantly veiled in cloud.

At first light yesterday, however, they had woken to a clear sky and a view of the mountain rearing to its full height above them, cold and crystalline.

'Let's go,' Martin had said to Pasang. They were the stronger pair. Taking minimal food and protection with them, they had planned to climb to the rock head and assess how serious an obstacle it really was, then return to camp to rest and prepare a load to carry for the assault. The next camp would have to be established above the Moor's Head.

They would be back that evening, Martin assured their American companions.

The two men set off up the slope, chipping their way upwards until they were no more than black specks moving amid the rock and snow. Finally they were swallowed up in the immense distance.

By mid-afternoon of the same day, an ominous nimbus encircled the sun. The wind began to blow and clouds whipped across the upper heights. The two men left behind watched and waited, but as darkness fell the snow and rising wind drove them into the inadequate shelter of their tent. They waited all that night, and through the following day, but the storm only gathered force. They couldn't retreat, any more than they could go upwards, and the younger one was now suffering from chest pains and disturbing intervals of dizziness and confusion.

The elder lay as quietly as he could, assessing the situation.

Brunner and the sherpa had with them only basic supplies. They would have had to bivouac in the open overnight, and now the second night was upon them. It was inconceivable that they could survive two successive nights outside in conditions such as these.

Once the storm had blown itself out he himself would have to help his companion down to where their support team waited for them above the icefall at Camp I, and he thought they would be quite lucky to make it. There was no question of launching a rescue attempt.

Martin Brunner and Pasang Pemba would certainly be Nanga Parbat's latest victims.

He remembered the advice of the American consul back in Calcutta, who had warned him to take no risks that might have potentially disastrous consequences. Of course the consul was thinking in political as well as human terms, because the bestowal of permits for future American expeditions depended to some extent on the absence of a tragic outcome to this one. And as expedition leader, at least in name, he didn't think they had been reckless – just unlucky.

But, considered separately, Martin Brunner was a different matter. He climbed with implacable strength and determination, almost like a machine, and this brutal focus meant that he was careless of the weather and of himself.

'If I have to go solo, I will do that,' he had said once. 'But I will get to the top.'

The leader understood his determination. He knew that Martin had been to the mountain before, and on that expedition his companion had been carried to his death in an avalanche.

Martin had returned to Nanga Parbat for a boy called Matthew Forbes and his family, as much as for himself – he had always been candid about that. And the current team all recognised that this would almost certainly be his last chance of reaching the summit. During the war he had several times been refused a climbing permit on his own behalf by the British authorities, but the name he had been using during those earlier negotiations had been different.

On the new permit, the very first to be issued following the end of the war in Europe, he was named as Martin Brunner and that was what the mountaineers called him. He had thanked them, laughing as he did so, for their indulgence. The possibility of such subterfuges wouldn't endure for long. As the world slowly returned to normal, men, their names and their where-abouts would be more carefully monitored.

He said, 'There will be no more cloak-and-dagger days, no more now-you-see-me-and-now-you-don't times. We will all be ticketed and documented again, even more than before. So let us enjoy our conjuring tricks while we can.'

Shivering, the expedition leader lay down in his sleeping-bag and drew the frozen folds of it around him.

He must have dozed.

He was startled out of a dream by a heavy weight collapsing against the tent and the sound of a voice calling out. The wind had dropped and the canvas gently sucked and bellied in the remaining draught. He scrambled out of his sleeping-bag and tore open the tent zip. A man's boot blocked the opening, a huddled shape lay in the snow. Overhead, tatters of cloud streamed across a sky pricked with stars.

'Martin? Pasang, is that you?'

The body stirred and gave a groan. The leader saw that it was Pasang Pemba.

Between them the two Americans hauled him into their shelter. The man was more dead than alive, but they fed him sugared drinks and cradled his body between them until some warmth crept back into him. When they stripped off his gloves

412

they found that his thumbs and fingertips were frozen solid. He would lose them, but he would survive.

'Martin?' the leader asked gently.

The sherpa shook his head. The frozen fingers drew a flat line in the air.

More than two thousand feet above them, in the tiny scoop at the foot of a rock face, a hummock of ice infinitesimally stirred and became a man again.

He was in no pain now, even though his leg had been smashed in the fall.

He was flushed with warmth and his dreams had been vivid and detailed. He had seen Srinagar again, in the full glow of summer, and the lovely reflections of the city and mountains were shimmering in the mirror waters. A little girl had been running towards a woman, shouting a childish version of her name.

Rainer floated closer to the surface. It was night again but at last there was no wind, and there were stars overhead.

He turned his head with the greatest difficulty and registered that he was alone.

Pasang had gone. That was good. The sherpa would reach camp if he was lucky. He was a strong man; he had made only one mistake.

His head fell forwards again and was enveloped in the frozen hood of his parka.

The sense of a job not done, of dispensations that should have been made, was like a faint tinnitus inside his skull. But he was too far gone to attend to his conscience. The languorous dreams were rising around him again and he gave himself up to them.

His lips moved to form a word.

'Nerys,' he said.

EIGHTEEN

Mair spent that Christmas with Dylan, Jackie and their smaller daughter, after a run-up to the holiday behind the till in the bookshop where she was now working. She was back in time for New Year, after which Hattie and her latest boyfriend left for two weeks in the Caribbean. When they came back, suntanned and smiling, Mair knew that Hattie had finally found the man she wanted. The two of them were finishing each other's sentences, and had adopted a series of new pet names.

When Mair mimed sticking two fingers down her throat Hattie only grinned. 'I know, I know. But I'm buying into it. Coupledom, you know? I never thought I would, but . . .' She shrugged, delighted.

'Does being a couple have to include calling him Edbo instead of just Ed, and other cringey things?'

Her friend raised an eyebrow. 'I think you're jealous.'

'Of *course* I'm bloody well jealous.'

Hattie was just the same as she always had been, but happier. And busier, it also had to be admitted. She wanted nothing more than to be with Ed, and although the two of them regularly included Mair in their plans, there was simply less time nowadays for Mair and Hattie on their own.

Mair insisted to herself that it was Ed's monopoly of Hattie's company that made her jealous, not the quicksand condition of being in love.

The two women embarked on determined jokes about how Mair might compensate by taking up new hobbies and Internet dating sites, or even revisiting old flames to see if there was still a flicker of warmth.

'No way.'

'You're not making any effort.'

'I'll take up macramé then, how about that?'

'Really hot.'

But then Hattie became serious. 'Do you want to be with someone, Mair? I mean, it's not the only way, is it?'

'I do,' Mair answered, after some thought. 'But then again I don't.'

She didn't want to be any more explicit. There was nothing to be explicit about, in any case, just a vague longing that wasn't even as defined as a wish. She only knew that she was restless and incapable of fixing her attention on anything in particular because it was already subliminally, troublingly, focused elsewhere.

In February Mair heard that Tal and Annie were expecting a baby, and emailed her congratulations. A laconic message eventually came back from Tal, saying that it would be good to have another pair of hands for next year's lambing. This made her think of the last evening in the old house, when she had first seen the shawl, and the Williamses' sheep out on the hill had been crying for their vanished lambs.

The weather was harsh, with snow lying on the ground for almost a month, which meant that footfall in the bookshop diminished to almost zero. She asked her friend, the bookseller, outright whether she could really afford to keep her on.

Her friend said, 'It may come to that, but let's hang on and see what happens when the spring comes. If it ever does.'

The lack of job security didn't worry Mair any more now than it had done in the past, but what was new was a sense of impermanence and a growing detachment, as if she were somehow not quite occupying all the corners of her own life and couldn't make herself care enough to change anything. She kept busy with the humdrum affairs of the shop, with her wider circle of friends, and even began going to the gym again and practising some of the old routines she and Hattie had developed in their circus days. Being more supple and fit was a partial antidote to her strange and intractable state of mind.

During all this time she read and reread her grandmother's letters.

There were three dozen in all, written over the fifteen years between 1945 and 1960. Mair unfolded the pages carefully so as not to crack them along the folds, smoothing them out in order to puzzle over dates and the sequence of events before arranging them in chronological order once again. She concluded that quite a few must be missing, because some of the events that Nerys mentioned in passing were never related in full.

In her imagination, the young Nerys Watkins became her daily companion. And at the same time the known Caroline, the very old woman sitting with her leg propped up in the quiet room in a quiet suburb of Srinagar new town, merged with the sad unknown one who – Mair came to understand – was in a long-stay hospital somewhere within sight of the Malvern Hills.

The very first letter that she read, on the flight from Srinagar to Delhi, was an attempt by her grandmother to comfort her friend during her illness. From an address in Shillong, Assam in September 1945, Nerys wrote that it must help Caroline – even if only a tiny little bit – to have such a beautiful and perfectly English view to look out at from her window. And then, in the sad but reconciled voice of a missionary's wife who hadn't seen home for six years, she touched on the heat of India's summer, the latest epidemic that was overwhelming the mission hospital, and her wish to see her own Welsh valleys again before too long. There was some more Indian news, related with determined cheerfulness, partly of Myrtle, the dark-lipped beauty of the photograph that Mair had carried with her for so long. Nerys wrote that Myrtle and 'Archie', presumably her husband, had been up into the hills for a little break from the heat, but now Archie was back at his work in Delhi. 'Myrtle suffers, but puts a good face on it. They both do.'

No matter how many times she read the next lines, her grandmother's absolute faith in the mysterious pin-up never failed to strike her. The name 'Rainer' always jumped out at Mair. Nerys wrote that there was still no word or news from him, not yet. But he always kept his promises, Caroline knew that, didn't she? Zahra would be safe in Rainer's care; Caroline was to try not to worry; they would reappear like magic when Rainer was ready and there was no more danger, and between them they would make sure Zahra reached England. Caroline would be well again by that time, and Nerys would bring Zahra to see her: 'We'll have a picnic, sitting in the cool grass on the riverbank, you and me and the little girl. Hold your faith in that, if you can, darling. And of course Ralph need never know a thing about it – if that's worrying you in the least.'

But there was a note of underlying desperation in the passage about Rainer and the little Zahra – whoever she might actually be – and urgency even in her grandmother's handwriting that had troubled Mair from the very first reading of the letter. It sounded as if Nerys was battling to reassure and convince herself, as much as Caroline, that there would be a happy outcome.'Rest, Caroline dear, and let the doctors take care of you. You'll soon be well, and in the world again. Write to me when you feel up to it. With love always, Nerys.'

One of the first things Mair had done was to look up the address on the envelopes: Mrs Ralph Bowen, Carteret Ward, Calderton Hall, Calderton, Nr Malvern.

The top entry that came up under Calderton Hall was a property developer's prospectus. It showed a gaunt grey stone mansion set in sweeping grounds, now in the process of being divided up into luxury apartments with startling price tags

417

attached. There was no mention of the history of the place after the Calderton heirs had sold it in the middle of the nineteenth century, and it took some more digging before Mair discovered that for more than a hundred years it had been a secure mental institution.

Further researches drew her into an unexpected underworld of lunatic asylums, the gaunt institutions where families used to deposit their deranged, damaged or occasionally just egregious relatives, then largely and conveniently forget about them. Her laptop and its patient, dispassionate connectivity led her deeper and deeper into the history of such institutions, and into the sad individual stories of mental illness. She began to read widely, ordering books and pamphlets as her interest intensified. Calderton Hall Hospital had been closed down more than a decade ago, after public disclosures relating to inhumane treatment of the long-term residents. Several had been locked up for as much as fifty years and some had originally been no madder than it needed to be odd, or friendless, or the mother of an illegitimate baby.

Mair's sympathy for the unknown younger Caroline grew to the point where she felt as if she knew her, even though the real sequence of events that had taken her into Calderton, out again eventually and back to Srinagar, was no more than a tissue of guesswork stitched together from research and clues in Nerys's cheerful letters.

Mair worked out that Caroline must have suffered a breakdown in India, and on her return to England had been immediately committed by her husband to the long-stay Carteret locked ward at Calderton.

That made sense of the tiny amount of information Caroline herself had given Mair, and Aruna's strange manner, which seemed to combine servant and nurse with just a touch of jailer. And there in Carteret Ward Caroline had presumably stayed, until at least 1960 because that was the date of Nerys's last letter, or the last letter from her that Caroline had kept.

This one was short and written from the same familiar

address in North Wales as all the others, except the first few:

I have some very sad news. Poor Evan died five days ago, finally succumbing to pneumonia. We buried him yesterday. As you know, he had never been strong since our years out east. He was very peaceful at the end, I was with him all the time and Gwen was able to say goodbye while he was still conscious. We will both miss him so much.

If only I had talked to Mum, Mair thought. If only any of the three of us had ever thought to ask her about Grandma in India.

The shawl lay in its usual place, folded over the back of an upright chair where she could see it whenever she looked up from her laptop. The colours rippled in the grudging daylight reflected off grey snow. The shawl, the lock of hair and the letters themselves were Mair's only physical link to the story that remained full of obstinate knots.

One of Nerys's letters had described the joyful upheaval of the return to Wales. In 1950, almost shyly, she wrote about the birth of her daughter. After that the letters became domestic recitals, sympathetic but general attempts to keep Caroline in touch with a world that was steadily leaving her behind. Mentions of Rainer and Zahra in the chronology became less and less frequent, and the certainty that they would reappear seemed to fade into puzzlement and, finally, the sad silence of acceptance.

Mair had scanned the pages so often that she knew some of them off by heart, and there were no more obvious clues that she could follow up.

She had plenty of evenings to spare, though, and she devoted many to the Internet. The National Archives eventually led her to Captain Ralph Bowen's regimental records. He had been decorated for his bravery in Burma, and honourably discharged in 1945. He had died in 1978, without issue. There was no mention of a wife to survive him. Poor Caroline had been erased.

By searching the Scottish Family Records online, after many false starts she eventually uncovered Archibald Fraser McMinn of the Indian Railways. His wife Myrtle, née Brightman, had predeceased him, but Archie himself had lived on into the 1970s and had died in Edinburgh. The McMinns had had no children either.

Piecing everything together in the quiet evenings, the conclusion Mair eventually reached was that Zahra had most probably been Caroline's child, but that the circumstances surrounding the birth had been kept secret even from her husband. Zahra had in some way been entrusted to Rainer's care, and then the two of them had disappeared.

If this theory was correct, then Zahra was almost certainly dead. That Aruna had rebuked Mair for upsetting Mrs Bowen because she had lost her daughter long ago seemed to confirm this.

For the right dates, she found nothing under Rainer's name but brief and confusing mentions in some books on magic tricks (could this be a different man?) and a pre-war collection of mountaineering anecdotes.

There was nothing more.

During the long hours in the quiet bookshop, Mair related instalments of the incomplete history of the shawl to Mandy, her bookseller friend.

'It's really interesting,' Mandy said, over the rim of her coffee mug, before Mair went into the back room to unpack a new delivery of books. 'You've put such a lot of time into investigating it, going to Kashmir and everything. Maybe you should write about it.'

Mair looked about her. The books lay in tiers and slabs, their jackets like so many coloured leaves, bright and imploring. There were plenty of them, more than enough, and the shawl story was private, her own history. 'I don't think so,' she said.

420

Spring came, late but exuberant. Business in the bookshop picked up a little.

Mair took a week's holiday and went walking in Spain with some friends. A month later she was in Birmingham for Eirlys's thirty-ninth birthday party. ('I'm not mentioning next year's event,' Eirlys said.) She and Dylan had both been interested to read Nerys's letters, and they looked at the picture of the three women on the houseboat in this new light. They listened politely to Mair's account of her subsequent discoveries.

'Mental institutions were quite barbaric in those days,' Eirlys agreed. 'When Caroline's husband died and psychiatric care improved, they were probably relieved to be able to discharge her as mentally fit. Once the hospital was given notice to close, that would have been the convenient option anyway. How did she seem when you met her in Kashmir?'

'Frail,' Mair said, conjuring up the quiet room in Srinagar as she spoke. 'Forgetful. But not insane.'

Eirlys nodded, sombre with the weight of medical insight.

In June, during a spell of hot weather, Hattie called Mair to say that she would be coming round to Mair's flat to have a glass of wine with her after work. The door to the fire escape stood open and they took two kitchen stools out on to the metal platform, squeezing them in side by side. There was a faint breeze in the trees. Mair took a sip of her wine and waited.

'Ed and I are going to get married,' Hattie said.

Mair exclaimed, and hugged her friend. She said that they were made for each other, she was so happy that Hattie was going to do it, and Ed was lucky to have her. All this was true, and the dazzle of joy in Hattie's face was the best picture Mair had seen for a long time. 'Am I to be a bridesmaid?' she demanded.

'Just try to get out of it. I'm thinking of a pink theme, by the way.'

'I'd really prefer to be in turquoise.'

'Don't start being difficult. You have to do what I want. It's my ego trip, remember.'

'Fine, Bridezilla.'

Mair had a bottle of champagne in her fridge. They drank it, and in the end Hattie had to leave her car behind and ring for a taxi to take her home.

After she had gone Mair sat down in her accustomed place at the computer. The shawl caught her eye. She was just drunk enough for the snag of an idea in her mind to embed itself and become a full-blown intention within seconds.

She went into her email list and found the one message she had received and saved from Bruno Becker, eight months before. She didn't look at the contents because she didn't need to.

At Lamayuru he had mentioned the name Rainer.

The *click* she had first heard when Caroline uttered the same name repeated in her head, just as loudly.

Here was the real link, she was suddenly convinced, not archives or records offices. Several times in the past months she had thought of contacting him, but she had always dismissed the idea. Bruno and Karen were mourning their daughter, and she had felt too diffident to approach them, either with further condolences or superficial questions about family history. There had been no response to her message; neither had she expected one. What was there to say, in threadbare words, in the face of such a loss?

But now, she judged, flushed with champagne certainty, now was the perfect time to write.

She began to type, quickly and nervously, unsure as to what extent she was using the query about Rainer to shield her real wish, which was to have news of the Beckers themselves. Thick-fingered, she made a series of typing errors and urgently corrected them, altering the wording until she was satisfied with the result. The final message was just a few lines long. She wrote that the two of them were often in her thoughts and she wondered how they were now. If they felt able, she would very much like to hear from them. Then she added that Bruno had once mentioned the mountaineer called Rainer, whom she believed from discoveries in Srinagar and recent researches

422

might have a strange connection to her own family. Could he perhaps give her any more information?

She hesitated, then typed simply *With love from Mair.*

There was no question that Bruno and Karen wouldn't remember who she was. She didn't imagine that those days of waiting were ever far from their minds.

She pressed send. Then she sat staring at the screen for several minutes, as if a response might come immediately.

Nothing happened for two weeks.

Hattie and Ed were planning to get married just before Christmas.

'A winter wedding,' Hattie said dreamily. 'Perhaps a little cloud of a cream fur jacket with a stand-up collar. Ivy and mistletoe and sparkling frost.' From being an average-to-advanced cynic, she was melting into a dewy romantic. Mair humoured her, with equal parts of love and amusement.

Then, after an author reading event in the bookshop followed by a book signing featuring a free iced cupcake with every purchase, she came home late from the shop and found a reply from Bruno in her inbox.

He apologised for the late response, then said it had been good to hear from her and added that he had been away in the mountains. He thanked her for her kind thoughts, and said there had been some black times but he was doing all right, more or less, and so was Karen. About Rainer Stamm he knew little, only that he might have been killed in a motor accident in Kashmir in 1945. But no body or bodies had ever been found.

There were some other things he could tell her, but perhaps it would be simpler if she telephoned him. He gave a Swiss number. *Best wishes, Bruno.*

Mair looked automatically at the clock. It was an hour later in Switzerland, she was almost certain. Too late to call now, and also too eager-seeming. She smiled to herself about having become a lonely spinster bookseller. Right on cue the cat

423

belonging to the people downstairs appeared in the doorway to offer her his company.

She waited until the following evening, then dialled the Swiss number.

Bruno answered, just one word, but she knew his voice at once. The receiver seemed slippery in her hand.

'It's Mair.'

'Hey,' he said.

Afterwards she didn't remember the sequence of their conversation, just that it seemed to continue from where it had broken off in Lamayuru. He spoke more slowly than before, with a suggestion of hesitancy, as if all that had once been certain was no longer to be taken for granted. When she asked about Karen the pause was even longer.

'She is living in a consciousness-raising collective for the bereaved, in New Mexico.'

Mair groped for a response. 'A Buddhist one?'

To her relief, Bruno laughed. 'I'm not sure. Could be a one-size-fits-all-faiths sort of set-up. Karen and I split up, Mair.'

'I'm so sorry.'

'Thank you. It happened very quickly after Lotus died. Her death was like – an explosion, I suppose. Silence, then shock waves, falling masonry, shards of glass piercing what hadn't been crushed.' She could hear the rise and fall of his breathing. 'It became obvious almost immediately that Karen and I couldn't help each other at all. That forced us to acknowledge we'd have to separate. It was sad, but there wasn't too much animosity. Neither of us had the strength to be angry at that point. I expect Karen's working through her anger now. It's not unusual, I've heard, for couples to be blown apart by the death of a child.'

'What have you been doing?' Mair asked gently.

'I resigned from my job. I didn't know how to – to be a clockwork person. I came up here to the mountains. I'm surviving in a sort of cabin. I walk a lot. Sometimes I take a tent and some supplies and go even higher up to camp. That's

424

where I've been for the last couple of weeks. It's beautiful. You . . . should see the view I'm looking out at. It would remind you of Ladakh.'

'You sound as if you're doing better than surviving,' Mair told him. She didn't know whether she was more impressed by his honesty or the route to survival that he had chosen.

'I don't know. Sometimes it feels like less than that. She was so perfect. And she is so very conclusively and absolutely gone.' There was a silence. Then he said, 'Tell me why and what you want to know about Rainer Stamm.'

Mair collected herself, with difficulty. She explained as succinctly as she could.

Bruno broke in to say he remembered everything she had told him about tracing the history of her grandmother's Kashmir shawl.

Mair added, 'There are some letters. It turns out that Rainer knew my grandmother in Srinagar, and two of her friends. The shawl belonged to one of them – her name was Caroline. I met her, she's living in Srinagar again now. At the end of the war Rainer disappeared, taking a child with him. I think that child might have been Caroline's.'

There was a silence.

Then Bruno said, 'Prita died fifteen years ago, you know.'

'I didn't know. I haven't heard about anyone called Prita.'

'Prita was Rainer's Indian wife. She brought Zahra up as her own daughter.'

Mair thought she might have misheard. '*Zahra*?'

'That's right. Prita Stamm and the little girl were more or less bequeathed to my parents' care when they reached Switzerland after the end of the war. I knew them all the time I was growing up.'

Mair's thoughts tumbled over each other. *Here* was the link at last. Here was the continuous thread . . . Her eyes widened as she realised the significance. 'Is Zahra still alive?'

'Oh, yes. She's in her late sixties now. Prita and she went back to India after Zahra graduated from university here. We

425

keep in touch, but it's only a card now and again. We'd planned to visit her on the way home last year.'

Mair listened to the echo of his words. There was still too much to take in, and too much to try to say on the telephone. She said, on a sudden impulse, 'Bruno, may I come out to see you?'

'Of course,' he answered.

The train journey from Zürich airport took almost four hours on four different trains, but every connection worked to the minute. The last leg of it was on a little cog railway that took her up the side of a mountain through pine forests and past lush Alps dotted with brown cows. Through the open window flooded huge draughts of sweet-scented air carrying the jingle of cowbells. Mair craned her neck to look up at snow-covered peaks that brought to mind lake reflections in Srinagar and the circle of mountains enclosing Leh. She felt as if she had travelled back a year in time.

At last the train reached the end station. She stepped off in a shoulder-high tide of Japanese tourists wearing sun visors, and a surprising contingent of Hassidim in long black coats and wide-brimmed hats.

Beyond a little cluster of station buildings and hotels, the earth slipped away into blue air ahead and behind her, but to the right and left it was as if it had been grasped by a giant's hand and twisted up into vast monuments of rock and ice. A glacier slashed with huge crevasses hung over a dizzy rock-fall of moraine.

Mair stood still and gazed.

'Hey,' a voice said. A hand lightly touched her shoulder.

She swung round to see Bruno. His weatherbeaten face was noticeably thinner than the last time she had seen it, but he was familiar in a way she hadn't expected.

'You look surprised,' he said.

'This scenery? Awestruck would be closer.'

He nodded, his dark eyes on her face. Suddenly she heard

426

the chop of rotor blades and saw him with Lotus in his arms, running towards the helicopter.

'Welcome to the Oberland,' he said. He hoisted her bag and swung it over his shoulder. 'Can you walk up the hill? There's no other way to get to the cabin, I'm afraid.'

They left the Japanese and the Hassidim milling between café sunshades and souvenir stalls and began to climb. A ribbon of path zigzagged over the hillside towards a scree slope.

Mair put her head down and followed on Bruno's heels. Leaves and long grasses brushed her ankles – she saw now that the entire hillside was thick with wild flowers: blue campanula bells and starry marguerites, yellow doronicum, tangle-headed wisps of Alpine anemone and baroque spires of giant thistle. Dark blue veronica edged the path. If this was really the way to Bruno's house it was the loveliest station commute she could imagine.

The path angled vertiginously across the scree.

She was glad when they reached the shoulder and Bruno stopped to hoist her bag to his other side.

'Thank you for carrying my stuff.'

'It's steep. You're pretty strong.'

She was pleased by this. Turning back to look at the way they had climbed, Mair's breath was taken away again. Below them lay the station and the little green train, like a child's toy, winding its way back down to the valley. Across the saddle the giant peaks now seemed close enough to reach out and touch.

Bruno pointed. 'Jungfrau, Mönch and Eiger,' he said.

The face presented to them by the mountain called the Eiger was a black pyramid of concave rock rising sheer for thousands of feet. The sight of it made Mair shiver.

'That's the Nordwand,' Bruno said. 'North face.'

'At Lamayuru you told me about Rainer attempting to climb that.'

'Yes. His guide was my grandfather. They both came very close to death, and their survival forged a friendship.'

427

They stood shoulder to shoulder, staring across at the rock wall.

'Come,' Bruno said at length. 'It's not far from here.'

Downhill now, at an angle, winding deeper into a remote landscape of empty air over rolling turf with a pile as velvety as the finest Kashmir carpet. Far down in the valley Mair could see clusters of chalets and the glint of traffic on threadlike roads.

They scrambled over a ridge and a tiny lake of extreme blue appeared just below them, set like a sapphire in a green ring of ground. At the opposite bank, on a broad wedge of land, a small cabin stood among the flowers. There were four windows, two by two, each with a window box spilling scarlet geraniums.

In the doorway, Bruno bowed. He seemed more Swiss here in his own setting.

'Welcome,' he said again.

The cabin was constructed of logs, and there was a low pitched roof of wooden shingles. The eaves projected a long way all round, and in the shade at the front there was a wooden platform with two benches, one on either side of the door. To the left-hand side there was a flat wall of logs, stacked with such intricate attention that it would have been difficult to slide a finger between the cut faces.

Inside there were wide wooden floorboards and a square metal stove. At the windows were red and white gingham curtains and on a solid wooden table stood a blue jug of flowers.

'It's quite primitive,' Bruno said. 'Lake water, earth closet, candles or oil lamps. I've rigged solar panels on the roof, though. They heat a small hot-water tank for washing. I could make it more comfortable, of course, but I rather like it as it is.'

'Don't change it too much. It's one of the most beautiful places I've ever seen,' Mair said.

To her surprise, he smiled with pleasure. It was the first time this afternoon that she had seen him do so.

'Do you think so? My father used to bring me here every summer. It's just a shepherd's hut, really.'

He showed her the way up a ladder through a trapdoor in the corner of the beamed ceiling. Up here two small rooms were separated by a rough plank wall. Mair's had a single mattress on the floor, made up with white sheets and a patchwork quilt. There was a faded rag rug, and a row of wooden pegs on the wall, nothing more. The window was at knee height. She was touched to see a pale blue towel laid on the quilt, neatly folded with one corner doubled back. Bruno had prepared a welcome for his guest.

He withdrew his head from the trapdoor and she unpacked her few things and hung them on the pegs. As she climbed down again she glimpsed his room. There were piles of books, another single mattress, hardly more clothes on his row of pegs than she had brought with her for a stay of three days. It was clear that he lived simply.

Downstairs Bruno showed her out to the neat kitchen with its stone sink and modern bottled-gas cooker. A row of pots and enamel plates and two glasses stood on a wooden shelf. Outside in a lean-to was the lavatory. A tiny porthole cut in the door gave a circular view of a clenched fist of ice and snow high on the Nordwand.

A kettle whistled on the gas and Bruno made tea. Looking around her, Mair noticed a wind-up radio, a laptop computer. On a shelf of new-looking wood there was a photograph of Lotus in a Perspex frame. Her hair blew off her face like a cloud of white candyfloss. Bruno's gaze slid across it.

'Most days I walk down to the station buffet the way we came,' he said. 'My friend Christoph's the boss there. I drink an espresso and read the newspaper and they let me charge my phone and computer.'

They carried their cups outside and took a bench each.

Mair stretched out her legs and rested her head against warm, splintery wood. The snow and ice walls glittered in the crystal air. With so much space around her she had the luxurious sense that there was infinite time to ask all the questions that simmered in her head.

In his new, hesitant way Bruno told her about his life in the cabin.

'When I first came up here there was still snow on the ground. I'd wake up to find chamois and hare prints passing the door. I'd put on my skis and follow them as far as I could. If I'm in a hurry, I walk as far as the station and get the train on down to the village you came through to buy food and pick up emails, but there *is* no hurry. I keep a bike at the station so I usually cycle or even walk all the way there and back again. It only takes a couple of hours. At the . . . beginning, after she died, I'd walk and walk, from dawn until dark. As fast and as far as I could, until I was ready to drop. As if I could ever walk away from what happened. I realised, in the end, that that was what I was trying to do. It's better now I know that much.'

Mair nodded, full of sorrow and sympathy.

Her impulse was to jump up and hold him in her arms, but she resisted it. Bruno was tough, even though he spoke with such raw frankness. He didn't need her mothering.

They drank their tea and watched birds gliding over the ridge.

After a while he said, 'I collected this from my sister, when I knew you were coming. She lives in Bern.' He brought out a big album with heavy black boards split and frayed at the corners. He turned pages until he found what he was looking for.

'This is Rainer Stamm, with my grandfather, in 1937.'

It was a deckle-edged black-and-white photograph of two men wearing breeches with braces and flannel shirts. They were standing in front of what appeared to be a station halt somewhere in the mountains. Both of them were smoking, smiling, squinting a little against strong sunlight.

Mair looked for a long time.

The pin-up. Caroline's words.

'He was rather handsome, wasn't he?' she said.

'Prita was only married to him for a matter of weeks before he died, but she never took up with another man in Switzerland, or India, as far as I know. She told me once that the European ladies in Srinagar adored him.'

Remembering the picture of Nerys, in a moment of high happiness, Mair thought, *maybe*.

Quite possibly Grandma had been one of those ladies. It was wartime. There would have been the opportunity, after all – she knew from *Hope and the Glory of God* that missionaries were often away in the field. She found herself hoping that Nerys had indeed stolen some romantic moments with the pin-up. It would have given her some wicked, glamorous memories to help her through the Welsh years of chapel, village politics, and being the preacher's wife that must have followed. Mair had never envied her grandmother's way of life, or her mother's.

'Would you like some more tea?' Bruno's voice made her jump.

'Yes, please.' She smiled.

Later, while Bruno was frying potatoes and schnitzel, she leafed through the other Becker family pictures. In two or three Prita was a small upright figure, at the end of the line or standing a little apart. What must it have been like for her, she wondered, an Indian widow so far from home? But Mrs Stamm had an indomitable look. She was a survivor.

They ate facing each other at the wooden table, yellow-lit by an oil lamp.

'You're a good cook,' she said appreciatively.

'Karen didn't like cooking. It's strange to be making food for someone other than myself up here.' Mair listened to the silence that seeped around them. 'Strange but good,' he added. 'Thank you for coming all this way.'

Afterwards they took glasses of schnapps out to their benches. The sky faded from royal blue to infinite darkness, with the mountains radiating spectral light.

'We drank all that cognac at Lamayuru,' she said deliberately.

431

She didn't want to remind him but neither did she want there to be topics they had to steer away from. But he seemed relieved to remember the place. He had spent a lot of time alone recently and she guessed that the words came more easily out of doors, looking ahead into the darkness, than face to face in the lamplight.

He said, 'I remember everything we talked about. And the food they gave us, and the faces of the drivers sitting opposite, and the snow when we went out to the yard.'

Cold snapped suddenly out of the silence and drove them back inside the cabin.

'I go to bed very early,' he said awkwardly. She knew that he needed solitude.

Lying on her mattress, listening to the cabin creaking around her ears, Mair thought that this could be one of the most romantic places in the world, including the lake at Srinagar. The creaking wood even echoed the protests of *Solomon and Sheba* as it sank lower in the water. This sapphire lake was a miniature of the other, reflecting its own shimmering peaks. Even the wild flowers splashed the same colours as her grandmother's shawl.

She had a strange sense of time tucking inside itself, folding, dovetailing with minute precision.

On the other side of the plank wall Bruno was absolutely silent. He didn't clear his throat or turn over. She thought he must be lying on his back too, staring up towards the old beams.

Soon she slept.

There was a delicious smell of coffee and frying bacon.

She yawned her way down the ladder.

'Eggs with your bacon?' Bruno asked, holding up a wooden spatula. He brushed aside her protests, saying that they were going walking and she would need to fuel up.

'If you want to go higher into the hills, of course?' he added. It struck her that he was uncertain of her response, but that

432

he wanted to please her. The realisation made her skin prickle as if it had become electrostatic.

They set off from the hut, uphill along a high mountain path, then negotiating a moraine ridge. Bruno pointed to the chains of peaks and named each one for her. He also began to tell her what else he knew about Rainer Stamm.

The mystery of his disappearance or death had never been solved although the official explanation, that he had skidded off a Kashmir mountain road when Prita and the child were already aboard ship on their way to Europe, had enabled his wife – eventually – to inherit his estate. He had left everything he had to her, including a house in Interlaken.

'There is another story, though,' Bruno said.

'Go on.' Mair was panting for breath and it was much easier to listen than try to talk.

'In 1945 there was an attempt by a Swiss-American climbing team to conquer Nanga Parbat.'

'Nanga Parbat again?'

Tinley and his ancient uncle, smoking *bidis* in the graveyard at Leh and waiting while she read the inscriptions. She had discovered the memorial to Cambridge mathematician Matthew Forbes, lost in an avalanche on the mountain.

'Exactly. Again.'

Mair glanced back over her shoulder, towards the wall of the Eiger.

'There were three Western names on the climbing permit for that 'forty-five expedition. Two Americans and a Swiss by the name of Martin Brunner.'

'Yes?'

'Well, Brunner was killed. He had gone up with one of the sherpas to recce a higher camp and there was a storm. The sherpa eventually made it back to rejoin the Americans, but Brunner had been injured in a fall and couldn't down-climb. I tracked down the expedition report in the annals of the American Mountaineering Association, so I know the details.'

Bruno walked at the same sure pace, uphill or down,

whatever the ground. Mair had to watch where she placed her feet and it was a moment before she was able to ask, 'Why were you so interested in this Martin Brunner?'

He glanced at her, enjoying keeping her in suspense. The hesitancy in his voice had disappeared as they talked more. He was a good storyteller.

'Because he didn't exist. There are no Swiss records of a climber by that name. His details on the permit are false, too. They don't relate to anyone.'

'I see. Do I?'

Bruno raised an eyebrow. 'Come on. You can guess.'

'Brunner was really Rainer Stamm?'

'I can't prove it, but I believe so. My grandfather was guide to the Forbes family as well as Rainer, and he said that Rainer always promised Matthew's father that he'd go back and claim Nanga Parbat in the boy's honour. In the end it wasn't climbed until 1953, by Hermann Buhl, just a few weeks after you British knocked off Everest.'

'But why under a false identity?'

'I don't know. I don't think we'll ever know. Shall we stop here and have something to eat?'

Mair had begun to think they would walk all day but, to her relief, he led the way to a flat-topped rock. She sank down, resting her chin on her knees to marvel at the view. Bruno handed her a chunk of bread, some mountain cheese and an apple. The simple food tasted wonderful.

'Rainer would have had his reasons for the assumed identity and for faking his own death. He was a magician as well as a mountaineer. An illusionist.'

'Ah, I know about *that*.' Mair laughed. 'Because I looked him up too. It was confusing.'

Bruno was staring across to the black rock face where Rainer's life had been saved by Victor Becker.

Mair thought, That same man was perhaps my grandmother's lover, certainly her good friend. Her sense of time's intricate dovetailing grew even stronger. She murmured, 'It's sad, isn't

434

it? Rainer was newly married, he was performing some kind of disappearing trick with his own life, and then he actually disappeared trying to claim Nanga Parbat in memory of a boy who had already died on the mountain. I do know that for years afterwards my grandmother was waiting and hoping for news of him.'

Bruno said, 'Yes, that's sad. But perhaps she also understood what made him who he was. Many lives were lost on Nanga Parbat before Buhl climbed it. Sixteen men on a single day in 1937. Rainer would have known all that, but still he went. Perhaps he needed to live and to risk death in that way, because extreme risk was in the end the only reality he could subscribe to. Maybe the gravity of mountains and the weightlessness of magical illusion were always opposing within him. He probably hid the compulsion even from the people he loved. He must have been a fascinating character. Do you think your grandmother loved him?'

'Yes, I do. And, yes, I think you're probably right.'

The shawl, the photograph, the lock of hair.

The quirks of history that linked her to Bruno Becker, the vertiginous face of the mountain confronting them – all these things made a pattern that seemed, in that moment, part of a bigger and only partly intelligible design.

This realisation made Mair feel happy in a profound way that seemed entirely new to her.

'Now it's time to talk about Zahra,' she said.

Bruno stood up and shook breadcrumbs off his lap. Two Alpine choughs greedily descended on them.

'Later,' he said, the adept storyteller again. 'Can you remember the mountain names? What's that one?' He pointed at a vast tumble of rock and snow.

'Um, is it the Wetterhorn?'

'Good,' he said.

They ate dinner back at the cabin, and afterwards Bruno lit the oil lamps. They were sitting inside with the door closed because clouds had drifted across the sky and a chill wind rolled down off the glacier. He took another book off the shelf and opened it. With her head bent close to his, Mair saw that it was a more modern photograph album with sticky plastic interleaving the pages. Some of the pictures were even in fading colour.

'This is Zahra.'

A solemn little girl with dark brown hair worn in two looped plaits, lined up with a row of other children in school dresses. Her skin was darker than her companions', but not distinctly so.

'And here.' Bruno pointed.

She was a teenager in this one, short-haired, dressed in jeans and a blue-checked shirt. Her face was more clearly visible and Mair studied it for any resemblance to Caroline Bowen. She could see none at all. Zahra had aquiline features and dark eyebrows that almost met at the bridge of her nose.

'There's only one more. Mine wasn't a family for photographing every rite of passage.'

Zahra stood near the top of a flight of stone steps with Prita on the one above her. Their heads were level. Prita's hair was greying now, centre-parted and drawn loosely back. Zahra was perhaps twenty, solemn and formal in a dark skirt and jacket. Even in their Western clothes, Mair thought, they looked distinctly Kashmiri. Their features were quite different but they could have been taken for biological mother and daughter because of something poised about the way they looked into the camera, heads up and gaze unwavering. She reflected that the two of them must have been closer than many natural mothers and daughters because of their difference from their Swiss friends and neighbours.

Bruno answered an unspoken question. 'That must have been taken when Zahra was at university. Prita and she always had an understanding that once Zahra had finished her education they would go back to Kashmir.'

He collected his two glasses from the shelf and poured

schnapps, slid one across the table to Mair. 'My father told me that they often joked about it together. Before the maharajah finally acceded to India, he used to claim that he wanted Kashmir to be a sort of Asian Switzerland. Independent, neutral, on friendly terms with all its neighbours. Prita and Zahra would say that Maharajah Hari Singh originally had the right idea, at least. They knew that much from the real Switzerland.'

'So they went back?'

'Yes, not long after that picture. It was in the mid-seventies, before the really bad times of the insurgency, but you more or less know what they found.'

Mair did.

'Srinagar became a dangerous place. They settled eventually in Delhi. Zahra taught European languages at one of the universities.'

'Did she marry?'

Bruno gave one of his rare smiles, and drained his schnapps. 'Yes. She had three boys. I believe one is a pilot, one is a software designer, one is an architect.'

Mair beamed with satisfaction. 'How wonderful.'

'It is, rather. I'd like very much to have been able to visit her in Delhi.'

The yellow light of the lamp hollowed darker shadows out of Bruno's face. In the silence that followed they listened to the rising wind and the old cabin creaking like a ship at sea. Bruno's eyes were on the photograph of Lotus with her white hair blown into a cloud around her head. 'In a few more weeks, it will be a whole year since she died.'

As gently as she could, she asked, 'Will you be here on your own?'

'I don't think I shall be fit company for anyone else.'

'Bruno . . .'

'I know. She's dead and she won't come back, and those of us who are left behind have to pick up and carry on without her. I'm doing it, Mair. But it takes time and an effort of will.' His head dropped suddenly into his hands and he clawed his

437

fingers through his hair. With his face hidden he said, in a muffled voice made jagged by pain, 'It takes so much effort. To wake, to exist for another day, to sleep – or try to. Over and over again, living while all the time Lotus is *dead*.'

She got up from her seat and went to him. This time she couldn't stop herself. She put her hands on his bowed shoulders. 'I wasn't going to tell you to do anything any differently. I wouldn't have the cheek, when you're already braver than it seems possible to be. I was going to say that if you wanted someone to stay with you, even nearby, I'll be here. I was at Lamayuru. I saw how it happened. There would be nothing to explain.'

She had meant it in the sense that there would be no need to describe the sequence of those events to someone who had not witnessed them, but he flinched under her hands.

'She was so innocent and trusting and yet we couldn't keep her safe. I can never explain that away.'

'There's no explanation to be made. Not about what happened, or how. It was a terrible accident.'

He was choking now with sobs. Mair's face was wet too. She cradled his head against her ribs and waited as he wept.

In the end he raised his head and she immediately released her hold. Her hands retained the memory of his skull shape and the thickness of his hair. She went back to her seat and, after a last look at Prita and Zahra, she closed the photograph album.

'I could hear your heart beating,' Bruno said. There was an odd, disbelieving glimmer in his face that she read as hope. In a voice so low that she could barely hear the words, he added, 'Another human heart.'

He reached for the bottle and refilled their glasses. 'Let's talk,' he said. 'Can we do that? I'm surprised to realise it but I've enjoyed today. I'd forgotten what it's like to talk and have someone listen, taking in what you say and measuring it up and shaping an answer in a voice different from your own, instead of the monologue going on and on in your own head.

I've been alone too long. I don't want to talk about Lo any more, though. I will do eventually, if you'll listen, but I'm not ready yet. Is that all right, Mair?'

His words were falling over each other now, all the hesitancy obliterated.

'Yes,' she told him. 'That's quite all right. You could tell me some more about Prita and Zahra, maybe. Were they very close?'

He listened to the wind for a few seconds. Then he settled back in his seat, ready for the story. Mair found that she breathed more easily.

'Yes, they were. There were a few disagreements, I think. Zahra was my father's generation but she was quite modern in her outlook, and Prita was very traditional. But by the time I was old enough to notice anything, they were devoted to each other. They came back here two or three times while I was growing up to visit my father and their other friends. Prita used to give me Indian sweets in amazing colours, and I thought that was very exotic. Zahra taught me some words of Urdu.'

'Did she know about her background?'

'Oh, yes, Prita never concealed anything. Zahra knew that she was an orphan adopted from the mission in Srinagar.'

'My grandfather's mission,' Mair put in.

They looked at each other across the table. The two halves of the story that they held between them fitted together as neatly as two nutshells enclosing a single kernel.

'Prita was a widow whose own son had died at about the same age as Zahra was when they arrived in Europe. Prita herself was legally married to Rainer so, of course, as a wife and then a presumed widow once more she was able to come to Switzerland and inherit his estate. Zahra arrived with her, somehow or other, probably as the result of one of Rainer's magical flourishes aimed at concealing an illegitimate birth. That is, if all your theories are correct. Eventually Zahra became a Swiss national too. As far as we were all concerned, all of us who knew them, they were a mother and her daughter.'

439

Bruno paused. He added, in a lower voice, 'I'm quite certain that to one another they were mother and daughter too.'

Mair had the same thought. Yet she believed – no, she *knew* – that Zahra's natural mother was still alive, and living in a quiet house in a suburb of Srinagar. Should she bring them together, after so long? Was it right to intervene in other people's lives and play with their histories?

The two halves lay in her hands now, and Bruno's.

She had no proof: only a theory, a sheaf of letters, a lock of hair and a *kani* shawl. And a man sitting opposite her who had lost his daughter, just as Caroline Bowen believed she had lost hers. The agony of that loss was plain to see. Sixty-odd years might have diminished it for Caroline, but she had spent perhaps as much as half of that time in a lunatic asylum.

Mair sat upright. There was no doubt in her mind that the secret wasn't hers to keep, now that she had unravelled it. 'I'm going to go back to India to see them both,' she said, 'if you will give me Zahra's address.'

Bruno stared at the lamp flame and said nothing.

Mair waited.

Then she added softly, 'Or perhaps you could come with me and we could visit Zahra together. That was the plan, wasn't it?'

He did look at her now, remembering.

She saw something else in his face, a contraction of the eye muscles and tightening around his mouth, and she knew that it was fear.

Bruno was afraid to leave his shell, the safety of his cabin in the mountains, and venture out into the world again.

He shook his head. 'I would hold you back,' he said oddly.

'No,' she contradicted. 'I don't think so. The history isn't all mine, is it? Half of it is yours to tell.'

'I don't know.'

But he did: she could see that in his face too. Outside concerns were intruding into the isolation of grief.

In silence he battled with himself as rain drummed on the

cabin roof. Mair rinsed the glasses in the sink, put the bottle back on the shelf, and climbed the ladder to her bedroom while he still sat at the table. She was in bed, lying in darkness when his head and shoulders framed themselves in the doorway. 'All right. I'll come to India with you.'

He closed the door on her and the latch clicked.

NINETEEN

The house was in a leafy street in south Delhi, secluded behind rendered walls painted pale mustard-yellow. They waited at black metal gates as Bruno spoke into an entryphone.

They had arrived separately the night before, Mair from London and Bruno from Zürich, to meet at the anonymous hotel near the airport where they had arranged to stay. Eating dinner in the hotel's gloomy coffee shop, they had been awkward with each other after the ease of the cabin in Switzerland. Now that they were finally in India they were unsure what their mission really was, and it seemed too late to be agreeing on what they would say to Zahra or how they might say it. They made small-talk and went straight to their rooms afterwards.

Jetlagged and unable to sleep, Mair had slid open the balcony door and stepped out into the night. There wasn't even a shiver of movement in the scalding air, and the traffic noise from beyond the hotel garden was as loud at three a.m. as at midday. The orangey ribbons of elevated motorways snaked in all directions, glimmering with cars and trucks, and in their shelter were the awnings and refuse of colonies of destitute people. In the ten months she had been away she had forgotten the din, the surging motion and the brutal contrasts of India.

442

Was this all a mistake? Mair wondered. Should she have left history where it lay?

She shook herself.

A voice like the buzz of a grasshopper floated out of the entryphone grille and the left-hand gate swung open. They walked along a path between oleander bushes with the patter of a water sprinkler close at hand. A door opened at the top of some shallow steps and a small elderly woman stood there. She was light-skinned and she had Kashmiri features, but this was not Zahra. 'Mrs Dasgupta says please to come in.'

They followed her into a wide hallway, the polished floor laid with Kashmir rugs.

'I am Farida,' the woman said. 'Come this way.'

A set of doors led to a room full of dark carved furniture, kept cool and dim by lowered blinds. A stately figure came to greet them, her arms outstretched to envelop Bruno. She had styled hair that was more grey than dark, she was plump, dressed in a loose silk shirt and wide trousers, and spectacles hung from a cord round her neck.

'You are here,' she cried. 'Come, let me look at you.'

Mair stood aside as they hugged each other and spoke rapidly in Swiss-German. Bruno handed over the flowers and gifts they had brought with them, and Zahra exclaimed and remonstrated. Mair looked at the pierced china baskets filled with sweets, the coloured glass ornaments, teapots, and numerous framed photographs of boys and young men in variations of uniform, team-sports clothing or academic dress. She smiled to herself. This was a family home. Zahra's family home.

'I am Zahra Dasgupta.' A hand was held out and warmly shook Mair's.

Bruno introduced them: 'This is Mair Ellis, Zahra. Mair has become a good friend of mine since Lotus died.'

Once he had spoken Lotus's name he seemed to relax a little.

'I'm so sorry about your child,' Zahra said. 'So very sorry. It is a terrible tragedy. How is your wife?'

'She is in the States. We're separated now, Zahra.'

443

The woman's eyes moved from Bruno's taut face to Mair's, assessing them. There was a sharp brain behind the majestic exterior. Mair wanted to say, No, it's not what you think: there are these two halves of a whole that Bruno and I hold and we've brought them here . . .

'I am sorry for that too,' Zahra said. She took Bruno's arm and led him to a chair.

Farida brought the inevitable tray of tea with china cups and a brass samovar. She put out plates of cakes and embroidered napkins and Zahra rearranged them as soon as they were set down, the two of them getting in each other's way and telling the other what to do. It was evident that they were long-term companions and friends rather than employer and servant. At last they were both satisfied and they all sat in the heavy plush armchairs with cups and plates dispersed between them.

Zahra said to Mair, 'I knew this man when he was a small baby. A very sweet, good little baby he was. Growing up he was more like all boys, very noisy and causing disruption. He was driving his mother mad a lot of the time.'

'Zahra, Mair doesn't want to hear this,' Bruno protested.

He was embarrassed because Zahra was treating Mair as if she were a girlfriend, and as soon as she realised as much, Mair felt a dull red blush colour her face and obstinately stay there.

Zahra and Farida looked at each other.

'So you are making a holiday now in Delhi?' Farida asked.

Zahra interrupted her, 'No, no, no, you know that Bruno told me he had something most important to talk about.' She sat back in her armchair, slippered feet placed side by side and hands folded across her stomach. 'I am very curious to hear what it is.' Her glance slid from Bruno to Mair.

The room went quiet.

Mair felt breathless as she reached into her bag. She unfolded the shawl from its wrapping and spread it over Zahra's broad knees.

Farida instantly gave a grasshopper chirp and seized the nearest corner. Blinking, she held the soft fabric up to her cheek. 'This is *kani* weaving. From my home in Kashmir.'

Mair slipped the photograph from a folder and laid it on the arm of Zahra's chair. On the opposite arm she placed a little cellophane envelope containing a lock of gilt-brown hair. Farida had found the shawl's reversed BB signature. 'I know this work,' she breathed. 'From my own village.' Her face shone.

'What are these things?' Zahra demanded. 'Why do you bring them to me?'

'It's a long story. Mair will explain her part first,' Bruno said.

'Look at the picture,' Mair suggested.

Zahra settled her spectacles on her nose and peered down. She breathed out through her nose, almost a snort. 'Srinagar, I think.'

Mair pointed. 'This is my grandmother, Nerys Watkins. She and her husband were Christian missionaries in Kashmir during the war.'

Farida bobbed upwards. She grabbed the picture and gazed at it. 'Ness. This is Ness,' she cried.

They all looked at her in amazement.

'You *knew* my grandma?' Mair wondered.

'She was my best mother when I was a small girl. I remember all about her. There were songs and games. She was so kind, an angel.'

Mair held out her hand, and Farida grasped it in her tiny dry one.

Farida told her, 'I can see now, your face. You have something like her here.' She drew a circle round her own mouth and chin.

Mair thought, Whatever happens next, I am so grateful to have come this far.

Nerys had known this small, bright-eyed woman when Farida was a little girl. It was like holding hands with Nerys herself, across the divide of almost seventy years.

Yet again time rearranged itself, folding into new patterns.

She would almost certainly never know exactly what Zahra or Farida had meant to her grandmother, and why she had kept a lock of hair and a shawl hidden for so long, as if they were her most precious and secret possessions, but she had this human link that connected her directly to Nerys.

Bruno was smiling at her.

Mair pointed for the second time. 'This one is a friend of my grandmother's called Myrtle McMinn. And this is another friend of theirs, Caroline Bowen.'

Zahra shifted her weight. 'I do not understand any of this.' She pouted. '*I* found Farida, you know. My husband and I went to Srinagar when we were married and I made a visit to the school my mother told me about, a mission school, you see, where I was looked after. I was an orphan just like Farida,' she explained to Mair. 'There were many orphans in Kashmir. My mother Prita and father adopted me, took me away from that school to Switzerland.'

Mair couldn't help but glance down at Caroline Bowen's sweet English face.

'When Dilip and I came to see the school the missionaries were gone. This happens, especially in Srinagar, which is a place very much changed for the worse. But the school was still there and Farida was helping the teachers. We talked, and she remembered me when I was two years old. Can you imagine that?'

Farida patted Zahra's shoulder and laughed. 'I never forgot her. I loved her so much I thought she was my own baby. But then she went away and I cried for a long time. I was so happy to see her again, a married lady. I had no husband, and my two brothers went to Pakistan many years ago.'

'So she came here to live with me. I insisted on this,' Zahra said, in triumph. 'To be auntie to my boys, and sister to me.' She rattled the cellophane envelope. 'So. What are these other people to us, and this piece of hair?'

'I think,' Mair slowly said, 'this lock of hair is yours. It was

446

with the shawl, and we found it put away among my mother's things after my father died last year.'

Farida opened the envelope and tipped the contents into her hand. Zahra bent over it, pinching the hair in her fingers and holding it up to her head for Farida to compare.

There was no resemblance.

'No,' Zahra said.

'It might be,' Farida said.

They both laughed but uncertainty was kindling in their faces. They were apprehensive about what they might learn next.

Mair was glad to let Bruno take up the story.

'As well as being my grandfather's good friend, Rainer was a friend of these three women,' he began.

'It was wartime,' Zahra remarked. 'Many people made friends and lost them in those days.'

'That's true. In 1945, as you know, Rainer put his wife Prita and a child aboard a ship for England. They were met at Liverpool docks by an Englishman, a mountaineering friend of Rainer's, who helped them with their onward journey to Switzerland. And when they arrived there, they were taken in by Victor Becker and his family.'

'It was done for my father's sake. My mother was always proud. He was a special man, she said to me, to have such friends as your grandfather Victor.'

Bruno smiled again. Mair saw that the ease from the cabin was coming back to him, and there was more than that – he was alive with interest in Zahra's story.

Zahra leant forward. 'My mother believed always that Rainer meant to return to us. He was killed in the car before he could come. But he did not abandon us.'

He nodded. 'Zahra, Mair and I both believe that Rainer and his wife helped out a friend by taking her illegitimate baby out of India. By taking *you* away, to safety in Switzerland.'

'My mother told me she and Rainer took me, cut my hair, dressed me as her boy until I was on the ship. There was danger,

447

but Prita was not sure why. Naturally Rainer would have made everything clear if he had not died.'

Mair leant forward too, touching the tip of her finger to where Caroline smiled in the picture. 'Mrs Dasgupta, Rainer Stamm took this photograph. I think the third woman might be your mother.'

Zahra frowned. '*This* person, you think?' She turned away and indicated one of the framed photographs that stood on a low table beside her. 'Take a look, please. Here is my mother.'

In the picture Prita Stamm stood with her chin up, a small grandson hanging on to either hand.

'I meant the woman who gave birth to you,' Mair amended. 'She is still alive, and she lives in Srinagar. I met her last year and I showed her these things.'

Zahra lifted her cup, very deliberately drank some tea, replaced the cup in the saucer. 'If you know so much, then who was my father?' Her lower lip protruded and her voice had cooled by several degrees.

Caroline's lover must have been Kashmiri, and theirs could only have been a forbidden liaison, a wartime love affair, but she had no idea what kind of man he might have been. Not an honourable one, that seemed certain. Had Caroline loved him? Why hadn't Ralph Bowen stood by his wife? The mysteries seemed to thicken, even though she had imagined them solved.

She could feel Bruno watching her and she wanted to turn to him, but she plunged on: 'I don't know that. I don't think we will ever know, unless Caroline Bowen herself tells us.'

'Do you have any proof of this theory?'

'Firm documentary proof? No, none. There are only the letters that my grandmother wrote to Caroline and the story that Bruno and I have pieced together between us. But when I showed Caroline this shawl, she recognised it at once. "That belongs to Zahra. It's her dowry shawl," was what she said.'

There was a silence.

And then Zahra observed, 'Mine is not such an uncommon

448

name.' Her face showed her disapproval. 'And my mother Prita made sure that my marriage was a proper one, with a suitable dowry. My own theory is somewhat different. *I* believe, you see, that Rainer was my real father.'

Mair thought, Yes, that's equally plausible. Wartime, a magician mountaineer with pin-up looks, and a girl from the Vale of Kashmir. A girl Rainer couldn't marry – perhaps because of her father's anger or her brothers' defence of her honour – but whose child he vowed to protect. He found a wife, a widow who had lost her own son, married her, made a will, and took care to send the two of them away to Switzerland and safety. Only then, at the last moment, did his plans somehow go awry.

Triumph glinted in Zahra's eyes as she handed back Mair's photograph. 'Occam's Razor,' she pronounced. 'Are you familiar with this principle?'

Bruno laughed. He left his seat and went to Zahra, putting his arm over her ample shoulders. 'The simplest explanation is usually the correct one?'

'Good boy.'

Mair began to protest but Bruno warned her with a look. She was angry at this intervention. He wasn't going to stop her pronouncing what she knew to be true, not when it had taken her so long to uncover that truth. But his gaze didn't waver, and a different, entirely contradictory feeling swept through her.

It wasn't sweet or honeyed or even remotely comfortable – it was sharp, and thoroughly disconcerting, because she knew at that moment without any shadow of doubt that she was in love with him.

The words, whatever they were going to be, dried in her mouth.

Bruno's face showed a flicker of amusement. His glance said that they understood each other. She wanted to go and kiss him, but she made herself sit still and concentrate.

Zahra laced her fingers. 'I am right, you see. But these are

449

old, long-ago times. Why are we discussing them? Let's talk about young people. They are the future. Bruno, please tell me, will it be painful if I show you and your friend some pictures of my grandsons?'

'No, I'd like to see them,' he said. He was still looking at Mair and she felt hot in the over-furnished room, and confused. It was unthinkable that Bruno might suspect she was in pursuit of him. Might he think she had engineered this whole trip to India as a way of getting closer to him? Surely not, when she had herself only just worked out these feelings.

Zahra and Farida were replacing cups on the tray, clearing space among cushions to lay out photograph albums, telling each other all the time where to find what they wanted and how to make room for it. Farida laid the shawl aside.

Mair put her photograph in its folder and quietly replaced it with the lock of hair in her handbag.

'See, Bruno? This is little Sanjay – he is nearly six. He is a very clever boy. Already he is good at mathematics. His father tells us he is the best in his class.'

A long interlude followed in which Bruno looked at all the pictures and asked the right questions while Mair peered over his shoulder and made supplementary noises.

And then after the Dasgupta family news it was time for reciprocal questions about the senior Beckers and their neighbours, and commiserations because Bruno's father wasn't showing any signs of mental recovery. Farida brought in more tea and savoury snacks. Footsteps came across the courtyard and an elderly, oval-shaped man in a business suit appeared in the doorway.

Zahra called, 'Dilip, you are here at last. Say hello to our visitors.'

Mr Dasgupta was bald, smiling, almost as light-skinned as his wife. He was courteous to Zahra's connections from Switzerland but it was also clear that here was a man who was ready for his dinner. With polite formulations, invitations to stay and regretful refusals, the visit began to wind itself up.

450

Mair had worked out what she wanted to do. 'Mrs Dasgupta,' she began, 'I'd like to ask you a favour.'

With only a glint over the spectacles, she said, 'My dear, of course.'

'For my grandmother Nerys's sake, please will you keep the shawl? I'd like you to have it – you and Farida, of course – and I think that's what Nerys would have wanted too. For months I was on a quest for its history. I went to Ladakh and Srinagar, even up to what's left of Kanihama village to see where it was woven and embroidered.

'I feel that in the end the shawl would be closer to home here with you, closer to its own history, rather than in England with me.'

Farida's face blazed with joy. She said imploringly to Zahra, 'My village. My family made this thing. So much work.' She held it against her thin chest. 'And it comes from our mother Ness, you know, very long ago.'

Mr Dasgupta put on horn-rimmed glasses and studied the corner of the shawl that hung free from Farida's arms. 'The finest work. Good enough for a museum,' he pronounced.

Zahra pursed her lips. 'Dilip knows what he is talking about. His business is textiles. If this is truly what you would like,' she said, 'although this shawl has no real connection to me, I appreciate what you are saying. Therefore, thank you.'

'Just one more thing,' Mair said. 'I'd like to take a photograph.'

Quickly she brought out her digital camera and passed it to Bruno. She stood on one side of Zahra with Farida on the other, the shawl draped like a magnificent banner between the three of them.

Bruno took the picture.

Mr Dasgupta insisted that he must drive them back to their hotel but Mair and Bruno said they wouldn't hear of it. They compromised by accepting a lift to a busier street where a taxi or an auto-rickshaw would be easy to find. Zahra and Farida came out and saw them into the big black car that had white linen slipcovers over the seats. Bruno was warmly embraced, Mair was kissed on the cheek, and the car moved off at last.

Zahra waved energetically until they turned the corner. Farida stood in the wall's shade with the shawl still in her arms.

After Dilip had left them, with a stream of instructions about how to regain their hotel, Bruno let out a long breath. 'I need a *beer*.' He groaned.

The nearest bar was lit with blue and pink neon. It had giant Bollywood posters lining the walls and a clientele dressed in skinny jeans and oracular Japanese T-shirts.

Bruno said, 'That was rather clever of you.'

A waiter brought their drinks, the glasses deliciously beaded with condensation. They clinked them together. Mair felt as if she were already half drunk. Amazement and apprehension ran through her in unsteadying currents. 'What was?'

'You returned the shawl to its rightful owner, without the owner accepting the real reason for her right of possession. Do you feel sad to have parted with it?'

Mair shook her head. 'It was Zahra's all along. I couldn't keep it for myself. You do believe our story, don't you, rather than Zahra's version?'

'Yep. Anyway, scientifically speaking, the simplest theory most probably being the correct one isn't what Occam's Razor really indicates . . .'

'Oh, please.' She laughed.

'Zahra's is quite a success story, isn't it? I think, having come so far, it's her right to believe in whatever version of her past she chooses.'

'Yes. Thank you for warning me off when I was going to plunge on regardless.'

'You looked furious.'

She bit her lip, fending off embarrassment because of the revelation that had followed the anger. 'It was only for about a second. Was I wrong to have tried to convince her in the first place?'

452

'No. Deliberately to withhold the truth would have been wrong. Shall we look at your photograph?'

As they bent over the little screen Mair was acutely conscious of his hand and arm, and the weight of his shoulder against hers.

The picture was pin-sharp, and somehow Bruno had caught an echo of that other photograph of three women.

'It's good,' she said. 'Thank you.'

'I'll take it to the business centre at the hotel and run off a gloss print. We can take it with us.'

'Take it with us?'

'To Srinagar.'

She stared at him. 'We're going to Srinagar?'

After Zahra had so decisively stonewalled the news they had brought her, Mair had assumed they would have to abandon their original plan to travel on to Kashmir. She didn't see how they could find a way to tell Caroline that the daughter she had given up so long ago was alive and well, but had chosen not to believe in their relationship.

'Of course. We have to close this circle somehow, don't you think?'

As if to demonstrate, Bruno reached out to clasp her hand, lightly threading his fingers through hers.

Mair wondered giddily which circle he really meant. She loved him for taking up her quest and making it theirs. For that, and for everything else. Suddenly, Hattie and Ed floated into her mind.

'Would you like another of those?' he asked, nodding at her drink.

'I would,' she said.

Srinagar had changed.

On the way in from the airport, the roads were clogged with slow-moving traffic, held up at almost every junction by police or Indian Army roadblocks. Imperious young para-militaries toting automatic weapons patrolled the streets,

453

herding the crowds of pedestrians as they passed in a weary stream under the chinar trees. The blue air was thick with the fumes of idling engines, and crackling with tension. Around Lal Chowk there were bombed-out buildings, shabby bazaars and fine old brick houses blackened by fire or pocked with bullet holes. Everywhere they looked there were more troops, and more roadblocks. Mair knew that separatist insurgents had stepped up their activities as more of the militant young stone-throwers returned from the camps as trained gunmen and arsonists. The levels of violence against the Indian Army of occupation had lately risen almost to the point of open war, yet still she hadn't quite anticipated the atmosphere of dejection and the evidence of economic decay that riddled Srinagar.

The word that came to her was *extinguished*. That was how the place and its buoyant people seemed today, and the sadness of it struck through her.

In the taxi Bruno silently gazed out of the window. She had wanted him to love Kashmir at first sight because that was how it had been for her, and she found herself trying to excuse the present state of the city. She pointed at ancient tiered roofs in the distance. 'It's not always like this. It's really very beautiful. Look, there's the Jama Masjid, the Friday Mosque. Fourteenth century.'

Their driver sat hunched in his grey tunic, patiently waiting for yet another Indian soldier to flag him down and minutely scrutinise their papers.

At last they reached the hotel. Mair had chosen one of the Chinese-owned establishments on the Bund, not the one where she had sheltered from the grenade attack, but quite close at hand. They had passed *Solomon and Sheba* on the way, the old houseboat tilting even more rakishly towards the mirror surface of the lake. She didn't even point it out to Bruno. She had decided against booking a houseboat. For all their various states of decay they were raffish, romantic destinations, chosen by lovers and honeymooners.

As they checked in, they were told that a city-wide curfew would operate from dusk until dawn. They ate another coffee-shop dinner, this one without even the benefit of alcohol because the hotel didn't serve it. From not very far away they heard the brief, shocking rattle of gunfire.

'Difficult time.' Their waiter sighed as he put down bowls of reddish soup. 'Very difficult. You are tourists here?' There was always hope for more tourists.

'Not really,' Mair had to say.

'You are UN? NGO?'

'No, just visiting a friend.' Bruno probably didn't mean to sound curt, but the man withdrew at once.

They didn't talk much while they were eating. Mair knew that Bruno must be thinking of that other visit he had planned, with Lotus and Karen.

In her room, before she went to bed, she lifted layers of tobacco-reeking net curtain and peered out into the night. A police car crawled along the deserted street. Not far away, a building was on fire. She could see an ugly red glow licking the undersides of cushions of smoke.

The next morning they took an auto-rickshaw to Caroline's house.

The old bazaars were thronged with people and, instead of an army jeep, a mixed herd of goats and sheep scudding through the traffic held them up. Bruno smiled at the sight. 'I'm sorry I was so subdued last night.'

'That's all right.'

'This is a troubled place.'

'But a resilient one. It gets under your skin, I know that.'

'It must have been the same for Caroline. She made the opposite move to most of the British Raj, coming back out from England to live here, didn't she?'

Their little vehicle surged forward as the last of the sheep bounded out of their path.

Aruna answered the door of the house in its overgrown

garden and frowned at Mair as if she had last visited only the day before yesterday. 'Mrs Bowen very tired. Not at all well. I am sorry.'

Mair stepped closer, holding the package of Nerys's letters. 'I promised I would return these. We won't stay very long. This is Mr Becker, a friend of an old friend of Mrs Bowen's.'

Aruna received this information and the package with another frown, but she gave up the attempt to exclude them.

The room at the back of the house was quiet, except for Chopin on the CD player. Caroline sat in her usual chair. Both feet were now propped up on the stool and a walking frame stood close at hand. Sensing their presence she turned her head as soon as they came in, but Mair could tell that her eyesight had gone completely. She peered anxiously in their direction, listening intently through the piano music.

'Aruna? Is that you?'

Mair went quickly to her side. 'It's Mair again. Do you remember? Nerys Watkins's granddaughter?'

'Who? Who is that? *Nerys*'s granddaughter, did you say? My dear friend Nerys? I can't believe it.'

Mair hesitated, momentarily disconcerted by the memory blank. Bruno was equal to it. He came to the other side of the chair and said gently, 'Hello, Mrs Bowen. I'm Bruno, Mair's friend. My grandfather was a good friend of Rainer Stamm's.'

'Rainer.' Caroline clapped her hands. 'How extraordinary. Where is he? I'd like to see him. Do tell him so, won't you?'

Bruno took her hand and held on to it. It looked like a tiny claw caught in his big fist.

Caroline smiled, radiance lighting her blind face. 'Hello, dear,' she said. 'Thank you for coming.'

'Rainer's dead, you know. He was climbing a mountain.'

'Everyone's dead,' she retorted, still smiling. 'You get used to it at my age. I'm ninety, you know. Ninety. That's right, Aruna, isn't it?' She cocked her head, listening for Aruna's voice.

456

'Yes, ninety.' Aruna sighed. This was obviously a question that was regularly asked. She unscrewed a small brown bottle and counted out green-and-white capsules.

Caroline sat back, still clasping Bruno's hand. 'Isn't this jolly? You must tell me all your news. We should have a drink. Aruna, dear, what have we got?'

'Thank you, that would be very welcome,' Bruno said, giving Aruna a look. He had the measure of her.

'I'll see what there is,' she said, as she left the room.

Mair came closer. 'Mrs Bowen, do you remember when I came to see you last year and I brought the shawl? Zahra's shawl, you said it was.'

'Did I, dear?' The smile hardly faded. The CD stopped playing and the music centre emitted a small electrical hum.

Mair lowered her voice. There was no script for what she was about to say.

'I left the shawl with Zahra. Was that the right thing to have done? I saw her two days ago, in Delhi. Zahra survived, you see. Rainer sent her safely to Europe, all those years ago. Bruno and I met her, and her husband.'

There was a moment's pause.

'Did you? That's nice, dear,' Caroline said.

The electrical hum was like a mosquito's whine. Bruno began a move to switch off the player but Caroline gripped his hand. 'Don't go.'

'I won't,' he soothed. 'Do you understand what Mair is saying?'

The old woman turned, trying in vain to see their faces. Uncertainty clouded her trusting smile. 'Who? Who is this? Is Nerys here?'

Mair said, more urgently, 'Was it the right thing to do, to give Zahra her shawl?'

Over Caroline's white head Bruno's eyes locked with hers.

Caroline murmured, 'Well, I expect so. If it was hers. Where *is* Aruna?'

'She has just gone to fetch some drinks. She'll be back in a minute,' Bruno reassured her. He squeezed her hand and her face cleared again.

'Oh, yes. A drink would be nice. What did you say your name was?'

'It's Bruno.'

Aruna came back with a tray and glasses and a jug. She poured lemonade for them all, and when hers was placed in her hand Caroline gulped thirstily, like a child. Afterwards she gave a small belch. Aruna tipped two pills into her palm and she swallowed them with a refill of lemonade.

Mair wondered how long they had actually been sitting in the room with its view of the garden that Caroline could no longer see. It felt like a long time.

The thread that she had traced for so many months ended here. It had woven a complicated pattern, and even though she couldn't cut the ends free and finish them off with knots, like those of the shawl itself, she was glad that she had followed it all the way.

Caroline yawned. Her head fell back against the chair cushions and her jaw sagged. Bruno released her hand and folded her wrist into her lap. A moment later a snore escaped from her open mouth.

Mair was looking round the room. Pointedly, Aruna drew up a blanket and tucked it round her charge's shoulders. She picked up the glasses and replaced them on the tray as Mair and Bruno stood up.

'I'd like to leave this for Mrs Bowen,' Mair said quickly. 'It's . . . some old friends of hers who we met this week in Delhi.'

Caroline's chair was placed next to the brown-tiled fireplace. There was a shelf over it with a gilt-framed overmantel mirror so Mair tucked the glossy print into a corner of the frame. She and Zahra and Farida smiled out into the room. Aruna immediately came to peer at it, adjusting her spectacles to see more clearly.

458

She pointed. 'You brought this shawl with you last time you were here.'

'That's right.'

'She can't see it, you know. What does it mean?'

'Nothing. It's just a Kashmir shawl. And it's more that we – I, that is – want the photograph to see her. Is that all right?' She ignored Aruna's sceptical look. 'Please, may I use the bathroom before we leave?'

'I will show you.'

Caroline was fast asleep. Mair bent over her as she passed and just brushed the top of her head with her lips.

'She is asleep most of the time nowadays,' Aruna said, with just a hint of tenderness. She pointed down the little hallway to the open door of a green-painted bathroom and carried the tray into the kitchen. Bruno stood examining a series of framed photographs of polo teams that hung beside the front door.

Mair checked over her shoulder, rushed to the bathroom and loudly closed the door, staying on the outside of it. Caroline's room must be the one next door. There was a bed with a white cover under the canopy of a rolled mosquito net. She slipped in and glanced round. It was more like a hospital room than a bedroom, with a similar antiseptic tang in the air. Next to the bed stood a table with a single drawer.

She slid open the drawer, glancing at the medical contents. Then she tucked the cellophane-enclosed lock of Zahra's hair inside at the back where it couldn't be seen. She closed it and dashed back to peer through the crack in the door. The hallway was filled with the sound of knocking. Aruna bustled out of the kitchen, and while her back was turned, Mair popped out as if from the bathroom.

Bruno raised one eyebrow at her.

On the doorstep stood three women, faces framed by black *hijab* scarves. One of them carried a wicker basket, with the same red and green patterning as a *kangri* holder. Evidently Aruna knew her visitors quite well. She showed them to the old chairs under the shade of the veranda. Mair was thinking, But *I* know them too. How do I know them? There were two young girls with smooth olive cheeks, and an older one with a lined face.

Aruna accepted the wicker basket and opened the pot within. A heavenly smell rose to surround them.

'That's *good*,' Bruno said.

Aruna nodded. 'It is *tahar* rice, cooked in a special way with turmeric. In Kashmir we make it always when there is a safe arrival, an escape from danger.'

Mair remembered. Of course. They were Mehraan the *karkhanadar*'s mother and his two sisters. They recognised her too. The girls giggled and the mother inclined her head.

'I was going to pay a visit to Mehraan's workshop.' Mair smiled. 'How is he? How are you?'

There was an exchange between the women. Aruna said, 'If you would sit with us, the rice is to share. It is important. A . . . symbol. They have brought for Madam, but there is plenty.'

'Thank you,' Mair said simply. They took their places in a circle, the girls cross-legged on the floor. Aruna brought plates and Mehraan's mother reverently spooned the rice, a few mouthfuls each. It was eaten moistened with creamy Kashmiri yoghurt, sprinkled with nuts and fresh coriander. Mair and Bruno copied the women, eating in silence, using the bunched fingers of the right hand and chasing up every stray grain with an eager thumb.

It was one of the most delicious dishes Mair had ever tasted.

Aruna replaced the lid on the pot. 'For Mrs Bowen, when she wakes up. She will enjoy.'

There was more giggling and murmuring from the girls.

Aruna said, 'They would like to know, is this man your husband?'

Mair couldn't look at Bruno, but she felt his eyes rest on her. She was conscious all the time of his proximity, of the oddness of their being in Srinagar together. Now that all the pieces Nerys had left behind had been put in their right places, it would be time to think of home again, and separate ways.

Her heart contracted with dismay.

'No, he's not my husband. But he is my good friend.'

There was more smothered laughter, and some talk that Mair and Bruno couldn't follow.

Aruna composed herself and told them, 'Mehraan is good. He has come often this year, to help me. In the winter he brought wood and cleared snow. See? He mended the fence.'

New pickets of light-coloured wood were interspersed among the old splintered ones.

'That's very kind of him. Where is he? At the workshop?'

Aruna hesitated. Then she said, 'Mehraan is not in Srinagar. He has gone to a camp. He has crossed the Line, and his mother hears today that he is safe. So she makes *tahar*.'

Mair and Bruno both stiffened.

To cross the Line of Control into Pakistan-controlled Kashmir was a hazardous journey, and this camp of his could only be a training centre for militant Free Kashmir insurgents. Mair struggled to reconcile this information with her memory of the sombre young man whose responsibilities made him seem much older than his real age.

'I hope . . . he will be safe,' she whispered, imagining him returning to his mother and sisters only to be murdered by the army or paramilitaries.

Aruna wagged a finger at them. 'This is not what you will be thinking. It is not a war camp. It is for learning of Islam, for peace.'

The mother spoke rapidly and the two daughters turned their faces to her.

Aruna did her best to translate. 'For Mehraan and his friends, there is only one *jihad*. That is inside the heart of every man, alone, where there is no weapon except God's truth. It is to this camp, and the teachers there, that Mehraan has found his way. He is missed here, but it is right for him to go.'

Mehraan's mother bent her head. Mair found that she was

461

close to tears. There was so much sadness in Kashmir, and such fortitude.

It was time to leave.

Bruno and Mair thanked the women for sharing the gift of *tahar* rice, and Mair asked Aruna if she might call again to visit Mrs Bowen before she left Srinagar. Herself again, Aruna gave a barely perceptible nod.

Mair hugged Mehraan's little sisters and bowed over her folded hands to their remarkable mother.

A moment later she and Bruno were walking away down the lane, under apple and walnut trees touched with autumn colour. They were so full of their visit that they took no notice of where they were heading and after two minutes they were lost in a maze of high-walled alleys. A dog panted beneath some wooden steps.

Bruno stopped. 'Do you think it's this way?'

'No – we came from over there.'

They hesitated and he put his hands on her shoulders, looking down into her eyes. 'It doesn't matter,' he said. 'We'll find our way. What were you doing, back there?'

'Leaving Zahra's lock of hair beside Caroline's bed. It's not much of a connection, is it? But it's better than nothing.'

'I'd never have thought of that. But it's the best thing you could have done. That, and the photograph and the shawl.'

He was bending his head towards hers when there was a sudden yell, and the thud of feet pounding towards them.

In the other direction the dog leapt from its shelter, a quivering strip of tawny fur with its red mouth stretched in a snarl.

Bruno grabbed Mair's wrist and dragged her away from the animal, running full pelt towards whoever was coming the other way.

Into Mair's head flashed the image of a troop of soldiers with their guns raised. But with Bruno beside her she ran anyway.

From round the corner a mass of children flew at them. They almost collided, but Mair and Bruno jumped aside and let them race by. They were five-year-olds to teenaged boys with white skullcaps, all in neat dark-blue *kameez*, satchels bobbing, elbowing each other out of the way as they ran along. School was out for the day. The dog turned tail and crawled for shelter, and Mair and Bruno were left flattened against the alley wall as the children ran off. Shouts and laughter echoed behind them.

He let his head fall back and exhaled with relief. 'Sorry. Sorry about that. I'm afraid of dogs.'

'It's all right.' She took his arm. 'They must all be heading somewhere. Shall we follow?'

They walked in the wake of the slower children. A hundred metres brought them out to the banks of a stream, one of the Jhelum tributaries, bordered by a little meadow. There was a fringe of poplars and silvery willows, and grass worn bare in dusty patches. The children were already running and kicking a ball between a pair of discarded satchels. Another group had set up cricket stumps, and a bolder contingent was swinging from a knotted rope over the water. The rope swung further out and higher up, a child clinging to the end like the weight of a pendulum.

Bruno and Mair sat on a grassy bank to watch.

The afternoon light was fading as the chill of the evening crept up from the stream, but they still sat there. The games were universal, and the joy of the participants seemed to rub out the troubles of the city beyond.

'They look so happy,' Mair said.

Bruno nodded. 'And hopeful. Even in a dangerous place, with an uncertain future ahead for most of them. Hope's the most powerful redemptive force, isn't it? Do you know something else? While we've been watching them, I forgot to think about Lotus. I've done that several times since we came to India. Like when we were eating celebration rice just now, sitting on that veranda without the pressure of talk or barriers of language or faith. It's never for very long, but when I do remember her again I feel a pain inside myself. It's as if to experience even a moment of happiness is to deny the memory of her. As if I'm obliged, somehow, to nourish my sense of loss in order to honour her properly.' He shook his head. 'I don't know where real grief ends and self-indulgence begins.'

'You're not self-indulgent,' Mair said quietly.

'No? I'm always thinking about what I think. I'm not sure I understand anything in the way I once did. All the old values have been turned inside out. What does anything matter, after what's happened? Ambition, work, success, even love.'

'I don't know. Those are big questions. I think what matters is this, here. And versions of it, everywhere.'

She gestured to the small world of the playground, thinking at the same time of Wales, and Tal and Annie's baby, and the peace of Bruno's wood cabin in the mountains.

And of Zahra's shawl.

'You're not ready yet to stop grieving,' she said.

He had been staring ahead, but now he turned to look at her. 'I'm not, no. It might take time.'

It was the gentlest and the most inclusive of warnings. She appreciated this candour, and the associated concern for her. 'I know, I understand.'

As they talked she had been half watching the rope game. Three of the biggest boys swung outwards until the rope was almost horizontal, and at the highest point they each let go and leapt for the far bank.

Mair's own muscles automatically contracted as she enviously measured the effort involved.

One by one the big boys made the return journey across a log balanced over the crusts of yellow scum that came flooding downstream. Now a much smaller boy grabbed the rope and ran up the bank to begin his swing. The last of the returning trio lost his balance on the log and kicked out as he lunged for dry ground. The log rolled sideways and collapsed into the water, but the little boy was too intent on his swinging to pay attention. His weight wasn't sufficient to create the high arc that the others had achieved, but he wriggled on the end of the rope, swung back and outwards again. The bigger boys were hooting encouragement, but behind them the other children had begun to filter away, playtime ending as the early evening slid towards curfew hour.

The boy swung outwards for the third time, the rope slackening as his resolve deserted him. But he wouldn't give up either, and allow the pendulum swing to carry him back to safety. For a split second he hung there, then sprang too late into empty air. Arms and legs flailing, he crashed into the water. He jumped up and tottered to the bank before falling forwards into mud and sand. When he stood up he was drenched to the thighs and the front of his blue *kameez* was coated with dirt.

Even at this distance Mair could see him trying to smile, but then he realised that the precarious log bridge had collapsed and he was stranded.

The big boys called his name.

Mair scrambled up. She ran the fifty yards to the rope and clamped her feet to the knotted end. As she swung she measured the distances by eye. There was a tree with a low-hanging branch in just the right place.

Exhilaration shot through her.

One more swing gave her enough momentum and the proper trajectory.

At the highest point she let go of the rope. The sky and the grass and the water revolved but she felt the point of stillness, the moment of glory when she knew that she couldn't fall or miss her landing.

She caught the branch and turned an entirely unnecessary somersault. Rough bark tore her palms, but she hung on.

Trapeze wasn't as good as sex, Hattie used to say. But it was up there.

Grinning, Mair dropped to the ground. The little boy stood with his mouth open. He forgot to cry, or even exclaim. On the other bank the boys leapt up and down and cheered.

She stooped to the child's level. His eyes were liquid.

'Hello,' she said, and held out her smarting hand. He

grasped it and they turned to the bank. Bruno was at the opposite side. He paddled into the filthy water and grasped the end of the log as the other boys bumped around him, eager to assist in this startling rescue. They hoisted it back to a precarious bridge position and Bruno balanced halfway across. Mair led the child to meet him and passed him over. As soon as the boy was deposited safely on the bank, Bruno came back to collect her.

'Be *very* careful. I wouldn't like you to slip and hurt yourself,' he said, taking her hand.

'Thank you for rescuing me. But you've got your feet wet.'

They laughed at each other as the boys capered around Mair, the small one already reabsorbed by the group. One who might have been his brother or cousin was trying to clean off the mud.

'Very good, where you from? England? Good cricket,' they shouted, as always. The biggest called a warning and they chased up the bank and across the meadow. Mair and Bruno were suddenly all alone.

'You are a surprising woman,' he said. 'An absolutely amazing woman.'

'I just wanted to do that.'

Wind riffled the dry leaves and smoke blew across the roofs of low brick houses. Bruno took her face between his hands and with his thumbs he stroked the corners of her mouth. They stood together, listening to the breeze and the ripple of water.

Mair remembered Leh, almost a year ago, and the day she had first met Karen and Lotus. And then came the memory of the terrible morning in the snow at Lamayuru. She had done a back-flip to please Lotus and the dog had streaked out of nowhere.

She closed her eyes, and opened them again.

A year had changed everything.

I won't do that again, she thought. No more acrobatics. The circus was over.

Happiness unexpectedly possessed her: its reality seemed as

466

perfect and as indestructible and as fleeting as the moment of flight itself.

'It will be dark soon,' Bruno murmured.

He held her hand as they headed across the meadow. At the margin a group of women in fluttering black *burqas* hurried by as the call to prayer sounded over the low roofs. This was a strictly orthodox Muslim neighbourhood, more like Saudi than Srinagar. Mair and Bruno released each other and decorously followed the path that led to the Jhelum river.

When they reached the smeared-glass walls of the hotel Bruno sighed. 'Do we have to stay another night in this place?' he asked.

'No, we don't. Where shall we go?'

He turned in a half-circle towards the glimmering waters of the lake. A handful of *shikaras* swayed at a jetty, hoping to pick up a fare before curfew. A pair of jeeps loaded with soldiers crawled by.

Across the water a few yellow lights winked in a row of houseboats. Dusk concealed their peeling paint and sagging timbers.

'What about . . . There?'

Half an hour later, without luggage or anything but the clothes they stood in, they had taken possession of the *Rose of Kashmir*. Proudly the house-boy conducted them through carved rooms hung with embroideries and miniature chandeliers. The boards creaked loudly underfoot and the ornate mirrors were veiled with dust.

'I make dinner,' he told them, and sprang down the plank leading to the kitchen boat.

Mair and Bruno stood out on the pillared veranda. A moon like a silver ball floated over the high mountains. The last *shikara* glided by, its wake punctuated by drips from the paddle.

He sighed. 'It's all very beautiful. But Kashmir would only be a picture postcard if it . . . if it were not for you. Is it all right to say that, Mair? I did say I'm not sure I understand anything any more. If I'm wrong about this . . .'

467

Tomorrow, she thought, there would be other questions, and no doubt some things that would be more wrong than right, but for tonight there was nothing out of place, nothing missing, nothing but now.

'You're not wrong at all,' she said.

It was dark, but still they could see each other's face.

From the trees on the bank an owl hooted.

Acknowledgements

Bob and Carolyn Wilkins originally drew my attention to the effects of the veterinary drug Diclofenac on the vulture populations of Asia, and the consequent rise in the numbers of feral dogs and the spread of rabies. Drs Wilkins were also wonderful companions on a lengthy trek in the Zanskar mountains of the Indian Himalaya, as were Jane Maxim, Stephen Barnard and Graham Francis. Our guide was the inestimable Seb Mankelow, who shared his deep knowledge and love of the region with us, and who helped in many ways with the early research for this book. Our local guide was Sonam 'Jimmy' Stobges, whose energy and good humour made long days in difficult terrain seem easy. I am grateful to him and to his wife who welcomed us to the family home in Padum, and also to the camp staff and pony men. Dr Tsering Tashi of the Community Health Centre in Padum gave me an afternoon of his time to discuss the threat and the effects of rabies. Another Tashi was my resourceful driver on the long and difficult drive across the mountains from Ladakh via Kargil to Srinagar in Kashmir.

In Srinagar I was greatly helped by the owners and staff of Gurkha Houseboats on Nagin lake. I am grateful to the spinners, dyers, weavers and embroiderers of Srinagar and the Vale of Kashmir who invited me into their workshops, demonstrated their working methods and patiently explained the processes involved in producing fine shawls. Thanks are due to Justine Hardy for her generous advice, and also to Sara Wheeler.

My brother-in-law Arwyn Thomas was born in India to Welsh missionary parents, and he gave me helpful information about their work.

I would also like to thank Lynne Drew and everyone at HarperCollins, Hazel Orme, Annabel Robinson and the entire team at FMcM Associates, the London Library, and my unsurpassable agent Jonathan Lloyd.

As always, thank you to my supportive family, Charlie, Flora and Theo.